Surrender the Storm

AWARD-WINNING AUTHOR
ELIZABETH
ST. MICHEL

Praise for Elizabeth St. Michel

The Winds of Fate Reviews:

The Winds of Fate "…captivating romance that takes us to the world of seventeenth-century London… Sexual tension and legal and familial intrigue ensue with the reader cheering on the lovely pair."
—*Publishers Weekly*

The Winds of Fate "has everything…full of passion, betrayal, mystery and all the good stuff readers love."
—*ABNA Reviewer*

"Original…strong-willed heroine…I love all of it… the unlikely premise of a female member of the aristocracy visiting a man who is condemned to die and asking him to marry her."
—*BNA Reviewer*

Surrender the Wind Reviews:

Surrender the Wind won the **National Excellence in Romance Fiction Award** and a prestigious **Holt Medallion** Finalist. "The lush descriptions of the

southern countryside, the witty repartee between the characters, the factual descriptions of battles woven into the storylines, and the rich characters kept me glued to the pages."
—*Alwyztrouble's Romance Reviews*

Surrender the Wind received the "Crowned Heart" and National "RONE AWARD" finalist for excellence. "With twists and turns…and several related subplots woven in, no emotional stone is left unturned in this romance."
—*InD'tale Magazine*

Sweet Vengeance Reviews:

Sweet Vengeance: Duke of Rutland Series I received the **International Book Award.** "Elevates historical romance to new heights with an elegance of writing both electric and magnificent…a tangled web of love…deceits and adventures bursting into one fantastic journey across the seas."

Only You: Duke of Rutland Series III Reviews:

Only You: Duke of Rutland Series III won the American

Fiction Award and National RONE Finalist. St. Michel's unique voice and talent shine through this exciting tale of loyalty, love and danger."
—*American Fiction Award Winner*

"Characters bring unique elements on a lush tropical island with the road to love filled with twists and turns."
—*InD'tale Magazine*

Lord of the Wilderness:
Duke of Rutland Series IV Reviews:

"An extraordinary writer, a master storyteller, and a superb historian, Elizabeth St. Michel has created a powerful, poignant, and touchingly far-reaching epic of romance and adventure. With vivid characters, arises an evocative love story that is intricately woven in the American Revolution. This extraordinary tale will captivate readers like few others and sweep them away to another time and place."
—*International Book Award Winner*

"Powerful, magnetic characters… St. Michel is a master at crafting realistic characters who tug at your

heartstrings."
—*Forward Reviews Bronze Medallion "Book of the Year"*

"*Lord of the Wilderness* is a fresh, unpredictable story with feisty, complex, and complicated characters that magnetize. The author has obviously done a massive amount of research about the American Revolutionary War era and area, and her plot snares you fast, from page one. A raw and rugged story, I was enthralled with Ms. St Michel's writing ~ not your typical, generical romance but one packed with realism and vigor and a love that dares even the threat of death itself.
—*New York Times Bestselling Author Parris Afton Bonds*

Surrender to Honor

—InD'tale's RONE Award

Surrender the Storm
Copyright © 2021R Elizabeth St. Michel

All rights presently reserved by the author. Printed in the United States of America. No part of this book may be used or reproduced in any manner whatsoever without written permission except in the case of brief quotations embodied in critical articles or reviews.

This novel is a work of fiction. Names, characters, places and incidents are either products of the author's imagination or used fictitiously. Any resemblance to actual events, locales, or persons, living or dead, is entirely coincidental. No part of this publication can be reproduced or transmitted in any form or by any means, electronic or mechanical, without permission in writing from Elizabeth St. Michel.

LCCN: 2021913099
EBOOK ISBN: 978-1-950016-05-1
PAPERBACK ISBN: 978-1-950016-04-4

Cover and Interior Design

DEDICATION

For Matthew
The most important mark I will leave in this world is you.

We shall not shiver from whence the Storm
To stir the ashes in the fire
To rise a passion, you and I.
The war that weds scorched earth and sky
No fear to be swept in its track
The storm comes to clear a path.

CHAPTER 1

Spring 1864, Northern Border of Virginia

SISTER GRACE BARRETT RAMMED A stout branch at a drunken Yankee deserter. He zigzagged, a dog's whisker away from the spiky end piercing his abdomen, and then twirled around and yanked her nun's cornette off her head.

"Hell, Captain, look at that light gold hair as pale as cornsilk," sneered one of the greasy Yanks at the raucous laughter of his companions.

Again, she thrust her primitive weapon at the Yank deserter, keeping herself between the marauders and her fellow sisters. How was she to protect them and their precious medical supplies from these vile gutter rats? Her heart panged for the sisters' two bloodied guards slumped dead on their wagon. "You are the worst of humanity. I'll fight you to my last breath."

The greasy man prowled, his lank and filthy frame shuffled through the grass, a dance of sorts.

"She got spark for a nun. Can't wait to sample what's under that tunic like we did to that southern sympathizer's wife and daughter."

Ice water surged through her veins. She held tight to her weapon, drew back and shoved. Again and again she thrust the pointed tip. The renegade came at her, dodging each lunge, his yellow eyes as hard as agates, and his superiority bred on the insulting cheers of his comrades crumpling the notion of her defense.

The branch lay heavy and Grace's arms trembled. The sisters prayed. Horses tied to trees farther in the orchard reared their heads, blowing loudly into the chill air. A hawk cried overhead.

"Sister, you better let me sample your charms before any dirty Reb gets a hold of you. That's when you'll really taste fear and wish yourself back in our company. The Rebs are beasts compared to us." He laughed through rotted teeth and even at this distance, she recoiled from his fetid smell. His loathsome companions clapped and hooted.

She shivered. What horror could be worse than this band of swine?

In one sudden move, the Yank leaped. Grace lunged. He dodged the spiny end, then spun around, ripping her weapon from her hands and tossing it high into the branches of a peach tree. Cold, white fear shot through her. She screamed.

A bullet burst through his head followed by an unearthly shrieking that shattered the Valley, froze her brain and rendered any logical thought impossible. The deserter's eyes rolled back, and he toppled over.

From high atop a hill came a burst of demons. En masse, Rebels surged out of the trees, riding forward, then rising like a huge gray wave. A splintering burst of flame and smoke hailed in a vast eruption of gunfire. Minie balls whizzed past her ears so close she felt the breeze, another tore a jagged hole in her gown.

Her breath came in burning gasps.

The Rebs are beasts compared to us.

"Run, Sister Grace, run. Death is upon us," came a chorus of panicked female voices. Infected with terror, the other sisters cowered behind a peach tree. Did they believe the gnarled trunk shrouded their existence?

Her fingers dove into her rough woolen tunic. She could not move if she wanted to. Her mind told her legs to move but they would not obey.

The scene took on a dreamlike quality. Lined up, the Rebs…butternut-clad horsemen came at them, flying over hedgerows, one after another, like swans, elegant in their movement.

She stared from the edge of the peach orchard, thick with white blooming blossoms, their flowers like so many tents, pitched above the ground. She caught the fragrance, sweet and amazing, a small flicker of civility in the great horror that erupted before her eyes. She imagined the number of arms, legs, wings, teeth, claws, horns, the rapid assailants might host. They howled like banshees, closer now, the pounding drumbeat of their horses' hooves, descending on her.

The Yank deserters scattered behind narrow trees, emptying their muskets, their faces ashen beneath the grime. "Give 'em hell, boys. They're just filthy Rebs."

In one crashing discharge, smoke and flame blasted straight into the line of Rebels. Even the best aimed did not meet its mark. The Rebs responded with guns targeted. Bullets cracked and slapped against the twisted trunks, sheets of lead sliced through the peach trees and churned the ground.

The Rebels were too close and too many. Smoke swirled around her. The Yanks struggled to reload. One rolled over, flat on his back, his eyes open to the blue sky.

All around her, she watched as the brilliant canopy of white blossoms shattered, and a steady shower of white drifted down upon her head and shoulders. Like snow it was; her paralyzing fear shifted and, something else called her away, the bizarre and beautiful image…so many men plying their wicked vocation, and yet there was a peacefulness, the firing so steady it seemed like a hard wind, and all the while the air around her brought a piece of home…a horrid snowstorm.

Sister Josephine's ragged voice pleaded through the din and swirl of snowflakes. "Come, Sister Grace."

Grace fingered a delicate blossom. The angel of death had come for the wicked and she deserved every bit of his punishment. She killed her loathsome stepbrother. He'd attacked her. She pulled the trigger. It wasn't an accident.

Grace swallowed. Mercy meant death.

One Yank struggled to reload his musket, fought to pour powder into the barrel, slid the ramrod down, and then tilted the musket up. Before he fired, a musket ball blew through a "v" in the tree, shattering his arm in splinters. With his other arm, he raised his musket, and then lurched backward, his limbs splayed out, his musket falling slowly down across him. Burning gunpowder and fresh blood drifted up and roiled her stomach.

"Retreat!"

The able deserters clamored on rearing horses, the rest, a heap of bodies.

Frightful beasts chased away the Yanks and entered into the dazzling light of the orchard. Acrid smoke of stale gunpowder stung her nostrils, and she coughed, glanced down. Dazzling snowy flowers covered much of the ground. Giant steeds pawed deep black ruts into the earth with sharp hooves, desecrating the carpet of white. She lifted her head, expecting to see a legion of twisted and macabre faces. Men. They were mere men, fanning in an arc about her.

Except for a rider who barreled alongside her. His Hardee hat veiled his face, half in shadow, half in light…a vision of Dante's Inferno? He was a center of ominous stillness in their frenzied energy. He rose head and shoulders above them, looking down upon all in his range by the sheer necessity of his looming height. His was the steely fist that kept a tight rein on the motley crew. His was the command they obeyed without question.

Die bravely. Die swiftly.

Another huge Rebel with a scraggly beard that climbed his face like last year's raggedy vines after a severe winter, spat a vitreous stream of tobacco on the ground. "What do you want us to do, Colonel Rourke?"

She cricked her head back. "Colonel Rourke? The

Gray Ghost!" she said, her voice a whisper. A cluster of tentacles clutched her abdomen.

The other nuns blessed themselves, fell to their knees with the death grip on their Rosary beads, and recited Hail Mary's.

Wasn't he marked with blasphemy, a great beast that rose from the bowels of hell, seven horns upon his head? He was the worst the Confederacy offered, causing night terrors for children of the north to wail beneath their blankets. Yet wasn't she a sinner to be claimed by a demon and thrown into a boiling tar pit?

"He's not a cyclops. See, he has two eyes." Grace's voice trembled as she allayed her fellow sisters' fear. And actually…pinned beneath his eyes, too luminous to be blue, and gleaming in the dappled sunlight like two smoldering cobalt ingots…to allay her own fear. "He doesn't have sharp pointed teeth like a wolf. See, Sister Clara?"

The drone of Hail Mary's swelled in crescendo.

His gaze passed over their two dead drivers, and then settled on her, and didn't vacillate for a disturbingly long time. His expression never altered from flinty and appraising. Though something about the tension between his eyebrows, and the slack in what must have been a normally rigid jaw captured the hint of an emotion that bewildered her.

Grief? Guilt?

"Yankee deserters killed them," Grace said. "The deserters were accosting us—"

"I know."

She waved her hands through the air, her hands unable to decide where to be. Which was anywhere else but here. She registered the fact that she faced the notorious Reb commander who'd incensed Grant's army, enraged President Lincoln, was legendary for his ferocity in battle, his rapid-fire crisscrossing movements on horseback, perplexing Union cavalry, and remaining peerless among Rebel cavalry leaders because his methods were so unorthodox and unpredictable.

"What are you doing in the middle of a war zone?" His voice, like a thunderclap shook a new cascade of petals from the trees and beneath the weight of his unrelenting stare, she found herself identifying with the fox ripped from its den by a zealous hound.

"We are Sisters of Mercy, nurses making our way to a Union camp. When pursued by those evil men, our wagon axle broke. If one of your gentlemen…"

His men's eyes gleamed with feral hunger.

"…would assist and fix our wagon, we would be most grateful."

The Reb colonel smiled, but it was a small one, and Grace got the impression that he was not a man who smiled often. He nodded vaguely in her direction.

"Captain Gill, are you thinking what I'm thinking."

She looked to the Viking-like, scraggly bearded soldier he addressed. A niggling feeling tingled up her spine. She didn't like the direction of the colonel's thoughts at all or the fact that his face lit with a maniacal gleam. To distract the man and to calm her quaking, she said, "It is a pleasure making your acquaintance." *Stupid.* Had she really voiced a social pleasantry?

"It's a tragedy to make his acquaintance," spat Sister Jennifer Agatha behind her. The other sisters prayed louder to drown Sister Jennifer Agatha's ill-timed slur.

Unable to take her gaze from the Rebel, Grace said, "We must always be kind, Sister Jennifer Agatha. Charity is the fruitfulness of the heart." Grace glanced toward Sister Jennifer Agatha, her eyes imploring the nun to stay calm.

"Not to a dirty Rebel," said Sister Jennifer Agatha. Powerfully muscled, he filled out his gray frock coat well and looked far too harsh ever to be termed handsome. "He's not dirty. He's a little dusty," Grace affirmed in an attempt to present strong leadership.

"They have a bounty for the scalps of Union sympathizers," Sister Jennifer Agatha spewed in her dry and crackly voice.

Captain Gill snorted. "They think you're going to feed them to the lions, Colonel."

"They have lions?" cried Sister Clara.

"Of course not." Grace swung around to shush them.

"Those Yank deserters said the Rebs are murderous cowards prone to rape and plunder," affirmed Sister Jennifer Agatha, continuing her tirade.

Grace groaned. To reverse gravity would be easier than to silence Sister Jennifer Agatha.

There was no sign on the Reb colonel's face of disturbance except for a tick in his jaw. Yet, she couldn't stop staring. Lord, as much as it pained her to reevaluate her earlier opinion, he was a beautiful man. Not overly so. His looks were not soft, more like Hiram Powers' chiseled marble likeness of Andrew Jackson. Solidly crafted to evoke strength, a quantity of indomitable will, a measure of indifference, and… she couldn't put her finger on it. Oh, yes, hard and unyielding as hickory lay stubbornness.

Beneath his hat, his brown hair shone with a darker more phosphorous accumulation of bronze; a touch overgrown and curling behind his ear. She had an itch to smooth it back.

"What's in the wagon, Sister?"

Sister? It took Grace a moment to understand he was addressing her since she was so fascinated with his eyes that displayed obvious intelligence, but they also seemed hooded with pain and skepticism. Grace found him very mysterious, indeed.

And she needed to act like a holy sister.

She swept her hair to the side and looked behind her. "Only Bibles and…our under—" Her cheeks burned with the lie. A lie so enormous, it eclipsed the sun.

"I bet. Men look beneath that tarp," Colonel Rourke ordered.

Her heart skipped a beat.

"Medical supplies," Sister Clara blurted.

The blood drained from Grace's face. Why did Sister Clara have to be so truthful, informing the Rebs what they could steal? Grace backed against the wagon, splaying her arms across the tarp before the Reb soldier could throw it back.

"Fix that axle. We're taking the wagon with us." The acerbic slash of his hard lips opened to bark out the order.

"You are breaking the Sixth Commandment," Grace protested.

"I'm far from committing adultery, Sister—"

"Grace." Her cheeks burned as she turned to the other sisters to confirm her mistake.

"Seventh," Sister Josephine corrected.

"The Seventh," Grace said as she turned back to him.

"Thou shalt not steal."

"Add that to my list of sins."

"And coveting thy neighbors' goods." Grace bristled at his rudeness as she tried to pry the Reb's hands from the tarp.

Colonel Rourke tapped his finger on his saddle horn. "What about breaking the commandment of lying?"

Grace picked up her cornette and plastered it on her head. "I don't understand."

"You lied when you said you carried only Bibles and undergarments."

Her nerves frayed as a tired gallows rope. "I didn't lie entirely. There is a Bible and—"

"Where exactly are you headed?" he snapped.

Grace lifted her chin. "I am assigned to do the Lord's work at Brigadier General Benjamin Jensen's camp to give succor to Union soldiers." The general was her father's dear friend. He'd help exonerate her with a plea of self-defense. He'd believe she didn't mean to kill her stepbrother. Wouldn't he?

The Reb colonel's nostrils flared with the mention of Brigadier General Jensen's name. He narrowed his eyes at the sisters cowering behind the tree. "Are you all nurses?"

Sister Jennifer Agatha found her voice. "Very good nurses, except for that one," she pointed her contempt at Grace. "She's a doctor."

"Did you hear that Colonel Rourke?" said Captain Gill. The lines on his face drew together, etching a story of an unhappy soul.

"A woman doctor?" the colonel repeated.

Grace straightened. He said it as though she were a newly discovered species deserving of public scrutiny. She sighed, accustomed to the disbelief and scorn against a female in a male profession.

"I'm not a real doctor."

"She is, too," emphasized Sister Josephine. "She's better than a doctor, trained under her father who was the best."

Grace pressed her lips shut. Her fellow sisters shouldn't be so free with information.

"We could use nurses and are especially in need of a doctor, Colonel, even if she is a woman," Captain Gill pressed.

Colonel Rourke rubbed his square jaw, no doubt mulling possibilities she in no way wanted to entertain. "I must protest, Colonel. As I said before, we must get to Brigadier General Jensen's camp. He is expecting us. It is our calling to give support to the Union Army. We have been ordered to do so."

Colonel Rourke leaned over in his saddle. "Did God order you on this mission?"

"Well, not exactly." Grace cleared her throat, and then, inspired, said, "It was Mother Superior. You must understand, the ranking in the Sisters of Mercy is like the military, yet Divine. From God to Mother Superior. If you break that command, you will forsake eternal salvation."

No emotion, not even a twitch except for the horses lowering their heads to munch on the grass, the jangle of their bridles, and the strain of men lifting the wagon to affix a wheel. The Rebs and their commander were immune to the threat of zero absolution.

One of the Rebels picked up her medical bag with her father's precious instruments, the last slice of cherished memory she had of him. She hooked her fingers around the handle and yanked, but the Reb refused to let go. She kicked him in the shin. He yelped. She knew it hurt because Mother Superior had furnished her with hard leather boots.

"Tie the bag behind my saddle," Colonel Rourke ordered. His command rolled like honey over thunder.

"You can't take my instruments." Grace clawed at the ropes. Too tight and as immovable as the implacable expression on his face. "I will pray for you because you are my enemy, but I doubt your deliverance," she warned.

"Heathens!" Sister Jennifer Agatha held up her cross and shouted exorcism prayers.

Colonel Rourke fixed a glare on Sister Jennifer Agatha and she scampered back like a mule with its tail afire. He angled his head to his men. "Finish the wagon. Bring the supplies and the sisters to camp."

Grace dared to pull down on the reins of his horse. "There are newspaper reports you practice unconditional surrender with no guarantees to those surrendering. When you are done with us, what then? Prison? Lynching? We will not go unless you promise not to execute us."

Sister Clara swooned. The other sisters fanned her face.

The colonel's brow raised; his eyes turned a darker cobalt. Her knees shook from his continued silence. Oh, how the demon would take delight to poke and push her under bubbling pitch with grappling hooks and pitchforks, just like a cook submerges bits of meat in a soup. Then he did the most surprising thing. He kneed his horse forward, swooped her up and placed her in front of him.

"You will answer your God-given calling to give succor to Rebel troops."

CHAPTER 2

"I DEMAND YOU ESCORT US to Brigadier General Jensen's camp," said Sister Grace, her posture rigid and unbendable as iron as she struggled to maintain a circumspect distance from him.

"You think I'm a lunatic." Her unpleasant pronouncement of his burning her and the sisters at the stake grated him.

She turned to look behind and her blasted hat caught him in the eye.

"Are the other sisters coming?"

He didn't answer and spurred his horse into the woods. He'd already given the command to have them follow and knew his men would escort the sisters without question.

She clamped her cornette to her head. Like a giant seagull ready for flight, he hated the folded prim and starched white cloth. He was tall and, annoyingly, she was near his same height. He stretched to see in front of him. Couldn't. Manners be damned. He tossed the offending contrivance to the ground.

She gasped. "What you have done is sacrilege. I demand you return my cornette to me."

Not a prayer was he going to ride where he couldn't see what was ahead of him and invite a Yankee bullet. He'd just been through the Battle of the Wilderness. The damning stream of piercing bullets, the howling infernos of the arid forests ignited by ear-splitting cannons, and the shrill cries of terror of men burned alive. *Francis.* He'd promised his mother he'd look out for the boy, and now he lay in the camp hospital fighting for his life. His brother, General John Rourke was missing or dead. No way could his brother have escaped those blistering fires. He tightened his hands around the reins.

A pity he'd make the nun suffer with his silence.

Her hands held a death grip on his saddle horn. "Oh, how I'd wish you'd talk. I'm not nervous. It's that I'm overwhelmed with the need to fill every silence with words. Silence to me is a void in the world that could suck us all in. It is my mission to block the deadly void with words and save the world."

Ryan was amused by her lilting candor.

"I don't trust anyone who speaks ill of someone, and I don't trust anyone who doesn't speak at all."

She shook her head and a cloud of pale blonde hair like the essence of summer veiled his vision. He swept it from his face.

"Sister Jennifer Agatha says my rapid tongue means I'm proud and given to the devil's work. She says I must kneel on rice and pray for hours. Do you have an opinion?" She waited. "All right. I won't say another word—not one. I know I talk too much. It's a trial for me and one I'm trying to overcome. Even though I say far too much, you have no idea how much I really want to say and don't, and I know you'd give me credit for it."

If words were turnips, he'd have a trainload. He inhaled a lungful of her scent. She smelled like peach blossoms. A faint hunger rose in his chest.

She turned to him and smiled…a bright white smile that lit up her whole face…a smile that made a man pay attention. She had a smile that made a man pay attention. "I just wanted to make sure you were there. In case you'd forgotten me."

He stole a glimpse of her face, but couldn't get past her lips. Lips as lush as petals, pink, full and exquisite. All he could think about was what she would taste like.

"Of course, when someone does not have the courtesy to speak when spoken to, it means one of three things…it could mean you are addled."

As she searched his face for idiocy, he grunted, looking deep into her violet eyes.

"Oh, a sound. That's better. I think we are on the way to communicating. Maybe we could work out a system of grumbles to communicate. Two grumbles yes. One grumble no. That should work, don't you think?"

He suppressed a grin. She was obviously trying to distract him…and doing a great job at that. Her eyes were the deepest ocean, so full of life yet uncertain. The violet hue carried his emotional currents, and before he could breathe, he drowned.

"No grumbles? Well, then that gives me reason two which means your mission to shoot up the world and leave death and destruction has left you shy and awkward. Don't be shy. You can talk to me," she coaxed, and then shifted facing forward apparently forgetting to maintain her distance from him.

He urged his horse through an icy stream, water sloshing over his boots and the hem of her shapeless black shroud. He leaned forward and kneed his stallion up the opposite embankment. Her breasts rubbed against his arm and made him wish he'd made her ride in the wagon, but he must get her to his camp with haste.

Another part of him had a mind of its own, especially with the movement of rounded hips massaging his groin. He hadn't lain with a woman for some time, but his body hadn't forgotten how.

For a single, wild moment, a vision flashed of the assignation they might find if he turned from the forest path. On a soft bed of green moss, framed by the sweet scent of ferns. Of what she might allow him to do to her while his men veered off to camp.

Of what he might allow her to do to him.

He imagined lifting soft white thighs, discovering the feel of her skin, the scent of it. Uncovering the sounds she made in pleasure. Would she sigh? Would she cry out?

He froze. A nun? He took a deep calming breath, thrust his lust aside.

He should be purged to hell for such thoughts.

Riding sidesaddle, she flexed her legs, and sighed. "It

must be reason three which means you have taken the vow of silence to celebrate your holy celibacy."

He looked heavenward. Celibacy was the last thing on his mind.

"What do you know about me, *Sister Grace?*" He almost choked when he recalled her kicking one of his men in the shin.

"Oh, *it* talks! The immortal has condescended to talk." She twisted around, looked him up and down as if he were the milk cow she hadn't bothered purchasing.

He ignored her slight, *it*, figuring she had a propensity to fill in the silent gaps.

"Only what the northern papers have praised. That you have the reluctant respect of Union commanders."

He disbelieved that. "Is that all?'

"I like to remain positive, Colonel Rourke."

"I take it the rest is not so flattering?"

She waved a hand. "I think that there are defects in editors and their opinions. I wouldn't want to hurt your tender feelings."

She lacked any pretense of deference. "Hurt my tender feelings…or are you afraid of me?"

He felt her stiffen, and then relax, as if deciding not to be angry. "I'm not afraid of you in the least."

Pure bravado on her part.

"The northern newspapers have decried you to be barbarous, boorish, untamed and vulgar."

"All that."

"Those were the complimentary words."

He raised a brow. She wasn't afraid of him. "I don't care about newspaper reports. I hate newspaper men. I've learned to ignore most of the caterwauling written by bugle-mouthed reporters who believe wisdom comes from a job that allows them to hold a pen. They are more to be feared than a thousand bayonets and decry my greatest battle maneuvers as scandals more interesting than Sodom and Gomorrah. No doubt, I'll be killed on the field of battle and they'll misspell my name."

She laughed.

He liked the sound of her laugh, but the discussion left a sour taste on his tongue. Did she actually think he'd execute a bunch of nuns?

"Why do you feel compelled to kidnap a nun knowing it is against God's wishes?

From battle after battle, he fought to remain detached from any feeling. "I need a doctor who takes pride in saving lives, not killing them."

"Your raids are legendary, like the barbaric Atilla the Hun and his horde sweeping down on innocents."

She didn't let go of her newspaper mantra, almost singing it like a refrain. He'd educate her. "A raid is a predatory incursion against supplies and communications of an enemy. The object of a raid is to embarrass an enemy by striking a vulnerable point and destroying his subsistence."

"Thievery comes easy for you. Stealing me away from where I want to go."

"Comes with the art of war...to appropriate the enemy's goods."

"You dare call it an art?"

"A peculiar trait my men have acquired." He chuckled. "I must admit, my men are largely in debt to the Union."

"And you are their leader, imitating a Greek dramatist who brought down a god from the clouds to assist in the catastrophe of tragedies."

"My men are eager for a fight to win more laurels."

"Not to mention the spoils of war."

"Everything that is not used by our army, is given to the people. The rest of the spoils are divided among the men with no difference between officers and men. It is an act provided by the Confederate Congress as applied to the principle of maritime prize law to land war."

"Of course, there is a law to support your thievery by an illegitimate government. You are irredeemable, Colonel Rourke. Besides warmongering, I assume robbery and kidnapping can be added to your list of sins. Your mother must be weary praying for your soul."

"Do the Sisters of Mercy train all the nuns like you?"

"I have an accepting nature."

He entertained her illogical belief in the occurrence of the improbable.

She patted his horse's neck. "You have a fine horse."

His horse whickered.

"He's the best of horses. Had him throughout the whole war. Are you a good doctor?"

She turned...impaled him with a look that could freeze Virginia in the heat of August.

"With male disbelief, I have learned that it is a part of their brain activity brought with their evolution from monkeys. Have you evolved, Colonel Rourke?"

He quit smiling. "I'm not ready to start another war." No doubt, she'd have him skewered and stuck on a spit over a blazing fire. "I need a good doctor to attend a soldier. I feel he will die, or at the very least, lose his arm."

"Why is this particular soldier important to you?"

"He's from back home, I promised his mother I'd care for him. He also saved my life. I'll not leave him to the sawbones."

"How bad?"

"He was shot. Lost much blood. I'm worried."

"I will use my skills to try to save his arm. I can't promise that I will, but you must promise to return the sisters and me to Brigadier General Benjamin Jensen."

He choked on that request. "How about your mother?"

"My mother?"

"Isn't she praying for you?"

She lifted a shoulder. Let it drop. "My father would be very protective of me."

She made no reference to her mother and talked of her father in the past tense. In a flash, he sensed just how lonely Sister Grace really was. Sister Grace possessed layers.

He wasn't certain what he thought a nun should look like, having met few in his experience. More like the two older crones, especially the one that spat venom like a copperhead. "I thought nuns chopped off their hair."

"I'm not a full-fledged nun yet."

He slowed his horse to a walk, enjoying a canopy of trees that provided a tunnel of shade through the forest. "There are different degrees?"

"I need my cornette."

Her beatific voice had brought him back from the

dark beckoning abyss above which he floated. Barely.

"Your hat is gone with the wind."

Little did she know who she was up against. He was her captor, and she was his prisoner. The sooner she came to terms with that fact, the easier all their lives would be. He straightened, his back board-stiff and clenched his jaw. He knew all the manipulations of war.

The sun passed its zenith, pouring out its brilliant hot oranges and reds into the horizon like a pot of molten lava, leaving the air so heavy, he could cut his saber through the thickness. He didn't know if it was his terse reply or exhausted nerves that silenced her, but over the course of the next hour her back relaxed by incremental degrees. Eventually, her shoulders leaned into him, her head nodding forward, and soon, he heard her soft snores. The large buttons on his coat must be digging into her back. He unfastened them with one hand, shifted her effortlessly, settling her back into the circle of his arms as though she'd often been there.

He tucked her head beneath his chin, her breaths coming out against his neck in a soft caress. A silky strand of her hair flew up, tickled his face, and then twined around his neck, like a slight, powerful tether, lacing them together. Was she a lantern in the dark, leading him from a cave of pain, a spark of yearning to be drawn into one flame?

Her hand rested on his chest, luring him closer, her movement a faint whisper of soft flesh against the threadbare cotton of his shirt.

He traveled over the hills, among chestnut and red

oak forests. A breeze kicked up and the trunks and massy foliage were the harps and strings of the evening. The day's decline flowed steadily over them as they crossed yet another ridge and descended into shadow, into the sapphire bowl of evening and the harkening silence of the night. With the exodus of sunset falling to the west of them, the cozy glow flickered, then extinguished. Guilt reared its ugly head.

Ryan sighed. Soldiering came easily. He was an excellent rider and quite handy with his Colt revolvers. He took risks that he knew he should avoid, but amidst the horrors of war, it became apparent that there was no way he could possibly survive the carnage. And if by some stroke of fate he managed to come through with his body intact, he knew that his soul would not be so lucky.

Four long years of war had passed. He was a respected leader because he cared for his men, except for one ill-advised maneuver that remained buried in his bones and haunted him still.

CHAPTER 3

GRACE STIRRED FROM HER SLUMBER and blinked. A string of campfires like a marmalade-colored pearl necklace disappeared into a distant obsidian landscape. A nearby fire crackled, projecting long shadows on the surrounding area. The light cast by the flames danced across the dark trunk of trees, tents and soldiers, twisting and curling in obscure shapes and providing a small radius of light. A soldier added more wood, poked at it with a sword. Orange flames celebrated with a wild flickering dance, ready to devour the new offerings.

A chill rioted up her back. She existed in the belly of the dragon.

"Good evening, Corporal Anderson," said Colonel Rourke.

"It's good to have you back, Colonel," said a giant of a man with biceps as big as smoked hams.

The colonel dismounted then lifted her down. Her

legs gave out and she melted against him in a quivering pool. She cursed her unsteady legs. A moment passed and she straightened, blushing under the curious stare of a giant soldier seeing his commander with a nun.

"How is Francis?" The colonel handed his reins to the soldier.

"Not good. Took a turn for the worse. Old Sawbones showed up and wants to work his awful occupation. He needs a real doctor, sir."

"I left orders that Dr. Damodam was not to go anywhere near Francis. Damodam's a quack. I doubt he has any medical training."

The colonel took her by the elbow, and she had to run to keep up with him. He threw back a tent flap, charged through several rows of cots and stopped.

She saw a boy, barely a man, saw the mouth that must have known laughter at one time. Grace swept a hand over his brow. Hot. His eyes opened yet masked the ordeal inside. Not good.

She pulled back the blanket, lightly examined his arm. The wound was nothing like she'd expected from her extensive experience. Instead of a neat reddened hole it was oozing with dark congealing blood and the putrid smell was enough to initiate a gag reflex. The ball had hit his upper right arm bone. Had it completely shattered? She kept her face passive while she panicked inside.

A man shoved his bulk between her and Colonel Rourke. "Yes, sir. His arm will have to come off."

The famed Dr. Damodam? Connected with sideburns, his face supported beard on top of a beard that left little in the way of the confidence of his abilities and presented a living specimen of a man who had gone into hiding and was peering out behind the bushes. Grace wrinkled her nose from the whiskey fumes emanating from man's heavy breathing, and her voice shook with authority. "His arm does not have to be amputated."

The doctor turned his attention to her as if he couldn't believe what she'd said. The blood began to drain from her face. She straightened her shoulders, and in clipped, crispy syllables, she answered the drunkard. "I said his arm does not need to be amputated."

"He'll die if I don't remove his arm," the doctor warned in a Texas inflection graveled by years of pipe tobacco use. "Would you look at that! We have a camp follower giving us directions, Colonel." He laughed and turned his back to her. "Bring me my saw boys."

The boy on the table whimpered. Grace's heart went out to him from the doctor's callous behavior.

"You will remove yourself, Dr. Damodam." A cold note of steel came through the colonel's teeth with his command.

Orderlies snapped their heads up. Injured soldiers inched up on their cots to regard the bitter altercation brewing. Everyone stilled except the doctor emboldened by his drink. Grace had the distinct idea no one ignored a command from Colonel Rourke.

"I traveled a day to get to your camp. You can't order me to leave, Colonel. I'm the only chance this boy has. If I go, he dies."

Grace had seen a number of inadequate arrogant Union doctors enamored with their love of spirits and the damage they wreaked. No doubt there existed an equal number of Confederate doctors spewing their own hubris. She poked a finger in the doctor's back, "You, Dr. Damodam, are a disgrace to your profession."

"And you would know what a doctor is?" he snorted.

She clenched her hands. "I am a doctor."

The doctor weaved, caught her eye, and made a pouty face. "A woman is unfit for such occupation. It's not becoming of her sex." He turned his back on her again to address *all* the men in the hospital. "When you are healed men, this woman can attend to your *other* needs."

Grace picked up an empty bedpan and whacked the lout over the head.

That got his attention.

Oh, dear, she was not acting like a nun at all and had promised Sister Frances Gerard, Mother Superior in Maryland, she wouldn't draw attention to herself or bring shame to the Sisters of Mercy. Sister Frances Gerard would be horrified. Grace looked at her mud-spattered black gown and her tangled hair. No wonder Dr. Damodam believed her to be a camp follower.

He grabbed the front of her tunic, lifted her, her toes grazing the ground and raised his fist. Panic seized Grace, enough that she had to fight little spots of darkness in her periphery. Grace ducked the wild blow.

Colonel Rourke leaped forward, spun the doctor around. A right hook cracked into the doctor's hairy chin. Grace took a step back, stared wide-eyed for a full two seconds. The doctor pooled in a heap at her feet.

She glanced around the tent. No one moved. Blank stares, open mouths. Blood drained from her face to her toes. Now the enemy will have a real reason to despise her.

A roar of applause drowned around them. Whoops and cheers from the men.

She gaped.

"Good for you, Colonel. Old Sawbones is worthless."

"Like to see the worms eat him," a soldier hooted.

"Is that angel really a doctor?" praised a soldier from a nearby cot.

Colonel Rourke stepped over the doctor's prone body. "Get him out of here."

Despite her knees shaking, there was no time to sit down and gather her wits. She needed to talk to Colonel Rourke alone. "A word," she said, indicating for Colonel Rourke to follow her away from everyone's interest.

Outside the tent, they stopped beneath the wide-spreading arms of a giant live oak. Gulping air, she looked up above, peered higher, and blinked. How odd, a crow was tied to a branch.

"Francis' pet," the colonel allowed. He leaned forward, his one eye veiled in firelight, invading her space, her air. "Did I hear you right? His arm doesn't have to be amputated?"

She swallowed, felt like a bunny in the jaws of a wolf. "Not yet. I need my bag. I need my instruments to be boiled. I need clean bandages. I need the supply wagon. I need Sister Josephine to assist." *I need a miracle.* She listed several other items she required. Without a doubt, the colonel would balk at taking orders from a woman. However, this was a decidedly unusual situation.

"We have nothing. You'll have to use whatever is in

your bag. Who was your father?"

Shifting her shoulders back, she said, "My father was Dr. Edward Barrett. He graduated from the University of Pennsylvania School of Medicine, was an expert and lecturer in the practice of medicine, anatomy, pharmacy, chemistry, surgery, and most importantly earned a renowned reputation in resection of limbs."

"Resection?"

"Exactly the type of surgery I want to utilize to save young Francis' arm."

She hadn't been aware of her trembling until Rourke leaned forward, pressing his lips very close to her ear. "How many times have you done this procedure?"

She swallowed. "Twice."

In a carefully controlled tone, he said, "And you expect me to let you do this procedure on Francis?"

"I know what you think. I'm a woman with no experience. But I grew up learning medicine at my father's knee. I love medicine. I thrive on it. From the time I was five years old, I accompanied my father everywhere, assisted him in every surgery. I can operate on Francis blindfolded."

She took the cigar out of his mouth and on a stump, she smashed it with the heel of her palm.

"That's a good Cuban cigar," he shouted.

She retrieved another from his pocket.

"I did not give you leave to—"

When she slit the second cigar with her fingernail, he looked at her as if she were the wicked witch who had pushed the children into the oven. If she wasn't so worried, she might have found his reaction comical.

"You no doubt stole it and I have no time to suffer

fools." She held up the crushed cigar. "This is his arm as it exists." She slid the slitted cigar over the rough ends. "I'm going to cut here and salvage the two ends of his arm."

She held her breath.

"Say that again, Sister Grace," the colonel said in a voice that was calm and soft in spite of the fact that his eyes were positively radiating fire.

Grace held up the joined cigars again to demonstrate. She'd never cared for the way men thought that by virtue of their sex they were superior to women and could simply order them around and tell them what to do.

He drew his hand across the back of his neck. "I'm trusting you with that boy's life."

His words rumbled all the way down her spine and skittered along her skin until every hair rose to vibrating attention. "I can't make any promises. He will be maimed if I'm successful, but a maimed arm is better than no arm. However, from what I can tell from my examination, there are no serious lesions of the vessels and nerves of the limb. Many resection surgeries have positive results. But this late in the game, Francis has been compromised."

"Compromised?"

She lowered her chin in what was supposed to be a nod. "Amputation or death. We need to move as quickly as possible before the boy goes into shock. Since the sisters are not here, I'll need another man to help. I want you to be there because he may not follow my orders."

After her instruments were sterilized and under a bright lantern, Grace took a leather thong and secured her hair up in a topknot. She tied on a clean apron, and then washed her hands in a basin. She laid out her tools, then she glanced at Colonel Rourke, guarded and dubious of her skills, yet depending on her skills to save the life of someone important to him. How she wished her father were by her side.

She placed a few drops of chloroform on a sponge, and then placed the anesthetic on top of a cone, covering the boy's nose and mouth. Minutes eclipsed until he was sound asleep.

You'll never amount to anything.

Hands shaking, she tamped down her mother's cruel taunt, picked up a scalpel. The metallic instrument flashed in the light. She felt Colonel Rourke's eyes bore holes into her. No way could she make a mistake.

She made an incision from the tip of Francis' shoulder to his mid-arm. She searched for the long head of the bicep and divided the rotator cuff and capsule, mindful to stay opposite the main blood vessels and nerves.

Despite the colonel's stillness, she could feel his restless energy snapping through the air. "You must be patient. This surgery takes special care."

With her elbow, she wiped the sweat beading on her brow.

You have a unique gift, Grace.

Her father's words bolstered her confidence. With a Gigli saw, she excised the humerus, dividing the bone at appropriate locations. She eradicated bone splinters and pieces of clothing, cursing the new type of bullet or Minie ball that caused so much damage. She sewed him up.

Straightening her back, she placed maggots on the wound. "To eat the infection." She wrapped her patient's arm with clean bandages, careful to keep the maggots in place. The bloodied bandages and water pan were given to a soldier to discard.

Tired lines drew about the colonel's eyes. He had ridden for hours while she slept.

"What do we do now?" he asked which translated to Grace, *what's taking so long?*

"You obviously are accustomed to getting what you want and quickly. Healing takes time. We apply cold water dressings and wait. We'll know in twenty-four to thirty-six hours. You can go and rest."

"I'm staying." He signaled a soldier to bring a chair and seated her.

Grace busied herself checking and rechecking the boy's bandages. Under the fringe of her lashes. She watched Colonel Rourke visit with the other injured soldiers. He had a special affection for them and they for him. From what she had previously gathered about his reputation, she didn't know what to think.

She sat and held Francis' good hand, willing healing into him. The long night yawned ahead. She watched the boy's chest rise and fall, and then her gaze drifted to outside the raised tent flap, the darkness superimposing her chaotic journey. She brushed a watery tear from her eye for it was the one-year anniversary of her father's death. He had dropped from a massive heart-attack and there was nothing she could do to save him.

He had died in her arms.

Two months had passed and, ignoring all scandal, her

mother married Senator Henry Dawson. Her mother, a beauty, and with an expected fortune coming to her from her late husband's estate, caught the eye of the ambitious politician. In exchange, her mother, who had been dying from obscurity while married to her introverted husband, received the notoriety she craved.

"Prince Henry" was the Senator's nickname, partly because of his aristocratic manner and his fondness for theatric hand gestures, partly too, because of his flared mustache, luxuriant sideburns, gaudy clothes and imperial height that matched the bloated sense of pride of his accomplishments.

Grace's mother, a vain, selfish creature, was predisposed to luxuries and disdained her late husband for his chosen medical profession instead of taking up his family's banking business. She did however enjoy the fruits of the vast financial fortune. To her only child, she showed derision and had shunned her. *How could she have born such an ugly child?*

When the will was probated, Grace's mother went into an apoplectic rage and the power-grasping, greedy Senator Dawson demanded a contest. The estate attorney affirmed the will was ironclad and Grace was the sole inheritor to the fortune with her mother to have the home and a small allowance.

Grace's life changed dramatically. Lost in the grief of losing her father, Grace spent added time with her beloved horses and in the stable her father had built, a stable that was known throughout Maryland as the best in the state. Soon she was forbidden to go to the stables by her mother. Then the Senator Dawson chimed in with her mother, discrediting Grace for her medical pursuits and demanding that they cease, improper as it was for a woman.

Then her two stepbrothers arrived, adding to her misery.

The eldest, Carl Dawson, was well-dressed and the more handsome of the two brothers. Surpassing his father's greed and avarice, he existed a sneaky, idle man. Oh, he was charming at first, but Grace saw his propensity for women and gambling, preening himself, always thinking ahead and maneuvering for his own benefit. Carl, she discerned was the most threatening of the two.

The youngest brother, Thomas, slothful, indolent, obese, and slept until noon, valued comfort above all else.

When Grace rebelled against them for forcing her to give up medicine, she was moved into an attic room while her two stepbrothers and stepfather lay ensconced in luxurious quarters below. The act was to break her and force her hand to sign her money over to her mother that the greedy stepfather, no doubt would seize as his rights by marriage. Then the next bitter ruse employed was for her to accept her oldest stepbrother's hand in holy matrimony, so they could claim her fortune through marriage. She refused and before she could escape to friends, she was locked in the attic until her attitude adjusted. For a week, she suffered isolation. In her loft, she saw people come to the front door below, asking for her services, and her heart went out to them in their time of need. They were turned away by the butler under her mother's orders, claiming Grace remained in mourning.

The servants were appalled.

During the night, the butler unlocked her door. "I had to wait until they were all abed, Miss Barrett." He thrust a satchel and small derringer into her hands. She turned and tucked the gun into her garter, and threw her arms around her favorite servant and hugged him. Under the light of a crescent moon, she crept down the back stairs, into the dark stables, and mounted her saddled mare.

In a flash, she was yanked from atop her horse. Her head smacked the stone floor. Air whooshed out of her lungs. She rose to her feet, but her attacker tackled her, threw up her skirts.

"Where does Miss Too-big-for her-boots think she's going? Too good for us?"

"Thomas?" Grace kicked and clawed her younger corpulent stepbrother.

He slapped her. Her head banged on the floor again. Stars flashed before her eyes. The barn became a black-edged blur; her head throbbed as if a million shards of glass pricked her skull. Tears came to her eyes.

He reached down and unbuttoned his pants. "I'm going to compromise you. Then you'll have to marry me. I heard my father ordering my brother tonight to get control of your money but I'll beat him to it."

And she had thought the older brother was more dangerous.

His weight pinned her; his fetid breath hot on her face. His hands were everywhere on her body. His slimy rum tongue licked her neck, his plump hands pinched her breasts. Her horse reared and pranced inches from her head.

Think, Grace.

"You don't have to do this. We could have a proper wedding. I've had a fascination for you from the time we met," she blurted out, gagging on her words and the flaccid flesh loosened above his pants as he pressed against her thighs.

He lifted and, in that hesitation, Grace reached down and snatched out her revolver. The shiny metal flashed, he caught sight of it, and they wrestled for the gun. Grace's finger pushed through the trigger opening and she pulled.

He slumped on top of her. The sticky sensation of blood congealed on her hands from the top of his head. She panicked. Dear God, she had killed him…a man. No one would believe her. No judge would listen to her plea of self-defense. Not against a powerful senator's son. A gallows rope swung in front of her eyes.

She shoved him off. Lights came on inside the Barrett mansion. No time. Grace mounted her horse and galloped off in the night. Where would she go? The only man to help her was her father's best friend, Brigadier General Benjamin Jensen but he'd been commissioned farther west.

Her only recourse to get to him had been through Sister Frances Gerard. Grace's father had done an extraordinary amount of work for the Sisters of Mercy. She'd ridden like the wind, hoping no one would realize where she'd gone. As soon as she'd reached the convent, the wily Mother Superior had demanded a quid pro quo to disguise Grace as a nun. In return, Grace would devote her valuable doctoring skills. And who knew, affirmed Sister Frances Gerard, perhaps

Grace might become a Bride of Christ.

Colonel Rourke gazed down on the angel asleep, her head turned to the side on the table next to Francis. Cascades of long thick hair, the color of sunshine, had loosened from her leather thong and hung in graceful curves over her shoulders and down her back. Sooty lashes dusted delicate ivory cheeks.

She stretched her hand, entwining her fingers with Francis as if it were a natural thing to do. Falling from her lips were sweet words of comfort like drops of raw honey and divining the boy's salvation. To have seen her surgical work reassured him their world was safe in her competent hands.

How would it feel to have her hand's gentle touch on his? A mixture of jealousy and admiration stirred in his chest, yet a mocking inner voice cut through his thoughts

Could she save him?

In the dim light, he heard a sob.

He frowned. What dared to cause her sorrow?

His men had called her beautiful. Even with her hair askew, and her gown and apron bloodied, he concurred with his men about her loveliness. How could anyone that striking be a nun?

Francis' eyes fluttered open. "Colonel?"

Ryan smiled. Francis was back from the dead. He lifted the boy's cool head, careful not to move his arm, and gave him a drink of water mixed with herbs Sister Grace had prepared.

"Is my arm?"

"Yes," he said, smiling. "your arm will be okay."

His angel of mercy had performed a miracle.

The other soldiers observed Francis awaken and began to shout out a cheer, but Colonel Rourke raised a hand to silence them. Instead, he picked up the angel and carried her to his tent. Hardened by years at war, he'd sleep outside beneath the oak.

CHAPTER 4

SOUNDS OF POTS CLANGING AND the pleasant drawl of soft voices surrounded her. Fighting through a deep sleep, Grace lifted heavy eyelids, and regarded the flapping canvas overhead.

A tent? She was in someone's tent…but whose?

Her gaze roamed the interior. She saw a desk with dozens of unopened letters and a carved brass plate on a cigar box.

Colonel Ryan Rourke, CSC.

With one hand, she brushed her hair from her eyes, threw back the heavy wool blanket, and swung her feet to the floor. Her eyes burned. Her body seized, engulfed in tides of weariness and tenderness. Had he loaned her his tent? She looked at the bed, eyes widening. Had he slept the night with her?

A sudden vivid recollection of the night's earlier events came to the fore. Her patient! How negligent she'd been. Grace flew to the door and threw open the flap, the bright light of day blinding her. Captain Gill crossed the camp with a cup of coffee and offered it to the colonel who rested with his back against a tree and a blanket across his legs.

Grace exhaled. The colonel had been a gentleman and given her his tent. A twinge of guilt washed over her for he had sacrificed his comfort for hers.

Other soldiers had seen her depart their commander's tent and stared at her askance. What a mess she appeared with her blood-soaked, bramble-torn gown and Medusa-like hair. No. They must think her a harlot.

Her patient.

She stomped over to Colonel Rourke and kicked his leg. "Where is the hospital tent?" she demanded, and standing with her feet apart, she crossed her arms.

The crow above with ink-stained wings cawed, and having loosened itself from its tether, alighted from its perch. She did not wait for an answer. The crow would take her to its owner.

They hastened over to the hospital tent, she and the crow, and went inside. Like a mother hen, the crow tottered above her patient's shoulder, watching Grace with a suspicious eye. Francis cooed to his pet, and then smiled at Grace. "You saved my life."

She passed a hand over his forehead. No fever. Overwhelmed by his improvement, she checked his wound, satisfied the maggots were doing their work.

"It itches like hell." Francis croaked.

"That's a good sign. It means your wound is healing. The maggots eat the old skin and any infection that may rise. You must remain very still and give your arm time to mend."

The crow cawed again as if echoing her command.

Grace smiled, placing fresh cold-water bandages on his arm. "What's his name?"

"Lucifer, 'cause he's a black devil and steals all the time, yet he always does what I tell him."

In a circus, she had seen a trained crow perform a variety of stunts. "What tricks have you taught him to do?"

"He's real good at sending messages and can fetch things. He's smarter than a dog."

The crow allowed Grace to give Francis a drink mixed with her best healing concoction. With the boy improved, the colonel would be grateful, and return her and the other sisters to Yank lines. She bit her lip. Wouldn't he?

She wrinkled her nose with the pathetic hospital facility, its lingering stench, woeful lack of supplies, and added to the list of changes she'd started in her head the night before. Before she departed, she would mention to Colonel Rourke the changes that would be helpful to his men. No doubt she'd run into a brick wall.

The clump of horse hooves, jangle of reins and loud voices drew her attention. She hurried outside.

As though she were thistledown, Sister Josephine was lifted off the back of the wagon by a giant soldier, who then turned to assist Sister Jennifer Agatha.

"Get your hands off me, you oaf," Sister Jennifer Agatha shrieked, springing from the wagon and like a ball of yarn unfurling, unraveling a string of insults upon the giant. He stared at the ground, his face blanched, the same hue as a calf standing before a butcher. In an instant, Grace's stomach knotted and she drew into herself, wrapping her arms tight against her chest, her mother's tirades echoing in her head. *You're ugly. You are nothing. You'll never amount to anything.*

"Enough," snapped Sister Josephine. "The soldier was being helpful."

At the sister's words, Grace came to attention, too. Her mother wasn't here. Couldn't hurt her…as long as she stayed incognito.

Sister Jennifer Agatha scanned the grounds like she was stepping through the gates of hell. "In this rabble of the rebellion, there are nothing but illiterate farm boys from cotton country who know nothing of soldiering, except having an alarming talent to shoot straight."

Oh, how Sister Jennifer Agatha possessed an aptitude for complaining. Her brows knitted together in a perpetual frown. Like deeply plowed soil, her face possessed a myriad of furrows, highlighted by a large charcoal stained mole on her chin. Her old gray skin coloring appeared rotten through and waiting for a last gust of wind to blow out the black dry dust inside.

"You will remember we are at the disposal of our captors. I suggest prudence and refrain from further offenses," Grace said.

"Where is your cornette? You will suffer many penances for the breach." Sister Jennifer Agatha reached into the wagon, grabbed a soiled cornette, no doubt the one Colonel Rourke tossed to the roadside and crushed the cap on Grace's head. "And who are you to champion lice infested, opossum eaters whose morals are as scarce as hen's teeth?"

A lanky soldier with a lock of hair the color of hot chocolate curled against his forehead tied up the reins on the wagon. "Colonel, you gave me the job of escorting the sisters and supply wagon. I've survived Antietam and Gettysburg but the whole trip back with that nun…" he pointed at Sister Jennifer Agatha, "…her caterwauling makes me want to drive railroad spikes in my ears."

Everyone swung around to see Colonel Rourke, his jaw clenched as he glared at the aged nun. "Private Johnson, you may go."

"You will address me as Sister Jennifer Agatha," she snapped.

"You have been making assertions, Sister Jennifer Agatha?" As cold as stone, an edge of impatience lined the colonel's voice.

Sister Clara shrank against Grace. Stern-faced Sister Josephine stilled. Sister Jennifer Agatha glared.

Grace closed her eyes. She needed to get to Brigadier General Jensen as soon as possible. If he received word of her crime, he might not help her, believing the worst. Her plan was to convince the Confederate colonel to return them since she removed the bullet and repaired Francis' arm. With certainty, Sister Jennifer Agatha was making a mess of the situation.

Half in fear and half in morbid curiosity, Grace opened her eyes and she saw the gathering ragtag Rebels. Dappled sunlight created sinister specters of the soldier's faces. They stared with such concentration. Any reprieves she'd won by saving Francis evaporated. Grace choked on a panicked protest in her throat, but then she shored up her reserves, and pulled herself up, knowing the importance of what she could do…save lives. All she had to do was make sure Colonel Rourke believed that, too.

Why couldn't Sister Jennifer Agatha see Colonel Rourke was the law in his camp? To go up against the barbaric, ruthless genius of guerrilla warfare? His bloody raids, savage tactics, tormentor of Union generals, carrying out blistering attacks on Union positions, destroying rail lines and bridges before vanishing into the forests. How could she not see the danger?

Sister Jennifer Agatha spat, "When will we be returned?"

"I expect you to act like guests. As working guests." His voice, tautly controlled, was more threatening than if he'd screamed the words.

Seeing the incalculable fury seething beneath his air of indifference, Grace placed herself between the colonel and the aged nun. "I will remind, you, Sister Jennifer Agatha, that we are in the heart of the Confederacy."

"You may cater to this spawn of Satan, but I will not. I have the full power of the Vatican to protect me." With that pronouncement, the beak-nosed nun stomped over to a stump and plopped down, satisfied at delivering a final blow to her abductors.

Grace swallowed. With certainty, the pope would not form a crusade to save the contrary nun or any of them. Colonel Rourke pivoted and disappeared into his tent with three of his men. She must rectify the situation as soon as possible. Dare she penetrate the lion's den?

She wavered for several minutes, and then straightened her shoulders and marched into his tent. "Colonel Rourke—"

There was so much of him.

Built like a Roman warrior, he stood tall, clad only in his cadet gray trousers, pulled tight against his thighs and molding to long, thick legs. A neat diamond of hair on his broad, powerfully muscled chest tapered to a narrow waist that boasted not an ounce of fat. Bronzed from hours in the saddle, he was an amazing specimen of primal masculinity, both dangerous and deadly. She had seen plenty of men during her practice, so why did Colonel Rourke affect her?

Surely, no man on earth should be as handsome as this one. He looked remarkably like his voice sounded. Like a low, liquid rumble. Like temptation. Like sin.

As he shrugged into a new shirt, his muscles flexed and relaxed with the flow of his movement. A wicked, feral smile curved his lips and her face heated in a blush as if she were fourteen instead of twenty-three.

Eyes, Grace. Focus on his eyes.

Instead she averted her gaze to the interior of the tent, his personal tent, remembering what it had looked like when she had awakened in the morning. There was an ink bottle and pen, a crate of rolled parchments, a lantern, a canteen and mirror hanging from a center pole. Guns and cartridge boxes were placed alongside a washstand that contained a shaving brush, razor and strop. Everything was arranged neatly and in impeccable order with all soldierly accompaniments, masculine and reflective of him.

He laughed then. Dark and barely humorous, sending

an unwelcome thrill through her.

Knees shaking, Grace looked at the other three occupants who had entered.

Colonel Rourke put his remaining arm in the sleeve and buttoned his shirt. "You've met Captain Gill. This is Sergeant Craig Hutchinson and Corporal Amos Anderson."

All three men doffed their hats. Unlike the fierce, stone-faced Captain Gill, Sergeant Hutchinson possessed a good countenance with a great vivacity and sparkling sharpness as if he viewed the world with jocularity. Corporal Anderson had broad high shoulders like a bull buffalo's, his head set meekly on a thick neck, and the full-cheeked, ruddy-colored, rounded Irish face shone with clear eyes, of pale sweet blue cornflowers.

He was the gentle giant that Sister Jennifer Agatha had berated, and with certainty, Grace felt it incumbent upon her to repair the damage.

She took a deep breath. She'd use her best diplomacy. With these men? More like showing up with a gun in one hand and cornbread in the other and asking which they preferred.

"I must apologize for Sister Jennifer Agatha's reaction. You all must understand she is old."

Colonel Rourke jabbed a shaving brush in a cup of soap, and swirled it like a tornado. "I doubt she has declining mental facilities. She is a vituperative woman. Meanness and spite course through her veins."

"A point impossible to disagree with," Grace conceded.

"Don't let us forget our manners." Sergeant

Hutchinson frowned at Colonel Rourke and seated her.

With the shambling gait of a bear, Corporal Anderson moved to the chair on her other side. She was unsure of the structural stability of the chair to hold his great weight.

She was sandwiched in by Sergeant Hutchinson who sat to her left. He had dropped his joviality, and even though his face was severe, she swore he winked at her.

"Sister Jennifer Agatha is like an angel," Hutchinson said.

Captain Gill snorted.

The giant exhaled the absurdity.

Colonel Rourke applied the soap to his face and bestowed upon his sergeant a baleful eye.

Hutchinson explained, "When someone breaks her wings, she'll simply continue to fly…on her broomstick."

Captain Gill grunted which was as close to laughter that he'd apparently allow.

Corporal Anderson's waves of belly laughs near shook the tent.

Grace knew she shouldn't laugh nor join in their hilarity, but she couldn't help herself given the horrid but accurate picture painted of Sister Jennifer Agatha.

Hutchinson said, "I want to tell you, Sister, what you did for Francis is remarkable and we are beholden to you." Gill grunted again. Corporal Anderson's eyes sparkled in agreement.

To receive such sincere approval. Grace felt a warmth from the tips of her toes to her head. Rarely did men tell her she'd done a good job or admire her work.

She inhaled. No praises came from the colonel which reminded her of her mission. "About being your guests. I need to get to Brigadier General Jensen's camp."

"I'm not a fan of Brigadier General Jensen." The colonel sharpened his blade on his strop.

Uncomfortable with the intimacy of his shaving, she shrugged. No doubt, after she had operated on Francis yesterday, he felt she was accustomed to male personal activity. "You are familiar with Brigadier General Jensen?"

"We have a history."

"Here, join me with a cigar," Captain Gill said, pulling four cigars out of his pocket, offering one to his fellow officers and leaving one on the table for the colonel. "You don't mind, do you, Sister Grace?"

"Guard your cigars. Sister Grace has a habit of making short work of them," said Rourke looking into the mirror and taking a swipe.

She ignored his remark. "Not at all. My father smoked a cigar in the evenings, and I loved the smell." She liked the familiarity and casualness of the men. Accepted. Other than with her father, she had never felt this way before in her professional life. Always scorned.

"Nothing like the best of Virginia tobacco," Gill said, taking a lucifer and scratching a flame to light his cigar.

Corporal Anderson studied the cigar in his hand. "Won't it stunt my growth?"

"Good God, you're as big as Aristotle," said Hutchinson. "If you get any bigger or hairier, Sister Grace will begin to think you a wooly mammoth."

Grace placed a hand over her mouth to conceal her amusement. What was the history between Brigadier

General Jensen and Colonel Rourke?

"Isn't it addictive?" said Corporal Anderson. "My momma said to stay away from tobacco."

"I've been smoking ten cigars a day for twenty years and don't have the habit," said Hutchinson.

That drew a chuckle from the giant who leaned over to her soft and confidentially. "About Brigadier General Jensen. The Yank general has a rabid dislike for our Colonel Rourke."

Hutchinson held his hand up and silenced the giant. As if not to be outdone and unable to keep a great tale, he continued with the story. "One time, we brazened into a Yank stronghold during the coal black of midnight. Since our Reb uniforms were cloaked in darkness, everyone thought we were Yanks. Colonel Rourke walked upstairs to Jensen's headquarters to find him snoring like a baby. With the side of his sword, he spanked the general on his bare back. Upon being so rudely awakened General Jensen indignantly asked what this meant. Colonel Rourke asked him if he had ever heard of 'Colonel Rourke, the Gray Ghost'. The general replied, 'Yes, have you caught the rascal?' 'No, but he has got you. I am Colonel Rourke.'"

Hutchinson slapped his knee and howled with laughter. Captain Gill never cracked a smile. Corporal Anderson rollicked with hilarity, his chair creaking and cracking. "We captured a general, a captain, twenty-nine men and fifty-eight horses without firing a shot."

Colonel Rourke took another swipe, examining his neck in the mirror. "Jensen will not forget his humiliation nor his inability to get promoted nor what Lincoln said about him."

"What did President Lincoln say about him?" Grace asked in awe.

"Lincoln did not mind the loss of the general for he could make another in five minutes, but those horses cost a hundred and twenty-five dollars each."

"That might be a sticking point," Grace averred.

Colonel Rourke finished his shaving, dried his face, and then wiped his razor on a towel. She regarded him with gathering interest. Without the day's growth of beard, he was strikingly handsome, his aquiline nose, and the sharp planes and angles of his face seemed etched into stone by wind and weather.

"And you wanted to see me because—"

Her heart scurried and her nerves rattled through her veins. The man moved to a different subject with dizzying speed, and she hadn't yet framed a response. She looked at the three other officers. What she had to say was to be done in private.

"You're dismissed," Colonel Rourke told his men. He picked up his cigar and lit it. When the men left, Grace shifted uncomfortably in her chair. She swallowed. It was one thing to be in the company of his men and another matter to be unaccompanied. She patted her cornette. Her claim with the Almighty would protect her, wouldn't it?

She turned her gaze on the crates of books lining the west wall of the tent. French novels, Greek classics and many English writers, Thackeray, Dickens, Collins, Eliot and Tennyson. Most she had read and had found delight in discovering varieties of nuance and coloring among the words she'd stored in her mind. Just like people, she realized, words could imply many varied and even contradictory meanings. Like the North and the South's attitudes and undertakings, and...like Colonel Rourke.

"Go on," he ordered.

Oh, he was a rascal, aware of her discomfort and capitalizing on it. "You mentioned that we were short-term guests. How short-term?"

Annoyingly, his scent enveloped her, shaving soap, male sweat and something dangerous. He made a long-exaggerated sigh like she was wasting his time.

"I could make life better for your men in exchange for a quid pro quo. For our early return to Northern lines..." she tempted him. "I've started a list of improvements—"

"What kind of improvements?" He clamped the cigar in his teeth. Definitely not committed.

Rankled by his obvious unwillingness, she clapped her hands in prayerful repose, her fingers pointing heavenward. "Oh Lord, bless me with patience...not opportunities to be patient, I've had plenty of those and they don't seem to be working." She darted a look at Colonel Rourke who was immune to her prayer and plunged in with her requests.

"Of primary importance, scrupulous cleanliness must be enforced. I'm a big proponent of Florence Nightingale's discoveries and methods. Men lying on the bare ground are seven times more likely to die from disease. The hospital linen, cots, clothing, furniture, utensils, grounds and surroundings, and patients need to be boiled, baked, poached; whatever it takes to sweep the area free of vermin.

"From Vienna, Austria, I follow Dr. Semmelweis'

practice of hand washing, making it a priority. Despite the naysayers of the medical community who want to blame diseases on 'basic humours' of the body, his discovery and practice have dropped the death rate to near zero."

She took a deep breath. "Our wagon has supplies but I believe by the state of things those supplies will run out in a short amount of time. There will be a dire need of morphine, bandages, quinine, chloroform, and tincture of opium. I will not allow the practice of bloodletting, blistering or purging. And I demand a real hospital, not a tent."

"Is that all?" he said laconically.

"Above all, we need to get the men better food."

"Do it."

"Do it? You are allowing me free rein?" She couldn't believe her ears. Did he have that much faith in her? Could she believe him? Doubt grew into an ocean of suspicion.

He lowered his voice. "I saw what you accomplished last night with Francis."

She blinked. His proclamation was the closest to a thank you she'd get, yet the hairs went up on the back of her neck. "About the duration of our stay. How long?"

"Until the end of the war."

She blasted out of her chair, her cornette plummeting to the floor. "The duration of the war! That could be years."

"Not if the Northern aggressors stop invading my country."

Grace slapped her hands on his desk. "Oh, to

summon the futile meaning of this war, Colonel. Did you listen to the politicians in their tailored suits with their flair for the poetic, spouting bombastic speeches while standing on their cracker boxes?"

He hissed around his cigar. "I agree. Those fire-eaters in South Carolina went too far. Sure enough, they would pay, we'd all pay the price, bringing down the wrath of the Federal army. I thought it was pure stupidity to shell a government installation, but shell it they did. Fine, what's done is done. But even then…I held out hope that perhaps…perhaps those cannons in Charleston would drive home our point, and that Lincoln would back down. I was convinced that none of us would ever be called upon to put an army onto the field, to fight a war."

Oh, how he thought he'd use every contention of the war as a reason to keep her in the Confederacy. She stiffened her spine, lifted her chin. "Yet the fire-eaters prevailed."

He drew on his cigar until the end flared a fiery red. "Where was the sanity of the Congress of the United States that had every opportunity to stand up and take the hammer out of Lincoln's hands, and instead…they chose up sides, like boys in a schoolyard brawl."

Grace gave a sharp bark of laughter. "And it's a bloody one. Each side ready to spill more of the other's blood. And the men chosen to lead the Southern armies were for glory and romance of the Cause with the stark reality, a bloody military campaign. You parted, with final farewells, and short tearful kisses that tempered your lust of the Great Fight. So, no matter how heroic you might become, what kinds of trophies of war you might bring—"

He took his cigar out of his mouth and pointed it at her. "If southern leaders had any hope of defeating a far more numerous and better equipped enemy, they had to do it on their own soil, and make the Yankees fight on our terms."

Grace swept her hand over his desk. "A case of the tail wagging the dog."

Colonel Rourke rubbed his brow as if he had a headache, and she hoped it was colossal.

"The southern child that the north believed was in need of a good spanking had itself unexpectedly risen up and wrested the rod from the parent."

Grace scoffed and picked up her cornette. "No logic comes to your argument. Let us return north."

"You are my prisoner."

"And if I try to escape?"

"You won't," he countered. "Your vows won't let you forsake injured or ill men."

"Impossible! I must get to Brigadier General Jensen's—"

He leaned over until his nose was inches from her face. "Why?"

She took a step backward, felt the blood drain from her face.

Because I'm a murderess.

"I promised Mother Superior."

He narrowed his eyes. "There's more to it." As he spoke, his voice, harsh and grating—well-suited to his disposition and features dropped into a parody. "I thought nuns were devoted to prayer and hymn singing, not politics."

She snapped her mouth shut so hard she thought she'd cracked a tooth. A nun would not be so free with world affairs.

It was impossible for her to say anything more. She was an unpolished and an uncertain liar because she constantly intended and expected she would always only tell the truth.

He adapted an expression of sardonic amusement, no doubt toying with her, much as a cat batted a helpless mouse, teasing it until its death arrived.

Mother Superior's instructions on humility rang in her ears.

Speak as little of oneself as possible.

But the devil incited her, she argued.

To accept insults and injuries.

Yet the colonel seemed to know everything about her, every perceived flaw, every vulnerability and he knew where to put the pressure.

To be kind and gentle even under provocation.

Grace raised herself up to her full stature and looked him straight in the eyes. She would be magnanimous. She'd offer up her sufferings to a higher power.

And with certainty, she'd be a master of passive resistance and tactful disobedience.

He would not see the storm coming.

CHAPTER 5

RYAN HAD RIDDEN A BROAD reconnaissance, left the road to wind through loblolly trees, the air scented with resinous pine, the dry needle duff and rock, crushed beneath the horses' hooves. The slope fell away abruptly to the water's edge. A great chunk of the shore had been bitten out by a spring flood and the scar was masked by bluebells, growing down to the water in flowery terraces. Reins jangled as horses dropped their heads to the water to slake their thirst. The shadow of the embankment covered him like a shroud. The water ran faster, frothing and foaming. Ryan stared at a dizzying eddy.

The nightmare came on except he was awake, and he could not stop it. Invisible, a rapid river current surfaced with a sudden brutal ferocity, sweeping him away, engulfing him in despair, surrender or fight, drowning, sucking him down in the murky depths with malevolent force. His hand tightened on the reins and his eyelids shut tight.

The orders spelled suicide. Maneuver the left northern flank. Horses kicked up billowing clouds of dust. Impossible to hide. In front, Union cavalry charged. Murderous numbers. To their rear, the Yanks surged.

"Kill! Kill the enemy. No mercy. Charge!"

Trapped.

Rifles roared. Bullets flew. Men swept away. Blood spurted from the stallion's shoulder. A Yank on foot ran forward, pistol aimed. He kicked his spurs into his horse's flanks. Just in reach of his sword, swinging, striking the enemy across his neck.

Cannons to the side spewed canister. Screams of horses, cries of men trampled, scarlet cloaked the ground. His men fell. Hundreds of them…in wicked contortions…agonizing cries, shouting for water…praying to God to end their agony.

Jaws of death.

The mouth of hell.

Retreat! Retreat! His horse went down, rolled over him. He squeezed out from beneath… grabbed a wild-eyed mare. The horse reared. He swung up on its back, catapulted over bodies of men and horses. A bullet slammed into his side, ripping flesh. He plunged into a battery of smoke.

When he arrived back at camp, only three of his men had survived. What was done could not be undone. The burden of the aftermath was like kerosene in his gut. His insides burned with the poison, needing no more than a spark to set it ablaze, and leaving him a hollow shell of a man.

His hands were clammy and sweat dripped from his brow. He forced his hands to stop shaking. He'd been through a myriad of battles. Immune to all of them except that one, the one that branded him forever. He glanced to the side, at his men, and breathed deeply. Sergeant Hutchinson looked at him curiously. Rourke raised his hand. "Back to camp."

He rode ahead of his men. All was quiet in the Valley. For now.

Why had he been such a callous brute telling Sister Grace she was his prisoner, when she'd miraculously healed Francis? He had doubted her ability but her long slender fingers wielding such skill amazed him. Confident. Beautiful. Precise. Faultless in judgment if there were such a thing. Reliable hands that comforted and protected humanity. He could watch her work for hours, saving a man's life…and his arm.

That she prayed over her patient touched his heart. That her prayers might have extended over him may well be his saving grace.

Grace, her name meant so much more. The free and unmerited favor of God, as manifested in the salvation of sinners and the bestowal of blessings. His dark soul needed her like a parched desert needed rain.

He had a stunning sense of anticipation, looking forward to seeing Sister Grace. His spirits lifted at the thought of her, his chest expanded and a smile grew from within until it reached his lips. He nudged his horse into a strong canter. "Let's move it, men. At this rate it will take a week to get back to camp." The sooner he got back, the sooner he'd get to see Sister Grace again.

The thought jarred him. Good God. He was attracted to a Catholic nun. A mystery. Yet, she lit up the firmament with a graciousness and luminescence.

Her laughter was like a chorus of angels.

Intelligent for sure. Hadn't she debated him on the finer parts of the war? Brave, too. Hadn't she stood in the middle of a firestorm between Yank and Reb? Hadn't she scorned his leadership, even dared to ask if he'd yet evolved from monkeys? Loyal, too. Hadn't she flung herself between the hag nun, Sister Jennifer Agatha and him? He grinned, recalling how she hit Dr. Damodam over the head with a bedpan.

Sister Grace was an enigma, an anomaly of perfection and irony. She dressed like a nun but did not act like one.

Ryan passed the pickets and edged through several tents and dismounted. His camp was a flurry of activity. Extra tents had been pitched. Men running everywhere. In his absence, had a new company arrived?

"Colonel, she has us carrying bedpans and emptying chamber pots."

Three more soldiers arrived filthy from head to toe and one rubbing his backside. "All day long, we've been digging latrines."

What the hell?

No doubt, Sister Grace created the havoc. She needed to be afraid. With fear came caution, he reasoned.

Still in her bloodstained garb, the object of his interest ran out of the hospital tent, unaware of his presence. She woke one of his soldiers and hurried him to do her bidding before entering another tent.

Ryan's curiosity won out over his surprise. Sister Grace was not as serene as she pretended to be. After a split second's hesitation, he headed in her direction. Her head snapped up as if she heard his thoughts. She came forward, came to stand right in front of him. Their eyes caught and held. A strange electric connection seemed to pass between them.

He shook his head and broke the spell. Did she feel it too?

A soldier came forward palms up. "I'm a soldier and that Yank is ordering me around like she's General Lee."

Ryan narrowed his eyes. "What is going on?"

She straightened despite his menace, stared him in the eyes. "You did give me free rein."

"Free rein? Obedience must be at war with your nature." He'd be sanctimonious and remind her of her vows.

They stood no more than a foot apart, neither of them moving an inch.

"I see you are confused, Colonel. We must make haste then, not only because you are aging daily, but also because the concept of things and the understanding of them cease with your increasing dotage. Remember. In your tent, before you went on your pleasure trip, when you said I was your prisoner."

"I said that?"

She sighed, her eyes though a serene violet appeared uncommonly piercing, as if they held vast knowledge rarely seen by a person her age. "You were magnanimous. You said I could do whatever was necessary."

"Why are my men emptying chamber pots and digging latrines?"

She sighed as though he were a child with the lowest intellectual capability.

"Nothing requires more care than the removal of the wastes of the sick; urinals, bedpans, and chamber pots.

They must be removed from the tent as soon as used and under no circumstances be allowed to remain to contaminate the air with unhealthy emanations and must be buried. Additionally, some idiot had ordered the latrines dug above the camp. The latrines have been removed to a better location below and far away from the camp and water supply."

She caught him staring at the new tents.

"I ordered separate wards established for those with disease to contain the sickness. I've seen two men with measles, am suspicious of typhoid, pneumonia, and with the way some men are running from the tent, presume dysentery."

One couldn't escape the rich vibrations of her voice. He would not desire to do so, which gave wicked curiosity, crafting images to his body. He stopped, grimaced. She had insulted him twice. With certainty, she knew he was the *idiot* who ordered the location of the latrines, and then had the gall to intimate he possessed senility.

She gave him an innocent glance that didn't deceive him in the least. "My talents are used in the service of others and offered as sacrifice and penance."

He didn't know what annoyed him more, her insults, her turning his camp upside down or her standing there mute, like a saint readied to be thrown to wild beasts. Every bone in her body vibrated with silent insurrection.

A shaky hand tugged at his sleeve. "Sister Grace is a blessing, Colonel. We're lucky to have her. Cured my quick step. Cleared Hank of his coughing fits. Lanced Elias' painful boil." The soldier on his cot continued to enumerate many things Sister Grace had accomplished.

The unfortunate thing was that Ryan needed her. The improvements were necessary and ones he failed to think of or had the lack of knowledge to do so. She'd won his men's hearts.

He guided her outside of the tent. "I'm aware of your quiet revolution. I'll concede to the illusion of your charity, Sister Grace. For now."

She blinked as if he'd surprised her.

"You think I'm that manipulative?"

"Absolutely."

She seemed stunned that he could see through her so easily.

"I have your best interests at heart, Sister Grace."

"That would require you to have one."

"I agree with you. He doesn't have a heart," snorted Colonel Horace Lawler, pushing forward on his well-shod Morgan.

Ryan groaned. His nemesis' arrival and his private war with Sister Grace could not have been more ill-timed.

He had to stand tall with Colonel Lawler while suffering under his savage criticisms all the way back to the President of the Confederacy. The grand martinet, a man who believed in no one's abilities but his own, whose jealousies toward everyone else's success had created discord and confusion throughout his command.

"Is this a social call or something relevant? I'm busy," said Ryan.

Lawler took off his gloves. "Your lack of manners and good cheer, I find insulting."

"And so did your backbiting and all the lies you spun about me with President Davis. You think I didn't hear about that?"

"I stated the truth."

"With several convenient twists, leaving interpretations that castigated me and glorified you."

Lawler swished his gloves to swipe away the flies. "Sad fact of war."

"I don't argue with idiots, they just lower me down to their level and beat me with their experience."

Lawler ignored him and turned his gaze on Sister Grace. "Since when do you have the Holy Orders available to give comfort?"

Ryan clenched his hands into fists. He wanted the treasure of Sister Grace and her doctoring skills kept secret. "Sister Grace, don't you have duties to finish in the hospital?"

A slow smile spread across her countenance. She'd enjoyed his interchange with Lawler. Didn't want to go anywhere. She dug her fists on her hips. "Since we have been kidnapped—"

"Sister Grace, I order you to attend to your patients." Her blatant disobedience regardless of the consequences fired his temper, and the fact that he had kidnapped nuns was not information he wanted shared.

"Your flagging confusion has caused you to forget, Colonel Rourke, I'm not in your army." She stared right back at him. To strangle a nun? How many years in Purgatory for that crime?

Lawler laughed. "Looks like you have your hands full, Colonel Rourke. And Sister Grace," he coughed out, "how is your treatment thus far with Colonel

Rourke?"

"He is the colonel. But you should not allow that unhappy circumstance to color your prejudice of the man." She huffed, turned on her heel and returned to the hospital and yanked down the tent flap.

Lawler slapped his gloves on his hands as if it added to his cognitive thinking, a useless endeavor which Rourke considered nonexistent. "Kidnapping the religious? I wonder what opinion the pope will have. Lee must be apprised."

"No doubt you'll be the first to inform him."

"By all means, Colonel Rourke. I believe the entire south must be informed that a Holy Crusade might be forthcoming. And then there is the fact your hostage has alleged your loss of mental faculties."

Ryan stroked his chin. "Perhaps the exaggerated limp you claim from a bayonet in Mexico but was really from a whore in Louisiana should be brought to light."

Lawler heeled his spurs into his mount, scattering men out of his way. His men followed, their horses kicking up billows of dust in their wake.

"Give me honorable enemies rather than ambitious ones, and I'll sleep more easily at night," he told Captain Gill who had come up beside him.

"Unfortunately, he's in a hurry to share the news with anyone who will listen," Gill said. "I hear it's best to keep your enemies close."

Ryan said, "Whoever said that didn't have many enemies."

CHAPTER 6

THE NEXT DAY DAWNED BRIGHT and cheerful as Grace entered the hospital tent, wishing the arrogant Colonel Rourke to perdition. An early morning disagreement with the man over the rapid depletion of supplies had drained her and she had too much to do to waste time on further dispute. Of course, he dogged her heels, his hovering presence buzzed around her like a fly she couldn't swat.

His intense regard turned the innocuous walk from one side of the tent to the other into a perilous, heart-pounding journey. She stumbled once, caught her hand to the side of a soldier's cot and mumbled apologies. Cheeks burning with mortification, she stopped at Francis' cot, sat on a lopsided stool and checked his wounds.

Colonel Rourke sidled next to her. "How is the patient doing?" he drawled, his voice even and infinitely impatient.

"He's healing nicely. I want him to get up and around soon."

Adopting an expression of disdainful scorn, Sister Jennifer Agatha said, "What's a cripple like that supposed to do?"

Grace glared at her fellow sister as an asphyxiating cloud of woodsmoke drifted in from a campfire, making her cough. "He is not crippled, and his recovery is as can be expected. His arm will be shorter but functional."

Why was she plagued with her two least favorite people in the world? Grace motioned to the young nun sitting with her hands folded on the other side of Francis. "Colonel Rourke, this is Sister Clara. I've assigned her to be with Francis during his convalescence. She is very capable."

Trembling, Sister Clara stared at her hands. Grace felt sorry for the young nun who experienced great distress around so many men, and whose terror of the Rebs was fostered by Sister Jennifer Agatha's acidic tales and Colonel Rourke's omnipresent glacial stare. Which of the two should she kick first?

To lessen the young nun's great angst around so many men, Grace had designated Sister Clara one person to care for, balancing it out with the one soldier that needed personal attention. Francis was gentle. The way the crow hawked around him said a lot about his soothing demeanor. Grace had to shoo away a horse and a couple of camp dogs that had come in the tent to visit him. She'd never seen such a natural affinity with animals. In addition, he possessed the unique ability of drawing a powerful response from people, involving his fellow soldiers and Colonel Rourke. Francis was good for Sister Clara.

The huge bulk of Corporal Amos Anderson had tread too many times on her foot. The man was so much of a nuisance that she consigned him to assist Sister Josephine. At first, the timid soldier was terrified of the stern nun, but under her direction and kindness, he responded to her great love. They had become inseparable.

Captain Gill stood to the far side of the tent watching her. Grace had the distinct feeling that he was there under the colonel's orders to make sure the men were cooperating. She studied the stoic giant with the deep-set haunted eyes. Like Lazarus from the grave. He possessed the face of a man who had lost something valuable, and the knowing did not soften the desolation.

"Sister Grace, I need your help," said Sister Josephine.

Sister Josephine was one of Grace's favorites, tall, fair, and plump, with everything in her person, round and replete, though without indolence. Her features were thick, but there was a graceful harmony among them, and her complexion had a healthy clearness. Her gray eyes were full of light, a wide, firm mouth, which, when she smiled, drew up her cheeks. Despite her forty-five years, she possessed a youthful spring to her step, was a picture of simplicity and kindness, and yet could be stern when necessary with an unruly patient. Her maternal mentorship and years as a battlefield nurse provided a great asset to Grace.

Grace crossed to where the older nun assisted a

patient. The man's howling moans demonstrated his misery. He gave Grace a wild-eyed look and shook his head. "I got to have a man doctor," he cried out.

How many unwilling soldiers had refused her when she only wanted to help? From every other man came the cultivated arrogance, and forthcoming masculine bigotry where women were relegated to cooking and cleaning despite how she had saved Francis. Their lack of confidence and scorning of her skills grew tiring.

Sister Josephine delivered a well-meaning look. "He feels like he's pregnant."

"I see," said Grace glazing her hand over the huge bulge in his bloated belly. "How long?"

The soldier gasped for breath. "Two days. The pain is terrible. And I'm not pregnant."

She must catheterize him. "Two days is too long. We cannot wait for Dr. Damodam." Nor did she want the quack to reappear.

"Let the monster suffer," said Sister Jennifer Agatha.

Grace turned on her. "The Rebels are not monsters; they are just men and deserve your respect."

The soldier gripped his groin. "I'm not about having a woman attend me."

She frowned listening to his Virginian accent that pronounced anything with an "ou" with a long "o" vowel sound. About sounded like "a boat". "Very well. Not voiding for that length of time can cause kidney failure then death. Your choice." She'd let him wallow in his male pride until he changed his mind from the horrid pain and beseeched her help. Grace turned to leave.

"Is there a problem Sister Grace?" said the colonel

and she jumped. How did he sneak up on her like that, and how did he have the talent to enunciate every syllable in a whisper threaded with steel?

Grace swung around, her tunic scraping the ground. Of course, Colonel Rourke plagued her steps in the fluid, long-legged gait of a predator. Every word, movement and breath infuriated her. Was he questioning her expertise? She narrowed here gaze. "No problem. This soldier prefers to wait for his kidneys to fail before letting a woman physician help him. That's his problem, not mine."

He stood immobile, his face hard and implacable, his harsh glare directed to the soldier, not her. "I command you to allow Sister Grace to assist you, and that's an order."

The soldier shut his eyes and nodded. "Hurry."

Grace blinked. She could count on one hand how many times she'd been struck speechless. He wasn't second guessing her. What's more he enforced the man's obedience to her.

"Listen up, men," he spoke loudly, addressing everyone in the hospital. Grace suddenly felt as if a strange power emanated from him, a force that communicated itself to all. As if a spell had been cast over them, the soldiers grew silent, their eyes riveted on him. Then and only then did Colonel Rourke speak. His deep voice rang out in the unnatural stillness of the hospital, carrying with it the power and force of thunder.

"Whatever Sister Grace bids you is a direct command from me."

His harsh gaze slashed across them for one breath-stopping, threatening moment, and then he turned to

Grace. He reached as if to take her hand, then suddenly stopped…pulled back.

Her heart swelled and she basked in the moment. Tears threatened, but she held them back. She had to remain strong so the men would believe in her ability to do the job Colonel Rourke entrusted to her. Around them, Corporal Amos Anderson and Captain Joshua Gill clapped. Twelve more soldiers clapped and, soon, the entire tent was thunderous with steady clapping—not the sort of unrestrained acknowledgement that scored heartfelt zeal, but rather the rhythmic reaction of the spellbound who are awed by a power too potent to resist.

Captain Gill nodded. "How I'd like to have a delivery and response like that. May I have a word with you for a minute?"

Colonel Rourke excused himself. She watched his broad shoulders as he departed, and then she took a rubber tube from her medical bag and performed the procedure, her mind still dazed by his incredible thoughtfulness. Like a waterfall, released urine flowed into a bedpan. The soldier's face relaxed. "Thank you, Sister."

Grace washed her hands, checked on more patients, and replayed Colonel Rourke's command, wishing he'd never issued the orders so she could go back to disliking him. She could not. He had given her his full support. Extraordinary.

That he accepted her? That he expected his men to accept her? Never had she had such freedom in practicing medicine always being relegated to some other inferior status. The morbid, sterile, hateful fits of being considered second rate vanished and she luxuriated in feelings of deep and all-pervading satisfaction. Like writing the last line of a poem, winning a horse race, or performing a concert with a standing ovation, nirvana had come to her and her heart beat harder with the unexpected windfall.

Colonel Rourke moved from soldier to soldier, listening to their woes or stories of back home, offering sympathy to homesickness, instilling confidence, and sometimes sharing a humorous anecdote to make the men laugh. He had great love of his men and they, in turn, showed respect, admiration and loyalty. He led and men followed.

A different conversation drifted to her ears, a feminine laughter and light masculine chuckles. Grace glanced up to see Francis encourage his crow to do another trick to the delight of Sister Clara who melted and flourished from his tenderness.

"What will you do once you are healed? You won't return—" said Sister Clara.

"I'm pretty much useless." A pang of regret could be heard in his young voice.

"You will not be useless," said Sister Clara. "You have survived, and you will be of great use when you return home."

"I have nowhere to go. My family is gone. Before the war, my home caught fire…my mother, brother and sisters lost. I survived because I had been out hunting for a week. Nothing was left, just a smoldering ruin."

"I'm so sorry," Sister Clara whispered.

"I joined the army. This is my family."

"What do you like to do?" asked Sister Clara. "Surely

you can look forward to what endears your heart."

A camp dog wagged his tail and put his paws up on the side of the cot and barked. With his good hand, Francis patted the dog. "Ah, my good friend has returned."

"You have many good friends," laughed Sister Clara. Unmistakable adoration shone in her eyes for Francis. "I feel like the ark has been released to your bedside."

Grace mused how Francis and Clara were similar. Like Francis, Sister Clara with her bright blue eyes was an orphan. No doubt, she chose the sisterhood more from her lack of funds and no place to live, yet spiritually driven. Unlike Grace who stood an imposter.

She slipped her hands into her apron pockets. Maybe it would be best to hide in the south. Her greedy stepfamily could not get her and, no doubt, Brigadier General Jensen had heard of her crime. With that knowledge, there existed no way to plead her case and demonstrate her innocence. The senator's machinations would have her hanging from the nearest tree.

Considering her own need, she reminded herself of her ill-fortuned past and the shine of providence to be safely ensconced in the south where she could practice her first love—medicine. Treating injured soldiers here was no different than the north she rationalized, especially with the added bonus of the freedom to do so. Yet the scarcity of supplies bothered her.

Even more troubling, what would a man like Colonel Rourke do with the lie she told? He could do anything he wanted with her and no one would say anything about her. A man of Colonel Rourke's stature and discipline would allow no dishonor or deceit. He was a man of integrity, honesty, and loyalty and expected the same from those who served under him—especially her…a nun.

Evening arrived and with it came the soothing comfort of the soft melodious voices of the sisters singing, preceding the time of vespers. The musty smell of canvas and the night sounds of men settling in for the night surrounded her. Like a mother putting her children to sleep, she looked over the men she had attended. The Rebels were good men. Like the Yanks. Just divided by inane ideologies. She sighed with the futility of war, failing to understand the political thought processes of the war, of men, seeing it as a waste of humankind.

She bent to check an ailing soldier's gunshot wound. He'd make it. She straightened and found Captain Gill next to her. He gruffed out an inaudible sound. She glanced up. Like a fine claret, the blush spreading across his cheeks took her by surprise. Whatever he wanted to talk about embarrassed him.

"Shall we go for a walk?" she offered.

Once outside, he looked at the starlit sky. She waited. The man possessed a maddening economy on words, and she diagnosed his problem by the way he rocked side to side. *Dysentery.* "I have a special herbal concoction that will cure your problem." Grace said nothing more but handed a packet of brewing herbs from her apron pocket. "In twenty-four hours, you'll be a new man. But boil the water first."

He grunted, turned sharply and left.

She yawned, eager for a bed in private quarters. Frankly, sharing a tent with all the sisters was fatiguing.

Sister Jennifer Agatha snored loudly and suffered severe flatulence.

She wandered over to the line of horses, saddled at all times, ready for the next mission. In the early part of the war, the Rebels made quite a picture, full Confederate gray uniforms, cocked felt hats with long black plumes, and high cavalry boots. With the interminable war-torn years, they maintained threadbare uniforms and tattered wool Hardee hats.

She picked out the exceptional stallion Colonel Rourke rode. The way he carried himself on his fancy black mount appealed to her senses, and she remained stymied by the fact that when he rode in and out of camp, she couldn't take her eyes off of him.

Back in Maryland, she had seen fine horseflesh. Many of Marylander's gentlemen possessed beautiful animals. Her father possessed a keen eye for a well-bred animal and procured many horses for their renowned stable. She had acquired the same skill. Even from a distance, she could tell this man's horse was exceptional. His lines were perfect, his muscular frame was one of power and poise, just like his master.

She took a step toward the spirited stallion and placed her hand on his withers, stroking the beast. "That's it, darling, stay right there. I know you're a little lost. A little frightened. Let me soothe you."

She skimmed her long fingers over his face and the horse nuzzled her chest. "I'm here, darling. I'm here."

She kept on soothing and petting his fine glossy coat. "You're so handsome. So perfect."

From the shadows, Rourke spied Sister Grace

caressing and cooing, her soft capable hands touching, stroking, soothing the horse like she did so many of her patients. He could almost feel the palms of her hands on his skin, feel the bunching and quivering of his stomach muscles where her fingers toyed with the top button of his pants.

His teeth ground together. Grace belonged to God. In his case, luck belonged to the devil, who looked out after his own.

She looked up, saw him, and startled by his presence, laughed at herself. Her smile was breathtaking, sending a current of awareness beneath his skin with warmth.

He stepped into a triangle of firelight. "I am in your debt, Sister Grace."

"There is no debt, Colonel. I'm only thankful I was able to help."

"As am I. *Very* thankful." The muscle along his jaw twitched. He took a breath and moved toward her. "You are fond of horses?"

"Actually, horses are my first love with my warmest memories riding and caring for them. Your stallion is exceptional."

Crowned with her wide cornette, she raised her head and, at last, he could see her eyes. He looked into their beautiful violet depths and his breath caught. "Never had a horse for quickness and spirit. He's as fleet as the wind and as active and quick as a cat, no fence or ditch can stop him with my weight on his back. No rattle of gunfire or artillery blasts faze him. When I first received him, I led him out, looking sleek and fine, but with the devil in his eyes. After much coaxing, and running alongside, I put my foot in the stirrup and hand on his mane, and that was all I needed his consent for. When I introduced the saddle, he reared and bolted. I gave him a half-mile at a full run, and then gently but firmly pulled him to a moderate gait."

"What's his name?"

"Archimedes."

"After the famous Greek mathematician?"

"He's a smart horse. Pick any number from one to ten."

Her cornette bobbing, Grace leaned her head to the side and raised a feathery brow. "Eight."

Archimedes raised his front right hoof and stomped into the soil for the count of eight.

"I can't believe it!" She stroked the horse's withers and her fingers brushed against his hand. Ryan looked into her eyes, dropped his gaze to her mouth. So close…

Pink spread across her cheekbones. "Fascinating. You have a gift with horses."

He felt the heat of a million burning suns glow within from her praise. He loved horses and to have someone who shared an interest as well was refreshing. He glanced at her from head to toe. Her gaze locked with his and she touched her covered hair and, cheeks warming, she looked down at her soiled gown, grimier with the day's work

"I was going to offer you an opportunity to freshen up," he said.

"If only there were a bath?" Her words were a little rushed, her voice a bit breathless. She was nibbling at the corner of her lower lip. He gripped his hands on the saddle horn to keep from reaching for her.

"I don't have the luxury of a tub available. I have the next best thing. You could bathe in the river."

Her gaze rose and met his. "I'm afraid—"

She referred to his men, about her privacy. For him, it was a conundrum. He couldn't order one of his men to do it. "I'll guard you."

They plunged through the woods on the way to the river, the snow-white flowers of bloodroot and trillium sprang moonbeams in the dappled light. With a fresh change of clothes under her arm, she walked beside him, wading through hip high feathery ferns, the strong musky woodland scent drifting up through the air.

"What do you want to do after the war?" she asked.

He rubbed a hand across the back of his neck. "Not much. I'm a simple man. My dream is to have a horse farm and raise thoroughbreds. Even though my parents' homestead is huge, I'd never take their charity." He didn't tell her his family's farm was the size of half the county. "To get started, I'll need my own place and livestock, and that takes money."

"That's a nice dream."

"The war is endless, and those dreams are naught." Twigs cracked beneath their feet breaking the silence of the night. "Can you swim?" he asked.

"Like a fish," she said, laughing.

In her voice, he could feel her exuberance. He was glad he could give her a small pleasure.

On a mossy bank by the river's edge, water toppled over rocks and she stopped and put down her pack.

The first trace of nervousness flitted across her face. "You won't look?"

"I'm a gentleman," he lied and retraced his steps farther into the forest.

Soon he heard her squeal of delight, splashing through the cool waters. Behind a three-hundred-year-old oak, he shifted back and forth. A choir of locusts in the flanking woods spun out a long canto of music, like the acolytes of a singing-school practicing the rudiments of psalmody. The varied concert fell faintly, and only seemed to measure an unfulfilled silence. What did a nun really look like? He recalled her soft curves against him on the way back to camp, how her full, soft breasts rested on his forearm when he held her sleeping form.

He had lived through this war for years which seemed enough for a hundred lifetimes. The past was dead. The future was resignation and fatality. The present was here, right now, with her in the river. Before he drowned in gathering numbness, before he felt nothing, he'd allow one guilt-free transgression.

Accustomed to stealth from years of reconnaissance, he used the impenetrable darkness to conceal his form as he moved with noiseless steps. There in the moonlit river stood a breathtaking siren with all the power that ethereal beauty held, and for the life of him, he could not move. His breath caught. She was more luminescent than the dazzling moon itself.

Ryan moved closer. Her back was to him, and a delicate and heady scent of roses filtered in the air and teased him. No doubt from the cake of soap she smoothed over her breasts and farther. His nostrils flared.

Her hair hung in thick heavy ropes down her back. She turned and his mouth went dry. The unobstructed view of her long, pale throat, her creamy shoulders, and…water sluicing down her high pert breasts, and puckered from the cold, taunted him. A hard hum of lust sizzled through his veins with salacious wicked images. To drag her out of the water, lay her on a grassy woodland path and bury his face between her breasts, drawing one nipple at a time into his mouth would be as close to heaven as he would ever get. To taste her, every bit of her. To run the palms of his hands up and down her silky legs and rounded hips. To mold his rock-hard body to hers.

Beyond frustration, he leashed every primitive instinct, bolted down his hot, raw carnal attraction. His honor rose its fiery head and goaded him not to cross any lines he'd regret. A damned heavy price.

She waded on the slick bank and he melted into the forests while she dressed. She called to him and he appeared, startling her like a doe caught by a hunter.

He clenched his jaw, the shapeless garb she wore tamped down his cock. He wanted to burn her clothing and the horrid cornette she tucked her damp hair beneath.

In silence, they walked back to camp. Not once did she have a hint of the iron control he exercised, yet better him than one of his men. He might trust Gill and Anderson, but that thought soured his stomach. With any other man, there would be no guarantees of her safety, and in the future, he wasn't sure there would be with him.

"Will you promise to escort me to the river tomorrow

evening, Colonel?" asked the architect of his madness.

CHAPTER 7

"YOU STOLE THE BRANDY FROM Colonel Rourke's tent?" Sister Josephine looked heavenward.

Grace glanced over her shoulder to see if the cavalry had returned. They had ridden out early in the morning. "I borrowed it. There's a difference."

Sister Jennifer Agatha's rheumy amber gaze skewered Grace. "You can steal from them all you want for they are idiots, except calling them idiots is a compliment and an insult to all stupid people."

"That is unkind, Sister Jennifer Agatha." Grace tired of Sister Jennifer Agatha who refused to do any nursing, and like a repeater rifle, hurled blistering insults at the soldiers.

She directed a soldier with jug ears and a splotchy face to place an ancient wooden case on a plank table. "Nathan from Chester, Virginia has been helpful in fashioning crutches and scouring the camp for badly needed items. He even informed me that there might be alcohol in the colonel's tent for us to use. I did try to find Colonel Rourke, but he'd left the camp. So, I explored myself."

"By the Holy Angels!" said Sister Josephine. "Are you sure that is wise?"

Grace gulped. No need to tell Sister Josephine that she'd waited early in the morning for Colonel Rourke to leave before scrounging. He'd be gone for a few days, maybe a week, wouldn't he? During that time, she would come up with a perfect reason why she was pilfering his tent. "We need to preserve our limited supplies as much as possible. We can't go to Union warehouses and resupply, can we?"

She grabbed cleaned bandages and began to roll, her thoughts turning to the colonel. Why had he turned cool and aloof the night before? No matter what she thought about, no matter what she did, or more accurately, tried to do, her thoughts circled to Colonel Rourke. The way he'd looked at her when he escorted her to the river for her bath. There had been such warmth, such softness, such…trust…in his eyes in those last moments. And then, when they returned, the warmth and amiability was gone. What had she done to make him withdraw like that?

Her frown deepened. She'd never felt like this in her life. The man confounded her.

She sighed. Who was she to guess the minds of men?

Sister Jennifer Agatha slammed the flat of her hand on a fly, making Grace jump and waking some of the sleeping soldiers. "The Rebs are the ones who have taken and must pay most dearly in return. These heartless devils tear entire Union detachments apart without shedding a tear and then sleep like babies."

Grace sighed. She needed to say extra prayers for the middle-aged nun whose large bristly mole, the size of two Indian head cents, worked up and down with the movement of her jaw.

"Do you think the colonel will mind being separated from his spirits?" Sister Josephine asked, the mirror of conscience.

Grace blew the grime off a brandy bottle. Very expensive brandy. Her father had stocked the same kind of French cognac. The colonel might mind very much if his precious spirits were commandeered. "I need it for cleansing wounds. He'll have to sacrifice."

"No doubt they will drown us for your theft, and that's if they're feeling merciful. Especially Mephistopheles, their leader," spat Sister Jennifer Agatha.

"They'll do no such thing." The colonel melted out of the shadows like Hades emerging from a realm of spirits to claim his most recent soul.

With the brandy in her hand, Grace swung around and gaped at him.

He moved like a cougar. Silent and predatory, with the languid ease of a beast at rest, secure in the knowledge that he was a creature to whom all in his environment showed obedience.

He gently but firmly pried Grace's hand from the bottle, deposited it back in the box, and then handed the case back to Nathan who half-heartedly accepted it.

"You must not be hard on Nathan. He has nothing to do with this," Grace demanded. Maybe not so demanding. In reality, her words escaped as a half-murmur, half-query and her gaze settled somewhere in the vicinity of his neck.

"You presume to steal from me, and then order me about my own camp?" Amusement shaded his smooth baritone.

Her limbs shook. "There is a difference. The bottles were in your tent collecting dust and I thought you wouldn't mind if I found another use for them, so I borrowed from you." She clamped a hand to her heart, mustering the nerve to meet his menacing glare.

"Stolen. The case is dusty because the brandy is old and very rare."

She didn't like being afraid and stepped into his space. Oh, the urge to kick the man who kidnapped her, and then destroyed any chance of exoneration from the law she might have had, and now he was questioning her for taking his hoarded brandy. "I'm using the brandy to cleanse the men's wounds. If you have a problem with that, then that is on you."

A few masculine chuckles erupted around her. Injured soldiers sat up on their elbows. From outside, others craned their heads to watch their commander and the nun.

Her heart sank further. Sister Clara whimpered, and wild terror bled from her eyes. Sister Josephine quietly prayed. Sister Jennifer Agatha sniffed as if the air around her was sulfureous. Poor Nathan dipped his head so low he looked as if he wanted to jump into the case of brandy.

She took the colonel's arm and her body tensed at the feel of strong muscles clenched beneath. Oh, she was bold, but she was going to have it out with this Reb. With little inventory to work with, she had sweated and strove to get the hospital in some semblance of order. With a nod that would have done an imperious queen proud she indicated the area beneath the oak where they could converse in private.

Nathan followed, one hand up. "Colonel, don't you—"

One look from the colonel silenced him, and Nathan skedaddled back inside the tent. Grace guided him to the oak tree where golden sunlight cascaded the area, spilling over the colonel. He regarded her with his hard blue eyes that glittered like cobalt ingots.

She dropped his arm. "Is gratitude difficult for you, Colonel? Indeed, I should be very stupid or ungrateful if I did not congratulate myself every hour of the day on what coincidence brought me under your thumb. Not only are you unwilling to acknowledge appreciation owed me but to let me suffer the poverty of your complaint, especially since I need the brandy for medical purposes."

Corporal Anderson huffed up alongside. "The latest communications, sir."

Rourke rifled through the papers.

"Is something wrong?" she asked.

"You will have to move the hospital at a moment's notice," Rourke said, his voice crisp.

"Impossible. I've just made this hospital functional. To move wounded men, tents and supplies—"

Corporal Anderson's eyebrows disappeared into his scalp. Apparently, no one countermanded Colonel Rourke's orders.

"Did I hear you right?" Colonel Rourke circled her with the unhurried but absolute concentration of a shark drawn to blood. "Let me inform you, Sister Grace, that Yank troops are moving in this direction with the possibility that this encampment may be the center of a battle." He struck a match on the leather bottom of his boot and lit a cigar and rested his booted foot on an empty powder keg. "Do you have trouble following orders, Sister Grace?" asked the Colonel. "Aren't there obedience rules you sisters have to follow?"

Julius Caesar might be cowered under that stare. Not Grace. Yet how could she argue when he was right to think of everyone's safety?

"I demand unquestioned obedience from my soldiers and to hell with the consequences."

"May I point out, I'm not one of your soldiers, and I don't care for your blaspheme."

Over the fiery tip of his cigar, he stared. "Do you struggle with humility?"

"It is a flaw I admit. Pride has not been burned out of me. I seem to fail in obedience, too. I like to think that contemplation draws us toward fruitful action. Through it, God shapes us for what is needed now. I must think of the more frail men. It would be hazardous to move them."

There, she said it, hopefully shaming him into his rightful place like Mother Superior in Maryland who wielded the divine art of admonition. She stuffed her hands in her pockets with the lie she told. What a fraud she was to employ the higher moral ground.

He snorted. No way did he buy her virtuous condemnation. Was she that easy to perceive?

Irked by the way he commanded her, having the burden of moving her established hospital, she clapped her hands together in an entreating pretense to mock him. "I am among you as one who serves," she said sweetly, quoting the Bible and permitting the narrative to linger over and strangle him.

To her vexation, Colonel Rourke burst out laughing. He was such a serious person that his transformation left her dumbfounded.

"Sister Grace, it is my considered opinion that your exercise—" he choked, "in humility is as deliciously surprising as finding a sudden hickory nut in five pounds of maple taffy. Those glorious moments, although not making life actually worth living, perhaps at least add spice."

She huffed. "I find your indulged hilarity with the same zeal one may experience mixing caviar with vinegar."

He positively howled, slapping his hand up and down and could barely breathe for laughing. At once, every man in the camp stared at their commander, and she took a step back, doubting his stability. His laughter filled the dusty air and spilled into the morning sunshine. Rocking back on his heels, his amusement became so infectious that she found herself grinning.

It served her right for being pompous.

"Sister Grace, I thank you for that moment." She swallowed, mystified by her captor. He had thanked her for making him laugh?

"I'd like to make a peace offering," he said.

"Peace offering?" Didn't the lord of the underworld offer Persephone an enticement to drag her down into his lair? She gauged him warily.

"I can assure you that your next location will be a real hospital. Also, I've noted all the improvements you have made to the camp and to my men. I'm hosting a dinner in my tent this evening and you are an invited guest."

Grace blinked. If she had wings, she'd fly away, but promises of a real hospital beckoned. She narrowed her eyes. "Is the dinner invitation an order?"

Any ire died when she noted his threatening mouth tilted in an earnest smirk. "In exchange for your thievery."

CHAPTER 8

THE FACE THAT STARED AT Ryan in the mirror was nice-looking enough in a woman's eyes, he supposed, but what did Sister Grace think of him? He frowned and smoothed his hair again, straightened his collar and shrugged into his frayed butternut coat, looked himself in the eye and shook his head. He'd never before had this hunger for a woman's approval. This gnawing eagerness, this need to have one look on him with favor. Sister Grace, and her seemingly cool demeanor that could be provoked into a fiery temper had changed all of that.

He turned from the mirror, rolled up maps on the table and straightened papers. The mere thought of seeing the woman had his stomach taut with anticipation. Sister Grace was not as distant as she sometimes acted, and he couldn't wait to look into her beautiful violet eyes and watch the warmth come into them as he shared a simple dinner.

That she had worked herself to the bone despite him kidnapping and bullying her said volumes about her gentleness. She was the most self-sacrificing woman he'd ever met. Many of his men had been treated by her and survived where other doctors had left fatalities. That she performed the overhaul of the camp hospital, cleaning, boiling, sterilizing for her purported enemy disclosed her capacity for charity and empathy.

She had the hands and intelligence to help others. She had the eyes to see misery and want, and the ears to hear the sorrows of his men.

Yet a wisp of mystery surrounded Sister Grace. He twisted the cork from his brandy and poured a drink, swirling the amber liquid in his glass. He took a drink, casting back through his memory. He recalled her lack of enthusiasm about her mother, and then how she became like a panicked bird in flight with her driven need to get to Brigadier General Jensen. Why was she so adamant in the beginning, but now seemed to forget all about Yank brigadier general?

He let the brandy burn down his throat, shaking off his agitation. She didn't seem the nun type. Nor had he seen her singing with the nuns or saying devotions during evening prayers. Instead she worked solidly, hour after hour, with her patients.

Yet he craved her goodness, the invisible stroke of her fingers against his cheek. Wasn't it why he had always sought her out, inviting the power that swirled and danced around her? Was she a heavenly messenger sent to help him fight the raging beast inside him?

He had been selfish, stubborn, arrogant and

undeserving, yet he somehow hoped her light would never be lost in the universe, and that a tiny amount might flow from her vessel into his.

He knew he would die in this war, that he'd lasted this long astonished him. But before he took the last bullet, he'd capture a crumb of Sister Grace's divination.

That little chin of hers raised like a flag of warning when she was feeling…what? Threatened in some way? But the truth of her nature was found in the softness and warmth of her eyes when her emotions overcame her…he frowned. The word that came to mind was…defenses.

What really threatened Sister Grace? She was an enigma…a challenge. He'd figure it out. He never backed away from a challenge.

CHAPTER 9

WHY WASN'T GRACE SURPRISED HE'D use extortion to get what he wanted? Well, what did she expect, sneaking into his tent and borrowing his brandy? The wind blew, flailing her unruly cornette. She tucked a few strays of loosened hair beneath the starched garment, and then looked down at her worn and soiled tunic. No matter. As Sister Josephine had told her, she was not to seek vanity doing the Lord's work.

In front of his headquarters, Grace came to a dead halt, and puzzled over the colonel's uncharacteristic behavior. The mistake was thinking that there could be an antidote to that uncertainty. Should she cross herself for added protection?

He threw open the flap, and she jumped back. Had he known she was dithering?

She eyeballed the table service set for two and wasn't so sure about the unconventional arrangement. "No one else is attending?"

"They were otherwise occupied."

No doubt they were otherwise occupied because he'd not invited anyone else.

He tied the flaps back with sureness, to have less intimacy, and to make her feel comfortable. She was grateful for that. He seated her at a table set up with fine food. At least as fine as the teetering Confederacy allowed.

She inspected the food artfully laid out. She could have been at the table of a fine southern aristocrat. Heat rose from warm flaky biscuits, smoked ham, peas, and potatoes, and then there was strawberry jam, fresh cream and butter. Little coils of steam rose from a tin coffee pot. Her mouth watered. Despite him being her enemy, her stomach was not.

"It's not real coffee like the Yanks have, it's ground okra seeds and the best I can provide."

Her gaze slid to the brandy box that had caused the tumult earlier in the day. A burnt umber brand on the side of the box appeared that she'd missed. "Property of Colonel Philip Sheridan, Second Michigan Cavalry, United States Army." She recited and then burst out laughing. "You stole that brandy from a Union commander."

With feigned innocence, he bestowed a boyish smile and used her own words. "I borrowed it."

She blew across the surface of the coffee and took a tentative sip. "You are a thief."

"Subtract that from my superb qualities." He grinned again, a quick flash of undiluted charm. "I like borrowing from Sheridan. Have made it my mission."

He tilted his head in thoughtful admonition. "I'd like it better to *borrow* from Senator Dawson."

She took a bigger swallow, and then spread her fingers out in a fan against her breastbone unable to believe what she'd heard. "Senator Dawson?" she squeaked.

"He's corrupt. The particular shipment I stole was meant for the grand senator. That stump orator has promised to flog, lynch, and then throw my body to the buzzards. I'm his favorite target and the reprobate castigates me every chance he gets, supplying eager newspapers with his infinite tirades against me, so they can sell extra copies while the publicity he obtains garners votes for him."

He shook out a *New York Herald* and read. *"Colonel Ryan Rourke is the worst of the world's villains. He loots and plunders the women of the north, is a dictator, and human scum. It is said he practices cannibalism…"*

Wincing, Grace looked down into her cup, swirled the coffee up close to the rim as he continued reading.

"…he is a monster, a swindler, murderer, thief, and predator. In summation, he remains the north's greatest atrocity, and I hold the Union Army accountable to capture and hang him."

Ryan slapped the tattered paper on the table. "I'd like to come face to face with the coward who hides safely behind enemy lines and uses me to advance his popularity. How outspoken would he be staring down the end of my Colt pistol?"

Grace swallowed, remembering her stepfather's bloodthirsty taunts to the press concerning the Gray Ghost.

"As easy as a child blows the down off a dandelion…is exactly how hard it would be for me to tear the limbs from

Colonel Rourke's sockets."

What if the colonel learned of her relationship to the infamous senator? Would he exact revenge on her? "We must always be forgiving," she said, not for her stepfather's sake but for hers.

In the column next to her stepfather's rant on Colonel Rourke was a notice about her. Gooseflesh rippled up her back. A sizeable cash award was offered for any information of her whereabouts or return. *Dear God.* They were looking for her. She inched her hand over the newspaper and folded it to conceal the announcement. "Forget Senator Dawson. Let us not waste the evening with his acerbic defamations."

Colonel Rourke settled his long frame in the chair opposite her. "Wine?" he asked and when she nodded, he leaned over and filled her glass, and then she thought better of it for a nun should not be drinking.

She picked up her napkin and placed it on her lap, her knuckles white from gripping it so tight. "Borrowing instead of thievery? You are incurable, using my own words against me." Oh, how she was dying to get off the topic of her family. She thought about his dream to own a horse farm. Wouldn't he be surprised to learn that her family possessed the finest horse farm in the northeast? "I like your dream of having a horse farm after the war. Noble and worth pursuing." She took a sip of wine. "I imagine your mother had a difficult time with you in your childhood."

He tilted his head back and scratched his neck. A dark shadow stubbled his sculpted jaw. "I do remember one time...my older brother, John had a prized horse, black as midnight. He went on and on about that horse to the point where I decided to give him a lesson in humility. I wove stories of a rare horse disease running through the county. I painted his horse white, and then with great alarm hauled my brother to the barn."

Grace arrested her spoon of potatoes midair and blinked. Was this the scourge of the north sharing boyhood anecdotes?

"My brother went into fits, wailing about his horse. Then he saw drops of paint on the floor I hadn't cleaned up. By that time, I couldn't stop from laughing. Like a wild banshee, he went after me, and for sure if he caught me, I would have had a good licking. Fortunately, I could outrun him. The downside was that my mother made me scrub every inch of that horse. Took me two whole days."

"I'm sure that wasn't all," she taunted, relaxing her limbs. He must have bathed in the river before dinner, and she caught the way he smelled, like the forests, and good sharp brandy, underscored by something she couldn't at all place. Something that couldn't strictly be identified nor reproduced, like the scent of rain or woodland ferns.

He stretched out his legs, and then clasping his hands behind the back of his neck, he stared up at the canvas ceiling. "I tied my other brother, Lucas' shoes to the table leg, and then told him there was a whole new batch of rabbits born. He tore out of his seat and fell flat on the floor. Everyone laughed except my mother for he had upended her shepherd's pie that had taken all day to prepare. I did get reprimanded behind the woodshed by my father and couldn't sit down for a week."

She sipped her wine and studied him over the edge of her glass. The good-humored manner in which he delivered his past was underscored with something else.

Something desperate and *bleak*.

"Were you always of impeccable character, Sister Grace?"

His question landed in her belly like hot coals tumbling out of the hearth. His mouth barely turned up at the corners, but the register was of such depth and resonance that it vibrated through her, spearing her chest with a possible duplicitous meaning.

Did he know about her crime?

She put her mind at rest knowing Colonel Rourke was the kind of man who would confront her if he'd learned of her wrongdoing. In the spirit of the moment, she grinned sheepishly. "When I was a child, we had a servant who was superstitious. She'd spill salt over her left shoulder, avoid black cats, kept rosemary growing by the garden gate. I made a stuffed, lifelike dummy, lowered it off the second story balcony to where she was shelling peas. The servant dropped in a dead faint."

He lifted one dark brow. "Sister Grace, that was very bad of you."

She let out a peal of laughter and his lips twitched in amusement, and then he absently massaged his fork between the ball of his thumb and forefinger. "I have a matter I've been mulling and would like for you to answer. You and Sister Clara dress differently than Sister Josephine and Sister Jennifer Agatha. What exact kind of nun are you?"

Grace dabbed her napkin around her mouth. His directness had taken her off guard. "I'm what is called a novitiate."

"Like a nun in training?"

"It means, I have not sworn my final vows."

His eyes rested on her lips. "So, you're not a full-fledged nun yet?"

Swallowing around a tongue gone suddenly dry, she said, "I have sworn my life to God."

He paused and pulled back, pondering her statement, let the words he was about to say remain voiceless.

She rubbed her sweaty hands across her thighs. Perhaps she should have not agreed to the dinner arrangement. "I haven't told you much about Sister Clara. She is so sweet and gentle."

He scowled. "She is scared of her own shadow."

Grace rose indignant. "With due cause. Her husband fought for the Union and was killed."

"There are many men dead in this war from both sides."

"I'm not judging who was killed. Her husband's death was a blessing, and I tell you this in confidence. He was a drunkard and beat her regularly. When he died, she was left a pauper for he left his estate to his brother who evicted her. With no place to go, and no financial means, she joined the Sisters of Charity. Because of her great fear of men, I placed her with Francis. He is very kind."

"Francis is special."

"I noted his affinity with animals. The crow never leaves his side. To my chagrin, dogs, skunks and porcupines flood the hospital tent, vying for his attention. He is magic. While Sister Clara helps him to recover, it is my hope, he will heal her."

"What about the other sisters?"

He was all agog. She imagined the colonel was curious about women with special devotions and she warmed to the topic. "I love Sister Josephine, and you will, too, as you get to know her. Imagine a bulldog whose ferocious exterior covers a heart tender to the point of sentimentality, and you have Sister Josephine."

Not desiring to place a pall on the evening, she didn't talk about Sister Jennifer Agatha knowing Colonel's Rourke's opinion of the irascible nun.

The lantern suspended overhead sputtered, creating competing shadows over the sharp angles of his face and were just as enticing as the illumination of the single flame.

He tilted his chair back on two legs, his body made perfect with the promise of hard, lean muscle. There was a slow roll in her stomach, the tripping of her heart. She stared at the pulse throbbing in the base of his strong throat and her libido stirred in all kinds of forbidden ways. Her eyes caught his heated gaze and held her.

The thin walls of the tent created an isolation from the gritty conversation of men around campfires and the noisy clanging of their cookware.

In the distance, the first slow stroke of a bow across a violin created a crescendo that seeped into her skin like warm water. The violin spoke, rousing her gently as it unwound, rising and tensing. It was poetry and seduction and light and shadow and every contradiction she could think of. It was impossible to breathe. The music undulated across the camp like a quintessence, like a thing alive and weighted with passion.

Why was he looking at her like that? Was it hunger and longing?

With certainty, she was imagining things. Wasn't she? She smoothed a fold in her gown and frowned. It was such plain, serviceable gown. Certainly nothing like the satin confections she had worn seemingly so long ago. As her mother had told her many times, no ornamentation would bring her beyond plain.

Yet to be a woman. A strange yearning to dress in something pretty and ladylike, to be treated as a woman. Oh, to be able to smile and laugh with her own feminine joyfulness, instead of having to curb the softer looks and inspire holiness.

The charade she must play each day bred its own repugnance. To don those wretched clothes and assume the hallowed persona grew more grueling. Little by little, the masquerade had stripped her of her womanhood.

How would Colonel Rourke view her?

In her mind, she observed the tall, lean form of Colonel Rourke swoop past, and on his arm, a woman elegantly dressed. His face was animated and attentive as he wooed the lady, and on bended knee he vowed his love. The woman's hand extended as if bequeathing knighthood upon the handsome head, and his lips marked the slim fingers and traced a path along the bare, white arm. The vision broadened, and then the image of a noose came to the fore.

The dream in which "Sister Grace" could share no part vanished. Doubts beat a wild tattoo. The walls of her beliefs like thistledown in the wind, blew away and disappeared. Simple. Austere. Unappealing. She wanted to shake her fist to the heavens. She looked at her hand and stared at an empty palm. Nothing. Nothing deterred fate's lot.

"You mentioned Francis saved your life," she said, suppressing her musings.

He glanced out the tent and beyond to where she heard a dispute growing in a heated game of cards between soldiers. "We had gone out on reconnaissance to discover the position and strength of the enemy when we were fired on by Yank cavalry. My horse slipped, fell on me, leaving me senseless. Francis, under heavy gunfire, returned for me and brought me back."

Under her skin, she itched, sure there was more to the story, more he wasn't telling her, and that more haunted him. Shrouded in an invisible cloak, he had placed himself into a small space where he could not be detected. Yet, like a child peeking through a door crack, she perceived his wound.

In the distance, a bugler played the eloquent and haunting melody of *Taps* to signal the day's end. The melancholy song ended, and they sat silently, ignoring the flow of the outside world. She marveled at the pure silence, marveled at the activity where they were able to sit across from each other and not say anything and still feel content.

Yet, the undercurrents and things not said between them were as broad as a continent. The sun sank, and the last rays of light painted somber fingers of orange and magenta in the tent.

Grace peered up at him. "Captain Gill is a secretive man. No more than a half-dozen words beyond 'yes' and 'no' in a consecutive sentence."

Colonel Rourke dropped his chair on all fours and reached for his cigar box. "Do you mind?

"By all means."

He reached for a cigar, lit it with the scrape of a lucifer and tugged on it until its tip was a fiery red. The pleasant smoke spiraled and drifted out the tent. "Captain Gill's wife died in childbirth to a stillborn son. He was away at war. When the news came…I never saw a huge man crumble like that. It was more than crying, it was the kind of desolate sobbing that drained a person of all hope."

"Such a devastating loss. Men grieve in different ways. I assume he has withdrawn from the world."

Rourke nodded solemnly. "I'll depart before daybreak."

Grace started. Had he told her he was leaving to gauge her reaction? That she'd miss him? Forbidden.

"Leaving again?" Her heart somersaulted with fear that something would happen to him.

Why should she be concerned for her enemy?

"I'll shall pray for your safe return," she whispered.

"Will you?" His eyes bored into her, giving her a glimmer of hope regardless of her shortcomings, yet a ping of caution drove a spike in her chest. No. She could not get involved.

She jerked her gaze from his and like stopping at the edge of a frigid river, she willed impossible desires away. "I want to thank you for Corporal Anderson. He has been a big help, lifting patients and helping Sister Josephine. I sense he is not your typical soldier?"

"Amos, despite his brawn, folded at a battle, cowering under a tree fall and nearly had us all killed. I keep him employed other ways at camp."

To care for a gentle giant by keeping him out of military action? Her esteem rose another notch for the colonel.

He took his cigar out of his mouth and pointed it at her. "Don't we all have our secrets?" He looked at her until she squirmed. He was not a man slow to seize on an inconsistency.

A goading breeze blew, billowed out of the tent, poked a drift of smoke from an exterior wood fire, and stirred his hair. She clapped her hand on her cornette and grabbed her wine glass.

"So, how did you decide to become a nun?"

To bare herself? To tell him she wasn't a real nun? The impulse frightened her enough that she wrapped her arms about her middle in a foolish attempt to hold herself together.

"It was a calling," she shrugged. "I imagine with the same motivation as you entered the war. Why did you enter the war?"

He said nothing, just tilted back his chair again, his gaze steady on her and assessing.

"I see sadness in you, Colonel Rourke. If you ever want to talk to someone, I'm here for you," she offered with saintly comportment, relieved she could hide behind her Holy Orders.

In the uncomfortable stillness, she glanced around at his arsenal of weapons. His sword gleamed in the light, a brace of Colt pistols, knives, rifles and on the floor, boxes of bullets, everything that depicted a warrior. "Chronic remorse is an undesirable sentiment."

She should know.

Something in his manner made her want to confide things to him. Painful things. Shameful things. She didn't know how badly she wanted to share them.

"My father was my world. I was always by his side and I have many fond remembrances. He took me to New York City one summer to a concert with the famed Jenny Lind. After that, I was sold and wanted singing lessons. My father promptly procured the best of voice teachers. Unfortunately, my calling was not to be on stage. That was one of many fond memories I have of him. My favorite however was how he held my hand when I was troubled. Before he let go, he'd give me a slight squeeze that told me everything was well in the world."

She took a deep sip of her wine, swallowed hard and a sharp pain lanced through her heart. "I live with the grief of the loss of my father. Despite all my medical training, I was unable to do anything. I cried for days. I cried until my eyes ran dry and my chest heaved violently." She caught a sob.

"I'm sorry for your loss." He stood up to adjust the overhead lantern, invading her space, towering over her like a wall of heat and muscle, as though his body formed a protective cage around her. "Your mother? Did she have influence on your life decision?"

His words slipped over her, low and compelling. Grace paused, put her wine glass on the table, and then placed a hand low on her belly where it seemed an entire flock of birds flapped and churned their wings in equal measure to the violent memories she felt. The hurt of all those years brought a bitter taste to her mouth. She didn't want to nor did she know how to talk about her mother.

All her formative years, if only she'd had a normal relationship. She supposed it wasn't her mother's fault. Her father had told her to be patient with her mother who was brought up with cold, insensitive, demanding, and dismissive parents.

Grace had learned that her father had been older when he was sought out by her mother who asked *him* to marry her. As a shy, gentle bachelor with no desire to spend time away from his practice, he took her to wife. Yet the moment he said, "I do" her whole demeanor changed to a demanding witch. As a gentle person, her father did not possess the coping mechanism to deal with his difficult wife and let her rule. Grace knew that to protect her from her own mother, her father kept her at his side, providing the love she should have had from both parents.

Grace set her jaw to keep from saying more and, for a long time, she scratched her plate with her fork, pushing around her peas. But the anger she had carried for so long drove the words from her. "The ball was to be fantastic. The ladies' dresses—silks and velvets for the dames, tarlatan and Swiss muslin for the younger, adorned with white water lilies from Paris and other fine flowers of French make. Like a fairyland it was…I was all of six summers and was enthralled with the excitement. I wandered into my mother's boudoir and sat at her vanity. I knew it was wrong for I was never allowed in her private quarters, but I couldn't resist. I touched her shiny silver brushes and crystal perfume bottles and felt ever so elegant. I picked up the mirror, fingering the fine silver scrollwork and looking at my reflection.

"'What an ugly child.' My mother jerked me off the chair by my hair. 'How could I have brought into this world such a horrid progeny?' The mirror fell from my hands and broke into a million glass shards. My mother dragged me through the broken glass, thrust me from her room and slammed the door behind me, screaming at me never to enter again."

Grace drew a long, ragged breath and returned her gaze to him. "In the end, I learned the girl in the mirror wasn't what I wanted to be, and her life wasn't the one I wanted to have."

His calm posture was deceiving, she realized, as his muscles were coiled tightly as a predator ready to spring. Though his expression remained indecipherable, a unique sense of leashed violence wove through the air between them, though his placid, enigmatic features never revealed it.

As he withdrew from her, she stared down at her twisting hands. Weren't they a mirror of each other's souls? Yet the mirror came with costs.

CHAPTER 10

A DAY LATER, IN THE WEE hours of the morning, Grace had awakened to a terrible cacophony. They had been roused from their beds, struck camp and traveled many miles on bumpy lumber roads, evading retreating Union troops. A battle had occurred near the town of New Market. Rumors claimed many wounded and killed, and she worried about Colonel Rourke and his men.

The mist swallowed the base of the mountains, smothering the greens of the leaves, the grasses and the underbrush. It leached out their color, turning everything a stony gray. The mood was apprehensive, matching Sister Jennifer Agatha's unsympathetic complaints that crawled over Grace's skin. How many times had they been lost to retrace their steps?

She jumped at the sound of gunfire.

Their driver leaned back. "Don't worry, Sisters.

Some skirmishers and many false alarms, probably a hog rooting or an old hare on its late morning round that's drawing the fire of a vidette."

He scrutinized the terrain ahead and with a razor-sharp turn, thrust the wagon into brush to conceal them. Her fellow sisters cried out and fell into her. The driver placed his finger to his mouth to silence them.

"Over here," shouted Sister Jennifer Agatha.

"Hold steady, Sister, or I'll blow your brains out," hissed a private, holding his revolver to the side of Sister Jennifer Agatha's head.

Grace held her breath. Had the Yanks heard Sister Jennifer Agatha? With certainty they'd be caught in a firestorm.

Canteens clanged against other accoutrements, officers shouted commands, tree branches crunched underfoot in rhythmic design. A Union infantry line advanced on the road they'd left behind. Through the mist, the blue line hummed like swarming bees. Men cursed. So close. She might reach out and touch them with her fingers.

Sister Jennifer Agatha's shout had poured kerosene onto the spark of fear in Grace's belly. Despite the morning chill, her skin was drenched in sweat. Grace told herself that the fear was simply her overactive brain, and then attempted to analyze the situation from the outside as if she were reading fiction. What would the character in the book do?

Her character would be strong and protective of her fellow sisters. She reached out a trembling hand and held Sister Clara's clammy one.

When the last of the Yank line passed, she let go her

breath, and barely declined the urge to slap the nasty nun. "Sister Jennifer Agatha, you could have gotten us all killed."

Sister Jennifer Agatha pushed away the soldier's gun. "You stinking pile of codpieces."

The heat of the sun broke through as Sergeant Hutchinson and another Confederate soldier galloped toward them. "Good morning, Sisters. We are here to guide you to your hospital. Hurry."

A real hospital. Grace straightened with hope to do good in a valley of wretchedness. Colonel Rourke had promised her a real hospital and had delivered on his promise.

Their driver tapped a whip over the mules' rears. More miles stretched before them, passing burned homes, barns and the charred remains of corncribs. They entered a small town and, in the distance, countless bodies were laid out for burial. The sisters crossed themselves.

Homes were commandeered for temporary hospitals. In outside tents, surgeons stripped to the waist stood splattered with blood, some holding the soldiers, while others, armed with long bloody knives and saws, cut and sawed away with frightful rapidity, throwing the mangled limbs on a pile as soon as they were removed. Many men were stretched on the ground awaiting their turn, many more were arriving, either limping along or borne on stretchers, while those upon whom operations had already been performed calmly fanned the flies from their wounds. The fortunate prospect remained she would have a hospital.

After a few more miles, the driver pulled the wagons

to a halt. Like a swarm of bees, men carried the injured on stretchers.

"A barn? This is not the hospital I was promised."

The cavernous gray structure, rose high from the ground, clinging like an aphid on a meadow's skirts, and shaky as though the wind might blow it into the forests.

Squealing pigs and baying sheep were shooed from the barn. Men removed a ladder laying against the open hayloft above, shifting a flock of startled pigeons from their roost. Cows lowed and dray horses snorted in the paddock adjacent to the unyielding structure. She stepped down from the wagon and sank into the mud. Shrieks came from Sister Jennifer Agatha who slipped on a pile of manure, her hands skidding in the muck.

"At least the roof don't leak. Cots will be coming shortly," said Sergeant Hutchinson, smirking at the flailing nun as Amos helped her up.

"Leave me alone!" She slapped him away, terrifying the poor giant. "You traitor, anarchist, infidel and blasphemer."

Grace's heart panged for the trembling giant and she stepped between Amos and Sister Jennifer Agatha. "That's enough. It is one thing to berate me but I'm sick to death of you bullying Corporal Anderson. He is the kindest of men."

"It still doesn't change the fact that he is a turncoat, fanatical rebel." She pushed out her chin like the blade of a shovel, flopped down on a barrel and continued her mutiny.

In the barn, Grace grew dizzy with the influx of

injured men. "Put those men on the clean straw on the right side of the barn. You there," she commandeered five soldiers, "I want everything swept clean and fresh straw to be placed down until cots arrive."

With Sister Josephine, Grace flew into a flurry of activity, assigning degrees of wounds in the order of treatment. There were so many, moving like a shoal of fish, and she viewed herself as part of that moving mass. Men ashen, blood soaking their chests, legs, if they had legs that weren't blown off.

She knelt in the straw, her first patient gut shot. Always fatal.

"Tell my wife," he said in between stunted breaths, "I shall wait for her in the heavens above."

Before she could administer morphine to ease his journey into the next world his eyes froze over like the surface of a winter puddle.

Sister Josephine's Rosary bead belt rattled as she moved next to Grace. "His pure heart will shine and make the face radiant in that realm above which giveth the peace that passeth understanding."

Grace closed his eyes, and then nodded her head for soldiers to take him away.

The grief she felt when she lost her father started all over again, raising its dreadful head. The heartache sneaked up on her, and took her under its arms in an instant. Every memory played over and over in her head. That sane part of her she grasped with clinging fingers but vanished in thin air. The onslaught came in waves, the darkness engulfing and overwhelming her and there was nothing she could do to get out from under it.

"Water. Help me." Cries deafened her ears, men clutched at her sleeves, begging for help.

Sister Clara cowered in the corner next to Francis whom they had brought on a stretcher. Warm reassurances came from Francis, encouraging Sister Clara that she could help.

Dear God. So much devastation. Grace's blood ran cold, and like the bilges on a ship, confidence leaked from her. She flinched at the screams, her breath bursting in and out to see so much suffering. Seeds of doubt, the terror of failing, fear cutting deeper than a sword. To flee. She turned away.

Sister Josephine grabbed her arm and shook her. "Get a hold of yourself, Sister Grace. I have experienced many battles and for every battle my fear is like the phoenix. I can watch it burn a million times and nonetheless it returns. This is your first real battle and I understand how overwhelming it is where death is so terribly final. You must focus on life; it is so full of possibilities. Use your God-given gifts."

Adrenaline surged through Grace's veins, fight or flight, stand or run, be a hero or a coward. Sister Josephine's message pierced her brain.

"Believe in yourself and you're halfway there, Sister Grace. Courage and determination. Faithful and fearless."

Sister Josephine's words like her father's, rang with the knowledge, carrying aplomb and could not be duplicated any other way. Grace washed her hands and knelt beside a soldier. Her mouth fell open when Sister Clara knelt opposite her, and then handed instruments as Grace called for them. Two of them had overcome their fright.

She began digging into the soldier's pitted flesh to remove shrapnel, found a ball, and then picked up a bullet forceps. Unable to get a hold of the slippery shell, she tossed her instrument aside and used her fingers to dig through his sticky flesh.

The soldier's intense silence somehow screamed through his whole body. Eyes widened with horror, mouth rigid and open, chalky face gaunt and immobile, fists clenched with blanched knuckles with nails digging deeply into the palms of his hands.

Sister Clara held the man's hand, cooing assertions. "Sister Grace is a doctor and the best there is."

Grace's fingers grasped the ball and, holding tight, she pulled the dented sphere out. She left the bandaging to Sister Clara and moved on to her next patient.

For hours while soldiers swept, stirring up a cloud of dust motes to clean the makeshift hospital, Grace worked, her knees raw, her back aching. Men who needed limbs removed, she passed on to another surgeon, devoting her time to those she could salvage with resection. Cots arrived for the patients, then blessedly a table for her to lay the men on while she worked on them.

Without any apparent effort, she had full command of soldiers, orderlies, nurses, sisters, and her patients, impressing them so forcibly with the idea of her vigilance.

A flood of boys from the Virginia Military Institute were brought in on stretchers. No more than sixteen summers, the bloom of their youth snuffed out, and for what purpose? To scream at the world, to tear her hair out with the senseless maiming and waste of lives.

A boy shot in the leg held up a pencil and paper. "Will you write my mother a letter?"

Another boy clung to her sleeve. "Will you read my Bible to me?"

She heard a rush of horses. No doubt more wounded. Then she heard the colonel from outside, knowing his irksome voice anywhere. His every word laced with command.

To have a hospital in a barn, in the middle of a farmyard was of no consequence. Visions merged. Colonel Rourke shooting and cutting through a swath of men as if removing wheat from the chaff. And then laid before her, an unconscious boy with golden hair and a cherub face.

Bitterness ate at her like cancer, spreading fiery acid through her gut. It was Colonel Rourke's fault this innocent was injured. The war was his fault. She wanted to pound the man with her fists and keep on screaming until she dropped.

CHAPTER 11

ALL THROUGH THE BATTLE, HE'D detached himself, knowing he'd go to her. Away from the field of battle, the field the color of blood. Her hands, delicate and fervent, would shelter him from pain. Her voice, a tentative whisper, would soothe him and strengthen him. She would make him *feel again*.

She was a nun. A creature of a distant and saintly profession. Untouchable. And yet, she'd showed him a warmth that he'd been without for a long time.

Chronic remorse is an undesirable sentiment.

How well she knew him, how she chopped down his resisting walls.

She had offered him redemption.

Riding through miles of the Shenandoah, Ryan thought of the many sides of Sister Grace. Frankly, he was surprised by how quickly he'd lost his temper with the woman. The fact that she said no to him, and in hindsight, he realized no one ever said no to him—especially a woman.

Yet, she had not the least compunction to say no, and said it as easily as she might have to a child. He'd been shocked by her standing up to him, giving him orders and sending him on his way like an eager schoolboy excited to do her errands.

He was the colonel. He was the one in command and his men were solicitous, no matter how small or meaningless the orders he gave. If it had been one of his soldiers, he'd have court-martialed him.

And this woman could insist in the most contemptible manner. How she tilted her head in that all-knowing way and say, "a word" and then thread her arm through his and drag him from his men. The fact that she commandeered his brandy. What else was missing in his personal effects? And she had the gall to call him a thief.

No southern woman in his experience would ever attempt such a thing. He would hazard a guess no other Yankee woman would, either.

This woman—he'd never encountered anyone quite like her. She was attractive with her light hair miserably hidden beneath her cornette, unusually bright violet eyes and soft voice that climbed inside him.

And yet she was different from the many attractive belles he'd met in his life. At first, he'd not understood why, but then, upon reflection, it had become clear to him—she didn't look at him with adoration in her eyes. She knew who he was, and yet, she didn't look at him with any particular reverence other than as a hopeless penitent. *None.*

It was oddly disconcerting. He didn't know how to return the gaze of a woman who saw through him. He didn't know how to feel not being pursued and desired. It felt out of step with his everyday life.

Everything lately made him feel out of step with his life.

His feelings for Sister Grace were growing beyond a strong attraction. He wanted to kiss her. And that want was getting stronger every time he saw her. The evening weeks ago, during dinner in his tent, he'd had all he could do to keep from taking her in his arms.

He'd wanted a wife and family of his own for some time now but had met no woman who had drawn his heart. Nothing in his life had ever prepared him for the immediate, strong attraction he'd felt the moment he looked into Sister Grace's eyes. Nor for the way that attraction continued to grow, to deepen every time he saw her.

He dismounted and handed the reins to a private. "Give Archimedes a ration of oats and brush him down."

Rourke went to his tent, snuffed out the light his sergeant had left on for him and collapsed on his bed. He laced his hands behind his head, let out a frustrated growl, flopped to his side and yanked his pillow into place. *I can't figure out what is going on, and I don't dare trust my heart.*

His hands curled into fists. In a rare moment, when she'd let her guard down, he'd witnessed what was written in her soul. *Unwanted, contemptible, a disgrace.* That she endured a hateful, selfish mother who had abused her intelligent, beautiful daughter was reprehensible.

Grace had been cheated of a good mother. A woman with a head, a heart and soul. A woman capable of listening, of leading and respecting a child, and not drowning her own defects in her. Someone whom a child would not only love because she's her mother but will also admire for the person she is. Someone she would want to grow up to resemble.

His own mother was perfection. She had been there to teach, to temper the hurts, to encourage and inspire. He smiled. Her reprimands had the sting of a feather. Her intense love did not measure, it just gave.

Fortunately, Grace's father had shown a sensitive girl love and had shaped her into an extraordinary woman. Yet her father's death had dealt a devastating blow.

How he'd like to take her away from the pain of loss, a life of cruelty and mistreatment. To heal the wounds of her past.

He could not. She was sworn to a higher vocation. Or was she? She had said she was a novitiate, like a soldier who hadn't earned his stripes. For a moment, her status gave him a shine of hope.

Yet he was pledged to the war and who knew if he would live or die. No. He'd not leave her a mournful widow, or worse, a child brought into the world without a father.

He frowned. That he entertained the notion of marriage and family? If it was to be anyone, it would be Grace. She frustrated him, made him laugh, possessed the truest smile, had generosity of the heart, and tendered a friendship. Perfect.

Ludicrous. She was devoted to her calling. Hadn't

she told him so?

For Rourke, hell was no longer a place, but a state of being. His prison did not consist of four walls guarded by men, but by the sacredness of her vows. She was a nun and he dared not contaminate her with his impurity.

War had taught him nothing was permanent. How better than to remain numb and let his emotions float away. To not care. Detachment was preferable, no risk of vulnerability. But he knew it as a delusion, to keep himself occupied and deal with the struggles and realities of the maimed and dead.

"Please place the boy on the table, Corporal Anderson." Grace closed her eyes. To save his arm? She felt a bright light fall over her, opened her eyes and glanced up. Colonel Rourke nodded quietly and adjusted a lantern overhead.

Had she missed him? Her heart panged with the forbidden admonition, but an unforgiving demon took hold of her. "You look tired." Her voice held no mercy. If he noticed her aloofness, he ignored it.

Other lamps were lit as the night fell. Grace stretched, looked at the moonlight slanting between boards.

She felt his eyes on her as she placed a cone of chloroform over the boy's nose and mouth. The boy laughed hysterically then with his good arm rounded a fist and slammed it toward her chest. She jumped, missing the blow. A reaction she was accustomed to with the anesthetic.

"Get more men over here. Hold him down," Colonel

Rourke ordered.

Soon the boy's limbs went limp, and the men stepped back. She made her incision to begin a resection. She prayed while she worked to save the boy's arm. For hours she worked on the boy, the colonel staying with her the whole time and assisting.

Despite her roiling anger with the colonel, his presence was comforting.

"I noted you do not wear a gold sash, stars or trim to decry your rank," she said, her voice cold and flat.

He leaned a shoulder against a barn beam and ended his spell of silence. "I don't want to summon a Yank bullet. Officers are shot first."

"It doesn't bother you to be called land pirate or horse thief?"

"I take those terms as honorable and demonstrative of my success."

She plucked out the last metal shards, and then she reached for her needle and thread.

He folded his arms in front of him. "The Battle of New Market is won. A makeshift army of forty-one hundred Confederates up against ten thousand, defeated Union Major General Franz Sigel and his Army of the Shenandoah. We stopped Grant from threatening Lee's western flank. The crops of the Shenandoah will be saved."

Her anger rising, she braced herself against his smooth, deeply accented Virginian drawl that feathered along her nerve endings, and then she pulled a stitch closed. "So many wounded and dead…no good can balance such evil."

"Unfortunately, I am the remedy, however futile, to

that wretched reality."

Her hands shook as she drew another stitch and looped it closed. His callous admittance that they had won the battle when the boy she worked on would have a dramatically altered life. "We are doomed to repeat history where no amount of collateral damage is too much, where the wicked and stupid masses are easily manipulated into war by corrupt politicians, arrogant academics and pious religious leaders, spewing their propaganda in the name of God."

He leaned over, only inches from hers, a mask of steely determination. "We cannot give up when facing the impossibility. We will not be defeated," he said, his voice rigid, uncompromising.

"Why were schoolboys allowed to fight?"

"They are men. They proved themselves out on the field of battle. Do not demean them."

She clipped a thread. "Your folly, Colonel is your excessive pride. Though you deceive yourself, deep down below the surface, a voice rises that says something is out of tune."

"It's a sad fact of war."

She threw her instruments in a pan, wiped her hands free of blood and flung down the towel. "Sister Clara, I will leave you to bandage the boy. I'm going to get some air." Her stomach a ball of knots, she turned on her heel, the hem of her gown swishing the floor as she darted from the barn. Anywhere he wasn't.

Once in the open air, so many injured men lay on the ground, crying and moaning. Like an opera without music, she surveyed the devastation that was fiftyfold of what inhabited the barn.

Predictably, Colonel Rourke joined her, and she stared daggers at him. "It's more than that. It's your self-righteous, patriotic tribute to tragedy."

She'd hit a nerve and pursued her sentiments. "Victims of war are constantly drowned in tidal waves of guilt, regret and pain. I see glimpses in your eyes, no matter how much you try to hide it."

His voice came cold and steady as stone. "Perhaps I should return you to Union lines."

She paled. "I don't pity you, Colonel. Only the people who must put up with your boorish behavior."

They stared at each other. Rourke seething. Grace fuming. He stormed off. She shouldn't have picked a fight. Nor could she hold him responsible for the madness. The young boys sent to slaughter were not under his command and she had a niggling feeling if it had been under his control, he'd never have sent them into battle.

From across the yard, Captain Gill pushed from a tree and joined her, and then watched Colonel Rourke slam down the flap to his tent.

She glanced down at her bloodied apron. It was beyond wearable. "How angry do you suppose he is?"

As was his normal communication, Gill didn't reply, and she expected no more than a long stretch of quiet. How odd that Gill would talk to the colonel but not to her. Like a gaping void, his reticence vexed her, and she craved for him to cease his smothering stillness and fill it with sounds, words, anything. His silence stretched thinner and thinner, like a balloon blowing big, until the temptation to rupture it was too great to resist, and she said, "You impress me as a man of limited capacity who acquired a reputation for wisdom for not saying anything—the story of the owl?"

He practically hooted with that notion, took out his pocket watch, sprung open the timepiece and snapped it shut. "On a scale from one to ten."

She did a double take. The warrior aspired to partake in conversation? "If you think his mood would fit on a such a scale."

"It wouldn't."

She resisted the urge to look at him for fear he'd stop talking. "My next question is why do you suppose he is so angry with me?"

"He is impassioned, yes, but always tortures his logic." He took an exaggerated breath. "He's not angry with you."

"That is like calling me a wise fool for we were apparently not observing the same person just now."

"He's not angry with you. He's not accustomed to having his life disrupted. He'll come around, he's not entirely unreasonable.

"Not unreasonable?" Her mouth dropped open. *Are you lunatic?*

"It's more like he's afraid of you."

Grace blinked. "I beg your pardon."

Captain Gill let play out a long moment of silence. "Let's say he's hurting."

"Do you know what happened?"

"That's something the colonel should tell you. What I can say is, one incident in the war changed him. Changed him a lot. It was a bad maneuver and he holds himself responsible."

Grace swallowed but it did little to ease the lump in

her throat. "I don't know what to say."

"There's really nothing to say. Or do. That's the problem. Some men go out and get drunk. Colonel Rourke internalizes everything."

No wonder he was angry. She had all but accused him of the atrocities that befell the cadets and further burdened him with failing in which he'd no culpability. "But surely he realizes that in this war there are no guarantees and it wasn't his fault."

"A man like that keeps churning things in his mind."

Soldiers brought in another man on a stretcher. She'd have to attend him.

Captain Gill shook his head. "Takes a woman with spirit to—" He stopped.

"Please finish what you were going to say." She watched a bearded soldier under a tree shovel beans from his tin plate into his mouth.

"Sometimes the right woman can tame the beast."

Grace twisted her lips somewhere between a smile and a grimace. "He certainly is a beast."

"But it takes the right woman…the right woman with spirit."

"You've already said that." Realization dawned on her. "You aren't saying what I think you are saying? I'm a Bride of Christ."

"You're no more a Catholic nun than that horse tied over there."

Grace stood speechless for a moment. So astute he was. She kept her gaze on the soldier who continued to trowel beans into his mouth that now decorated his beard. After a moment, she gathered her wits enough and said, "I am of the Sisters of Mercy performing

God's work."

Beneath a tangle of brows, Grace saw a slash for the captain's mouth, then a slight upward tilt of his lips. For the first time since she'd met the long-suffering man, he cracked a smile, bursting into a full-blown grin as if a flock of bluebirds escaped from his stomach, lighting up his eyes and spreading into every part of him A strange sound came from his throat, strained like he was on the verge of choking until it arrived in the low, rumbling boom of thunder.

"You're no more a Catholic nun than that horse tied over there," he repeated, and then hiccupped into full-blown belly laughter completely unsettling her and making her question his sanity.

"I'm Catholic," said Gill. "All my uncles were priests. You don't even know how to genuflect." More laughter burst from him like ripples across a still lake.

"I'm getting better at it," she swallowed. Was she that discernable?

He howled, slapping his hand up and down almost involuntarily, could barely breathe, his laughter flowing over the firmament.

Grace frowned as he hooted, and everyone in the camp turned to see the normally stoic Captain Gill wipe his eyes, and bend over in laughter.

"When you bless yourself, it's like swatting flies." He broke out in more guffaws.

Grace blushed, furious with the attention they were receiving and her failure to maintain her masquerade. "Get a hold of yourself, Captain. We are gathering too much attention."

Captain Gill said, "The colonel finds you fetching,

but he's an honorable man and respects your *supposed* vows."

"I find this conversation ridiculous."

"You're a great doctor, even beyond that. But to my estimation, you joined the Sisters of Mercy because you're hiding from something or someone." He stepped away from her.

Grace's mouth dropped open and she ran to catch up with him and caught his arm. "You are a wicked man."

He threw back his head, his laughter echoing through the camp and over the Valley, filling the dusty air and early dawn. Men from around their campfires stared at the sight. "I have not laughed in so long," he said, gulping mouthfuls of air.

When he gained some control, he said, "What scares Colonel Rourke the most is that he's attracted to you. Can't put any more sins on the man's shoulders for being attracted to a Catholic nun. He'd not forgive himself. Yet, horrors of horrors, what if he were to fall in love with you?"

Grace didn't see that as the worst horror in the world, but she kept her thought to herself.

"The colonel's struggles entered his life as an unwelcome guest."

Grace blinked. "You are putting too much responsibility on me to heal—"

"Your obligation is to reach as deeply as you can and tender your exceptional and genuine gifts as courageously and beautifully as you are able."

Grace shook her head. "To mend a battle-scarred man? Like moving mountains and pushing the borders of impossibility way beyond my capabilities."

"It is a matter of believing…it is possible."

Grace had her doubts. "You won't tell anyone of our conversation?"

He laughed again and clamped an arm around her shoulders, and she stumbled forward before he righted her. "Sister Grace, it has been a pleasure. I'll be like a fish with its mouth closed, one that never gets caught, so feel safe that I'd never betray a confidence. In time, I'd hope you'll be honest with Colonel Rourke for he's like a brother to me and he needs healing."

CHAPTER 12

A TALL REBEL RODE UP ON his horse. Grace had seen him before, after she had performed the surgery on Francis and recalled Colonel Rourke's obvious contempt of the man.

He was thin, all boney elbows, long shanks and protruding knees. He looked to be in early middle age, had a black beard streaked with gray, sharp nose, slanted cheek bones, and unlike his counterparts, he wore a brand-new gray uniform, polished black cavalry boots with nary a scratch.

From high upon his horse, the man looked down his nose, a perfected and seemingly perennial sneer. "Good Sister, do you know who I am?"

"I don't believe I caught your name." He glared bright-eyed and bristling, as if his identity needed confirmation.

"I am Colonel Lawler."

Should she genuflect?

"And you are—"

He knew who she was. "Sister Grace," she said.

He glanced around the camp. "Where is Colonel Rourke?"

The man reminded her of her oldest stepbrother who communicated in jibes and sarcasm. Every observation curious and morbid. Every reply an insult. "Perhaps he is in his headquarters. Have you checked there?"

He chafed his gloved hands. "What is the news in Colonel Rourke's camp?"

He was snooping about Rourke to cause trouble. "I'm not privy to gossip, Colonel Lawler, nor do I partake in it."

Apparently immune to her rebuke, he dismounted and pulled off his hat. What was left of his hair banded tight all around like someone had circumcised his head. Her hands itched for her scalpel to finish the job.

"Good point. Has Colonel Rourke been advertising his good qualities? His good qualities are he is a drunkard, liar and braggart."

"You should not be spreading falsehoods about Colonel Rourke," she said, lifting her chin. She pursed her lips and clasped her hands.

"Must I restate the obvious?" he said, his voice raspy as a rat tail file across iron.

If Grace herself had been asked to christen this pompous man with a nickname, it would not have been a spider but an armadillo. There was something about Lawler's mocking voice that reminded Grace of an armored, long-nosed, snuffling, anteater…leathery scaled, malevolent and unpredictable.

"Actually, I came to talk to you. I understand you are a good doctor. I'm going to have you assigned to my camp, kind of a holy promotion." He laughed at his little joke. "What do you think of that?"

She suffered his platitudes with the same affection she had for smallpox. "I believe Colonel Rourke is in command of this camp and will be making the decisions." She smiled benignly. Lawler's overreach was outrageous and defined his presence a pity that Noah and his party made it to the ark.

He towered over her, stared unblinkingly, yet she maintained eye contact, despite the urge to pull away.

"Colonel Rourke," Lawler drawled, taking her arm, "cannot make intelligent decisions regarding where you'd be better off, so I'll make them. Now run along dear, gather up your fellow sisters. We leave within the hour."

"Your order rings in my ear like a hen that cackles as if she has laid an asteroid." She jerked her arm away and strode across the yard to find Colonel Rourke. She glanced over her shoulder, Lawler bounded toward her, his shiny boots kicking up puffs of dust and jangled her nerves.

She walked faster, her gown dragged and she tripped on it, but quickly righted herself. Several injured soldiers tried to rise to assist her. She waved them off.

Lawler caught up with her, grabbed her hand and pulled her back across the camp, his strength surprising her as did his boldness. "No more than you deserve for your insubordination. Once you are under my command—"

A few men sitting by a fire singing in accompaniment

to a banjo, stopped and stared at her rough treatment.

"You will take your hands off Sister Grace now," shouted one of the men.

"She is a prisoner of war and I'll do as I see fit," said Lawler.

Grace pushed at Lawler. "You have the disposition of a warthog."

Lawler laughed.

A few men shouted out, some rose on their crutches, and then they crowded around her in a protective circle. Guns went up. Grace blinked.

Lawler glared at the men. "How dare you point your guns at a Confederate officer? I'll have you hanged for treason."

Silence snapped the air. The men glanced uneasily at one another from the possibility and lowered their guns. Where was Colonel Rourke? Grace shook. With certainty, Lawler descended on Rourke's camp because he knew the colonel wasn't present.

She scratched at his hands to pry his fingers loose, grimacing as rancid tobacco breath wafted into her face. Her stomach roiled. His strength overpowered her and she nearly let out a string of curses at him. Instead, she said, "God made fools first, Colonel Lawler. That was for practice. Then he made you." She wiggled and jerked back, pulled at his fingers and still unable to free herself, she drew back her knee and brought it up hard against the Rebel colonel's groin.

The men's laughter drowned out the pained sound that escaped from Lawler. A moment later he said through clenched teeth, "You will rue the day you dared to injure me—" he began in raw fury, and then hobbled after her, a murdering menace vivid in his eyes.

A pistol shot split the air. Everyone jumped. Lawler swiveled.

Pushing through the intimidating horde of Rebel soldiers glided a considerable man. A threat of violence came off of him in waves as thick as the smoke of a green bonfire.

Rourke.

His dark hair ruffled in the wind, the expressive sweep of his dark brows, and the sensuous bow of his lips radiated a mix of brutal predatory instinct, and irrefutable authority. It seemed that at any second a trembling mechanism could give way in the wily brain behind those burning cobalt eyes to unleash a crushing bout of destructiveness.

His right hand rested on the handle of his pistol, the leisurely grace of long habit. Rourke ambled to within inches of Lawler. "Be aware, I ask just once, after that, I'll not be provoked further. Nor will I allow my hospitality to stand in the way of my exerting what is critical and polite." He made an all-encompassing sweep of his arm. "You have many of my men with guns and itching to use them. So, you see wisdom suggests that we make amends, wisely raise our generous hearts to the predictable, and offer you to be so obliging to release Sister Grace?"

"I see," said Lawler. He planted his hand on the silver handle of his revolver. With unpolished gallantry and smooth aloofness, he took his measure of the Gray Ghost. "Indeed, there is much fervor in what you say."

"It's with healthy optimism, you ease my sentiments.

For it would not seem inconvenient to shoot you myself," snapped Colonel Rourke, his tone one that would make the devil jerk to attention.

Lawler's eyes played over him like tips of steel "President Davis will have a different opinion."

Ryan's lips curved with blatant disregard at Lawler's threat. "Unhand her now or perhaps more generously, I'll start slowly from the top to bottom to dismember you. It won't be pretty."

"You are a buffoon to think you can keep her. A buffoon, you hear?"

Rourke leaned over, plucked a piece of Timothy grass and chewed on the sweet end. "I have been summoned to General Lee's headquarters."

Lawler looked aghast, dropped her arm. "General Lee?"

"You weren't summoned? How odd."

Grace gauged Rourke had hit a sore spot, and he chuckled mockingly. "You're not intelligent at all, Lawler. Moronic, yes. Intelligence comes with forethought. A moron, however, doesn't stop to think or reason. He acts on instinct, like an animal, convinced he's doing good, that he's always right, and sanctimoniously proud to go around besmirching or accosting anyone he perceives to be beneath him."

"You tell him, Colonel." The men surrounding them murmured their approval.

Lawler seethed.

Rourke gave a careless shrug. "Do you have any important business?"

Lawler didn't respond.

"I thought not. My men will escort you to the

edge of my camp, but leave with one final word of warning. Never touch Sister Grace again, or some dark night while you are silent and content, and in the gray shadows of your sleep, a ghost will appear, a very wrathful ghost."

CHAPTER 13

RYAN GUARDED HIS FOOTFALLS, FOLLOWED her to the top of the hill until he came up behind her.

"Did you think I meant to escape?" She spoke to the firmament in front of her without turning her head to look at him.

He moved shoulder to shoulder watching the line where heaven touched earth. The majesty of the sunset hauled him into its net as orange gold stretched far and wide, the color of fire hearths and tangerines. "Up here," he said, "the peace comes to me. I wish I could stop moving forward and exist in this moment. Not breathing. Not thinking. Watching the mauves of the dusky sky intensify and the cotton bale clouds blush at the warm touch of *the* sun."

Grace said quietly, "I come here to get away from everything. Yet to find that mirage of peace? You above all people should know that more challenging than war is waging peace."

She referred to their argument earlier about the cadets placed in harm's way. He knew she was upset and held him responsible. Silhouettes of birds flew across the sky that was now magenta, the battle cry of the night closing in on them. "Can't you ever say anything approving?"

She sighed. "You are better than Colonel Lawler."

"That's not a comparison."

"Hmmm. You have a fine row of teeth."

Ryan gave an impatient snort and after a stretch of time passed, said, "Do you realize you've made it thirty seconds without a pointed barb shot at me?"

"That long?"

Silence hung in the air, thick and heavy like a blanket interrupted by a soothing breeze, and the music of cicadas, yet forsaking the gentle energy of the landscape to wash in.

No matter what he thought about, no matter what he did, or more accurately, tried to do, his thoughts came to Sister Grace, to the way she had looked at him in the hospital when he'd first arrived. There had been such warmth, such softness, such…trust…in her eyes in those moments as if she'd missed him. And then, in an instant, it was gone.

The woman had him elated and hopeful one moment, deflated and despairing the next. Was her withdrawal only to do with the injured cadets or was there something more? "Despite the abuse and recrimination you heaped on me, I did not give the orders for the cadets to be used."

"I was wretched to put all the blame on your head.

If you would forgive me?" she said.

"Forgive you? Forgive perfection?"

They stood nearly eye-level as the last of summer's warming rays stretched over them, giving way to fingers of darkness, and then flushing out the biggest star, yielding to thousands of stars. What was it about her that drew him like this? It was as though he were a ship flung about in a tempest, and she a siren tempting him to his fate. In her presence, his body was consistently at odds with his mind, and refused to obey him in any regard.

He feared his happiness and his vision would diminish if he reached for her. Even so, his hand glided down her arm, his fingers lacing with hers. Palms kissing, he could feel the fast thud of her heart through his single touch. It was that time in between. In between war and wretchedness and what was forbidden. When the world was quiet for just a moment and nothing else mattered.

She gave a half-hearted shrug. "There were rumors and rumors of war and the superstitious thought it was predicted in the sky. One summer night in 1861, I saw the whole canopy of the heavens obscured by mottled clouds tinged with color as red as blood. Such a phenomenon has not been seen before by those who saw it then, nor has it been seen since. Speaking figuratively, the ominous clouds burst and deluged the beautiful land with blood."

Resigned and weary, he said, "The disagreements and animosity between northern and southern states had been escalating for years, but when the cannons fired, those disagreements were replaced by mortal combat.

I suffer with the decision every day of my life. It comes with the job. I had my own myth, cherished it, did not understand for many months how wrong I was. I truly believed that all the outrage against Lincoln could be contained, that matters could be handled peacefully."

Her hand held warmth. She was not horrified, neither did she pull away. In the spaces between each other's fingers, their hands fit perfectly. When just for a little while, to breathe life into each other and appreciate one of the best gifts the world could give.

They didn't look at each other and he wondered if she felt as he did that the spell might be broken if they did. No word passed…the silent communion of the splendor of the night and the human spirit loaded with troubles instinctively sought each other. It seemed a natural thing to do, that comfort and protection. So, they stood hand in hand like two children with peace in their hearts for all the dark things that surrounded them.

When all I desire is to have your heart beat close to mine, knowing all of what I want the most is so near yet held so far away.

Finally, he said, "Coming to you, to be healed by you, will break me. For to come to you is prohibited, yet to stay away is pain. So, here I remain, locked in—I apologize. I should pull my mind back within the confines in which it is permitted to roam."

Whenever he opened his mouth to speak, a dread of her repulsion, of her retreat, wrapped their icy fingers around his throat. Choking him into silence.

If he stayed very still…she wouldn't leave. If he remained silent, he'd not offend her.

If he didn't breathe, maybe she'd not abandon him.

Grace's heart fluttered, and then sank. Fate was cruel to play this trick on her. The proud colonel all but declared his intentions. Grace breathed in the heady scents of ferns, pines and —the scent of him, felt the heat from his body next to hers. Every breath wove into her brain and spiraled there. In the stillness, she could hear his heartbeats, feel his pulse pounding along her nerves. She glanced at him. There was something powerful about the forbidden maleness of this man. It was almost as if the perfection of his face and form were at constant war with the scarred part of his soul. A flash of sympathy softened her discomfort. The warm evening lulled her. The moment felt so perfect…so perfectly right. It was possible to imagine…

No. As the night deepened, random lights of fireflies blinked woefully in the canopy below. She did not delude herself. Like poisoned fruit, any relationship with him remained prohibited. To partake in the sweetness may have momentary satisfaction, but devastation remained in the end. "I have affection for you, as a dear friend, Colonel Rourke, and I appreciate your respect for my vows."

"I'll take your friendship."

She realized then that for the colonel the real enemy was not so much the outside world but the enemy that hid deep within and perhaps explained why he was attracted to her. He was a master of men who ruled his company with a discipline of fear, though the fear was not of the colonel's violence but rather of his disappointment. He was a man whose approval other men sought because he seemed a master in his own brutal world. But there remained a wound far deeper in Colonel Rourke. Something he hid well. Fooled most. But not her.

"Do you ever fear?" she said.

"Every day, I fear. I fear my inability to assess the terrain and enemy strength correctly. I fear ambush. Mostly, I fear my men dying."

He showed her one of his open palms, as though to demonstrate the stains of blood. A darker emotion underscored the pain and pity she felt for this man who seemed to have experienced all possible tragedy, and to have multiplied pain and suffering.

She looked him square in his eyes, shadowed now. "What happened?"

He pulled away. Heat gave way to cool air. No. She grasped his hand, refusing to let go. "Tell me what came to pass," she demanded.

He shifted. "I've never said it to anyone else. Perhaps I'm telling you because I want you to understand that I—"

He brought his other hand to his dark hair, looking about, as though searching for permission from the elements to speak. "More than most, I grasp that my mind has become a sort of prison. The walls are blocks cemented with remembered screams. The bars are the remembered torments. My body struggles to be freed of it all. Of me. Of the days elapsed. And the revulsion that I feel douses me until an elusive sort of detachment takes over…and removes me altogether. I want to rip myself apart. Rip others apart. Or the whole world. Immediately, I feel violent and indifferent and—" He broke off, his grip on her hand hardening.

"It occurred with a glimpse of the enemy whose very existence seemed to inspire so much hatred in my men, a hatred I embraced. The fight had been at Green Tavern. I had been ordered to the battle knowing it was foolhardy when so many Union troops were reported to be in the area. It was supposed to be a brief affair that did little to turn the tide of the war. But there was more to the results than the casualties shared by both sides. With three hundred horsemen, the enemy surprised and attacked us with a force of nearly one thousand Federal cavalries. They double flanked us, and combined with a full-frontal assault, we were shaken. The Federals stood their ground. The action manic, went badly. A serious rout. The aftermath left most of my men dead. Oh, the boys so proud of their uniforms, suddenly washed by the horror of splashing blood, the guts and brains of a friend, screams and dismembered corpses. Every battle, the horrors grow worse, the sum and stink and pieces of men. The guilt is like ice in my guts. It can be a hundred degrees out and I'd still be frozen inside."

As the sun disappeared, nothing breathed. The hour of silence. Everything was transfixed. Only the grasses bowed upon a melancholy breeze.

Grace swallowed. He succumbed to the same panic and revulsion as the men who looked to him for… what? Rescue? Salvation? He carried that with him long after the fight, that when the enemy was there, death followed, and it wasn't clean.

He'd lost some piece of himself, had become a shell of a man like a crumbled pumpkin husk, soft and able to poke your finger through, he condemned himself for his failures, nurturing his demons.

And then she spoke. "There is a luxury in self-reproach. When we blame ourselves, we feel that no one else has the right to blame us. It is the confession not the priest that gives us absolution."

"It is an irreparable lapse laid at my feet, one that I can never make up."

Her heart ached for him. "Guilt is just another name for impotence, for defensiveness and destruction. Guilt becomes a device to protect ignorance and the continuation of things the way they are, the ultimate protection for changelessness."

He leaned toward her and her heart hammered. "You are very wise for one so young."

She shivered. *I have lived life.*

And that was when he did the unthinkable.

He kissed her, and the world fell away. It was slow and soft, comforting in ways that words would never be. His hand rested below her ear, his thumb caressing her cheek as their breaths mingled. Unexpectedly he deepened the pressure with his strong, hard lips, his day's beard chafing her jaw, and her cornette fell off. He kissed her hard, as a lover would, crushing his mouth down on hers—and instinctively, she parted her lips. She moaned with the taste of him, felt the kiss deepening in ways she'd only been able to imagine before that moment.

That shocking, magnificent, earth-shattering moment.

He drew back too soon, and Grace stood there trembling.

"I never should have kissed you," the colonel said.

Grace stood there mute, thinking of the time she'd dozed off in the hayloft and fell ten feet to the ground, landing on her back. The impact had knocked every wisp of air from her lungs, and she'd laid there struggling to inhale, exhale, to do anything. That's how she felt now, trying to remember how to breathe, unable to speak, totally stunned as the impact of the kiss bounced around in her skull.

He let go of her shoulders and raked his hand through his hair. "I'm leaving tomorrow."

"Can't you quit?"

"To entertain such a luxury? No, I will not. I'm honor bound. My cavalry troops are needed to guard infantry against entrapment by enemy forces. We insert ourselves between enemy divisions and offer protection served as screens for infantry armies. We are successful at mounting attacks on Federal supply lines and frustrating the outmanned Union cavalry's efforts to check them. Long distant raids are designed to attack supply lines. It is my hope to maneuver the Yanks from their positions all the way back to Washington."

Couldn't he see that the justifications he was making to continue the war were excuses for himself? "What about the losses at Gettysburg, Fredericksburg, Vicksburg?"

His face became a mask of granite and it frightened her.

"So easy to fall prey to the losses when we can win. The South must never give up because that will be the place and time that the tide will turn. I guarantee Federal soldiers will limp back to Washington where

Lincoln can watch them stretch out in front of the White House and commence drinking."

Before she could say a word, the colonel pivoted and walked away, heading to the camp in long, angry strides.

Grace stood paralyzed. She could not go back to the hospital, could not steal into her tent and hide beneath the blankets. Her feet were rooted in cement. She simply could not move.

Damn Colonel Rourke. Damn him to the depths of hell. No man had ever kissed her, never sent pleasure of awful, dazzling desire shuddering through her like splintering shards of lightning. She touched her fingers to her lips. No, never again would she feel like this, during and after the colonel's mouth landed on hers. In some mysterious way, it was as though he'd hazarded a claim on her, conquered her so thoroughly and so completely that she could never belong to any other man, as long as she lived.

The colonel had stirred an uncontrollable desire within Grace by merely kissing her and at the same time, satisfying that desire. In that brief sojourn to the deepest, truest part of her nature lay the harshest reality. The colonel cultivated a satisfaction that had exposed what a man's attentions—one certain man's attentions—could be like.

She pressed her fingers to her temples. He left her wanting. Desiring more of what she could never have. To tell him she wasn't a nun? To tell him she was a murderess?

Oh, how she worked to explain his shameful kiss to a Catholic nun. The more demanding the reparations her subconscious required, the worse she knew it existed.

She gulped. So exquisite were her lies, she could almost weep with them.

Hadn't she preached redemption to him? Far more reprehensible was her fraudulent disguise, and that disgrace corroded every part of her. It squeezed her brain, obliterating the thought of excusing her own actions. She had to think of a way to return north. To get her life back.

CHAPTER 14

GRACE HAD FINISHED CHECKING ON her patients with Captain Andrew Albury. His unit was new to the camp. Their numbers had been downsized due to casualties and combined with Colonel Rourke's. He possessed crisp fair hair and a frugality on words.

"Sister Grace, there is a mother here with her injured son. Can you help him?" Captain Albury asked.

The boy was sandy-haired, his eyes resembled wild violets dipped in buttermilk.

"I'm Emily Ferguson," said the boy's mother. The woman was Grace's size, very pretty and with the same colored eyes as her other children grouped around Grace. Emily also possessed tired lines, mirrored by so many women left home with the burden of running the farms and raising their families. Grace's heart went out to the woman.

The boy's shoulder was visibly out of place. With

his good hand he rubbed his eyes to wipe at tears and Grace felt the boy was crying more from the ignominy rather than the pain. Compared to the many war wounds she'd treated; a dislocated shoulder was so fixable. Grace bid them to follow her into the hospital.

"Are you going to do it?" asked the young boy, unable to mask the incredulity in his voice. His footsteps shuffled like sandpaper against the floor.

"I'm a doctor," said Grace.

"There is no such thing as a woman doctor," he scowled, tamping down his tears. "I want a man doctor."

All four children gazed at her with sudden focus. How many times did she have to meet resistance, even among the young?" She motioned for Amos to lift the boy on the table. "May I at least look at your shoulder?"

The boy sniffed, staring wide-eyed at the giant Amos.

"What is your name?" Grace asked the boy, maneuvering in front of him and examining the huge bruise developing on his shoulder.

"William, but most call me Willie."

"Willie, how did this happen?" She grabbed his wrist and extended his arm forward in slow movements.

"I fell out of a tree. Ow!"

His arm popped back in the socket. "Does that feel better?"

The boy nodded.

"I'm going to put on a sling. No more tree climbing for a while. Promise?"

She guessed the boy was near twelve summers. Willie didn't even look at her, so awed with Amos, afraid if he didn't do her bidding, the giant would eat him alive. "Yes, Ma'am."

"Doctor," his mother corrected and extended her hand, "I-I can't afford to pay you."

Grace smiled. "Don't worry. Do you live around here?"

She pointed to the nearby farmhouse layered with untended weathered clapboard and where a badge of grass, like a green brooch pinned at the breastbone of the edifice. "That's where we live. My husband and I farmed this land but he's been missing and presumed dead."

Grace helped the boy off the table and led them outside. Lucifer appeared and sat on her shoulder; his dark head tilted in expectation for the cornmeal she kept in her pocket. Grace laughed, retrieved the cornmeal and deposited some in each of the children's hands. "Hold your palm flat, and he'll eat from your hand," Grace instructed.

As each child took turns feeding the crow, Grace said, "Do you bake, Emily?"

The woman looked at her with a quizzical expression. "I do."

"How would you like to be under the employ of General Lee?" Grace embellished the truth as an indirect way to save the woman's pride. Her services would be paid by Colonel Rourke who worked for General Lee. "To earn money for your family…" Grace encouraged.

The woman's eyes widened. "Anything for General Lee."

"Your skills would save us time and trouble. Amos and a few other men can chop wood for you, if you don't mind." They were slow at the hospital, having sent many of the badly injured on to hospitals in Richmond. The woman could use extra help.

"Filthy, diseased bird." Sister Jennifer Agatha swept the children's hands away, the cornmeal dropping to the ground.

The girls began to cry. Lucifer flew to an upper branch, shuffling his feathers and tail, and then alighted to a higher branch as if shaking off the indignity of the foul human. The bird's antics made the children laugh.

Sister Josephine replaced the departing Sister Jennifer Agatha and brushed the hair back from one of the twin girls. "What are your children's names?" she asked Emily.

She placed her hand on the oldest child's head, "This is William, the twin girls are Sylvia and Renee, and my two-year-old baby is James."

Sister Josephine raised Sylvia's chin. "How are you doing with your schooling?"

Sylvia squinted up to her mother. "Schooling?"

Emily rushed in. "There's been no opportunity for schooling with the schoolmaster off to war—"

"That must be rectified," said Sister Josephine sternly. "I was a schoolteacher before the war. I can devote a few hours a day to their schooling. We will begin this afternoon. Amos and I will come over at that time, won't we?"

Sister Josephine was radiance and steel to the giant, showering him with affection and kind words. He bloomed like the unfolding petals that produced a fully bloomed rose. He had become her constant companion.

"That would be wonderful," Emily said, darting

a glance at the giant, her emotions as warm as the touches of the gentle rays of the sun.

Sylvia and Renee flanked the giant and grabbed each one of his hands. "Can he come with us now? We want to show him a baby robin's nest by the porch."

Grace laughed, picturing the giant with the two little girls. "Of course."

CHAPTER 15

THE FERGUSON HOME WAS A large, old-fashioned plank house with a porch wrapped around part of the front to the side and another porch in the back to catch the coolness away from the morning sun.

In the kitchen, crocks of various sizes, some with lids, some covered with cloth, sat on the floor or on a bench along the wall. Eggs were piled in a bowl. Grace's lips curved. As a young girl, she remembered slipping into her kitchen quarters back home to sneak cream from the top of the milk.

Far from this agreeable Virginia dwelling existed her ancestral home, large and ostentatious to the point of intimidation. The grand edifice was laid out in red brick with wings to the east and west, a gated entrance, and long driveway with leafy trees, and manicured hedges. Only the golden days spent with her father had given her home any warmth. But once he'd died, Grace sought to bury deep her cold and desolate history. She had left the fastest way possible.

Don't look back. Vanquish it.

There was an allure to the unpretentious, rambling Ferguson home. Built at different times, and furnished with less sophistication, the house had eroded from exposure and insufficient means. Yet, shaped by Emily, and the children, the home brought on simple pleasures. Warmth and magic dwelled inherent in their love and hope and dreams. Oh, to have something as wonderful.

She shouldn't woolgather over what she could never have. She'd done everything she could to distract herself from her thoughts, but it was no use. She could not stop thinking of the blasted colonel. She couldn't stop thinking of how his gaze had darkened, how he had grabbed her hand and revealed his story.

Her obsession was ridiculous. She'd gone from wanting to punch him square in the jaw to wanting desperately to kiss him. But it was foolish to entertain such an absurd fantasy.

With several loaves of fresh baked bread in a basket, Grace stood on the Ferguson porch. The heat and humidity lay upon her like a flatiron, and she was grateful for the noonday shade. Across from the house and under a spreading honey locust, Grace eavesdropped on Sister Josephine continuing with the children's school lessons.

"Here we are," said Emily, coming out on the porch from behind her. "I've pulled a fresh plucked chicken and wrapped it in cheesecloth for you to take to the sisters."

"Emily, the bread you bake for the men is heavenly

and well-appreciated. And the pies—"

"I can't take all the credit. With the children about, I get nothing done. Amos volunteered to take them berry picking and kept them from under my feet," said Emily, gazing upon Amos with fondness, and then sliding the chicken into Grace's basket.

"At first, the big man scared me. His face is chiseled from stone, his hands are as big as paddles, and his outward appearance terrifying, yet he is timid, and his heart is made of gold. Corporal Anderson has been so helpful, and the children adore him. He took them fishing and swimming, has helped in the garden, carried the wood, has plowed a field and organized a baseball game between the soldiers and the children."

"I heard the laughter. What a refreshing sound. So good for the convalescing men as well."

"Do you know the man played with the twins and their tabby kittens yesterday? My children follow him like the Pied Piper and are so much happier. Their own father never had time for them, I suppose too busy with his chores," Emily said, her bittersweet regret unmistakable.

Slates on their laps, Amos sat between the twins, each girl leaning against him.

"Write 'cat', and then obtain Corporal Anderson's approval," encouraged Sister Josephine and the children scribbled letters on their slates.

"This is a 'C', this is 'A', and this is 'T'". Sylvia held up her slate and pointed to the letters for Amos to see.

Amos nodded his head.

Grace hitched the basket up her arm. How wily Sister Josephine was. She had discovered Amos couldn't read and used the children to teach him, saving him from embarrassment. Grace's esteem for Sister Josephine raised another notch.

Suddenly, the twins leaped up and ran screaming toward their mother. "A snake. A snake."

Grace dropped her basket and raced toward them. Amos put his hand up, warning her not to move. Beige with dark brown lateral markings, cat-eyes, and a diamond shaped head capped with signature copper, the snake lay coiled in a nest of leaves next to Sister Josephine. With the excitement, little James tottered toward the aged nun and in the direct path of the snake.

Amos thrust the boy away, and then grabbed the snake by its neck. The snake's venomous fangs bared, its furious tongue darted in and out, and the tail whipped angrily back and forth.

Her hand held to her heart, Sister Josephine rose, and plucked up the wailing James in her arms.

Amos snapped the snake's neck and threw it into the bushes.

"Jesus, Mary and Joseph. You are the bravest man I've ever known," said Sister Josephine. "You are the embodiment of your Greek name, Amos, which means brave warrior."

Grace had never seen a man so large move so quickly. "How fearless."

"You saved their lives," whispered Emily, her awe and gratitude shown in the tears streaming down her face.

Unaccustomed to all the adoration bestowed upon him, Amos brightened to a deep shade of red. The twins hugged each one of his legs. "Are you all right, Corporal Anderson? The snake didn't bite you? We don't want anything to happen to you. We love you."

And then, Amos did the most unexpected thing. He snatched up the girls in his big brawny arms and bawled.

Sylvia pulled his face to hers. "Why are you crying?"

"No one has ever told me they loved me."

CHAPTER 16

FOR GRACE, DAYS MELDED INTO more days. Before the wavering haze of distant meadows, she paused beneath the dappled shade of a sycamore tree, longing to take off her shoes and feel the coolness of the grass beneath her feet. She tugged at the neck of her woolen tunic, the muggy heat pressed in on her, trickling down her neck and breasts like warm soup.

The Virginia summer months lazed upon her hot, sticky, and humid. The mercury rose to the ninety-eighth degree of the thermometer in the shade, the atmosphere seemed to glow, as if fires were kindled around her. The sun appeared as a ball of red-hot metal making the air seem thick and smoky, and making breathing almost impossible. Nor were the nights less sultry and distressing to her in the days.

Oh, to have a glass of sweet lemonade with real chunks of ice.

For weeks she'd been trying to forget…locking up the slaying of her stepbrother and burying it deep in her memory. No one was going to defend her for murder, no one would keep the noose from her neck. And no matter which way she sought self-validation, she knew in time, the tightrope she walked would break.

In the two years since her father's death all she had known was loneliness and pain. Grace had received the lion's share of her father's estate that had precipitated her mother's anger and jealousy. Memories rekindled of how her mother had looked the other way while Grace was subjected to her stepfather's cruelty.

The perfect consequence was she had begun to stop trusting her own feelings because there was no one to hear her agony. For her, there had been no way out and no sign of hope. Each day that went by, a part of her had died. Sometimes, like now, the feelings returned, panic, pain and desperation.

In the weeks that passed, Colonel Rourke and his men were gone most of the time, but oh how she rejoiced every time he returned to camp alive. Despite their short period to rest and feed their horses, he had avoided her, and that stung.

She banished the hurt and sometimes imagined Colonel Rourke meeting her stepfather. The idea of the confrontation brought a smile to her face. With certainty, her stepfather would shrivel at the first sight of the fearsome Colonel Rourke. She rather liked that picture.

Hadn't he been overly protective of her, saving her from Colonel Lawler? She didn't want to read anything into it. Of course, he didn't want to lose his doctor. Yet she felt safe with him, protected.

After the Battle at New Market, time had marched quickly. The red-haired and relentless Union General Tecumseh Sherman marched south from Tennessee, no doubt with Atlanta, Georgia in his sights. General Lee had successfully stalled Grant's drive toward Richmond at bloody Spotsylvania Court House. The flamboyant and beloved Confederate Calvary General J.E. B. Stuart died, yet successfully blocked Union General Sheridan's cavalry. Other faraway places like Trevilian Station, Jerusalem Plank Road and St. Mary's Church were spoken of yet seemed remote with none of their triumphs or losses turning the red tide of war.

Then the Grim Reaper reaped a bountiful harvest at Cold Harbor. Grant had launched a frontal assault against Lee's army where five thousand Confederates and fifteen thousand Yanks died. Each side was not allowed to pick up their injured or bury their dead by orders of General Grant or risk being shot. Roasting in the torrid Virginia sun for three days, injured men cried out for succor with nothing to slake their thirst or anyone to tend their wounds. Many died.

Her thoughts returned to Colonel Rourke. She couldn't grasp the exact instant when their friendship was molded. Like filling a pitcher drop by drop and making it run over; so, in a succession of kindnesses there lived one last drop that made her heart run over.

At intervals, Grace listened to the sullen hammer of a lonely woodpecker on some withered trunk. She sighed. As of this late date, no man had ever been the object of her desire. There never seemed to be any time for any romantic feelings. Love had been pushed from her mind as though it was nothing more than an old dress she'd outgrown.

She missed Colonel Rourke, and melancholy anchored her feet, disallowing her to surface and feel the sunshine, that feeling of soft joy forbidden to rise within.

She clung to the shadows watching the men who were recuperating from their wounds sit around, some smoking their pipes in an unconcerned manner while they lazed in the sultry afternoon. The Virginian accent displaced vowels and consonants and what had once been foreign to her became more familiar. "Y'all" for "you all", "fahhne" was "fine", "hose" for "horse", which translated to "Y'all have a fahhne lookin' hose."

Some men played dominoes; some wrote letters while another struck up his harmonica with another soldier tapping out a rhythm with bones. A bullet-ridden Dixie flag lifted softly in the breeze. One man was in a deep sleep, gradually snoring from a lower to a higher key, until he woke himself by a sudden and alarming burst that resembled the bark of a mastiff.

Apparently, Rourke's men enthusiastically filled the ears of injured cadets, their eyes as big as dinner plates as they sat in awe of tales of the Gray Ghost. How much was myth opposed to actual fact?

Rewarded with a rapt audience of cadets, Sergeant Hutchinson's voice stayed jovial and fond of a joke. His imagination vivid, his harangues, a source of much entertainment. He was a gifted storyteller and he sat induced to spin alive his folklore. Grace wasn't immune.

"We were up in the northern towns. A wounded Yank complained Rebs stole his canteen. The colonel got off his horse, filled his canteen, and then allowed the Yank to slake his thirst. Our colonel has a good heart. I'll never forget that."

"That was when we found ourselves up against six thousand Union cavalry ready to take us down. We had only two hundred men, yet those were Rourke's counties we patrolled, and the people were favorable to us. So many times, we were a hair's breadth away from capture. There's a huge reward on his head like Robin Hood," said a toothless soldier, his jowly voice reminding her of steam wheezing from a tea-kettle before it gathered enough strength to whistle.

Seated on a stump, his giant body crouched, Corporal Anderson moved his knife quickly over a block of wood. A score of shavings piled at his feet. He carved giraffes under palm trees, elephants, peacocks, and the like in such an artistic manner, and inevitability, toys for the Ferguson children.

"Colonel Rourke's speed and range made us into a great reconnaissance force," said a gaunt soldier labeled Stringbean. "Commanders rely on us for location, strength and enemy movement. The Union General Pope has bragged how he'd seen the backs of fighting Indians yet has been concentrating a large force around Culpepper Courthouse and has made himself a terror to the women and children through which he's passed by brutal and stringent regulations about citizens. Took Colonel Rourke two weeks to send him into retirement."

Sergeant Hutchinson slapped his knee. "What I like most about the colonel is how, on a hushed night, he can trail the Yanks, dancing between trees as the moonlight flickers, and then melts into the darkness with the arrival of dusk, and then disappears into nothingness."

She had heard about Colonel Rourke's legendary ploys, riding circles around his opponents, mounting surgical strikes, and then vanishing. The men enjoyed lionizing Rourke's deeds. What would the Gray Ghost do next? Walk through walls, raise the dead?

A soldier who had lost all of his hair, leaving his skull to look like a newly hatched egg, waggled his finger. "Colonel Rourke's reputation precedes him. He strikes terror in the enemy, moves like a supernatural entity, a specter in the fog, seeming to rise like a shadow of the underworld."

Grace rolled her eyes. Indeed, his raids struck fear into the citizens of the north, generated by the rabid newspaper accounts that amplified his reputation. With conviction, his men added to the lore.

A soldier from Atlanta, Georgia with large ears stuck out at starboard angles poked at the food on a tin plate, and then stuffed it into his mouth. "Colonel Rourke, I'd follow him into battle anywhere. He has nerve, moral courage and decisiveness when the dogs of war are to be loosed. His relations with his men are like those of a brother. Quick and warmhearted in his feelings. But mostly he keeps to himself. In action, Colonel Rourke showed the greatest advantage. I have never seen his superior on the battlefield. No one is quicker in detecting inefficiency, or wanting of courage and coolness in danger, or any departing from the course of a thorough gentleman."

"Hear, hear!" The men lifted their tin water mugs in

salute.

Grace grew dizzy following one of the soldier's odd ways. He'd start up on his feet, animated in conversation, and with the eagerness of his thoughts, wildly gesticulate, walk about the yard, and then plop down on the grass. "I hear he's fond of merry company and of ladies' society and music and dancing."

Grace was all ears. Was the colonel a philanderer? Of course, his rank, handsome countenance and legendary feats would attract women like bees to molasses taffy.

"That's all when he's entertaining the bigwigs. Other than that, he is a man to himself."

Grace wondered why a man Colonel Rourke's age and esteem had never married? Most military men had wives and family. Had he come from an unhappy home life?

Sergeant Hutchinson leaned back on the stump he was sitting on. "Here comes Wade. He was so drunk one night he led a charge on his own father's house."

The soldiers guffawed.

"How'd that go?" asked one of the wide-eyed cadets.

"His old man boxed his ears for a week. More brutal than a Yank incursion."

This was followed by another round of riotous laughter.

Sister Clara helped Francis settle in a rocking chair where he could enjoy the men's company. Three red coonhounds lolled at his feet. Pigeons and mourning doves gathered on the arms of his chair to the objection of Lucifer, who flapped his coal-black wings in indignation to the invasion of his territory. A horse pulled from its tether and dipped his muzzle near Francis' ear. Sister Clara laughed at the sight, her fingers lingering on his good arm overlong. The glowing looks between the two were unmistakable.

"Can I get you anything else, Francis?" Sister Clara asked, her voice lowered in dulcet tones.

"You've overworked yourself and deserve a rest. I'll send Lucifer for you."

Sister Clara remained hesitant and both couldn't tear their eyes from each other.

The soldiers winked. "I'll bet my brogans on what you're thinking boys. Anyone want to bet their coffee?"

Sister Clara colored and fled.

Had the men referred to a romance between Sister Clara and Francis? Was there more than a blooming friendship right beneath her nose? Of course, the two had been inseparable during Francis' convalescence.

"Tell us, Francis, how you rate a private nurse?"

Francis didn't answer ,his eyes glued to the back of Sister Clara.

Sister Jennifer Agatha stalked through the middle of the men, mumbling ills to lazy, indolent Rebs.

Sergeant Hutchinson slapped his knee. "There goes Sister Crow."

Lucifer squawked his complaint; no doubt being compared to the harridan.

Hutchinson rocked back and forth; extreme pleasure lit his face. "Sorry, Lucifer, didn't mean to give your kind a bad name."

This brought another round of laughter.

"I'll bet my food the old biddy will insult us on the count of three." Hutchinson stuck up his index finger, followed by his middle finger, then his ring finger.

On the rise of the third finger, the elderly nun turned on them, her Rosary bead belt clacked like rock on rock. "What can one expect from fools, cretins, lunkheads and heathens. You will all be dipped in hellfire."

The men's laughter drowned her out.

Hutchinson could not contain himself. "Men, you shouldn't worry about Sister Jennifer Agatha. You should worry more about that hairy mole crawling off her face and eating us alive."

A soldier with an extended overbite, tagged as Beaver, said, "Of course, you'll bet your food. Hard tack and greasy pork. If the bullets aren't brutal enough, then the food isn't much better."

"One time, I found a soft spot in my hard tack. I pulled out a penny nail," said Stringbean.

"How you always whine. Did the quartermaster give you a parasol?" said Beaver.

Stringbean held up a blubbery mass. "This thing's got hair on it. Still growing."

"Eat it anyway," Beaver chastised.

"Can't do it."

Beaver lurched forward, grabbed the meat, and tossed the blob of white pork into the pot. "Lord Almighty, Stringbean, you gonna waste food, throw it my way. Even though the Valley provides food, I remember when times weren't so good, and I heard the bellies of every one of you pea-brains bayin' at me all night. You need to keep your gut filled."

"Can't keep anything filled up. I eat those damned crackers and they can't slither through me fast enough. Been drinking water out of the river. I see things swimming in it."

Grace grimaced. It seemed like every soldier suffered from camp gripes. She must remain steadfast about boiling the drinking water.

"I sure miss those women back in Richmond," said a wistful Elias Hart, a young, golden-haired soldier with curls like Adonis.

"God's manna from heaven," agreed Beaver, chewing noisily on what was supposed to be sowbelly. Hair and all.

"Boy were those ladies happy to show off their patriotism and devotion to Dixie," said Elias.

Beaver gave a loud belch and patted his stomach. "Except you caught critters and been scratchin' at places that shouldn't itch."

In quiet and calm tones, the men sang, *Beautiful Dreamer* in sweet, mellow, gentle harmony, capturing the sentimentality of a lover oblivious to worldly cares and unaware that he may be deceased.

An anchor of sadness weighed down her heart. How she wished for a hug, or to reach the sunshine, or take a walk among the soft hymn of trees, hearing how the wind played in the leaves.

Her attention was drawn to a couple brought in by Captain Albury. The bedraggled woman was beautiful and escorted to a tent with a guard. Her companion, a Confederate officer was tied to a tree… and possessed…a familiarity. My God, he was a mirror image of Colonel Rourke. She'd take food and water to the prisoners.

"We need you right away," said Amos.

Grace pushed from the cool shade and ran after

Amos. She'd have to get the food for the prisoners later.

CHAPTER 17

EXHAUSTED, RYAN RETURNED TO CAMP and collapsed on his cot. He woke to the bright sun of the afternoon, choking on the same bloody nightmare he'd constantly had. His limbs didn't thrash, as some did when they dreamed of death. Nor did he talk or scream or carry on.

No, his nightmare was a paralyzing one. It seized him like a demon and sealed him inside his bleakest places, creating sleep a prison and his body his jailer. Sleep was an indisputable torment, unfortunately not one he could escape.

His life was careening out of control. He hated the sensation of helplessness his existence brought, and then more drastically, he raged against his desire for Sister Grace. Like a lovesick fool, he strove to lick the crumbs she threw.

He swung his legs to the ground, clutching his head.

He needed her for her valuable doctoring skills. That was all he needed her for.

If only he could convince himself of that notion.

Hell. So, he made a mistake in bringing her into his camp. No harm had been done. He would be more cautious in the future, obey his oath to stay away from Sister Grace. He'd keep his sanity by leaving her strictly alone.

He could do that. He could.

And for his next feat, he'd sprout wings and fly to the moon.

He remembered crushing her to him, her soft curves melding into his in a kiss that was beyond gentle and reverent. Holding her was heaven, a place in the mist. Time did not exist in that enchanted moment. Nor did any of the thousand reasons he should not make her his own.

Lately his thoughts hadn't been sweet nor innocent.

She was doing something to him. Rousing his lust and his protective instincts. He wasn't used to responding this way toward anyone. He'd felt protective toward those he loved before. Never had he felt both urges at the same time.

Never.

And it worried him.

Surely, he'd be damned for that and every other part he took in this war. Just add it to a whole host of sins, including kissing and lusting after a Catholic nun. In his bones, he felt she'd never been kissed most probably to the nature of her calling. There emerged both male satisfaction and disgust in that impetus.

He walked past men convalescing in the yard and

heard an unusual sound. Children laughing.

With children standing beside her, Grace burst into laughter that sounded so bright and carefree that if he hadn't been so perturbed, he would have laughed with her. She had a lovely laugh, the sort that settled on a person like a warm sun. Unnoticed, he watched Francis demonstrate Lucifer's talents with tricks to entertain.

He narrowed his eyes. Why were children in the camp? He'd have Hutchinson's hide.

The children laughed at an anecdote she shared and clung to her sides, clamoring and competing for her attention. What would it be like to have several of their own children? He banished the thought.

She moved away then, the children tagging after her. Why did he feel like a man who had discovered fire to have it instantly doused?

She turned as if she knew he were watching her.

"Oh, good morning, Colonel Rourke," she said and gracefully glided up to him as if nothing was amiss, and then boldly took his hand. Through his anger and despair, she retained a hold on his hand, her gentle grasp held him more captive than any chain or manacle would have.

For a moment, Ryan forgot where they were or his objections to children in the camp. All he could do was gape at her. He could stare into her eyes all day and never categorize all the hues. The ring at the center of her irises was decidedly brown, and then bled with color to the violet edge. From a distance, the sun's rays turned them a brilliant amethyst.

He tried to respond with an equally casual "good morning" but his jaw seemed to be locked in the open position and he could not move his mouth to shut it.

"There are children in the camp," he finally said.

She let go of his hand and cast him a dimpled smile that he found irritating.

"Children in a military camp?" he emphasized.

He swallowed hard, his traitorous mind and body recalling the softness of her.

Her eyes rounded in innocence and she still wore that annoying smile.

"You said that already." She picked up a toddler who sucked his thumb and the rest of the children sidled against her for protection. They stared at him as if he were a giant squid. "These are the Ferguson children, and this is their farm, so to be precise, we are trespassing on their land."

Oh, she was clever on her feet. And so very pretty, if he allowed himself to think about it. He particularly liked her smile, in spite of how many times she used that lovely smile to laugh at him.

He frowned. "Are you trying to manipulate me?"

"I would never manipulate you, Colonel Rourke. I like to think of myself as a skillful contriver. The children are learning from the men, and their mother bakes bread for them in return. It's a win for everyone, don't you think?"

She arched a brow, a silent question about his perusal of her and the children. "Oh, dear. Did I mistakenly forget to ask your permission? I assure you that was not my intent." She smiled again, her eyes sparkling with delight.

It took him a moment for his brain was working very slowly just now. "Why are the children staring at me?"

"They are in awe of the Gray Ghost. The men have been telling tales of your legendary exploits. This is James." She kissed the head of the child in her arms, and then placed an airy hand on the oldest child. "This is Willie, and the twins are Sylvia and Renee."

He could imagine what tales his men told. "What have you told them, Sister Grace?"

"That when you pass the ladies clasp their hands to their breasts and topple over in a swoon."

Ryan grimaced with the undisguised amusement in her eyes.

"Need to talk to you," said Captain Albury from behind him.

"What now?" After one last look at her tempting mouth, he followed Albury back to his headquarters. Why would he want to stay and talk to the infuriating woman who lived to mock him?

Five minutes later at Ryan's headquarters, his brain stuttered for a moment when he faced a woman claiming to be his wife. With certainty the beautiful woman's ruse intrigued him. He dismissed Albury and threw down his tent flap. "Since I do not have a wife, could you explain your scheme for I am not in a good mood."

"My name is Rachel Rourke and I'm married to your brother, Lucas. He's being held prisoner in your camp."

"I'm going to get to the bottom of this." He ordered Albury to bring him the prisoner. The woman started pounding on his back with her fists, regaling him with profane oaths, and kicked him in the shins. "Silence," he gritted out and set her aside.

Every thought process went on pause when he came face to face with Lucas. "Do you mind telling me why you are this far south when you are stationed in Washington, fighting for the Union? I'll remind you are on very precarious grounds."

Both men stared at each other for a long time, each taking his full measure. He'd hated his brother, Lucas for taking up the Union gauntlet. Had a hell of a fist fight that last day before they left for war and vowed to kill him if he laid eyes on him again.

"It's been a long time, Ryan," said Lucas.

"Too long. But not long enough where brothers can't keep their common sense and help each other out."

Ryan saw the anxiousness relax in his brother's frame.

"I didn't know how you'd actually feel," said Lucas.

"I know you helped out John. Admirable."

"John had been critically wounded, captured by Yanks and shipped north. Apparently Union soldiers thought he was dead and threw his body from the train. As luck would have it, a school teacher nursed him back to health but he was very vague about it. Irish thugs were about to hang him when I discovered his location. I tried to keep him out of the war. I didn't want him in a Union prison or shot dead in battle. Even found a foolproof place to keep him locked up during the war. Or so I thought." Lucas grinned at the memory. "But you know our brother, John. He escaped. I don't know the rest of it."

Ryan pulled out papers then frowned at Lucas. "Your *wife...*" he choked, "has been regaling me with the kindest of words. Before she has me boiled in oil, I find it desirable for you to save me from her further physical assault."

"You must not let that unhappy circumstance prejudice your opinion," she said.

"Introductions are in order. Ryan, this is Rachel."

Ryan raised a brow from his experience with the hellcat. "I'd like to think that someday, we'll all be back home and consider this time a bad dream." Ryan picked up a pen, dipped the nib in ink and began writing. "These passes will see you through the next five miles south where you can run into Union lines. There are two fresh horses in the back of my tent."

He unrolled a map and pointed. "There's a parting of troops at Brook's Crossing. You should be able to get through easy enough. I will warn you that you could get shot." Ryan angled his head to the Confederate pants Lucas wore, "or hanged as a spy."

"I'll take care," Lucas promised. "I owe you an extraordinary debt." He extended his hand but, instead, Ryan threw his arms around his shoulders and embraced him. They were brothers after all. War did not change that. He turned to Rachel and kissed her on the cheek. "Welcome to the family."

Albeit treasonous, Ryan alleviated their dire situation which left him bemused and satisfied. He shook his head. What was more extraordinary was the fact that Lucas had married.

He didn't have time to ponder further for immediately, a dispatch rider rode in and waited while Ryan read the communications. He picked up his quill pen, dipped it in the ink bottle and quickly wrote messages for the rider to return to General Lee from his recent reconnaissance. He took a drink of brandy and offered a glass to Captain Gill and motioned outside. They sat outside, the sun setting in the sky as fresh colors upon an artist's canvas, as if those rays were destined to create a great work of art, melding brilliant reds and oranges, hints of pink and smoky amethyst.

"It will be another hot day tomorrow," said Gill. "Could use a storm to break up the heat."

"We have orders to move out again and soon," Ryan said, allowing the warm liquid to burn down his throat and banish the urge to think of a certain Catholic nun.

Dammit. They'd shared one kiss, and it had been an idiotic impulse on his part. As for her, she had broken a vow of chastity of some sort. He was already going to hell. He certainly wasn't going to pave a path for her and have that added to his conscious.

Yet she was acting like he'd never kissed her, and he didn't know what to think about that, especially since he'd been fantasizing about kissing her night and day. What was more extraordinary was the fact that she had kissed him back. Why? Nor did she scold him afterward.

"Our Sister Grace sure is saintly, isn't she, Colonel?" said Stringbean, resting with his back to a tree. He rose and gave Ryan and Gill what was left of a fresh baked loaf of bread.

Ryan thanked the soldier, split the portion, giving half to Gill. The smell of tobacco and roasted rabbit spiraled through the air. He remembered his vow to stay away from Sister Grace.

Was that Sister Jennifer Agatha lurking in the shadows? She sat on her hoary throne of a stump. "She isn't saintly at all. She's not even a nun," said the aged nun.

He choked on his bread. "What do you mean?"

"I listened at Mother Superior's door. She's in disguise."

"Disguise?" He watched the nun's hairy mole jump up and down with the movement of her jaw, wanted to doubt every venomous word from her, but could not. Was Grace a spy? Had the sisters' sojourn to the Union camp been contrived so she would end up in a Rebel camp? Had he fallen for a brilliant scheme? He didn't want to believe it, but his men were at risk. "Isn't it a sin to be telling tales?"

"Believe what you want, Colonel."

Rourke stood, hammered his boots to where the nun sat. "Where is she?"

"I'm not my sister's keeper." She cackled and scuttled off her stump.

CHAPTER 18

LATE AFTERNOON LEFT LONG SHADOWS and a wood fire burning on Emily's hearth; a black pot hung from the crane in the center. Cabbage and a piece of pork were boiling together in the pot for dinner; the potato-bread baking in a skillet with a lid. Grace had completed the children's physical exams and they were all in fine condition. Now she rolled out dough to make pies, enjoying female domesticity and the children playing at their feet.

She grinned at the twins' antics, opened the door of the firebox on the stove, grabbed the handle and shook off the gray ashes. A few small, live coals remained. She opened the draft and added small pieces of kindling to coax the fire. Tongues of flame flickered, then licked hungrily at the new fuel. She added larger pieces of kindling, and finally a few small chunks of firewood and closed the door.

A little shiver ran through her. She really needed some chicory coffee or something to stop those tiny quakes in her. She picked up baby James and balanced him on her hip, all the while, a pair of deep blue eyes worked along the edges of her thoughts.

How she'd love to have a family and farmhouse of her own. Just like Emily's. Ryan said he wanted a farm to raise horses. Children? Perhaps he was a man who didn't want children.

Emily took James to put down for a nap. Grace poured a cup of coffee, lifted it to her lips and blew softly across the surface before sipping it when Sister Josephine ran up the steps, puffing loudly, her face near geranium.

"I need to talk to you, Sister Grace."

A tingling grew in the back of her neck as Grace read the urgency in Sister Josephine's eyes.

"The jig is up."

Thunderstruck, Grace sat down, her cup clacked on the chipped saucer. "What are you talking about?"

"Sister Jennifer Agatha. Apparently, she had her ear to the door when you were with Mother Superior in Maryland and has revealed the truth to Colonel Rourke. The tale has lit like fire through a hayrick, reaching all ears in the camp."

Emily grabbed Grace's arm. "What truth? If you are in any trouble, Sister Grace, I will help you."

Grace's stomach roiled and she cringed, betraying her good friends. No sense living the deception anymore "I'm not a nun."

"What?" Eyes popping open, Emily dropped Grace's arm, shifting the squirming James.

Grace stood, looked at Sister Josephine, and then back to Emily. The older children stopped their play and stared. "I want to apologize for the deception. It was something I had to do for survival."

Sister Josephine placed a reassuring hand on Grace. "Without betraying your confidence, Mother Superior informed me of the machination, and that I was to look after you. I'm sure her judgment was necessary. She does not mislead arbitrarily."

"You knew all this time?" Grace gave a self-deprecating laugh.

"That is not important. What is important is Colonel Rourke. He turned to stone with Sister Jennifer Agatha's disclosure and has drawn his own conclusions, believing you to be a spy. Like a lion with a thorn in its paw, he is turning the camp upside down looking for you."

Grace inhaled. "What do I do? To be at odds with the Gray Ghost?"

Sister Josephine rattled her Rosary bead belt. "Jesus, Mary and Joseph, the look on his face was too composed yet one could see the broiling undercurrent."

Grace's shuddered. "Death will be the least of life's penalties. What if he sends me to a Confederate prison?"

Sister Josephine scoffed. "I'm sure whatever you're hiding from is with good reason. But Colonel Rourke needs to hear the truth from you first."

Hands shaking, Grace looked to the low ceiling with dark beams, oppressive now and closing in on her. "You don't know Colonel Rourke."

Sister Josephine gave her a hard look. "I do. I see how

he looks at you."

"I haven't noticed him looking at me." But that was a lie, too. He had sought her out many times and even kissed her.

"He looks at you. He watches you," confirmed Emily. "I know that hungry look on a man. I have been courted, married and have four children."

"Both of you are ridiculous."

"I see how you watch him," accused Sister Josephine with a firm nod of her head.

"I think we all know what's happening here," said Emily.

"Do we indeed?" Grace drawled, and then crossed the room, turning her back to them to hide the heat rising to her face. She opened the oven door and pulled a pan of gingerbread from the oven.

"Holy Orders are not for everyone. There is a different calling for a man and woman to fall in love. Have you not seen how Sister Clara and Francis have fallen in love?"

Grace snorted. Sister Josephine a romantic?

"Love is always patient and kind; it is never jealous; love is never boastful or conceited; it is never rude or selfish; it does not take offense and is not resentful." Sister Josephine quoted Corinthians.

But this was different. Colonel Rourke was an entity to himself and a frightful one at that. "A man like Colonel Rourke will not forgive deceit."

"Nonsense," said Sister Josephine. "Who knows what Divine presence has had its hand in your life. How odd that we were on our way to a Union camp and found ourselves giving succor to the South." She shrugged.

"Is it fate alone, brought on by more than mere chance that brought you together?"

Emily reached for her hand and squeezed it. "You've fallen in love with him."

"Oh, for the love of Pete," Grace groused. She yanked her hand from Emily's, and then removed her cornette and dropped it on the table. "Since I've been unmasked, there is no sense in wearing this any longer. I must meet with the firing squad."

"You wait right there," commanded Emily. She disappeared into another room to lay James down for his nap, and then headed to the porch door. "Amos, be a dear and watch the children for a spell. I've important things to do."

She turned to Grace, looked her up and down, made rapid assessment, and then dragged her up the stairs. "Oh, this will be fun. We need to find you the right dress and I have so many. My wealthy cousin gives me all her throwaways and there is no possible way I can wear any of the confections working a farm. We need a gown that will cause him to do a double take. That will distract him when you make known your reasons to him. Come Sister Josephine. You can help too."

In a large bedroom, Grace fingered the folds of her stained and unappealing tunic. Despite coming from a wealthy family, she'd never had a Come Out, nor did she have an interest in the latest gowns. She wanted to be with her father and he was totally devoted to his calling. Truth be told, she loved medicine too. What joy was brought to her when babies were delivered into the world, children cured, the old swept clean of sickness.

A coming out? She'd been to a few of the outrageous displays, with the vain, inglorious, trussed-up creatures to be auctioned off amidst vulgar pomp repulsed her. She had begged her father not to put her through the humiliation. He, for once, overrode her mother's demands.

"I'm not sophisticated in the ways of the world. My whole life has been devoted to medicine."

"We need something with power to it," said Emily. She swung open the doors of a humongous armoire, the scent of lavender sachet spiraling through the room. They all admired the vast array of gowns.

Emily added a sultry tone to her voice. "Like a lower décolletage to capture his interest."

"Definitely," nodded Sister Josephine.

Grace swung around and stared at the older nun.

Sister Josephine raised herself up. "I have five younger sisters. I'm not slow-witted and neither am I unaware of female intrigues."

Emily giggled. "Oh, the intrigues we will cultivate."

Grace felt a slow smile on her lips. Oh, blast it—it was impossible to keep that telling smile from her face.

Emily narrowed her eyes on Grace. "I've seen that same dreamy look before."

"Me?" Grace looked at the ceiling and started giggling.

Emily frowned. "All right," she said, folding her arms across her body and wagging an accusing finger. "He has kissed you. Kissed a Catholic nun?"

Grace felt heat rise to her face again.

Sister Josephine sat so hard in a chair that Grace thought she'd fallen.

Emily fell on the bed in a fit of laughter. "This will be the story of the century to tell my grandchildren."

"You are making too much of it," protested Grace, but there were no words to describe what she'd experienced. That kiss had awakened something in her.

She couldn't stop thinking about it. She couldn't stop wishing for more of it, for all of him. She couldn't stop wanting all the things that had been denied her by her mother and stepfamily.

Emily and Sister Josephine didn't understand the way these things worked.

But Grace very firmly understood it, and she harbored no illusions whatsoever. This was a dangerous game she played, and she trembled to think what power Colonel Rourke possessed.

Emily jumped up and started taking out the gorgeous gowns and holding them up beneath Grace's chin.

"We must match her coloring," said Sister Josephine. "With her light hair, I like the silky pink gown, the color of peach blossoms."

Grace shook her head. "All this fuss, and I'll never be beyond plain."

Sister Josephine's eyes widened. "Plain? Good Lord, what devil told you that?"

"Nonsense." Emily laughed. "Your hair is an unmatchable exotic pale blonde and is sinfully rich… and your face is like…the goddess Aphrodite." Emily frowned. "And—I'm assuming under that dratted filthy tunic, a figure that would make a monk lust."

Yet years of Grace's mother's vicious conditioning could not wipe how Grace saw herself. She was convinced she was malformed and ugly.

Emily lifted the hem of Grace's tunic and pulled it off. Grace covered herself with her arms. "Your problem, Grace, is that you are disarmingly unaware of your beauty."

The women chatted on, and then left her to revel in a long, luxurious bath. Grace wanted to go to Colonel Rourke right away and acknowledge her pretense. Emily refused. It was good to make a man wait.

Grace rose from the bath and wrapped a sheet around her. Emily returned to help her dress, picked up a brush and angled her head. "I thought to pile your hair up on your head, but I think it's better long and glorious. Much more tempting."

How free Grace felt to not have the dratted cornette so tightly bound upon her head while Emily brushed her long, wavy hair until it shone.

A new cotton chemise was provided. Emily cinched her into a corset, and then threaded a gown over her head where Grace's breasts billowed out. "I cannot have this much revealing skin," she protested.

"Oh, but that's what is most important," chided Emily, and then continued with the buttons down her back.

Was that her? The woman in the mirror? She could scarcely believe her reflection. All these years she felt like the square peg in the round hole. Perhaps it was why she buried herself in medicine, so she had a place to belong. But this was a spectacular transformation. No longer was she plain, ugly or invisible. All the hideousness of her mother's cruel words evaporated in that instant. Grace pushed her shoulders back. She had emerged from the gray ugly duckling to the graceful and beautiful swan…and she felt as if she could conquer a small army.

"You are lovely," gasped Emily. "Colonel Rourke shall take one look at you and fall down dead. We'll try your new appearance on Amos first and see how he reacts," she said conspiratorially.

An army, maybe, but it was Captain Rourke she wanted to conquer, and he thought her a spy. They returned downstairs where Amos leaned back in a straight back chair in the kitchen with the children playing on the floor around him.

Sister Josephine dropped the wooden spoon in the stew she was stirring.

The children playing on the floor stopped their activity and stared wide-eyed.

"A fairy princess," breathed Sylvia.

Amos dropped his chair on all fours. "Sister Grace?"

Grace twirled and laughed. "I'm afraid that I must tell you that I'm not a real nun. Please keep this a secret until I've had a chance to tell Colonel Rourke."

Amos whistled through his teeth. "That's a big secret to keep. Why you're as beautiful as the stars."

"You must understand, I have had my reasons—"

Amos shook his head. "Whatever your aims, the colonel is going to take the news like a cannon blast to the head. He'll be tied up in a host of fits."

Grace lingered in the kitchen, searching for ideas to sidestep the situation.

"I'm afraid—" She heard the edge of hysteria in her voice.

With warm palms, smelling faintly of fresh baked bread, Sister Josephine cradled Grace's face, and with gentle eyes, gazed down on her. "When you endure distress, you will find blessings in many facets of color."

Grace's hands trembled and her stomach knotted, her emotions were running rampant. She shook her head with huge misgivings about Sister Josephine's wisdom. To face Colonel Rourke's wrath? To suffer the consequences?

"Do not loiter in winter when it is already spring," smiled Sister Josephine, knowing Grace was delaying the inevitable.

Grace wanted to be brave. Part of her was glad she'd been discovered but the other part feared the murder charges heaped on her head. There was nothing to do about it. She had stalled long enough. She swept off the porch, her skirts swishing over the plank steps. Clouds hung over the meadow, inching toward the mouth of the Valley with the promise of rain. She'd weathered storms before, the triggers of her past, the fear, and in those moments of the storm, she had found her calm.

She would not go to him. He'd know where to find her.

CHAPTER 19

Ryan came upon Captain Gill. "Have you seen her?"

"Who?"

"I'm through playing games. You know who."

Captain Gill fluttered his hand upon his chest. "The female heart is a labyrinth of subtleties too challenging for the uncouth mind of the male. If you really want to possess a woman, you must think like her, and the first thing to do is win over her soul. The rest, that sweet, soft wrapping, that steals away your senses and your virtue, is a bonus."

"What's that supposed to mean?"

"Oh, you have it real bad, Colonel. Should I draw a picture for you?"

"Shut up, Gill. Her past is as clear as a pall of coal smoke."

"Just what I said. You have it real bad, Colonel."

"And you are short of growing the horns of Satan."

Ryan looked sharply at Gill, his transparency laughable.

"You've done nothing to make you regret have you, Colonel?"

"Not a damned thing."

Gill eyed him a minute, then looked out over the camp. "Maybe that's the problem."

"Meaning?"

"Meaning that maybe you need a bit more to occupy that clever mind of yours. Do you ever dream of settling down, taking a wife, creating a child or two of your own?"

"Don't you think you ought to be minding your own business?"

"With a good woman," his captain said. "I had my time with my wife and the only regret I have is not having a lifetime with her. But some things in life are not meant to be. While we're on the subject of life, there's a mean outbreak of lice. The men are in a terrible temper."

"And so am I."

Gill scratched his chin. "But your temper doesn't come from lice. Do you think I'm blind? You're as touchy as Archimedes locked in his stall with a burr under his saddle. I saw it when you first clapped eyes on her when we rescued her from those Yank marauders. I see it when she crosses the camp, how you always find a way to be by her side in the hospital. And here you come like a conqueror of Rome, sweeping her up, all for the taking, and you don't know what to do about it."

"Watch your tongue, Captain. What I do or don't do is no concern of yours."

"You should allow yourself to seek what is seeking you."

"What the hell are you suggesting?" Rourke demanded. He damned well knew what Gill suggested.

"I've been your close friend during these years at war, and I see you attempt to wring from the unknown where there are no certainties and straight lines and denying yourself what you deserve."

"Don't tempt me to skewer you with my sword."

"I see how she looks at you."

"I told you to shut up."

Gill was free to give Ryan an effective sounding board, and unafraid to give his honest opinion. Even more, Ryan knew that any conversation between them stayed theirs alone.

"Her feelings are so evident, and you're a foolish to allow your guilt and pride to control you." Gill laughed, and then bent his head to speak low and confidingly. "You have the plague really bad, Colonel. I know of a cure."

He could never be cured. He must fight and there was no solution to the conundrum of war.

"Miss Barrett is good doctor. Perhaps we should ask her for a cure—"

Ryan decked him with a right to the jaw, knocking Gill out of his tent and sprawling on the ground. Gill lifted up to his elbow, roared with laughter. "Oh, how I love innuendo." When under a semblance of control, he said, "I know a man who strives to be perfect, measuring himself by unattainable standards. He should let go of his crippling ideals. He must accept and allow himself to love, before it is too late."

"When did you become Socrates?"

Gill rubbed his jaw. "I should remember you can box the ears of the best of the Confederate army."

Rourke offered his hand as a way of apology and pulled Gill up. "I accept your acknowledgement as a compliment."

"It wasn't meant to compliment. I despair and remain thankful you're on our side. If General Lee put you up against Lincoln, the whole Union army would flee to Canada."

He had searched the camp, getting stopped by couriers that he swore at, and then attending the constant needs of his men that took him farther away from finding her. He had sent Captain Gill and a few other men in pursuit. No one had seen her since earlier in the day and he grew more frustrated. He damned well wanted to get to the bottom of it.

Near dusk, he climbed to the top of the hill where a storm brewed in the distance. Why had he not thought to explore her favorite spot before was beyond his comprehension.

Coming upon her from a distance, his eyes bugged out. He gulped, blinked a couple of times, then looked again. Gone was the horrid cornette that concealed her rich platinum hair. Waves of light silk fluttered in the breeze behind her, enough for him to tangle his hands and bring her lips to his. Also gone was the shapeless nun's tunic and what lay beneath caused his hands to curl into fists.

How dare she look so appealing in her pink dress that served her slender figure, accenting her slim waist, the bodice edged with a pink satin ribbon, barely concealing her creamy breasts. She was a goddess and he was nearly overwhelmed at her loveliness. There were women in the south, many beauties he'd entertained, but she was beyond perfection. The suggestion of defiance in her unwavering eyes only made her that much more captivating.

He was unable to take his eyes off her. If his men saw her, all of them would be like dogs lolling at her feet. His stomach churned. Jealousy?

No, he would not succumb. She had made a fool of him.

Clouds descended, bowed deeper, and flew tattered and swift, hugging the horizon in a mist. Dry leaves were drawn upward as if scenting the oncoming rain. He took a step closer, towered over her. "You've made yourself impossible to find.

"I knew you would find me."

The look she gave him brimmed with an irony he didn't comprehend, but now he was too irritated to consider it.

"I looked for a nun...I see you've changed..."

She made a caustic, brittle sound, wrapping her arms around herself as she did so, hunching against the evening breeze as though the world had become too cold.

"You noticed?"

He flared his nostrils. Of course, he noticed. Enough to throw her to the ground and bury his cock in her.

Dammit! Women that beautiful should be thrown to the sharks. A normal sane man would lock her up, forever. Chaining her to his bed in his tent sounded like a good place to start.

"It is incumbent upon me to inform you that we have an immediate lack of medical supplies—"

"I'm not talking about shortages. You have some explaining to do, Sister Grace, or whoever you are," he said. "Before I left, I mistakenly gave you pertinent information trusting that you were one of the honorable Sisters of Mercy, yet you've made a fool out of me. Did you pass on what I gave you to the enemy?"

"I'm not a spy."

"What am I to think of such a deception? Nun? Woman?" He watched her fascination with the approaching storm. Did she really think she could get out unscathed? Sister Jennifer Agatha had insinuated she was a spy, but he had doubts concerning the repulsive nun.

"A storm is coming."

He didn't know what to think of that. He looked over the far hills to where a storm brewed. Breaking loose of the evening calm, the wind swelled, and the storm leaped from its lair in the western sky.

He turned back to her. "Do you not fear me?"

Her damp eyes met his, swimming with a potent emotion that made him catch his breath over an answering burn in his throat.

She shook her head, her hair drifting over and snaring him around his neck, and the sensation was more intimate than if she'd reached into his trousers. "There was a time that I was afraid of the whole world," she said. "But not now, and not you."

"Maybe you should be," he warned. If she understood what he was thinking right now. If she fathomed how near he was to tearing off her dress…despite her lies and fraud, or inherent wrongness of it all.

He wanted his mouth on hers again. He wanted her beneath him, her sweet breath on his damp flesh as he took her.

"All right," she conceded. "Maybe I fear you a little." Her lashes shielded her expressive eyes from him. "Sometimes, a storm doesn't come to destroy you…it comes to clear a path…"

Grace's voice suffocated as that pair of piercing cobalt blue eyes bored into her…cold, probing, speculative eyes. *Dear God.* She looked to the left and the right.

"Where would you run that I'd not find you?"

"If I wanted to escape, wouldn't I have done it by now?"

"I'm through with banal responses. I want answers now." His words rumbled against her ear, his breath was hot against the wet, sensitive skin of her neck, but his tone was as flat and cold as the James River. Her heartbeats stumbled and collided into one another, her nerves singeing with dread and alarm.

For Grace, the oncoming storm and the man in front of her both terrified and alarmed her. Time breathed in huge gulps as thunder roared its cannonade, and like convolving flames of scouting dragons, lightning split, illuminating across gloom-hidden glens, and for one instant she imagined she could taste the storm in him, the battering winds of misery and desperation that met her own, blow for blow.

Her past crippled her, but the truth must come out. He deserved her honesty. "Oh, the deception we conjure to justify the infliction of transgressions set against us."

"I don't like riddles."

"I can understand how upset you are," she said.

"Incensed is more like it."

She swallowed past a lump of guilt and embroidered a response. "My name is Grace Barrett. I had an inheritance and would have been most happy to share it with a family who loved and cared for me. My father loved me and had willed a small stipend and the house to my mother, but the bulk of the estate was left to me. My father was the sole inheritor of a banking family, had invested wisely, and over the years, the estate had accrued huge amounts.

My new stepfather is a very powerful politician. Oh, how he wanted to live in grand style, and desired to place a lien against my inheritance. When he couldn't get his hands on my money, he came up with the idea that I'd marry his eldest son.

"I refused. As a result of my denial, I was locked in the attic, leaving the nice rooms to my mother, new stepbrothers and stepfather—and me a prisoner until I decided to marry him.

"My mother screamed at me through the door, 'You are like the devil's own daughter. You are a plague, a pestilence.' I didn't like being compared to locusts, gnats, crabs: the bubonic plague; and oceans turning to blood."

Trees sashayed as a frightening darkness fell. A swift bolt hurtled through the lurid air, bleaching the Valley in pallid light. In the storm's ravaging fever, saplings bent, and her skirts plastered to her legs and belled out behind her. Despite her tremulous limbs and the ravaging wind, she stood firm in the wrathful chaos.

He took another step toward her, releasing his features from the darkness and she backed two steps against a tree. "My stepfather claimed I needed further convincing. My mother turned her back while he beat me. I had to get away and so escaped."

She couldn't tell him she was a murderer. She didn't know how he'd react. What if he possessed some southern code, sent her back where it was too late for any kind of justice. She trembled.

He took another step toward her and she placed her hand on his chest, a ridiculous barrier. "My father had performed many a favor for Mother Superior. I plead my case to her, and a quid pro quo was arranged. I'd perform my skills to treat Union soldiers in return for my disguise."

He gripped her upper arms with an iron brand. "So, you joined the Sisters of Mercy and are not a real nun?"

"No, I am not."

He laughed then. Low, dark and barely humorous.

Lightning ripped across the sky. The thought of going back tore up her insides. She wiped the tears and rain from her face. Her heart breaking, she said, "If-if you wish me to return—"

The forests creaked with bending boughs, the chaotic winds roaring upon the trees, waving, swirling, tossing their branches in frightful agony.

Those lips. Every single part of her remembered those lips. No more than a solid slash across tougher features. No longer elevated with masculine confidence but wound with mocking conceit. The transformation bewildered and confounded her.

He'd taken her hand to deliberately unnerve her, and then brushed his mouth over her knuckles. A tremor full of nameless fears and desires engulfed every bone she possessed.

Heaven's great ceiling poured down in a sweeping veil of rain, hammering, pulsing, soaking her until her hair hung in heavy ropes and her clothes plastered to her skin.

She was no longer afraid.

She had become the storm.

His fingers brushed her neck beneath her bodice. Grace trembled, but she held straight and still as a saint to a pillar as he explored the delicate skin of her nape. His fingers threaded in her damp hair and cupped the back of her head.

"Do you have any idea what happens to spies?"

"Do not give me an empty threat. I am not a spy."

"How about other threats?" His head fell until his lips skimmed her shoulder exposed by the wide neckline of her gown. Tremors speared her, rousing up from some echoing place with such power her belly contracted, before they exploded onto her skin in a cascade of shivers.

His arm ensnared her again with his rock-solid body, as the questing fingers of his free hand continued to delve into her hair. He whispered something against her skin, but her heart beat deafeningly in her ears so she couldn't correctly distinguish the words. Searing lips dragged over her skin, delaying at heart-jolting hesitations to haul in deep lungfuls of air as though he could gather her soul within him.

As she looked up to him, he took her in his arms and captured her mouth in a kiss that made her head reel. He slid his tongue across her lips, urging them to part, persisting, and the instant they did, he dove into her mouth. With the punishing rain beating down upon them, he slid his hands up and down her arms and over her breasts, then possessively across her spine to press her tight to his hardened thighs.

She knew his motives well, fueled with anger for her deception, he thrust his tongue deeper, to wield her passion, seeking to take full control, like a brand, searing her, having her.

His kiss both ravished and confused her. His arm tightened around her, pulling her so close and hard he could crack her ribs. She struggled to breathe but his hold did not loosen the smallest bit, and she felt she might expire from suffocation.

All the same, she groped his chest, firm healthy male flesh tingled beneath her fingertips. She desired him, wanted to touch him everywhere, to explore every part of him. She brushed her fingers over muscle, heat, moisture then slid her arms around his neck, sighing.

With every touch, he made her realize how very female she was. A wild sensuality stirred to life inside of her and she recognized it for the dangerous sensation it was. A wealth of hidden feelings leaped from her, blossoming, exploding with the volleys of thunder over them.

His lips left hers, abandoning them to cold raindrops. Then he released her enough so she slid down his body until her feet touched the ground, her arms still clasped to his neck.

A flash of lightning turned his eyes into silver embers, glinting hard and hot as tempered steel, and he pushed her away, not entirely, he held her shoulders. A myriad of emotions crossed his handsome face. The sadness of a man who saw himself merely a leaf blown by the wind, living and dying in uncertainty, or a thing destined like corn to wither in the sun.

Suddenly, his grip tightened, fingers digging into her shoulders. "Who are you to do this to me? To drive me to madness?"

Grace inhaled, words caught in her throat. She wiped the pouring rain from her face and her lashes.

"I cannot allow you into my life," he shouted.

"Why?"

They waited for the roll of thunder to end as though it were a raucous and brazen guest, and then he spoke through his teeth. "Because every day I face doubt, racing against time and numbers of the enemy. I don't know if I'll live or die."

Denial was mirrored on his face, like an outgoing tide, and the scariest thing was, he didn't seem to care about the loss.

"There will always be uncertainty," she said over the din. She saw a man imperfect and irresolute, but held together by the frayed and always fraying, destructive bonds of guilt.

So many silent protests rose in her throat and stung like vicious bees behind her lips, but she was too much of a coward to give them breath. It would be an exercise in futility for he turned apathy into an art form, and indifference into a religion. Her heart ached for him.

He escorted her back to her tent, the journey like walking endless miles in raging silence, and then he simply turned away.

Why should she spend any more time thinking of him? But she did. She had been afraid to open her heart because she'd been abandoned, neglected and very hurt, yet she'd fallen for his imperfections. She was a healer after all.

CHAPTER 20

RYAN DOWNED ANOTHER DRINK OF brandy. He rarely drank, at least not like this. His back pressed to his bed, he reached up and toyed with his sword dangling from the tent pole. Could he love her? He took another drink thinking about his enemies. Racing against time and numbers and most of all, he was yoked with self-doubt. She might be put in jeopardy and he cursed the risk.

Shrieks of terror drove him from his cot. His head pounding, he rose unsteadily, trying to erase the liberal amounts of brandy he'd consumed. He yanked on his boots, threw back his tent flaps and blinked.

What the hell?

Sister Josephine and Sister Grace stood in the middle of the camp clearing. He shook his head. Except she wasn't Sister Grace anymore. In the bright light of day and without her nun's garb, she was beyond exquisite. Her hair was an indescribable hue varying in shades according to the light thrown upon it, from honey to the palest shade of a sun's ray. Her shoulders rose gracefully, her manner grand, and her salutations were very charming; so elegant and lovely she seemed foreign to earth.

Dark circles formed beneath her eyes. Did she not sleep last night? Good. Because he didn't sleep either, fantasizing of warm creamy breasts against his chest and long slim legs wrapped around him. He straightened. He didn't believe she was a spy at all, but still he could not forgive her.

He dragged his attention from her and glanced at Sister Josephine who stood next to a huge boiling cauldron. Sister Jennifer Agatha gave the scene a final stamp with her cackling. Some of his men were stripped down to their underwear, their hands pressed in a fig leaf pose in front of their privates.

"Take off your underwear," ordered Sister Josephine, "or I'll throw you in the pot."

Despite the bruise growing on his jaw, his captain heaved with laughter. Dammit, why had he let his temper get the best of him. For years, he'd not seen the man with so much mirth.

"I fail to see what is so funny," said Sister Josephine, scalding Gill with a baleful eye, all while stirring the awful eye-searing brew. "You will set an example for the men and disrobe first. Once we've boiled your clothes in lye, you can go to the river and wash. I've seen enough vermin to last me a lifetime and my war with lice ends now."

That sobered Captain Gill.

Rourke moved up to the first row of men. A private appealed to him. "Colonel, I never remove my underwear. Atilla the Nun…" he aimed a creaky finger to Sister Josephine, "…demands we exceed the bounds of decency."

He flapped his hand to Sister Jennifer Agatha. "Without my clothes, she may take me to her bosom like a maternal boa constrictor. And that one there," he pointed at Grace. "She ain't a nun no more."

She certainly wasn't. A vein pulsed in his jaw as he glanced at his men. A tidal wave of randy grins and predatory hunger covered their faces. How naïve she was to expect these men, hard-driven men all made more so by war, to behave like penitents. Wasn't it Plato who said lust was the companion of all crimes? His camp would be turned into a nest of felonious delinquents with her presence.

She wore a simple green day dress except on her it was more a sculptured masterpiece, following every curve and line of her figure. The lace at her throat parted, and the hollow of her neck filled with shadows. Ryan stood transfixed. His gaze clung to hers, analyzing what laid beneath.

How dare she look so attractive? He enjoyed the advantage his height offered him; an alluring display of smooth flesh, exposed by the neckline of her gown. He clenched his hands, ground his teeth.

As a nun, she'd served as a sort of female eunuch, in effect, a nonhuman. With her transformation, he could well understand his men's unwillingness to disrobe in front of her.

With his mouth wide open, the soldier next to him

chewed noisily on a piece of pork rind. "Colonel Rourke, my mama brought me up with proper modesty."

Wasn't this the soldier who regaled his companions with detailed and glittering accounts of his romps with Richmond prostitutes?

Ryan took a step away. Couldn't tell if the foul smell came from the rancid pork rind or the soldier. With certainty, lice had a field day with the private.

"I don't want to be judging, Colonel, but my mama always said, *'Depart, depart, go out from there. Touch no unclean thing! Come out from it and be pure, you who carry the articles of the Lord's house.'* Matthew Chapter twelve." He dipped his head in the affirmative.

Ryan almost laughed at the high moral ground the soldier took. The soldier started choking on his pork rind, cleared his throat and commenced loud hiccupping.

"It's Isaiah 52:1," corrected Sister Josephine, stirring her brew with renewed vigor. "Yet, I'm thinking more of Ezekiel 36:25 *I will sprinkle clean lye water on you, and you will be clean.*"

"Lye water?" cried the soldier, lost amidst boisterous hiccups. "That will take the skin off me, Colonel."

Not a bad idea. Maybe the lye would pull off a layer or two or three of stench. "It's discouraging to think how many people are shocked by honesty and how few by hypocrisy."

Failing to interpret Rourke's reproach, the soldier stared blankly, his frenzied hiccups like a cat dying.

"My mama said it isn't good for your health to bathe more than once a year, and I find it a challenge to go against my moral principles," he said, his hysterical spasms annoying Ryan.

"You can die from hiccups," said Ryan.

"You can?" The soldier's shaggy eyebrows arched to the sky.

With an air of unequivocal authority not to be ignored, Grace came to stand before him. "The vermin are so plentiful, I'm petrified to sneeze, for fear the lice would regard it as a gong for dinner and eat me up."

Ryan stepped forward before anarchy took hold of his ranks, and said, "Surely Sister Grace, I mean, *Miss Barrett*, you can—"

"All bedding needs to be boiled in addition to their clothing. The vermin on the men is so profuse that I worry about a typhus outbreak." She took a step closer to inspect him and the hiccupping soldier held his hands up as if to ward off a vampire.

Ryan straightened. "I assure you I do not harbor vermin and I bathe regularly with soap."

"Can you believe one soldier told me that he couldn't sleep properly unless a few gray backs were gnawing on him? Another told me on a lively day of skirmishing he caught twenty fat lice. Did you know the men even entertain themselves with lice races, placing lice on their mess plates, and that one soldier was found to have cheated by heating his plate!"

Her cheeks were rosy from the sun, and that bare dip between her breasts—was there any defense?

He glanced at Sister Josephine, and then at Miss Barrett. "May I speak privately with you? I insist."

The older nun and Miss Barrett looked at him as if he'd just asked them to lift the hems of their dresses.

"Stay here, Sister Josephine and make sure none of them defect." Grace gave Ryan a withering look and walked ahead of him. They passed a smirking Sister Jennifer Agatha warming her rear on a stump. When Ryan glared at her, she scurried away like a rat.

"I have another concern, even greater," Miss Barrett spoke pompously over her shoulder. "Did you know some doctors in the village were giving the men calomel made from mercury, giving them the bloody flux? The staff for the two serving hospitals, what exists of it, is woefully behind in knowledge and are quacks with no qualifications. Most importantly, you must know you are undersupplied as of this last battle. I'm muddling through with what I have and equate it to the medical Middle Ages."

A courier pulled up and reared his mount. "Colonel Rourke, I have communications for you."

"You're dismissed," Ryan snapped and gave a curt salute. With long furious strides he moved around her and toward his tent.

Like a dog following a bone, she followed close behind. "You are impatient today, Miss Barrett."

"I made it through the day, refraining from hitting you over the head with a bedpan. I'd say my patient skills are improving."

"Your tolerance is remarkable."

"Which brings me to my next item. The food. The meat is so infected with maggots, it's a wonder it isn't carried off by the critters. The pickling of the meat makes it inedible. The salt horse when boiled carries a stench that no hard-core palate could tolerate. More men die from contaminated beans than bullets. Rice and other victuals have worms as long as your finger. Dysentery, malaria, diarrhea, yellow fever…we must have supplies, Colonel."

Her comment made him come to an abrupt stop, and she ran headlong into him.

He turned around, righted her, and then eyed the tantalizing rise and fall of her bosom. He dropped his hands as if they were scorched with fire.

His head ached from trying to keep up with the changes in her conversation, thinking that if she was around the camp any longer, he'd have to add saltpeter to the men's food…and his. "Do you think I do not have knowledge of the situation? What do you propose I do? Walk across the Potomac and beg Lincoln for his bounty?"

She blinked her pretty violet eyes, then squared her shoulders and looked like she'd like to do battle with him. "I don't know on what precise logic Colonel, Brigadier General, Captain, Lieutenant, Lord High Executioner Rourke you resist my pleas. Go out and raid some more."

One of his soldiers was leaning so far over, he fell off his stump. Other soldiers were openly ogling. It was dismaying to Ryan and his command during the war, too many secrets were unkept, the men seeming to delight in gossip. No doubt, every man was all ears in his camp, the colonel with the unfrocked nun, and now with the two of them bickering, there'd be plenty of fodder with the winks each man gave to another. He'd be the soul of circumspection. "A word," he turned and gestured for her to go ahead of him.

He tried to ignore her luscious scent. Her swaying

backside no longer hidden by her ugly nun's frock could tie a man in knots.

"You seem to be in an unpleasant mood today," she tossed over her shoulder.

She dared to mock him. "Livid is more like it. Put down the flap," he ordered, and he could tell she was rankled by him ordering her about. Excellent. She deserved it for looking so irresistible.

"I want to preface our conversation about last night," she said. "Things did not go well, and I thought to initiate a conciliatory relationship between us."

Damn. His cot was there, and he damned well knew what conciliations he'd like to make. Hell, she wasn't a nun anymore. He didn't say anything.

She took a breath and continued. "Right. I thought I'd offer a peace agreement."

He rubbed his hand across his neck. "It is I who should offer an apology." He knew he sounded cold and aloof.

She swallowed and he watched the dark shadows in her throat. He could dip his tongue there. She'd taste like honey because he had sampled her sweetness the night before. She was like opium to him. His brain battled against reason.

"It's not like I'm in any danger."

Her voice lacked conviction. "Aren't you?" His eyes raked appreciatively over her decidedly feminine form.

She flushed and stiffened, and then looked him straight in the eyes. "There is not one dishonorable bone in your body."

He let out a sharp bark of laughter. If she only knew what dishonorable thoughts he was thinking, she'd run.

His traitorous mind decided that it would like to get very fond of every part of her delectable body, and then his even more traitorous body reacted violently to the thought.

Grace was still upset from the night before. She bit her lip and stole a glance up at him. It wasn't like he was incapable of happiness, yet he held himself away from it. He felt underserving of it, mistrustful of it. The way he'd walked away from her after what he'd done to her. His guard had been put back up. The war had scarred this man very badly, but that didn't, however, mean that she would allow him to abuse her in turn.

Clear of his scars, she sensed something special in him, something fine and shining and very, very good. And perhaps all he needed was someone to remind him of that. She saw no reason not to throw caution to the wind and try to befriend him despite all the obstacles he was throwing in her path. Friendship. That was it. She'd develop a camaraderie with him.

In spite of that impulse, memories of last evening washed over her. He had captured her mouth in a soul-drenching, shattering kiss that had branded her for a lifetime. The unexpected wildness of the kiss, his tongue trailing across her neck and throat, even now sent shivers through her.

And then, he'd just pushed her away without cause or reason. Maybe he was one of those men honor bound by a code of chivalry. With certainty in his inebriated state he'd forgotten that he kissed her.

She should have known better. What did she expect?

Her traitorous face heated with the memory.

Looking at her, his eyes widened with a wicked cobalt gleam. The cad. He'd not forgotten, either.

He clutched the brandy like a dancing partner. "You best not join me for brandy. I have a terrible habit, you see."

She dipped her eyes disapprovingly to the bottle in his hands. "Just one?"

He shot her a look that said he wasn't amused.

She had never seen him like this before, so inebriated. Bottle in hand, he wavered back and forth, and then plopped in his chair, propped his feet on the desk and templed his fingers, his gaze considering her.

Her hands found her waist. "I need turpentine, quinine, bandages, morphine, and quinine sulphate. None of which I have."

"I'll just pluck your supplies from the air." He slammed down the bottle. "Am I taking you from something important? Lice removal must be a most wanted occupation of ladies."

The anarchy of her emotions intensified to full revolt. "Not really. I love taking time out of my busy schedule to explain something that should be common knowledge to a person in your position. Are you sure you are a graduate of West Point? Yes! That explains it. A mind that can credit the bleatings of military professors can hardly be expected to understand plain English."

She lifted a brow when he downed another drink. "I fully appreciate the defects of your character, but we must address this issue."

"What defects?"

"Right," she said, saluting him. "Would you like the short version or the long version?"

His voice was as calm as baby's breath, but his eyes stabbed daggers through her. "Do you have any idea whom you are speaking to? Men have died for less."

She snorted. "I have a proposal to improve conditions if you could take a few seconds out of your busy day to listen of what I have to say."

"Go ahead."

"I have knowledge of Union warehouses full of supplies and their locations in Maryland."

"I'm not going that deep into Yank territory on a fool mission. The idea is lunatic."

She sent him her most contemptuous look. "I don't take well to sarcasm."

"I know I don't have to be this sarcastic; but the world has given me so much material to work with… and I'm just not one to be wasteful."

She detested the slur in those words. "Then get me more medical supplies!"

When he remained mute, she said, "This isn't like you, Colonel Rourke."

"Don't you tell me what is or isn't like me," he hissed. "You have no right."

She never wanted to take a swing at a man so much, but oh, she wanted to punch him. Take a hefty swing and see him land backward on his Rebel arse. She didn't care how legendary or fearsome he was. Her blood ran hot through her veins that he spoke to her like she was an idiot. "You have kidnapped me. I have sewed up and mended your men. I have earned every right."

She could tell he was thinking of Green Tavern and she winced at the pain in his voice, "It wasn't your fault," she said quickly, "even Captain Gill said it wasn't."

His eyes narrowed in a threatening glare. "Bastard. He should keep his mouth shut."

"I came here because I desired to make clear that we will remain friends," she said.

He stood up abruptly and the chair rocked back, but he snagged it before it fell. A bit wobbly himself, he straightened, squared his shoulders, and then turned his back to her. After a moment, his broad shoulders rose as if he drew a deep breath, then sank again as he released it. "The things I've done. I'm not fit to be your friend. So, why?" he asked, his voice agonizingly harsh.

"Because I—" Grace stilled, stunned by what she nearly said. "I'm fond of you. I see you as a friend. I've had few in my life, so maybe I appreciate how special friendship is." She held her breath waiting for his reaction.

He whipped around to face her. "For the love of God, Woman, what does it take to get you to heed what I'm saying? For the last time, I cannot be your friend. I could never be your friend."

"Why not?"

"Because I want you."

She did not pull away. He'd been so blunt, so naked with his need—it startled her. "That's the brandy talking," she said quickly.

"Do you believe so? You are very unacquainted with men, my sweet."

"I know about *you*."

For a moment, he just stood there…filling the tent with his height. Grace's nerves thrummed as her eyes roamed over the shape of him, beautifully long, with broad shoulders and lean hips.

"Not half as much as I do about you, Miss Barrett."

"Don't mock me," she whispered. It was like caging a tiger, and suddenly not knowing how to tame the beast.

The colonel's brows dipped low over his eyes, sparkling with dark emotion. He moved closer to her. Very close. His considerable size made it necessary for Grace to tilt her chin up to look him square in the eyes. She recognized there was a time she might have been frightened by a rude Rebel colonel. When she would have demurely, with all expected haste done as he commanded her because young ladies were to be compliant. That was before she had been degraded by her mother, stepfather and stepbrothers. But now a demon of insurrection had burst from her and she refused to be beaten down anymore. And right now, the colonel was on thin ground.

"I've been watching you. All the things I know, all the things I've noticed."

Grace knew she should go, but his sleek, powerful magnificence mesmerized her into stillness, hypnotized her…seduced her with the potency of his masculinity.

"If I've learned anything in my life it's this, if you watch people long enough, they reveal themselves to you."

"Ryan, I mean, Colonel Rourke, I think you should—"

He placed a finger to her lips. "I'll start here," he

whispered, "with your mouth."

"My m—"

"Shhh. It's my turn." His finger traced the delicate arch of her upper lip. "So full. So pink. You've never been kissed before I kissed you?"

She shook her head, but his motion brought on sensual torture as he rubbed his finger rubbed along her skin. He seemed satisfied with her confession, and then stopped suddenly, leaving her bewildered and disappointed. Like quicksilver, his erratic moods destabilized and weakened her. How could he tease her so sweetly one moment and be so dark and forbidding the next?

Yet underneath, she couldn't shake the idea that he somehow *needed* her. He needed someone, *that* much was clear. Someone who could wipe away the pain that surfaced in his eyes when he thought no one was looking.

Despite warning bells clanging, she accepted the challenge, knew she'd slice through that conjured aloof façade, would chop through his cold exterior and sever his detachment. Oh, she could do that. Yes, she could.

He rounded his desk, exiling himself to the opposite side. A curtain had dropped. Drifting to business, he unwound maps. "Show me where the warehouses are located."

"Where did you get these?" she asked, her brain yet ensnared in a sensual fog. Yet the abruptness of his withdrawal left her abandoned and feeling the powerlessness of an unsupported child.

"I have a particular care for every item of intelligence calculated to enlighten me as to the design of my adversaries. These are stolen maps of Maryland and the region you are talking about."

Damn him for making her vulnerable. Still she must play her cards right to get him to agree to take her. She must have those medicines and pointed to the exact area.

He shook his head. "Unreliable at best. Geography plays a primary part in determining what is to be done and how various physical features make this place you are talking about a very difficult nut to crack. First, the bluff itself, the two hundred slate escarpment dominating the hairpin bend of the river at its base is unscalable for infantry let alone cavalry. It affords Yank guns at its crest and subsequent deadly fire. The only alternative is to come upon the rear and then make a wide swing east and approach it from that direction. I don't want to do it. I won't lead my men into a trap."

He couldn't let go of his long ago, ill-advised and costly military maneuver. With constrained eagerness, she pressed on for he must know the truth. "There's another problem. Binding east and west is a swamp with no roads for many miles. The terrain is impenetrable except to the smallest of parties engaged in the briefest of forays."

There was a long silence, during which he stared at her in an uncomfortable way, and then said, "Nothing cultivates Judgment Day like topography. How difficult is the terrain?"

"What? Oh, the terrain. About four or five miles of inland swamps with a myriad of off-shooting trails."

"Four or five miles?"

"And then some if you take a wrong turn."

"Damn."

She ran her finger over the vast blank area of the map with no delineated roads. "You can get through but there is a huge barrier of woodlands, hilltops and wetlands that you can easily get bogged down in and never return. Only one with a discernible eye can help get you through."

Ryan groaned. "You know of someone we could convince to guide us?"

"Me."

"Absolutely not. I'm responsible for you and I will not place you in jeopardy."

His whiskey-smooth voice poured out of his chest in words like the snowflakes of winter, allowing no other mortal to debate. She braced for a fight. "I desperately need those medical stores and must go to show the way. Don't you dare pull the dutiful chivalrous protector card. We can cross the river twelve miles above."

He arched a brow. "There is no, 'we' in this endeavor."

She watched his full, masculine lips as he spoke… inviting lips…kissable lips. "Oh, there's no 'we' because you know the area? That's why you're asking me about the swamps? This area is my backyard. It is where I traveled many times with my father."

After a look that threatened to scorch the fine hairs from her body, he perched on his bed and removed his boots. "An infantry line of action is not a wholesome place for a woman."

"I'll dress like a boy."

He laughed. "No one in the world is going to mistake you for a boy." More serious, he said, "Besides that, it's not a place for boys either."

"You'll get lost, captured, or worse. Every one of your men may lose their lives. The terrain is an abysmal labyrinth, and I know the environment like the back of my hand. No one will lose their lives if I can sneak you in the back way. I have no doubts whatsoever."

He stood, approached her in his bare feet, his gait as quiet as a hunter stalking his prey. "You must be the most irreverent, defiant person I have ever met in all my years," he said on a long sigh.

"Really! In all your years? Conceivably you ought to tour the world every so often, Colonel. I am defiant because I'm not one of your soldiers."

"Yes, you've made that exceedingly clear, *Grace*."

How her name sounded delicious when he said it in his deep soothing tone, with his alarmingly arousing drawl.

Oh, how he didn't want to take her. He wavered, leaned close to her. She smelled the brandy on his breath and how it mingled with his particular spiciness.

She waited. "Just quick in and out. There will be no trouble. I'm an excellent horsewoman and I'll do everything you order me to do."

"What, exactly, would you do for me?" He stood over her, his mouth hovered above hers, and his regard could set her to ash and embers and leave the rest of the world to smolder.

She inhaled at his heated question. Oh, he was hungry. Like the conditioned responses of any prey animal, she sensed his need with the tiny hairs prickling on the back of her neck urging her to run.

She placed her hand on his chest. Though her strength was feeble next to his, he halted his advance as though her hand were a wall. He stood still but the muscles twitched and tensed beneath her palm. The warmth of his body radiated through the butternut fabric, heating her chilly fingers. "I-I don't understand."

The colonel's brow lowered, his eyes turning dark with clarity. "You understand completely."

She snatched her hand back. Without the barricade of her hand, he crept forward, crowding her. Heart stalling and then sputtering back to life, Grace stepped backward.

He reached for her hair, and she flinched. He caressed the strands and twirled them around his finger. "Indulge me," he purred, his voice as heavy and resonant as torn velvet. "Pretend we are not in the middle of a Rebel camp. Imagine I've gone to Maryland to get your supplies." He leaned closer, his warm breath smelling of brandy and desire as his head dipped low.

Suddenly silent, he stared down at her, his eyes bright and fierce. So different from when she'd first met him, when all she'd read within his depths was a selfish, indifferent hunger.

Did he now consider her something other than what she was? Not a nun, beyond his grasp, but a woman? Someone who enticed and aroused him?

He gave no declarations or clichés. Yet, she grasped the likeness of herself mirrored in the hunger tightening his powerful features. In the reverence smoldering from his gaze. In the lash of his breath, and the heat of his sex now pressed against her.

A low moan slipped past her lips, a husky, helpless sound of want.

Then it turned sensuous and he lifted her gently on

his bed.

"I'll not take you."

A whisper of unease teased her senses, his words coiling, rioting, unleashing a restless throbbing in her veins. What did he mean? She was new at this, knew not what to do. Lying on the bed, she felt like a frail, boneless puppet held in place by a single straying string as his hot gaze drifted over her.

Damn him. He knew what he was doing. Teasing out a tension, leaving anticipation roaring in her ears and a marked warmth flooding the area between her legs.

Unable to wait, she raised her hand to him, and he responded immediately, descending on her, ravishing her mouth as his hands explored her body, where his eyes no longer could. She had one shadowy foretaste of dark lust on his features before he did, indeed, press her down. Down. Submerging her with the surrendering mattress below, and his hard body above in a cocoon of heat and want.

Some primitive force inside her urged her to move. To squirm against him as he took his time shaping his hands to her body. His fingers speared into the silky strands of her hair, and his mouth nibbled delicately at her jaw, her ear, the hollow of her throat as his hands traced the subtle shape of each dip and curve of her waist to her hips.

He stroked up her ribs, to the edge of her bodice, and then tugged it down, working his hands beneath until her breasts sprang free. Her breath caught when he cupped her breasts, heavy, weighted with need, his hot gaze intense as he dusted her rigid nipples with the palms of his callused hands, massaging and flattening.

His hands coaxed and caressed her, skimming down her back, and then reaching down to pull up her skirts as he took first one nipple in his firm, wet mouth.

She reached up, stringing her fingers in his dark hair, holding her to him, the sensations he produced brought every nerve ending brutally to life. His mouth laved her breast in tortuous agony, nipping and suckling, and then his tongue ran a sensual path to the other neglected breast.

All the time, his hands charted over her bare thighs, bunching up her skirts and smoothed over her belly. His hands continued their exploration, everywhere—but there. After so long, she made an anxious noise, flexing her legs, her quivering knees and wriggling impatient hips.

He was turning her into a wanton. But she couldn't help it.

He tugged her nipple with his teeth and let go, the glistening peak alone and abandoned.

Why?

He dropped a feather-light kiss on her lips and smiled.

Cool air doused her skin and he looked down to where her skirts were gathered above her waist. Clamping her legs together, she struggled to push her petticoats down, but a heavy hand on her stomach stayed her protests. No way would she risk losing the sensations he was making her experience.

An appreciative sound purred from his throat as he looked at her, and then spread her legs, widening the material of her pantalets. He kissed each thigh. When she gasped, he stroked his hand over her sex.

He petted her downy curls before parting them all the while watching her with those hooded cobalt eyes. His fingers cool against her hot intimate flesh.

"It is wicked," she breathed. "You must stop."

She heard a ragged murmur of satisfaction in his throat as she saturated his probing hand with moisture. For a moment, she surrendered to it, both the sweetness and the shame. He leaned over and kissed her then, with long, sweet promises, seducing her with hot, deep glides of his tongue.

The heat of his breath against her cheek distracted her for a moment, before his clever, careful fingers began to dip and toy with the slick desire her body released, drawing it up to the tiny place that swelled and ached for him.

Her body surged with painful throbbing, an elusive pinnacle she could not reach. Whimpering, she dug her nails into his shoulders and arched, bearing down on the fingers filling her.

He was breathing hard too, and she dared to look at him, to gauge his expression. Intent with lust, his color high and fevered. Trickles of perspiration dotted his forehead. His gaze on her was reckless.

But his hands, his maddening steady hands disproved what she read on his face. They made sly and circular motions around that place where her sensation crowned, leisurely, deliberate, even as she bucked beneath him, seized him. Panting wordless appeals for something she didn't grasp. Couldn't convey.

He laved her breast, tugging on the peak. Oh, how he played her body like an instrument, knowing where to touch her, drawing her strings taut on an excruciating journey.

Damn him. An infuriating smile tugged his lips, knowing he'd pushed her past maidenly inhibitions, beyond learned taboos, past caring about why she was here and what the future would hold, and possessing no idea where his touch would take her. He drew pleasure from her awakening. Savored it. So, unable to stand it anymore, she pressed her head back into the mattress and squeezed her eyes shut. Surrendering to the moment.

To him.

Ryan craved it for her. He pressed down the need of his throbbing cock, knew he was being selfish, ending her innocence to bring the dazzling silky path of erotic pleasure; to make her glorious sun set simply to rise again in a boundless instant of exquisite and intoxicating pleasure.

His finger found its way inside of her, to her maidenhood, and she jerked. With wicked, torturous strokes, he quickened his pace and rhythm until she surged in trembling, taut thrusts.

He slid another finger inside her, and she sobbed at the pressure of it. Breathing hard, he watched her, luscious, sensual, gauging her response, and waiting for her rapture. He had her riding his fingers as one might ride a horse, hips moving in time with his urging. He was rewarded with muted animal sounds.

All the while, he continued his ministrations, his fingers slipping easily into her wetness, pulled deeper by her grasping, pulsing muscles.

In that instant, he felt her thighs tremble, her belly

shudder, and he hushed her keening cries with his mouth as her hips rocked and her womanhood tightened in a convulsive movement, the heady perfume of her feminine essence washing over his hand.

Long after he withdrew from her swollen flesh, she twitched and shuddered. Letting out a breath, Ryan held her close, and with tenderness, reveled in the feel of her as he cradled her yielding body with his. He dropped a soft kiss on her forehead, cherishing the rapid beat of her heart against his chest, and closing his eyes to his searing agony of self-denial.

"Ryan?" she asked, her voice filled with dazed fascination.

"Hmm?"

She pulled down her skirts, and then nestled closer to him. In the distance, he heard the squealing of Archimedes, his loud snorts and pawing, and no doubt tearing at his tether. He'd have to move his stallion away from the undeniable heat of a mare. Ryan shifted, induced to pity for the animal's quandary. Grace's musk filled the air and he, too, could not ease his monstrous erection.

"This is new…I had no idea. I believe…it seemed a bit…one-sided. Perhaps I should—"

He nudged his chin into her silky hair, hoping his men had not heard her cries. "Grace, what you have experienced is a sample of desire." He played idly with a strand of her hair, telling himself to quit touching her. That it could go no further.

"I am curious why a trained doctor did not know what occurred between a man and a woman."

"I have led a sheltered life. My father and my

servants were my only companions and protected me fiercely. There seemed to be no time for frivolous acquaintances other than an occasional ball my parents held. Even then, the gentlemen were too old and the young ones frowned upon my odd pursuit of medicine which made me somewhat unsuitable for their tastes."

Her hand clasped his, and uncertainty made her voice shake. "Do I—"

He could see her holding her breath, waiting for him to declare his feelings, silently begging him not to hurt her.

"Grace, I gave you a little taste of what it is to be a woman. The rest will be supplied by your real husband when you marry."

She turned to her side and stared straight into his eyes, searching so deeply, he felt certain she could grasp the shaking soul he concealed beneath his sham veneer.

"I don't believe what you're saying. I know you have feelings for me."

He looked away, at the maps on the table and beyond, anything to escape her accusatory gaze.

When I see you, I smile. When I touch you, I feel. I love you, Grace. "No, Grace. You are wrong. I have a fondness for you, but do not mistake—"

"Bastard." She struck him on the chest, forcing his gaze back to her. "Damn you. Damn you to hell a thousand times."

He thrust her aside and jumped to his feet. "You make much when this was of little consequence."

"Of little consequence?" She sat up and drew her knees to her chest, her pale blonde hair in glorious disarray around her.

"Negligible," he said, shifting and attempting not to scowl at the mocking throbbing in his loins. "Trivial."

She angled her head, glaring holes in him. "After what happened just now, I will never look at you again—at myself in anyway unaffected. You call that of little consequence?"

"Yes," he snapped, his breathing ragged, and then someone cleared their throat outside the tent.

"You pig-headed, conceited, arrogant—"

Then came a louder clearing of the throat, yanking her out of her rioting emotions. Heat fired to her face for what they had been doing with an audience camped on their doorstep.

"Dammit." He hauled her up to her feet. She pulled up her bodice and pressed her wrinkled skirts into place. Her face was hot and flushed from their activity and she was probably fifty shades of red. She took the brush Ryan gave her. Hands shaking, she couldn't get through the hopeless tangles. He commandeered the brush and swung her around and brushed her hair. Where had he become so proficient in brushing a woman's hair? When they were both in sufficient order, he threw open the tent flap.

"What is it you require, Captain Gill?" He bellowed enough to wake Lazarus from the dead.

All smiles, Gill held out a copper mug. "I brought you a cup of coffee."

"Like hell. You never bring me coffee. Why the sudden benevolence?"

"Why the sudden temper?" Gill laughed.

Rourke's stare was enough to freeze the tropics. "Have you been deloused?"

"Why, I've been baked, boiled, steamed, poached, and all anew."

"You have the same clothes on you had two days ago."

"There is that." Gill dipped his eyes to the colonel's feet and raised a brow, apparently finding the whole situation amusing.

Grace cringed. *This couldn't be happening.* The interchange between the two men possessed as much subtlety as a hammer striking an anvil. Oh, to flee to the ends of the earth.

Ryan pulled on his boots, one at a time, blocking the doorway. "I happen to like long walks especially when they are taken by people who annoy me. What is it you want?"

Gill stroked his beard, pretending to look like a beguiling golden retriever who had buried his bone and couldn't quite remember where. "Now, what was it I came for? Oh, yes, I'd like to know what you intend to do about the shortages?"

Grace pressed her hands to her face. Dear God, had Gill heard everything?

No time to think about that now. She seized the opportunity. Storming right ahead, she grabbed the captain's hand, and ushered him around Rourke to the maps. "Do come in, Captain Gill. We were just discussing *our* next raid to Maryland."

CHAPTER 21

FOR TWO WHOLE DAYS AND one night they traveled in the rain without stopping. Grace had borrowed Willie's clothes and surprised the men by wearing pants, and then was chastened a hundred times with Rourke's harsh warnings. *You'll follow my orders to the letter. Do you understand?*

They had entered Maryland. The countryside looked very much like Egypt after a flood of the Nile, strewn with debris from Sheridan's army. The relentless rain made the roadways near impassable, slowing their travel with rivers of mud deepening by the hour. At risk using the main roads, it became almost useless navigating their horses through the dense thickets that lined most of the countryside. Breaks in the thickets appeared, opening to pastures, where the intense rains had made the fields so soft and deep and muddy, it threatened to swallow the legs of their horses. A long journey made longer.

She looked at Ryan's men and the total trust they held for their commander. She supposed there was something about war that forged an indestructible bond between men.

She peered at a barn, the promise of a dry temporary shelter.

Ryan must have seen the direction of her thoughts. "Spies everywhere. The mission is too critical and these men too few to be given up by a turncoat farmer. They may appear innocent to the eye with a harmless question, offering friendly conversation, or offer up a pail of milk or basket of eggs. They'll conceal maps in their pockets and walk miles, showing troop movements, identifying regiments and their commanders to a Yankee spy with a fast horse."

Soaked through her rain gear, she shivered. A waste of energy to complain. As if to add to her misery, the wind grew stronger, the rain harder still, the sharp breeze driving the rain into her eyes and ears. They were spread out within close sight of one another, still moving forward, the wagon wheels whispering a gummy accompaniment to the thud of the horse's hooves as they rolled along the mud slicked road.

The men gnawed on soggy hardtack while they rode, the rain working through their collars and shoulder seams and soles. Their slouch hats were soaked.

The silence grew tense. Grace cast a sidelong look at the colonel, caught his gaze on her and then watched him take out his compass to check their direction.

It was getting darker.

After two hours, Ryan ordered them to stop, and

then moved out of the column taking Grace and two officers with him. They dismounted and leaned in close to what made for dry place beneath a towering tree. The musty smell of stinking uniforms curled her nose. Rourke unrolled a map. "We're getting near to where you pinpointed the warehouses. We're depending on you to get us there."

Dear God! Had she led them on a wild goose chase? None of the terrain looked familiar. To waste energy gazing upward would earn her eyes full of rain telling her nothing. Grace swallowed and pointed on the map which was as useless as a milk pail under a bull. "If you can get me close, I believe I can get you there."

"Believe?"

She looked out over the frowning, rain-slicked men. Ryan demanded certainty.

She took a soggy breath of air. "I'm sure."

Two riders came up fast. Too hard to tell if they were friend or foe. The men pulled their guns.

"It's us, Colonel Rourke. We scouted the area like you told us. There's a Yank encampment nearby. Say about ten thousand."

An angry snarl curled his lips. "Have you led us into a trap?"

She fought the urge to wheel her horse and bolt. Not good odds. This escapade could get them all captured. The late afternoon rose darker as the woods became shadows that crawled over her. The downpour continued, the wind driving the rain through the trees like a flowing curtain. Fat streams and drops from the limbs above found the inside of her collar, her rubberized raincoat unable to keep her dry.

Despite weariness engulfing her, she kept pace with the men. She had to have those valuable medical supplies even if it was for her enemy.

Was it treason what she was about to embark on? Probably. But not treason against human suffering, she rationalized.

"If this isn't the damnedest rain," said Hutchinson. "Air so thick with water, catfish could survive in it."

Ryan kept his eyes focused, staring onward, willing the men to follow. Somewhere out there, the Yanks might be waiting to fire a barrage of gunshots into their sides. She sensed his awareness of every ravine, every mud hole, anyplace someone could be waiting. No matter what his scouts reported, no matter that the farmers had told them that the enemy was miles away, she felt his brain shout out with perfect clarity that they would come, and that his meager column might be swallowed by a screaming wave of Union troops.

Like an ancient monolith of Stonehenge, she saw the towering stone on the roadway ahead, kicked her horse to come alongside Ryan. "This is the place. We are not far. We take the path to the right."

He lifted his hand for the men to stop. "Are you sure?"

She nodded, and he nodded back. The reluctant smile she gave him thawed some of the ice bricked in his chest. She dismounted. "We need to put cloths over the horses' hooves to muffle the sound."

Heavy tree limbs concealed a barely discernible trail. They were a column of two now, traveling through a thicket of oak, pine and sassafras. Her heart pounded, her limbs remained limp with exhaustion, but there was excitement now, pressing against the dense thicket. Thick curtains of water on the tangle of branches showered over her. They moved past the familiar forest pond, crested a hill and halted. Through an aperture of trees, specks of lantern light shone, and she pointed below. This miserable mission had yielded numerous warehouses full of Union stores, a goldmine for the Confederacy. Wagons were lined on the side with a long lean-to to protect horses and mules from the elements.

Ryan turned his head slowly, scanned everything. He lifted his hand and signaled for his men to stop. No one spoke. Using only their eyes, the men gathered closer, in line behind the low cover of bush.

A couple of Union soldiers emerged from a building, their lanterns swaying in the wind. Ryan removed a single-lens spyglass, pulled it lengthwise, sheltering it from the rain. He scanned the entire perimeter.

Captain Gill whispered, "Pennsylvania Bucktails. The finest in the world—and so they are, as far as their tailors can make them."

Hutchinson spat on the ground. "Those Bucktails look like whores on a picnic."

"No other sentinels as far as I can see. With the rains, the guards are inside, keeping warm, thinking no way Confederate troops would find this nondescript place and so far in Maryland," said Sergeant Hutchinson.

"Remember your promise, Colonel Rourke," she whispered. She didn't want to be responsible for anyone's death.

The rain drove even harder now along with a deep rumble of thunder. Ryan grabbed her shoulder, a hard hiss in her ear. "If we are shot at, my men will defend themselves. You will remain here, out of danger."

She inhaled.

Ryan held up two of his fingers. Three of his men dismounted. He pointed. *Those two, get them. Bring them to me.*

His men crawled down the hill, their movements muffled by the rain and wind. The Union guards unaware of the interlopers, talked. With the butt end of a saber, one Yank fell unconscious, the other had a knife to his throat to halt him from giving warning to any of his companions.

The conscious Yank stumbled to his knees in front of Ryan, the smell of alcohol on his breath.

The Rebs hauled him up, held him tightly on both sides. "Don't move, Bluebelly. I'll put a ball in the back of your head."

The man whimpered, frightened into sudden sobriety. "Don't kill me, I got babies at home."

"Then shut up! Don't move!"

Ryan leaned close to the man's face. "You got the water out of your ears? Good. Now listen."

The man trembled. "Please don't kill me…"

Ryan rested a gloved hand on his shoulder. "Then don't give me a reason to kill you, Boy."

Grace felt sorry for him. There was nothing of escape in this Yank, the pure terror draining away any soldiering he might have brought to the uniform.

"Who are you?" the soldier asked sheepishly.

Ryan kept his voice hard. "Now that's your second mistake. I ask and then you answer. Your first mistake was walking in the rain and straight into a full regiment of the Confederate army's finest cavalry. What jack-leg officer ordered you to do something that stupid?"

Grace blinked, regiment? She understood what Ryan was doing. No one needed to know there were only four dozen Confederates with thousands of Yanks nearby. The question was a trick, and the prisoner fell flat face for it.

"Captain Crawford's orders. Told us to set up watch around the warehouses. He's inside with twenty other Yanks sick with the ague. It started with a cold then shivering and coughing and fever. They's been sick for three days with promises of reinforcements to come soon."

"Oh, for God's sake, Son, I asked one simple question. These reinforcements, how soon are they to come?"

"Uh…maybe I ought not be telling you this because these are Union stores. They said tonight."

"Listen Son, you know what a Texas toothpick is?"

"N-n-no, sir."

Somebody lit a match, a flash of light bursting between them. The Reb holding the prisoner held a blade to his face, the light reflecting the flicker of light. Eyes wild, he reared back his head.

The match went dark, and Ryan said, "We all carry them, Son. Keep them sharp. They're real good for gutting a hog, or, even better they'll split a Yankee from his chin to his soft nether regions. Now, you tell me what I need to know, or I'll show you how sharp the blade is, and then you can tell your grandchildren how you came face to face with the Gray Ghost one night and lived to tell about it."

The prisoner began to cry, hard sobs. Grace swallowed.

What terrified him more, the knife or the fact he was in the company of the infamous Gray Ghost?

"When are those reinforcements really going to arrive?"

"Captain said tomorrow."

"Whose regiment is close by with Yank troops?"

"That would be Brigadier General Crook, sir."

"How many men do you have and where are they all holed up."

"The building I came out of is the barracks. Ten men are in there sleeping except the captain."

Ryan hand signaled his men forward. "Tie and gag the boy. I want the element of surprise. No guns. I don't want to alert the Yanks bordering us."

They all dismounted, tied their mounts and crept down the hill. She saw Ryan slip inside with his men and marched out ten men and a very angry captain, and then marched them up the hill to be tied with the two other soldiers.

Grace edged her horse down the embankment and went to the north warehouse where she had collected supplies with her father.

Ryan spurred his horse to follow her. Dammit. How could he run this venture and worry about her as well? "I told you to stay put. There might be a guard we didn't get, and you'd be shot."

She peered at him under the dripping rim of her hat, her hand wiping water from her lovely face, and then disappeared into the warehouse.

With a crowbar, she pried a crate open, and like a child bequeathed with a million Christmases, she held up a bottle of quinine. She waved a hand over the marked crates. "These are the medical supplies I need. Chloroform, ether, bandages, medicines, gauze, scissors, needles, surgical instruments. Get the mules from the lean-to and have your men hitch them to the wagons."

Her smile was the key that fit in the lock of his heart. Despite her stubborn countermanding of his orders to stay out of sight, he would always remember this moment, when her face turned rapturous, when her joy bubbled over, and was infectious to everyone around her. Grace loved unconditionally, without selfish intent, without concern for personal gain, hazarding treason, and risking her life to procure medical supplies for her enemy in order to save them.

He leaned over, kissed her and her lips parted in surprise. "Men, bring the wagons around."

Soon a brigade was established, each man passing off crates and stacking them into the wagons.

Captain Gill's boots echoed on the plank floor. "Colonel, it's like being unleashed in a fancy candy store and not knowing what to take first. I checked the other warehouses. They's full of munitions, guns."

"Fill up whatever wagons you can muster. Will leave two men behind to set them afire once we're well from here. They can catch up with us later," Rourke bellowed over the pounding rain. His gaze raked the warehouses. A ping of caution erupted in his chest. They had to get out of there and make plenty of headway during the night.

"I worry if we get bogged down," said Grace, piling U.S. Army blankets in a wagon already overloaded. It was the first trace of nervousness he heard in her voice.

"If we have a problem, we'll toss off contraband to lighten the wagons."

Mules strained to pull the wagons, the wheels sliding back and sinking in the mud. At least the animals were well-fed and in top condition courtesy of the Yanks. His soldiers whipped the mules and finally they departed single file, tracking the way they came, passing the tall granite rock and onto the dark road.

Two hours later, they crested the top of a hill. Rourke swore. It was the most damnable rain he'd ever seen. Water flowed down and across every surface from flashing sheets of cold, crazy, chaotic drops in wild vortices one moment and hammering sheets coming every which way the next.

Grace never complained yet he knew she must be freezing. He stopped, pulled out a new oilskin courtesy of Yank contraband and placed it around her shoulders.

A huge explosion to the north shook the countryside. Fire lit the sky. His men had blown the warehouses. The vast accumulation of munitions set the sky afire and could be seen for miles, making night as bright as day.

"There you are, Grace. I did humanity a favor. Less bullets to kill men."

She huffed as vast clouds of smoke rose hundreds of feet in the air, and explosions of shells and other munitions detonated sounding like a major battle.

"We'll have every Yankee looking for us. Move with all haste." Ryan mounted, and then spurred his horse.

For Ryan, soldiering came easy. It was in his blood. He was an excellent rider and quite handy with rifles and pistols, swords and lethal with a knife. His job was all risk. Amidst the horrors of war, it became apparent that there was no way he could possibly survive the carnage. Nothing but a stroke of fate had brought him through this far. To think that he'd make it through the conflict whole? Or his body intact? Yet, he knew his soul had not lucked out.

Four years had eclipsed, and still Ryan managed to surprise himself, escaping death so far. Now he had the burden of Grace to think about. She trusted him as a child would to protect her from all evil and all danger. Her confidence in him served as a sort of deliverance. What scared him the most was not being able to protect her.

The wagons lumbered behind them, and the men whipped the mules to pull the heavy wagon through mud ruts. Escape would be a miracle if they weren't held up in this godforsaken swamp. Finally, the rain stopped and the skies cleared. They had traveled into a thick woods, still the darkness covered everything, the stars flickering through the treetops.

Two of his men who served as scouts rode up to him. "Yank cavalry, sir."

They had emerged from the flooding swamps which he'd crossed by an abandoned causeway. As the soldiers spoke, he heard the hoofbeats of untold number of riders. "We are in a tight place, and it's about to get tighter," he whispered to Grace. His men stayed stock still except those who moved in front of the mules, covering the animals' heads to keep them quiet. They stayed as silent as the unsuspecting Yank cavalry commander passed by.

With the cloud cover and darkness, he didn't know

which way was east, but he scanned what little horizon he could see. Nothing. Where were they? He checked his compass.

His men had settled in a line, each wagon close to the next, more men behind to protect their rear guard. They moved on for another hour.

Were his eyes playing tricks on him? Beyond a thin row of trees was an open field, deep rolling grass, surrounded by trees, more of the dense woods. He sat up straighter, heard droplets patter from the trees above, and then men talking, and the clank of their trappings. Shadows in motion, shapes suddenly appearing where none had been before. Then he heard a strange hum, coming from far across the field, from the woods beyond. The sound was distinct, the chilly air of the near dawn light blanketing the noises. Soon almost every man carried a lantern and the night lit with giant fireflies in the dark. Yanks were stupid to light the countryside. Illumination provided a way for an enemy bullet.

To his left rose the same sound. He posted a man in front of every mule team. An occasional bray due to lack of water could be deadly. The animals were silenced with the back of a saber over the head.

Gill came up beside him. "Not good, Colonel. The enemy is on both sides of us."

"I'm guessing a brigade or two of infantry followed by cavalry." The icy rain rolled off his hat brim and down his neck. Across the field, outlines of men formed. Damn. A formation of infantry moved. No doubt, the ten thousand Yanks his scouts had seen were divided to the side of them and they were smack in the middle.

His men heard it, too. Keep moving. Bluff their way through. Let the Yanks think it was a parallel movement of their own troops. A low, gray fog, clung to the trees, masking their progress.

"Looks like a Yank commander is aligned with us, Colonel, easy to make a feint by shelling our woods," said Sergeant Hutchinson.

Just as he said it, a rider galloped across the field. Ryan pushed his horse through thorns and briar bushes, and then through knee-deep grass, his oilskin covering his gray uniform. He didn't want the Yank captain to go any farther, to see all the Reb uniforms. They were sitting ducks with the heavily laden supply wagons. Two wagons were mired to the hubs. With certainty, his men had their rifles up. He didn't fancy a shootout with ten thousand Yanks especially with Grace present. Life was not always a matter of holding good cards, but sometimes playing a poor hand well.

"Hold there," Ryan commanded sharply. His calculation of success was based on the theory that to all appearances it was an impossibility. "Is that Brigadier General Crook's forces?" He used the info gathered from the private at the warehouses.

"Yes, sir."

"I have the supply wagons. What was that explosion?"

"Rumors that the damned Rebs hit our supply warehouses, but I'm convinced that all that racket we're hearing out there is coming from our own people. I'm not going to tolerate this nuisance anymore. Half the time it sounds like a damned barn dance, complete with banjos, fiddles and squalling house cats. But if there is

Rebel cavalry who think they can dance their way this close to spit on us, I want them found and every one of them killed or driven out of here. Reports abound, it was the Gray Ghost."

"I don't want to run into that rascal. He's a crafty Reb," said Ryan with pompous aplomb that would have made the showman, P.T. Barnum proud. "The leader of the gray raiders has no known rules of war. He's a law unto himself, doing the unexpected at all times and places. I find myself looking over my shoulder. How many supply bases has he looted, railroads torn up, bridges burned, depots destroyed, hospitals seized, and men captured?"

"Crafty all right. That son of a bitch is as elusive as catching this fog in your fingers."

Ryan stroked his chin; rainwater ran off his hat. "Gives me the shivers to think I might run into the Gray Ghost. I'd rather run the labyrinth with the Minotaur, fight Cerberus, the three-headed hellhound, or cut-off the head of Medusa."

"I'm sick of hearing all this talk about the blasted bogeyman."

"Bogeyman, you say. That is a new name for the Gray Ghost. I congratulate you on your creativity." Ryan angled his head behind him. "One of my wagons broke an axle and as soon as it's repaired, I'll hurry my men."

The appeased captain returned the salute. "Hurry it along. That thieving rascal would take all our stores."

"By the way," said Ryan as the captain turned his horse around. "Is the plan to still head due south?"

"Yes. We're going to enter Virginia. Got new orders

we are to link up with Major General David Hunter's army at Charlottesville. After Cold Harbor, General Grant wants to break the standoff with Lee, maneuver around his right flank, then draw the Reb army out of their entrenchments and into the open. At least that is our orders for now. Who knows? The situation is as fluid as this damned rain."

Charlottesville? No doubt tear up critical rail lines, too. General Lee would be interested in that bit of information.

"I hope to catch that bastard, the Gray Ghost. He's been nothing but a menace. When I take him prisoner, I'll laugh in his face and drink a toast."

Ryan snorted. "I'll make a bet with you, Captain, I'm sorry, what is your name?"

"Captain Maybee, sir." He saluted.

"Captain Maybee," Ryan repeated. "Let's make a wager, whoever catches that rascal first, will get a bottle of wine."

"Good enough," said Maybee. "Your men need any help repairing those wagons?"

"We have it taken care of. Thanks for the offer. Very helpful of you, Captain Maybee."

※

Grace gritted her teeth. Oh, how sly he was. "Didn't you overplay your hand with the head of Medusa? What if they had come into the woods and found us? You think that wise?" A hard gleam of warning underlined the levity in her voice.

"I've met superior numbers before. I'd give them a taste of our southern hospitality."

"With such sincerity and modesty, you have the craftiness of Satan's own tongue. All you have to do is sound commanding and the Yanks will do anything you want them to."

That brought a wry smile to his face. "You find that notion astonishing perhaps?"

"I find it cause to give you a good swift kick but have deigned to grant indisputable glorification."

He laughed. "Your tact exceeds your truthfulness. But it's a shame really. I just can't seem to help myself."

"You are a hopeless, irredeemable outlaw."

"That enhances my growing list of transgressions."

"Don't you ever repent?"

Ryan waved his Colt pistol in the direction he wanted his men to take. "Are you trying to bring a sinner to repentance?"

"You are far beyond redemption, Colonel, but honestly, I believe you are more saint than sinner. You just don't realize it."

He straightened in his saddle. "You don't say, Sister Grace."

"Quit calling me Sister Grace. I say plenty. I see plenty. I see how you care for your men, your horses. How you risked your life to get me medical supplies. You have shown kindness to me, your supposed enemy. You just don't want anyone to see what a big heart you have."

Captain Gill came abreast and bowed in her direction. "Always a pleasure to be out on a night like this."

She shifted her gaze from Gill to Ryan. "Have you noticed he likes to call me *Sister Grace* when he's irritated with me?"

Gill chuckled. "I'm going to scout behind us, sir." He wheeled his horse around and galloped off.

Ryan looked behind him to make a quick inspection of his ranks, and to see if anyone was following them, and then turned to her, so stoic and self-contained, so certain of his uncontested reign. "You have it all figured out, *Grace*."

Oh, how he resisted showing his vulnerability. "Somewhere far down, there is an itch in your heart, but you make it a point not to scratch it, afraid of what might come pouring out."

He gave her a wicked smile…promising.

Rain whipsawed then stopped, leaving a soupy fog enveloping the land. Ryan saw her shiver from the chill and cloying dampness. There was nothing he could do about it until they reached camp. A great blue heron lifted from its rookery and he watched the huge bird's uncertain flight.

"How will we ever be able to tell friend from foe?" she asked.

"Don't worry, Miss Grace," said a gap-toothed soldier. "Colonel has unmatchable instincts." The soldier's left hand drummed nervously on his thigh.

The ground to the west was steep, broken and wooded. To the south as ill luck would have it, ran a wide river. Escape was impossible. The mouth of a little valley opened on the road and covered with woods, large enough to hide his command. He turned his horse hard, slewing soil and grass through its hooves and led his men through the dense canopy of trees. A column of the enemy was in front, about one hundred and fifty yards distant. He could hear their conversation. In front of them, two cavalrymen appeared.

"Careful, Grace. I'm guessing Yank cavalry sent a man over the river to scout. Get in back of me. Now."

When they were in pistol range, the approaching Yanks fired. Ryan wheeled his mount. His men returned a barrage of fire. The wagons were hauled up front to protect Grace. Yanks snaked to their left flank.

Ryan's jaw went heavy with passionate rage. "Bring ten men, Captain Gill, and follow me."

They prodded their horses in the direction of the Yanks. Gunfire came hot and heavy. A bullet shot through his hat. Another grazed his shoulder.

Archimedes spooked, took off and would not obey him, taking him in direct contact with the Yanks' rear guard. The Yanks were as much surprised as if he'd dropped from the sky.

Three different groups of Yanks pressed in. In answering volley, his men charged with a Rebel yell, and panic seized the Yanks. Some had not bridled their horses and scattered in all directions. Yank wounded littered the ground.

Ryan led his men to the wagons. A riderless horse leaped over the wagon, its hooves missing Grace's shoulder. "Whip those mules and get those wagons across the river while the Yanks are in disarray," he ordered.

Captain Gill clawed his beard. "We were near captured by that Yank cavalry, Colonel. If you believe there is no hell, we convinced them that there was something mightily like it."

"The fire was so hot, but the victory was better than the feat of St. George and the Dragon," said Hutchinson, lighting a cigar and puffing on it as if it were a duty to be finished in the shortest possible time.

A soldier whose face possessed juvenile features braced by a neck the size of a mooring post, said, "Might as well have been chasing a herd of antelope."

Ryan watched Grace close her lovely eyes for a moment, then open them.

"I'm resisting the urge to scream, cry, laugh or do all three. How dare you make fun of near travesty, merrily amused as if watching a dog balancing a biscuit on its nose. We might have been killed by that Yank cavalry," she accused.

He had a tender spot for her unaccustomed as she was to battle. If it was possible, he'd sweep her off her horse and hold her in his arms, but there existed numerous enemies nearby to consider. War was one thing to view from afar but to come face to face with a heated skirmish was vastly different. His men were seasoned warriors and they were endeavoring to make the occasion diverting, to ferret out the worm of fear, with certainty coiling inside her.

Hutchinson said, "Miss Grace, they looked more like a procession of Canterbury Pilgrims."

"Mr. Hutchinson, would you please locate some dry cigars?" Rourke said, and then added, "We won by using strategy and deception."

Grace kicked her horse beside him. "Ha! Your tactics were as secure as that wild horse of yours. Archimedes won the hour, rendering your boast the same complaint made by the Austrians against Napoleon."

There was a scratching sound as he lit a cigar. "My dear Miss Barrett, in this life we can only prepare for the probable, not for every contingency. Believe that you can whip the enemy, and you've won half the battle."

He raised his hand to signal his men forward. "What are you waiting for, a choir of angels?

The driving rain returned making their journey miserable as they slogged their way over muddy roads and stared into the roaring violence of flooded streams to cross. Maps that said nothing of the weather. Thick clay coated the wagon spokes and broke off in chunks from the turning wheels.

Ryan's nervous horse had stopped blowing and shivering. Grace's watched Ryan when he stopped and stared southward down an open slope. The river almost capped an ancient and doubtful bridge. Could the wagons make it across?

Ryan went across first.

"Shaky but doable." He motioned them forward.

The bridge bowed and swayed, creaking and cracking, as the wagons rumbled one by one, across the angry waters beneath, craving to suck the heavy contraband into its jaws. She waited while the last of the wagons and men crossed. She and private Nathan, the soldier who had helped her steal the colonel's brandy remained. Her horse danced but she kneed the mare forward. A shadow passed to her left. Too late. A swirling log smashed into the bridge, cracking and shaking timbers. The horses reared, and pitched them into the icy water. Her breath halted from the shock of it, like a thousand tiny needles stinging into her pores. The weight of her coat dragged her down, holding her there. Swept along by eddying currents, she had no idea what was up or down, sideways or forward. Perhaps the strangest perception was that she would drown and not have to answer for the crime of killing her stepbrother. The universe sucked the world out in chest-squeezing panic, and a sense arose that the river held all the power. Shadows blanketed and fogged at the edges, in time with the river that swelled and surged. Must get out of her coat. She ripped at the buttons, shrugged free of the water-soaked garment, and kicked to the surface.

Coughing and sputtering, she sucked in gulps of air. Someone was shouting. It was as if he were calling from another world. Squealing, the horses swam toward the bank. Grace grabbed on to a tail.

Nathan cried out and she looked behind. His arms were flailing, and he went under. The soldier couldn't swim. She couldn't let him drown.

Grace let go of the horse. So fast. Like a river of liquid ice. Her medical mind told her she had seconds to get out before hypothermia set in. Nathan came level with her. He grabbed on to her, hugged her down, his panic uncontrollable. The relentless current held them in its tentacles. They'd both drown. She sank farther brought her hands up, pushed with all her might and broke free, and then swam behind him and grabbed the back of his collar.

All the while, the current swirled and eddied, sweeping them farther and farther away. Up ahead, a fallen tree hung over the river. She reached up, missed it. Her teeth chattered. Go with the flow. Don't fight the river. Ryan? Where was Ryan?

Another tree hung over the river. More shouting. Her numb mind said, one more time. She reached up, stretched her fingers, Nathan still in her grasp. She hooked her hand in the fork of the tree. Cold. Freezing cold water swirled around them. How long could she hold on with freezing water sapping her energy? Her arm was breaking with his weight and the water rushing over her.

Just as she thought she couldn't hold on another second, someone grabbed Nathan from her grip and then she felt strong arms pulling her up.

On shore, and shivering, she vomited. Her teeth clattered together. So cold. So very cold. Someone placed a coat around her. She had the remote feeling of being lifted.

I'm so tired…

CHAPTER 22

"COLONEL, SIR, MY UNCLE OWNS a cabin half-mile down in the hollow," the soldier with the juvenile face pointed. "He's in Richmond where his daughter is caring for him. I know he'd be honored if you'd use his cabin. Sister Grace, I mean, Miss Grace could warm her bones. We men will drive the wagons back to camp. You can meet up with us later."

Having been exposed to the rain for hours, and then a dunked in an icy river, Grace's lips were blue and convulsive shivering wracked her body. He must get her out of those wet clothes. Ryan nodded to the soldier. His men were weathered from years at war and could endure the elements. And they knew the roads they traveled were safe in Confederate territory.

Grace's teeth chattered so hard Ryan thought they would break. Her hair hung in wet ropes and her head dropped onto his chest. "Grace, I'm going to get you some shelter."

"So tired. So very tir—" she mumbled. "Why am I so cold? Who are you?"

She didn't remember her plunge into the river? Her confusion and slurred speech alarmed him. He held her closer, anything to protect her from losing more heat, and kicked his horse down a mud-caked road.

By the time he pulled up in front of a tiny cabin, she wasn't responding. He dismounted, carried her into the small house, laying her unconscious on the bed. His hands shook as he grabbed a lucifer off the mantel, knelt, banked kindling, and in three strikes, lit an ember. He added more dry tinder, and then log after log until a nice fire roared.

On the bed, she lay pale, her breathing shallow. A sudden dark fear gripped him. He'd seen hypothermia victims and once they lost consciousness, their demise twisted into a downward spiral. He had to get her warmed. He stripped off her sodden clothes, tossed them on the floor, and then covered her with soft, thick quilts.

He banked more wood on the fire, then checked her pulse. Low. Too low. He peeled off his sopping clothes and climbed beneath the covers, wrapping his body around hers to add his precious body heat. Her breasts rose and fell against his chest with shuddering, uneven breaths.

The firelight probed the shadows of her features. Ryan was drawn to the fine arch of gold winged brows, and then the sooty lashes that swept down over sculpted cheekbones, giving way to a straight nose and full, sensual lips. Her tangle of damp hair untethered from its tie, lay in long ropes of gold. He ran a hand behind his neck, kneading the tense muscles there. Why had he allowed her to go on the mission? The fool woman had almost drowned saving Nathan.

The dark silence enveloped him. He yawned and closed his eyes, yielded to its tormenting arms. His angel had led them to desperately needed supplies, gone through hellish lines under fire and saved one of his men. He tightened his hold on her. If he lost her…

Grace's heart beat faster and her brain pounded like a butter churn. The egg yolk sun poured through a window and waited for entrance into Grace's eyes. She worked to allow the visions of the night to give way to day, to move what she created on whim from imaginary to real. Thoughts of the vision in her sleep came and departed in waves, clinging to an elusive memory of the night but with little success.

Warm. Oh, so warm. Sighing, she burrowed deeper in the downy softness of the bed and gravitated to the hard rock heat emanating to the side of her. Heavy steel bands were locked around her. She rubbed the remainders of sleep from her eyes and stared straight into extraordinary, compelling, cobalt eyes. A slow smile greeted her. With a gasp, she hurtled back to earth.

"Glad to see you back from the dead. I thought I was going to lose you," he drawled.

Her mind was working with where she lay. "Lose me?"

"You rescued Nathan from a very icy cold river. He

is very thankful that his life is saved but the foolish endeavor nearly cost you your life."

Reality cut like a cleaver. She had almost drowned.

She stretched. She was nude, and so was he. Grace scrambled to the edge of the bed, grabbing the quilt around her. Black spots clouded her vision followed by a wave of dizziness.

He laughed, threw back the covers, got up, and then trod across the room stark-naked. He shrugged into his gray trousers, and she watched the sunlight shimmer over his backside, lending his form the exotic cast of Michelangelo's *David*. He tossed more wood on the fire. She tried not to notice when he lifted his wet coat and soaked shirt and placed them on a line strung before the fire while never taking his eyes away from her.

She tried not to note the flex and swell of his smooth chest as he lifted her clothes on the makeshift line to dry. It occurred to her that she'd stared for an inordinately rude amount of time. She slunk beneath the covers to abate her shivering, but now her trembling came from the close intimacy they shared.

He didn't prompt her to say anything. Something about the way he watched her…or perhaps the way he leaned against the mantel, relaxed, yet not relaxed.

The sinewy swells of his chest. The deep valley between them. The neat, symmetrical bunches of muscle at his stomach. Six ripples, she counted before they disappeared beneath the waistband of his trousers.

Swallowing around a parched tongue, she tugged her notice back to his eyes. This time, when the embers of his irises met hers, they glowed with something as dangerous as invitation. Something as sincere as admiration.

Did he want her to look at him? Did he want her to like what she saw?

Because she did. She always had.

So many questions lay on the tip of her tongue. Blinking rapidly, she found him staring across at her with a possessiveness she'd not expected from a face that had so far remained carefully unreadable.

"Would you mind telling me what transpired while I was asleep?"

His nostrils flared and he advanced to the foot of the bed. Only one corner separated her from him. And then he stood before her, a dark tower of saturnine grace. A man who moved with such finesse, she'd not marked his footfalls. It seemed his shadow reached her before he did, and now here he was, close enough to share breath. "You are a doctor. I'll not insult your intelligence."

Of course, he'd kept her warm with his own body heat and, for that, she was grateful. She pulled her knees up to her chin to test any soreness in her nether regions. None.

He saw her movement and spoke through gritted teeth. "I would never take you against your will." He picked up a lock of her hair, ran it through his fingers. "I can promise you that when I do, it will be because of your own desire—"

Grace found herself unable to move and his words evoked a quiver somewhere south of her belly. Memories flooded of what he had done to her in his tent and the desire he could easily stroke.

He poured a glass of whiskey and offered it to her. His callused fingers brushed hers, and her chest burned with his continued scrutiny as her heart hurled itself against its cage. Finally, her body compelled her to expel a breath she hadn't realized she'd kept stuck in her lungs.

The interchange pulled his regard to her bosom and an amused smirk came to his lips.

Looking down, Grace discovered that the quilt had plunged to reveal her traitorous pink nipples, the abundant flesh of her breasts quivering in time to the trembles of her body.

With an indecorous yelp, she jerked the quilt to her neck.

A flame from the fire flashed and turned his eyes into sapphire embers, glinting every bit as hard and hot as tempered iron. She stared at the pulse throbbing in the base of his strong throat.

"What if we were to entertain—" His inquiry came out as an order and it rankled her, yet his voice seemed less steady than before. Or had she imagined it?

"I am not one of your soldiers to bow and scrape to your commands," she said, pulling herself up with dignity.

Palm up, he gestured to where their clothes dried. "We will have a time to wait for our clothes to be ready—"

His voice was velvet seduction and she gulped the whiskey down, allowing the liquid to perform a slow burn down her throat. She became mesmerized by something both foreign and familiar in his dark eyes. He didn't blink. Never once did he break eye contact as both manners and nature's laws dictated.

They were alone. No one would know. Why not? To experience the love of a man? And not just any man.

A warning voice in her head said not to fall to his seduction and never would it be proper for her to entertain such a notion. Yet they were miles away, and no one was around to check on propriety. Her vow not to become involved with him was like an old wound that ached on a rainy day. The harder she tried to overlook the truth, the more it refused to go away. Her world whirled and skidded. Too fast. There was no future with this Reb. He would go on his merry way, back to war, leaving her with nothing but a broken heart. She would be the loser, for he offered her nothing. Her heart would not allow her to lose someone again.

"Your men have indicated you have a legion of society ladies at your beck and call. Am I to be one of your conquests? Is there no honor left in you?"

He kicked a chair over, jerked on his damp coat. "There is no question of my honor, and there has been no other woman since I met you." The disgust in his words ignited a temper she'd believed dormant.

"I'm going outside to get more wood from the woodshed." He paused. Blinked. Then seemed to change his mind. He reached out to trace her jaw, her cheekbones, her trembling lips. Pausing at the river of moisture at her temple, he swiped at a tear, rubbing it between his thumb and finger. "I've wanted you for *weeks*."

At that, he turned and headed outside. A cold breeze blew in on his departure and she swallowed. Rising, she wrapped the quilt around her and sat before the fire, hands clenched in her lap. Another hot tear dropped from her chin onto her cold hands.

She stared as the flames rose and fell along with her mother's dreadful taunts. *You are ugly and no sane man would want you unless it was bolstered by your fortune.* Loneliness and despair surged.

She brought her legs up, feet on the seat and rested her chin on her knees. In this tiny cabin, the old ache of loss had a new sharp edge, because now she was in uncharted territory. But wallowing in self-pity wouldn't solve a thing. She had been thrown into a foreign world with unfamiliar people, and rather than brood about her past, she'd deal with the present.

Grace thought about the very striking and startling sides of the colonel, and she wasn't at all clear she understood who he actually was. She had listened to his confession when he thought her to be Sister Grace and when he was most vulnerable.

Her sorrow for him was a huge painful knot. How he waged a battle with the reoccurring events at Green Tavern. She had seen the inner skirmishes that invaded and dominated his thoughts, riled his inner snipers, and held him hostage. Despite him being a trained and conditioned warrior, he was ambushed by an unseen enemy. She knew she could work to help him dissolve that terror. To eradicate the memory of guilt and become a safety net for him. The upset need not determine his future.

Just like her mother did not determine Grace's future. With that realization, the wall she spent so long fortifying shattered.

He could prick her ire easily, enraging her at times, but always manage to make her laugh. He regaled her with amusing stories of his *family* and aroused a passion and tenderness she had never before imagined. Most importantly, he protected her. She felt safe and cocooned in the strong confines of his arms.

As duty dictated, he should be with his command, not delaying or risking capture. Yet he stayed behind to revive her.

Without bias, he'd let her practice her profession. His faith in her snapped the chains that held her bound, lifting her from a tyranny of naysayers, and dogmatists, and setting her down a new and vibrant path.

She thought she'd mastered being alone, when everyone's life journeys separated from hers, when the only heart beating, was hers. The loneliness remained a vise over her spirit, squeezing with just enough pressure to be a constant pain. It killed her a little more each day, taking what was once her inner light and replacing it with darkness when all she wanted was a hand to hold or an arm about her shoulder.

She moistened her lips as images of their night together blended in sensuous shadows. He had lain naked with her to keep her warm. He had saved her life.

I've wanted you for weeks…

There was no denying it anymore, she was completely in love with Ryan Rourke. God help her.

Outside the cabin, he drank deeply of the cool midday air, hoping it would free his mind. With an ax, he chopped at the wood, splinters flying, his thoughts leaping around him like a serpent swallowing its tail. Her scent still clung to him, stretching over him, the haunting essence of the woman he craved. He brought the ax down harder, anything to resist her intoxicating pull on his desires, damn her.

His lips curled as his hands gripped the ax handle. He must manage his impulses. He wouldn't throw her on her back and take advantage, no matter how his starved senses screamed to do just that. Yet, he hated the sensation of helplessness his existence brought, and he raged against his foolish dreams, to one day break away from it all…of finding a normal life, a life with Grace. Yet the vagaries of life were as wide as they were severe. He had traded the long soulless death of a soldier, a cursed man, his chosen path to support the war.

In no time, he'd chopped a half-cord, and then returned. He dropped the wood into the wood box, and then picked up an oak log with a thick burl that would burn throughout the day and added it to the fire. Red coals shimmered and tiny flames flickered around a blackened chunk of wood.

He glanced at her solitary figure set before the fire. Deep in concentration, her pale hair rippled down her back. His throat constricted. He could not imagine a more contemplative or forlorn figure. They stayed in silence for a while, half a lifetime in the space between them.

He came around her chair and stood in front of her. "It's time to end this, Grace. I know of the regrettable loss of your father. I know of a young girl left to grapple alone with a heartless and abusive mother. I know the woman she became who bravely sacrificed herself to care for those in need. I know of your feelings of abandonment and the times you doubt yourself.

"I'm here to eliminate all the harsh words your jealous mother ever said to you. In my mind, you are the most beautiful woman I have ever known. Your beauty is so dazzling and shining, the brightest stars pale in comparison. Your smile lights my world, making a gray sky turn blue. Your glow shines like a sunrise, dashing away all dark and gloom. You are like a gentle breeze across the mountains or the fragrance of flowers in a forest. Wherever I am, your image holds me prisoner and until that day in the orchard, I had never met a woman who drew my heart."

He lifted his hand, cupped the side of her face and brushed his thumb along her cheekbone. He felt her tremble.

"I've fallen in love with you, Grace."

Grace pushed away from him and stood. Her heart panged. "No. I cannot do this. It is all wrong. It is not fair to you."

He took a step toward her. "What's wrong?"

"I'm wildly attracted to you, and I long to be with you but there is something—"

He stood feet away from her. A log burned through, broke into pieces and sent a shower of sparks up the chimney. He could haul her up into his arms if he wanted—he could do anything; he was that powerful. He knew it. She knew it.

"I'm waiting," he whispered.

Fear ruled her. Made her powerless, yielding to that crippling, crushing, stalling constraint.

She stared at him, trying to clear her brain, didn't know, couldn't be certain of anything other than the searing pain in her heart and her raw fear of the towering power in this man, a potency he tried hard to keep leashed.

He took a step closer. "You have to come halfway, Grace. You must tell me. It's all in your power. Take my hand. Do it. Come to me."

His fingers ran down her left cheek, leaving fire in their wake, as though he were branding her. The way he could draw her in, as though they were connected by a string. As though he could pull her to him, and she would go without resistance.

"Tell me your secrets, Grace. I'll not judge."

"My stepfather is Senator Dawson."

He shook his head. "Doesn't taint you a bit."

"When you kidnapped me I was on my way to Brigadier General Jensen's. I desperately needed his help. To exonerate me."

"What for?"

It is the end.

Her whole body trembled inside. Could she tell him? He would hate her? Turn her in? But if she loved him, she had to be honest. She had to bare her soul as he had done. She opened her mouth and, for a moment, she thought her legs might give out. She inhaled. Deep.

"The night I escaped from Maryland...my stepbrother found me in the barn...he tried to... to..." Tears welled within her eyes; her misery so acute that it was a physical pain. "He was on top of me...I fought but was powerless…before he…I shot him. He's dead…because of me. I killed him."

She couldn't look at him and paused, waited for some final word of condemnation. The pounding inside beat a rhythm to the words of her execution, the looming noose of Grace's judge and jury.

"Is that all?"

She blinked then, held up her hand to ward off the truth. "I am a murderess."

"You were defending yourself. If I was there, I'd have killed the bastard for you, and if there is ever a man who attacks you again, I'll show him the end of the world. It won't be pleasant."

Giving into a reckless impulse, Grace surged against him, threw her arms around his torso and buried her tears in his chest. For every few that fell, one or two were tears of relief, of gratitude, of wonderment that a man would come into her life and offer her salvation. "I thought you'd think I was terrible."

She needed to lean on something, on someone heavier and stronger than she was. If only for a moment, she needed to put the weight pressing her into the earth on someone else's shoulders. And his were so large, so wonderfully wide.

His gathered her into the welcoming warmth of his strong arms, and she clung to him, her sobs already beginning to lose their strength. With his hard-muscled chest against her damp cheek and ear, a stirring began that turned into a thrum. The thrum rose a beat, an ever-growing rhythm, and listening to it eased her. He forced her close, closer, cupping her head against his now racing heart. His other hand moved slowly across her back. And he stood there, soundless and unmoving, allowing her fingers to cling to the muscles of his back, her tears drenching his shirtfront.

He held no judgment against her.

Grace didn't know how long they stood there like that, but her crying had ended eventually, and she was reduced to a few sniffles. It astonished her how much better she felt.

He lowered his head and his breath touched her cheek. "The only problem I have is that you didn't trust me enough to tell me the truth."

He stared at her, the corners of his eyes crinkling. "I refuse to deny myself the simple pleasure of saying what is in my heart. I could shout it from the rooftops, from the summit of the Shenandoah if you like. I'm doomed, for without you, my life is a giant void."

Her chest hitched. "If I had a star for every time I thought of you…I could walk across the universe forever. I love you. I have loved you from the moment you hauled me up in front of you on your horse and threw away my cornette."

He laughed, and then his lips touched hers, soft… gentle…questing…she slipped her arms around his neck, went on tiptoe and pressed her parted lips against his in answer. His arms tightened, his lips parted, and he claimed her mouth fully. Time and place fell away.

He picked her up and placed her reverently on the soft bed. He shrugged out of his clothes, and one by one, tossed his boots, coat, shirt and pants on the floor. She sucked in her breath as he stood magnificently, like a fine stallion.

His nostrils flared, as did a spark of something wild

and dangerous in his eyes. He ripped the quilt from her naked body and stared as he regarded her. "You realize there is no turning back."

The air shadowed with a threat. Then a warning. Followed by a promise.

She quirked an eyebrow at him and smoothed the bedding next to her. "I'm a doctor. I understand what happens."

Everything declared and undeclared hung poised between them, and for the first time since she could remember, Grace didn't question her place. She was meant to be here. Now. In this bed, with this man, the scourge of the north. Yet, she lay unafraid and expectant.

She lifted her hand as an invitation and took his. Grace lost her breath in that instant and drew him down to her, his kiss slow, thoughtful, his tongue tracing the soft fullness of her lips, leaving her mouth burning with fire.

With a powerful, effortless grace, he enfolded her in his arms and rolled them until he pinned her beneath the heat of his body. The hard press of his manhood, heavy, forceful and throbbing against her hip made her pulse leap. Grace shivered.

Only when he seemed to have secured her, did he soften the kiss from desperate to reverent. His mouth didn't just take hers, he worshiped it. Every bit of him was so much harder than her. So much bigger, stronger, but for his lips. He simply drank pleasure from her mouth, and returned it in generous, overwhelming increments.

His kiss was rare and seductive. So close, the sight of

him blurred into flesh and flashes of eyes.

Gently, his hand outlined the circle of her breast, holding it firm, his head bent, his tongue caressed her sensitive, swollen nipple. He tore his mouth from her breast. She gasped. His hands touching pleasure points.

A wild jolt speared through her, a reaction to the possession she saw in those eyes. His hands touching pleasure points, and an unbelievable ache filled her core, her nipples rising in response. Grace licked her lips. He might be the Gray Ghost, but he was her lover. And he had every right to make love to her, just as she had every right to receive him.

Her chilly fingers grazed the warmth of his neck before threading through ebony strands as sultry as silk.

Their mouths meshed in a fiery web of passion, Grace clung to him, giving free rein to her won hunger. It was the purity of a spring awakening, and the ache of absolution all merged into one. Grace closed her eyes, and her womb clamped on a hungering emptiness and, as though he sensed her need, his body came down to spread her thighs, and she cared about nothing except the heated iron that entered her.

This was what she wanted. This was her love. This was her savior.

She found him. She found him in a world of madness. She found him in a realm made by war. She found him in the nightmares she wished he didn't suffer. In the storms he summoned.

She found him and never would she give him up.

The pressure of his mouth became more urgent, his tongue sweeping into hers with voluptuous strokes, doing things to her she never knew could be done. His kiss became many. His tongue working the harmony of music into her mouth, his lips creating the melody and crescendo, the ebb and flow, and like a conductor, holding the note longer and higher.

And his body. Oh, his body. Long and lithe, it rocked against her in a percussion so primitive, so necessary, it called to the very soul of her. To that answer and composed from the whispers of early ancestors, an evolutionary instinct responded, to weave her own pleasure—the one born to dance beneath him.

Her hands smoothed away from his hair, and over his muscled back. She feathered caresses over him, soothing him to relax deeper against her. To press himself down against her.

She arched toward him unconsciously unleashing a rousing melting sweetness. Her hands involuntarily reached to his lower back, the heat of his flesh hot and tingling beneath her fingertips. He pulled back and stared at her, raw tension in his eyes. She protested when he stopped, feeling cool air brush her wanting body, she looked at him questioningly.

He stared down at her silently, his eyes bright and savage. "Your virginity," he rasped. "It will only hurt for a second."

"I know."

Some astounding part of Ryan refused to move. Desiring, instead, to revel in her devilishly shy exploration of him. Her hands curved down his arms, outlining engorged veins forced against his skin by contracted muscle. Delicate fingers delighted down his ribs and seized all of his control not to flinch or shudder.

Her hands hesitated at his hips and they both ceased to breathe. Her violet eyes wavered, warring with curiosity.

If she writhed one more time, he'd lose himself. A primeval fear became a surge of satisfaction as her thighs parted wider for him, making a markedly charming cradle for his hips.

He plunged into her, his cock sliding into place, parting her soft folds, filling her completely.

He bent to her, surrounding her with his strength, hoping to lend it to her. Sorry for the pain he'd cause her. Wishing he could kiss it away somehow or take it upon himself.

He placed his hands on either side of her head, kissing her as he pushed into her gently resisting flesh with infinite slowness.

"Don't stop."

Flecks of silver shone in her violet irises and he fed her plea inch by agonizing inch. Her hot, wet flesh closing in on him, drawing him inside, inviting him to take his pleasure there. It was beyond heaven.

He plunged into her, filling her completely this time. She cried out and scrambled away. He stopped, holding her pinned to the mattress, his forehead touching hers, his breath fanning her cheek.

"It will not hurt anymore."

She nodded her permission to continue. He moved on her again, slowly, rhythmically, and she edged around his manhood, twitching and rolling her body and sending him spiraling out of control. Her little gasps of discovery stroked not just his body but gave him a sense of pure male satisfaction.

She clawed his backside, grasping for an elusive flame. In answer, he plunged with long, slow, deep strokes. He propped up his impending release until her head pressed back into the mattress, then began to twist from side to side, and a tremor inside her vibrated with liquid fire around his groin.

She hauled him with her into a luminous place. One made of harmonious gasps and staggering moans. Time fused with the storm, as a streak of lightning spiked the gloom, dazzling them as its counterpart pierced through their joined bodies. The indulgence just as sizzling and searing. The ecstasy just as blinding. And the passions as compulsory as a pact one engages with unequivocal fortune.

At last, Ryan lifted his head, drew in a ragged breath, rolled to his side, carrying her with him.

He held her head against his chest, his breathing unsteady and his heart stumbling to find its rhythm. "You are a rare find, Grace," he murmured, and nuzzled her breast.

"How's that?" she asked, no doubt swimming in a sensual haze yet uncertain she'd pleased him.

His slid his finger beneath her chin, tilted her head up until their gazes met…held.

"I love you, Grace. I'm not a rich man, but I've saved up from my years of soldiering and have enough to ensure you comfort and freedom from want. Will you marry me?"

She blinked away the tears, touched his cheek with her hand. "I don't care about wealth, Ryan. I grew up in wealth and it meant little to me. I've left it all behind.

All I need to make me secure is your love. I want very much to be your wife."

He sucked in another ragged breath and rolled her beneath him, claiming her lips in a kiss that promised forever.

CHAPTER 23

HE SLAPPED ON HIS FELT hat, tugged the collar of his dried Rebel coat and strode to the barn to saddle their horses. Riders galloped up behind him, and then stopped. The hairs went up on the back of his neck, instinctively knowing danger. Damn, he'd been careless. He'd left his guns in the house.

His horse was parallel to him and had a good view. Tightening the girth, he kept his back to the intruders. "How many Archimedes?

The horse stamped six divots in the muddy earth.

Ryan slowly turned. Six Yanks. With certainty, deserters and desperate. Bottom feeders. Ryan noted a doll with a pink dress on the giant's horse. His hands fisted. No doubt a trophy. What had they done to a little girl?

These were a brutal lot that thieved and preyed upon helpless Virginians, young, old and women while their menfolk were away. The same kind that had attacked Grace and the Sisters of Mercy that day when he and his men had luckily come upon them.

No doubt, the marauders had smelled the wood smoke and come for food—and to create destruction. No time to berate himself for such a colossal mistake. He had Grace's safety to consider and what these monsters might do to her.

"Well, look what we have here. A Rebel rat."

Seeing where Ryan's attention was focused, a rawboned soldier with his nose hanging down like a sausage, laughed. "You should see how we terrorized that little girl and her mother. Took their gold and food before we burned down their farm. Oh, how that little girl cried. Her mama, too."

A black rage bubbled in Ryan's blood.

The giant dismounted first. One leg of a tree trunk lifted over the saddle. Ryan looked up, acquired a crick in his neck. Nearly seven feet tall, the Yank's massive head and shoulders stayed framed by the firmament.

"Hey, O'Neal," snorted his rawboned companion. "Why don't we start the day with a fight."

"What, me against the six of you?" Ryan shouted loud enough for Grace to hear him. She was in the privy and he hoped she stayed there. His best hope was that she'd escape into the woods before they knew she was there.

The other five alighted and circled him. Not the brightest the North had to offer. They had guns and at this range they could have chosen which eye to plug him through. *If only he could get them to ditch their guns.*

"A fight you say?" Ryan repeated. "I won't fight

unless you drop your guns over there by the privy. Then we can have our fight. Although the fight is not fair," he added. "You should have brought more men."

The Yanks laughed. Behind him, one of the shorter Yanks said, "Hey, O'Neal, this would be amusing, wouldn't it? Why not?"

O'Neal the Irishman didn't look at all like he was in command of his brains. He was the furthest thing from his small dark-haired nervous companion on the left. The giant was twitching and throbbing with spasms. He looked deranged. His eyes were buried deep and his lower lip extended out way beyond his chin like his mother had stretched it out with a dinner plate since his birth. Many of his front yellowed teeth were jagged as if he filed them to canine sharpness, the effect to exact terror in his victims. His left foot lifted up and down in the mud, making a sucking sound. His right hand was bunched in a fist.

O'Neal didn't answer right away which gave Ryan a glimmer of hope. Maybe sucking his foot up and out of the muck took all his brain energy.

O'Neal nodded, an inch down, and inch up, the movement extraordinary considering his bulk. The giant lifted his hands. His fingers were long and thick. Not like railroad spikes. No. They were wider than that. More like whiskey bottles, jointed at the knuckles, with fingertips twice as wide as Ryan's, and nails twice the size.

He hooked those fingertips into his gun belt, unbuckled it, and then slung it into his companion's stomach. Whoof. The soldier plummeted in the mud and none too happy by the guffaws his companions gave him.

"Serves him right," said sausage nose. "He didn't guard the mother and little girl and they got away."

What happened next was beyond Ryan's comprehension. Perhaps the power of suggestion did work. One by one, the Yanks obliged, unbuckling their gun belts. That they deferred to the dumbest man in their band spoke volumes. Who was Ryan to argue his extraordinary luck?

Instead they left their guns on the porch. Three hundred yards from Grace.

O'Neal stepped back to enjoy the show. That was good because Ryan was sure he could manage the rest of them, and then chop down the oak tree last.

He'd fought and boxed with the best during his formative years. The famed "Boxing Billy", the south's greatest boxer, and his brothers, tested his mettle and made him a formidable force. No need to tell his current adversaries. They might run and he was brewing for a good down and dirty fight.

The men circled him like predators fighting over territory, eyes gleaming and feral, teeth bared, and muscles knotted beneath their coats. Each looking for a weakness in Ryan to exploit and finding none.

One dog-hungry Yank brought his hands up like a boxer, pretty high, so Ryan hit him in the gut, a tight body shot that sent him flying like thistledown in the wind. Another Yank crowded in like he was going for a bear hug, but he didn't get near because Ryan gave him a head butt that cracked in right on target, stunning him. Ryan seconded a bare-knuckled punch to the jaw with a resounding crack. A clean shot. The

Yank stumbled for two seconds and fell out cold. Two down, three to go, plus the giant. The giant would be a problem.

O'Neal grunted which was as close to any mustered language the giant probably used. In predictable triangular formation, the other three warily approached. One Yank rushed him like a wild panther freed from a cage, except twice as fast, crashing a right elbow at Ryan, like lightning, clubbing down. He wanted Ryan gone.

Ryan twisted, taking the majority of the man's force in the meat of his upper arm. Painful. Numbing. But he stayed on his feet, dodged, spun and kicked him in the groin with enough intensity to break a barn beam. The deserter rolled in the grass, clutching, screaming. He wouldn't be using his family jewels for a month. Maybe a year. Maybe he'd have no progeny.

The second soldier struck him in the eye and Ryan's head whipped back, blood spraying through the air in a fine crimson mist. His vision blurred and he wiped blood that dripped from his eyebrow and streamed down his temple. He shook his head through the struggling haze and danced back lightly on the balls of his feet.

With ham-sized fists, the next guy struck straight on. Ryan ducked the fierce blow and crouched, coming up with a hard fist to the deserter's solar plexus. Of course, his breathing stopped. He joined his comrades in the mud.

When he saw his companions dropped so easily, the rawboned guy glided his hand in his pocket and slipped out a knife. He hesitated. In that brief contemplation,

Ryan struck a direct punch that drove the bones of the man's nose into his brain. The guy soared. His resting place was a fresh pile of Archimedes' manure. He wouldn't be molesting anymore defenseless southerners.

Breathing hard, Ryan glanced back at the privy. The door swung against the side of the building. He made a quick survey of the yard. No Grace. Good, she'd hidden in the woods.

Ryan wanted more than anything to get this over with. Grace had promised to marry him, and he wanted to get her to the first church he could find.

With his fists up, he encouraged the giant. "Come on, O'Neal. You took the coward's way out and let your friends take the brunt."

He liked goading the giant. O'Neal didn't take kindly to the taunt. Like a bull before he rushed the matador, he stomped divots in the mud.

Ryan said, "Listen up, O'Neal. Here's the thing. I like your horse. I like all your horses. We could settle this now, and you could go on your merry way. Option one is agree right now."

"What's option two?"

"I advise you to choose option one."

"I get around on my horse."

"I understand that, O'Neal. But you need to understand who you are dealing with. Have you ever heard of the Gray Ghost?"

"No."

Confirmed he was not the sharpest knife in the drawer. "Think of me as your worst nightmare. Think of me as an ancient Roman warrior. Or Atilla the Hun.

Genghis Khan?"

"Who are they?"

Ryan figured there was more intelligence in the stump behind the Irishman. "Let's say, it is better for you if you don't get hurt."

"What if it's you that gets hurt?"

"Not likely."

"You're a dead man, Reb."

"How's that? Your guns are over there on the porch. I can run faster than you."

He didn't answer.

Ryan toed the motionless rawboned Yank in front of him. His sausage nose broke at a right angle. "You have a problem. Your men are unconscious and with broken bones. Not much help there."

The giant moved left, and moved right, and Ryan moved with him. Ryan was a couple of steps from him, which meant the giant was a single step from him. Close enough to worry about.

His brothers had taught him three rules of fighting. The first rule was for his mother to never find out he'd been scrapping which was hard to explain when he came home with an excellent shiner and his clothes torn and dirty. The second rule was regarded as an ethical rule. Never start a fight. The third rule was deemed the most important. Never lose one, either.

Ryan was clearly a rule three contender, even if that meant throwing the first punch, or he'd never win. As in, hitting the giant Irishman first before he hit Ryan.

"I've never lost a fight," said O'Neal.

"This will be your first time. You must pay for what you did to that little girl and her mother."

Ryan crashed a left hook into O'Neal's throat, and a short right to his kidney, as hard as he ever hit anything.

"That's the best you've got?" O'Neal snarled and charged, his left arm swinging viciously. Ryan dodged the incoming fist before it slammed into his jaw. O'Neal was big but slow. A good prizefighter's success was in quickness and a smaller man could beat a much larger opponent with rapidity. Ryan possessed speed and he counted on that.

O'Neal shuffled in, launched a right that Ryan saw coming a mile away. He ducked and the giant's fist buzzed over his head, and its momentum carried O'Neal onward in a curve, which meant his right kidney was exposed. Ryan hit it again and again in a series of blows that would have cracked a buffalo in half.

O'Neal swung wildly, the forward motion of the giant causing him to lean forward enough for Ryan to grab the Irishman's hair, yank his head down, and at the same time bring his knee up into his face.

Face red, eyes slits of rage, O'Neal grabbed Ryan by the throat, and held him aloft. His feet dangling, Ryan kicked the giant's knee, heard a crack and the giant went down still holding Ryan by the neck like a ragdoll. Can't breathe. Ryan tore at the giant's fingers and kicked at the other knee. Crack. Lights dimmed. Stars flashed.

Distantly, he heard a rifle shot, and O'Neal's grasp loosened. Ryan sat up, breathing in huge draughts of air, filling his lungs with blessed oxygen. He shook his head, looked at his opponent, eyes vacant and with a bloody bullet hole near his temple.

Grace stood on the porch with a smoking rifle in her arms. "I've killed another man."

"Unfortunately, you didn't. He's unconscious." Ryan took the rifle from her and held her in his arms. "I'm glad you shot him. It's my wedding day and I don't want to miss it."

CHAPTER 24

No way would Ryan allow Grace to set all the broken bones he'd inflicted on the renegades. As far as he was concerned, they deserved to hang for their crimes, yet her charity and concern for the miscreants touched his heart. After tying them up, he gave her several assurances he'd send someone along to give them medical attention. Time was short-lived, and he wanted to marry Grace as soon as possible.

With a line of tethered horses trailing them, they departed.

An hour later, he saw the sunlight bright on the shingles of the pitched church roof on the hill and just beyond it, a lush meadow with a flash of silver showing a stream that ran between two pastures. If the earth had a pulse, it rose through the mountains of the Shenandoah, where carved rocky outcrops covered with a rug of trees fell to lush green valleys, where rivers of the bluest of water, ran deep and cold and held a greater degree than mankind.

To have such land in a lush valley and raise horses with Grace would be heaven on earth to him.

In his heart, the sun glistening on the steeple was a good sign, a symbol of hope. Because sometimes a crumb falls from the tables of joy, sometimes a bone is flung to let him know that luck had come his way.

They rode up to the churchyard and a little girl raced out onto the porch. "My doll," she cried.

An old woman stepped out on the porch, nursing a well-aimed rifle in her arms. "Filthy Yanks burned down my granddaughter's house. I hope you got them."

Next to the house, a priest hurried out of the church and stood next to the woman who Ryan supposed was the parish housekeeper.

"The lowlifes are tied up at a house two miles west of here. Get the militia and have the Yanks sent to Richmond under the orders of Colonel Rourke."

The priest's eyes widened, and the woman lowered her rifle. "You're the Gray Ghost? You got 'em all by yourself?"

Ryan quirked his face in a half-smile from where it swelled. It hurt like hell. "I had to convince six of those men. You should see how they look."

Ryan dismounted, tossed the doll to the little girl and laid saddlebags over the railing. "These are filled with silver and gold pilfered from the countryside by the marauders. Take some to compensate your granddaughter and build a new home. The rest, disburse to neighbors who are in need. I'll leave a couple of horses. Hopefully that will relieve some of the suffering."

"It's what they deserve and worse for what they did to my granddaughter's family," said the housekeeper, wiping her hands on her apron.

"I need a favor and right away," Ryan said.

"Anything for the Gray Ghost," said the priest.

"We want to get married."

The priest, accustomed to immediate weddings during the war sprang into action, commandeering his housekeeper and the groundskeeper to act as witnesses. The little girl volunteered to be the flower girl. With a bouquet of Black-eyed Susans, a borrowed dress, and her hair down and shining, Grace stood regally beside him. He could not picture a more beautiful bride. After a brief ceremony that pronounced them man and wife, he was drunk with joy knowing Grace was his today and for all the tomorrows.

CHAPTER 25

They had ridden past Ryan's pickets and into camp in the dark of night, and then yielded to the privacy of his tent to commence their honeymoon.

Now, Grace plucked a hair from his chest and laughed merrily, drawing the attention of a pair of darkened cobalt eyes which heated her skin with the memory of a long slow night of their lovemaking. She found that she rather liked the warm weight of his body chasing the chill of the night.

Narrowing her eyes, she eyed him, her gaze flicking the length of him.

"Vixen," he accused.

"I suppose." She snuggled up to him. "You were going to tell me about when you finished West Point."

"When I graduated from West Point, I served in the third Seminole War up against Chief Billy Bowlegs. Next, my restless spirit took me to work in the exploration for the Pacific Railroad. I resigned after two years and farmed for a while on my family's homestead then answered the call to soldiering in 1861 to defend the South against the Union."

She liked how his hand stroked her hair, infinitely gentle, like the caress of silk against velvet.

"Farming, at the present seems a lot more preferable to soldiering. My officer's pay isn't much but what I have socked away might be enough for a farm, my eventual goal to raise thoroughbred horses"

He nuzzled her and his day's growth of beard tickled her neck.

She sighed. "I had a fortune before the war, and with certainty, my stepfather has seized it on the grounds that I killed his son. So in a way, my mother indirectly has my inheritance. Furthermore, I've married a Confederate colonel. The northern courts will look at me as treasonous and allow my stepfather to keep every penny."

"We don't need that money. We'll make it on our own."

Grace placed a cool finger against his lips, and then rose. She picked up a slice of bread and lathered it with raspberry preserves, the latter taken from the warehouse raid, including cases of lemonade, pickled oysters, eggs, canned beef and ham, French rolls, cakes and confectionary of all sorts, Havana cigars and coffee. "A while ago, there was a prisoner who looked just like you tied to a tree, and a woman who accompanied him kept in a tent. I saw them go to your headquarters, and then I never saw them again." She took a bite of the bread, jam oozing across her palm. "What happened?

Who were they?"

Ryan rolled to his side and propped his head on his hand. "You are very observant my wife. What I'm to reveal to you will be kept secret?"

She stopped licking her fingers in surprise. "On my honor," she whispered and laid down beside him.

"The prisoner was my brother, Lucas."

She widened her eyes. "I couldn't miss the resemblance, but why was he a prisoner?"

He lowered his voice so no one outside would hear. "It's a long story. Lucas fights for the Union and somehow found himself caught behind enemy lines."

Her breath hitched. "You helped him escape?"

"The truth is I never knew if I really loved my brother. And like any brothers, we irritated the hell out of each other, bickered and sullenly waited to grow up and get out. I hated him when he joined the Union. We had one hell of a fight and I swore if I ever saw him again, I'd kill him. So did my older brother, John. But you know, there is family blood the war cannot divide. Lucas, I found out, had committed treason saving my older brother."

"But you didn't kill him. He came to you for help, and you took care of your brother despite betraying your country."

"Yes, treason. When Lucas showed up with his bride, I gave him horses and directed him to Union lines and kept my men well away from his escape."

"Seems like there's been a lot of treason among the Rourke brothers. Admirable, despite your differences."

"That's what brothers do. They have each other's backs."

"Your family is remarkable."

"That's not the whole of it. My father kidnapped my mother, compromised her and forced her to marry him."

"Really? The fruit doesn't fall far from the tree." Grace enjoyed this domestic interlude and learning about him.

He chuckled. "When I was young, I was in the habit of blowing up trees."

"Useful in the military trade," she said.

He scratched his neck. "To interrupt our lessons with our tedious tutor, I blew up the tree in the front yard, fiery limbs hit the house and we had to climb up on the roof and put it out. The stump of the oak still adorns our yard. When we have children, I'll be a stricter parent," he said.

"Of course," she said. "But to remain clear, I want children. Lots of them. Maybe I'll give you all girls to torment you." She started to rise. "I must delay no further and visit *my* patients in that barn you gave me for a hospital."

He seized her, licked a drop of jam that had fallen on her chest and laved his tongue around her nipple.

"My dear, Colonel Rourke," she sighed. "What am I to do with you when you persist in being wicked? And what will your soldiers think when I emerge from *your* tent? They will conclude that I'm a harlot and I want their good opinion."

"To hell with what they think. I'm spending time with my wife." Unrepentant, he reached down and stroked her until she arched shamelessly. "Indulge me," he said huskily into her ear.

"You are a scoundrel, but your ministrations will not work, and the venture is unwise." Grace pulled away again, but he snatched her back in his arms.

"Tell me why," he prodded her.

Heat flooded her body. "Because you make too much noise when we…you know."

He rolled her over and buried himself deeply, the sensation of his damp skin sliding over hers, and his kisses smothering her cries of ecstasy. She was slick with sweat and…other things. Warm, languid, and fully pleasured.

They were silent for a long moment after, listening to the sounds of the camp around them breathe to life, the clinking and clanking of coffee pots and cups. Their breaths ebbing in complete harmonization. She could feel the tension escaping from her limbs and his, and she relaxed into the scandalous intimacy of the moment.

CHAPTER 26

FROM ACROSS THE HOSPITAL, GRACE gazed at Sister Jennifer Agatha as she attempted to force tea to an unwilling soldier. The soldier spat it out. "It tastes terrible."

"Young man, you must take your medicine," the elderly nun said sweetly, urging the man to drink more.

Grace stilled. The hairs raised on the back of her neck. Sister Jennifer Agatha never did anything nice for the Rebels. Grace looked to the table where the contrary nun had brewed tea.

White clustered flowers, purple spotted stems, fern-like leaves. *Wild hemlock.* Nausea, muscle and respiratory paralysis before death.

Sister Jennifer Agatha urged the soldier to drink again. Grace dashed around the other patients, slapped the tin mug out of the nun's hands, and sent it sailing to the floor. With her apron, Grace wiped the soldier's mouth inside and out. Thank God he had not ingested the poisonous potion.

Her insides shaking, Grace clenched her hands into fists and spat out, "You might have killed this man. How many were you planning to give the tea to?"

"As many as possible," the nun shrieked. "Until you stuck your nose in my business."

Sergeant Hutchinson's shadow covered them both.

Sister Josephine came up from behind. "What happened?"

"Grace tried to poison the men," accused Sister Jennifer Agatha with a haughty snort. "I caught her red-handed."

Sister Josephine frowned with the stunning allegation. "Nonsense. Sister Grace has just arrived."

Grace grabbed Sister Jennifer Agatha's elbows and lifted her forearms. Angry red blisters were plastered over the contrary nun's hands and wrists. "This is evidence from handling the toxic plant. She has tried to poison soldiers with deadly hemlock."

Sister Josephine gasped.

Sister Jennifer Agatha broke from Grace's hold and jabbed a finger in the air. "Poisoning them will aid in their spiritual growth."

Grace blinked, trying to process what she'd heard, the nun a fountain of spite and hate. "Why?"

"Pain and transformation are everything," said Sister Jennifer Agatha. She stood straight and tall and raised her chin in haughty defiance.

"You are the cruelest person I've ever met."

"All Rebel soldiers must die. The South must crumble to its knees. I hate everything southern." The sibilant antics of her dry tongue slithered from side to side.

Grace shook her head. "No. Your hatred…it's more than that—"

Sister Jennifer Agatha's face reddened, veins bulged out on her forehead, her lips curled into a snarl. "My father was a sadistic alcoholic—" she bellowed. "He was a fine southern man who raped me over and over again. I hated him and everything southern."

Grace's mouth fell open, her mind reeling. She vacillated between feeling sorry for what the sister went through and being repulsed by the woman's duplicity. Hiding behind a veil, Sister Jennifer Agatha harbored hatred and lust for revenge. To have innocent soldiers die as a bizarre means to exact vengeance against her father was contrary to every vow Sister Jennifer Agatha had taken. Contrary to every belief good Christians should have.

"Hatred has caused a lot of problems in this world and hasn't solved one of them yet," said Sister Josephine, obviously saddened by the revelation.

"What you have done is unspeakable, Sister Jennifer Agatha. You need to be reviewed. I'm writing a letter to Mother Superior," said Grace. "I'm also reporting you to Colonel Rourke."

"Of course," spat Sister Jennifer Agatha. She whipped around and ran from the hospital. At the doorway, she paused to kick out the crutch of a soldier with one leg amputated. The man sprawled headlong into the dust.

Sister Josephine helped him up. Grace raced by, grabbed Sister Jennifer Agatha and swung her around.

Eyes wild, the malevolent nun spat out. "I curse you

and the whole Confederacy. The south will swarm with frogs, locusts will devour every crop, wild animals will gobble you, hail and boils and pestilence will destroy you."

Sister Jennifer Agatha's arms whirled about, thrashing to get loose of Grace's hold on her, her words unintelligible babbling, cursing, and crying, and possessing a sudden brute strength, she yanked herself from Grace's grip.

"Sergeant Hutchinson," Grace ordered, "if you would please escort Sister Jennifer Agatha to someplace… anywhere…that humanity does not reside. And do not allow her near the men at all."

Sister Jennifer Agatha backed away. Her rail-thin body trembling, she waved her hand over the gathering soldiers. "The Rebels are beasts, their barbarism, natural. All of you will perish! The worms will devour your entrails—"

Sergeant Hutchinson gripped the older nun's arm. "Before you sink your fangs in my neck, I suggest you keep your mouth shut, Sister Jennifer Agatha, or you will find yourself digging latrines…or worse."

"I am a woman of God. Find one of your braying jackass Rebs to do your work."

Sister Jennifer Agatha broke from Hutchinson's hold, reached out and slapped Grace across the face. "You mock God's favor and your lack of abstinence is a surety of the devil's handiwork. You are nothing but a whore cavorting with the enemy."

Men gathered. Guns went up and Grace feared for Sister Jennifer Agatha. No doubt, word had gone through the camp like fire through a canebrake. To

Grace's relief, she saw Ryan move his way through a crowd of his men.

"Not one more foul word out of your mouth, Sister Jennifer Agatha," said Colonel Rourke.

Sister Jennifer Agatha kicked and spit on her jailer, provoking Hutchinson to say, "Colonel Rourke, before I shoot Sister Jennifer Agatha, please allow me to escort her back to Union lines."

"Go ahead and shoot me," screeched the old nun. "Did Grace tell you she's a murderer? Shot her own brother."

Grace's stomach filled with butterflies. Now Rourke's men would think the worst of her.

"Enough, you old crone," ordered Ryan. "I know everything, and it was self-defense as her stepbrother attacked her. I guarantee every man in my outfit would shoot her stepbrother for his nefarious deeds."

One soldier slapped away a mosquito that danced around his ear. "Yes, we'd certainly shoot him. Might be something you'd do, too, to that father of yours if you had the chance."

A soldier scratched under his arm and offered brightly, "Colonel, ain't no excuse for her trying to poison our men. We haven't had an execution yet and, doubtless the men would enjoy one to relieve camp boredom."

Sister Jennifer Agatha stilled and paled, and then pointed a yellowed corkscrew fingernail at Grace. "Harlot of the devil himself. You'll find no redemption in the fires of hell."

At her words, Rourke's eyes darkened, then ignited with a blaze that would make the fires of hell look small.

"Hutchinson," he growled through gritted teeth. "Get that woman out of my camp." His voice reverberated, his tone ice cold…and laced with murderous intent. "Let the Yanks contend with her."

The men cheered as Hutchinson and two other soldiers practically lifted Sister Jennifer Agatha off her feet and took her away.

Grace blew out a breath and before she could think more on the revelation, Ryan cupped her face between his big hands and captured her mouth in a good morning kiss. Grace flushed in front of his men. "That is inappropriate, Colonel Rourke."

"You better get married, Colonel, to make it proper," someone called out.

"If you don't, I'm going to propose," said Stringbean.

The colonel clapped his arm around her shoulders and pulled her in tight. The strident timbre of his voice boomed over the crowding soldiers. "We are married."

A cacophony of applause, cheering, hooting, clapping, and boot stomping, burst with palpable excitement through the charged air with wide grins, handshaking and patting one another on the back in hearty congratulations for the happy couple.

Captain Gill shook hands with Ryan and kissed Grace's cheek. Joy surged in her heart with the genuine felicitations and spontaneous outpouring of emotion.

CHAPTER 27

End of June 1864, Virginia

RYAN HAD RIDDEN THROUGH THE night to reach Lee's headquarters, now anticipating the worst. General Lee occupied a small frame house on the side of the road. He was already up and partially dressed though still long before daylight. The room had marginal appointments, a sofa pushed to the side, camp bed, maps tacked on the wall, a small writing table, camp stools, and a long oak table with chairs inserted neatly beneath. A newly printed book by Victor Hugo, all the current rage, lay on an end table.

Ryan knew command was a mountaintop, the air breathed there was dissimilar, and the perspectives seen there were dissimilar from those of the valley of duty. General Lee possessed a fervor for organization, and a genius for construction, which were qualities the wily commander utilized to obtain complete perfection. Lee had grown great because he saw from the top of his mountain, where he could mold, if he so willed, the teeming hordes below, including Ryan.

Ryan had been in service to General Robert E. Lee since the advent of the war and had imbued the man with angelic powers. He tried to erase an uneasiness with his sudden summons. Like a cat licking tuna off its paw, Lawler crossed his arms in front of him, watching Ryan carefully. The stare made Ryan even more uncomfortable. Thoughts raced through his brain. What does he know?

Lawler was a much older man and demonstrated a wholly inappropriate eagerness for taking command of the entire operation. He was a worthless political appointee, won by nepotism and considered negligible by every officer in the Confederate army. The two forays he had been ordered to command left all of his men dead.

Lawler had plagued General Lee with predictions of certain disaster, had insisted on Ryan's demotion. He had even passed the chain of command and gone directly to President Jefferson Davis, asserting his own expertise on just what Ryan's cavalry should be doing. After several such visits, even the patient Jefferson Davis had tossed him out.

Ryan clenched his jaw together remembering when Lawler dared to steal Grace from his camp. Give a man dominion over others and watch the worst of his character emerge. In terms of his subordinates, Lawler won first place for a dictatorship award for his fractious reputation.

No one said a word and as time wore on, the clock on the mantle ticked in the silence. The heat at the far end of the room began to suffocate him. Ryan blinked as sweat rolled down his forehead, threatening to sting his eyes. Colonel Gattis seemed more nervous than Ryan, glancing around the room as though searching for something. Ryan winced. Whiskey?

General David Moreland's face remained impassive. Of disagreeable nature, the Calvary general known as "Disapproving Moreland" possessed a penchant for sarcasm and a surly personality that tested the patience and the tolerant spirit of Lee, yet even Moreland remained mute.

Ryan rolled his shoulders to relax, then caught a continuous look from General Longstreet, saw the hint of a smirk. He still wore a bandage on his neck where he'd been wounded by friendly fire at New Market. Yet, Longstreet's relaxed confidence troubled Ryan, as if something had been decided, some secret that only Longstreet knew.

Lieutenant Colonel Andrews bowed to Ryan as if viewing his lifeless corpse and laying a rose on his coffin to acknowledge farewell condolences. Not good.

Lee walked forward and backward in his shirtsleeves in front of a bright fire, brushing his hair and beard. "Well, Colonel Rourke, what on earth compelled you to go on a raid so far into Maryland when I commanded you to guard the Shenandoah?"

Colonel Lawler gloated. Ryan knew where Lee had heard about his raid. Ryan had hoped he could slip in and out and make it back without comment. Yet Lawler had caught wind of his escapade and capitalized on it. No doubt, his nemesis twisted and convoluted the simplest of expeditions into a tangle of fabrications.

To be court-martialed?

Lee paced, ignored the other officers in the room, Trent and McDonald among them, who conceded to their commander's need for quiet and allowed him to vent his anger.

Lawler spoke again, staring at Ryan. "We need to revisit Colonel Rourke's foolish foray to Maryland."

Lee stopped, turned his frosty gray eyes on Lawler. "So you have frequently told me. Or are you insinuating that I need repetition to understand the simplest of concepts?"

Lawler uncrossed his arms. "No, sir."

"You will remain silent, Colonel Lawler. Obedience to lawful authority is the foundation of manly character."

Lee stopped in front of Ryan. "Pray tell what activity you came upon that caused you to invade Maryland without my direct orders?"

Perspiration trickled down the back of Ryan's neck. How he'd like to slam his fist into Lawler's sneering face. "To divert the enemy on their turf and to collect needed medical supplies, sir."

Lee smacked the palm of his left hand with the back of his brush. "I have a contest with General Grant." He referred to the recent Battle at the Wilderness, Spotsylvania and the conflict at Cold Harbor, an uncertain chess game with an aggressive Northern commander now entrenched in lines southeast of Petersburg, a crucial rail junction south of Richmond.

"My men are quite adept at a quick strike. I assure

you that there were no losses in Maryland, sir," said Ryan. "We brought back horses, pistols, ammunition, rifles, boots, shoes, blankets, tents, food and much needed medical supplies."

Lee's eyes flashed fire as he brandished his brush. "I have great appreciation for the striking power of your cavalry, Colonel, and your men have performed extremely well. But the risk—"

Ryan opened his mouth to speak but his commander held up his hand to quell his protest.

"As you know, gentlemen, our success at New Market has led General Grant to unleash General David Hunter. His scorched earth campaign across the Valley must be stopped. Burning homes. Helpless women and children left without shelter. The countryside stripped of provisions without a morsel of food left to feed the families. We are powerless to check or resist the brutal incendiaries."

"If I may interject, sir," said Ryan, getting up and pointing to a map on the wall. "During my reconnaissance, I touched Brigadier General Crook's brigade here. I learned Major General David Hunter was on the march to Charlottesville. Grant wants to attack your left flank and draw you out."

Lee took in that bit of information. "As to you, Colonel Rourke…I want you to join General Early who is now on the move to Lynchburg."

Ryan knew General Early very well. He was fluent in profanity and a great fighter.

Lee continued. "I assign you to the Shenandoah to protect our people and to crush Hunter. No discussion on this, Colonel. Do not take this as an insult. Your men have accomplished great feats and will continue to be a valuable service to this army. These are tenuous times." He looked off distantly. "I have lost General Stuart at Yellow Tavern. I cannot lose you."

Ryan was moved his commander thought about him. The loss of the cavalry General J. E. B. Stuart had been a terrific blow.

Lee went on. "We have stalled Grant's movement from the north to Richmond for the present."

Lawler spoke up. "Grant will be stalled for good with his losses and humiliation at Cold Harbor and go down in history as a failure like McClellan."

Lee crushed him with a glacial glare. "Do not mistake General Grant. His dogged campaigns in the west have proved his resolve."

Ryan stood alert. Lawler was another infuriating example of an officer who cherished the illusion that the gallant Army of Northern Virginia would wipe the Yankee threat away from the earth.

Lee gave instructions for each man to take a chair. There was typical formality in that order. General Lee was not given to friendly banter. The useless small talk that some generals exercised was nil with Lee. Ryan appreciated that and pulled out his chair.

Lee stood at the head of the table. "The area around Richmond is a noisy place right now with affairs changing rapidly. Colonel Rourke, your men have been in the saddle too long, and you must not drive them to exhaustion. Feed your men, rest them when you can. Do what you can to replenish and refit their weapons, and see to your horses, but you must catch up with General Early posthaste. I should mention your brother, General Rourke, has escaped the North's clutches and will accompany you on this raid. Talked to him the other day when you were on your imprudent sojourn."

"With all possible speed, sir."

Colonel Lawler, not to be ignored spoke again. "I feel Colonel Rourke should be reprimanded for his foray into Maryland."

Andrews and Smith groaned with Lawler's needling. The only reason Lawler got away with pressing Lee was on account of his close association with President Davis.

Lee said, "I appreciate your candor, Colonel Lawler. But we must move aside present difficulties, gentlemen. We must do what the country requires of us. If God has given me any hope, it lies in believing failure will be corrected."

Lawler drew a cigar from his pocket. "We are not going to discuss Colonel Rourke's failure?" Unfortunately for Rourke, the green-eyed worm of jealousy of his daring exploits became Lawler's focal point. The man lived to diminish Rourke whenever he had the chance.

"Excuse me, Colonel Lawler," said Lee. "I cannot trust a man to control others if he cannot control himself."

"Yes, sir," said Lawler.

"I should like to hear what Colonel Rourke has to say. Now, go outside and see that my staff provides Colonel Rourke with everything his men require. The rest of you have your orders and are dismissed. Above all, I thank you for your contributions, gentlemen."

Lee did not thank Lawler.

Lawler growled at the obvious set down.

Lee turned his eyes on Lawler and silenced him.

Lawler offered a brisk salute, said, "I wish only to serve, sir."

Ryan loved headquarters. Generals could slice their way through the thorniest of situations just by their authority.

Alone now, Lee said, "I've heard the most interesting tale. You kidnapped a group of Sisters of Mercy?"

"Yes, sir." Rourke watched with grim satisfaction as the author of those rumors was exiled to inconsequential duty. "They are nurses and were on their way to add assistance to the Yanks. I felt their efforts would be better served by the Confederacy."

"This is grievous behavior on your part. I trust they are treated well?"

Ryan sweated. "Very well."

"All of the sisters?" Ryan cringed. What had General Lee heard?

"Yes, sir. Very well."

"I have a letter from Mother Superior, Sister Frances Gerard in Maryland, via Mother Superior, Sister Veronica in Richmond, demanding the sisters' return. She has informed me the Sisters of Mercy are not combatants of war."

"Yes, sir." Was Lee ordering him to return the nuns? He'd fight it.

"My first thought was the honorable thing. Return them posthaste. But the Mother Superior in Richmond has since been in communication with Sister Frances Gerard and has waived their return because of a greater need in the south. However, if any wish to return, I expect you to return them."

"Yes, sir."

"I understand one of sisters is a doctor?"

"An excellent one."

"How unusual."

"She trained under her father, the late Dr. Edward Barrett, a renowned surgeon. She is willing to stay."

Lee paced the room, stopped and turned his eyes on Ryan. "Your position with her is chivalrous?"

Ryan thought of yesterday, sliding his hands under Grace's buttocks, cupping them and pulling her close to the edge of his desk. Grace had wantonly taken to not wearing undergarments, increasing his insatiable appetite, and inventing places where he might steal her away to take her next. Near the river, on a soft bed of ferns, in the forests, under the stars, shamelessly in his tent while his men worked around them. She was a drug. He could not get enough of her.

How her body melted as she exposed her naked limbs to his hungry view. He bent her knees up, gently kissing one then the other. How he remembered the blazing desire in her eyes as he stoked a burning fire, her hot scent warm and wet swirled, sending his nostrils flaring and luring him. How he built her arousal in the most primitive way, the soft gasps that caught in her throat when he thrust his hard cock inside her. How he gripped her bottom and slammed into her and within seconds, how she moved with him, in liquid, hot, intoxicating, exciting, her body gloving his…

Ryan cleared his throat. Lee had the eyes and ears of the Confederacy. Nothing got by him. He swallowed.

"We are married."

Lee looked at him gravely. "I appreciate your regard, Colonel Rourke, and I assume you are attempting to ease the strain I am under. But my capacity for humor is limited. Was the doctor willing to leave the sisterhood?"

Ryan's collar felt several sizes smaller. Lee had asked if he had compromised an unwilling bride, and the hastiness of a marriage after a two-month courtship. "No, sir. I mean, yes, sir. She was a novice and hadn't taken her final vows."

Lee stroked his beard, his smile gone. "I need the Almighty on our side and would not forsake one of His vestals. We are in a crisis, and I'm not certain what we can do to erase that. She accompanied you to Maryland? Highly irregular."

What didn't Lee know? "She knew where the warehouses were hidden and guided us to them."

"I'm thinking of having your wife's hospital moved closer to my camps. We could use someone with her talents."

Grace's surgical skills had reached his commander, but Lee's thinking was like a direct command from God. Ryan wanted Grace by his side. To have her removed nearer to Richmond? He'd rarely see her. "She is of much use to us in the Valley, General Lee," Ryan protested, and left his objection vague to stall the inevitable.

"For now, your wife can stay where she is. But when the time comes, I will place her under my protection. We must recognize where our best assets lie, whom we may trust and depend upon. Godspeed with you."

Ryan let out a breath. Lee was a great leader who shared as an equal in the trials and struggles, the demands and expectations, the hills and trenches placed on the backs of those he commanded. He was not motivated by power but by compassion. Such a leader was to be respected. And for that, Ryan loved the General Lee. "Thank you, sir."

In a fatherly gesture, Lee clapped his hand on Ryan's shoulder and followed him to the door. "It is well that war is so terrible, otherwise we should grow fond of it."

CHAPTER 28

August 1864

THE WEEKS OF SUMMER WHERE the earth smelled of wildflowers and the relentless sunshine spread like golden powder across the firmament and where the war was fought far away, created an oasis of peace. However outlying, the fringes of war bordered their doorstep, Grace was mindful not to be lulled into a sense of complacency. Oh, how she missed Ryan during his long absences. She had seen him only once or twice and not much was said during those reunions, as time was spent making love until his inevitable departure.

General Early's defeat of Union Major General Hunter at Lynchburg, and then his raid at Monocacy and Fort Stephens on Washington's doorstep to ease Grant's hammerhead blows on Petersburg, had gained the Commander of the Union Army's attention. So much so, he named Major General Philip Sheridan commander of the Army of the Shenandoah and unleashed "Little Phil's" inestimable numbers, and relentless destruction that rivaled Hunter's.

Colonel Rourke plagued Sheridan with guerrilla tactics. Scouts, raids, pitched battles followed in rapid succession, destroying supply trains, and breaking up means of conveying intelligence, thus isolating troops from their base, and confusing Union plans by capturing dispatches. Ryan's strategies were effective, compelling the use of large numbers of Yank troops to protect Washington and the Potomac, and railroads.

Grace sighed, watched Clara come out of the hospital and greet Francis with a brilliant smile. The shy little sister had divested her nun's garb and had declared her love for Francis. The two starry-eyed lovers had married and presently, walked hand in hand with Lucifer flapping behind them.

Tomorrow, escorted by the remaining soldiers, Francis and Clara would take the last of the patients to the Richmond hospitals. Amos, Grace and Sister Josephine would travel halfway, and then follow a soldier that would meet them for their reassignment from General Lee as ordered by Colonel Rourke. Grace had delayed two weeks due to two soldiers who needed extra care, and part because she enjoyed staying with Emily and the children, yet mostly, she hoped Rourke would ride into camp. He'd be furious because she hadn't followed his orders and moved to safety, but how joyous that reunion would be.

Lifting her head, she listened to the soldiers sing *Annie Laurie*. The blend of their deep male voices pressed sweet vibrations in her spirit. The poetic words were an ode to the universal love to a woman of their heart, be her fictitious or real. Each soldier became an island and, with it, they all merged with the same tidal flows and togetherness.

Their ballad sank her deeper and deeper into her own melancholy song. The loneliness and worry devoured her. It took her heart into its claws, squeezing every bit of life circulating through her veins. It craved her to suffer a life without Ryan's warm hands embracing her, or reassuring arms to encircle and comfort her.

CHAPTER 29

GRACE SHOT FROM SLEEP TO full wakefulness. In her nightclothes, she rushed downstairs and onto the porch. Without warning and under the chill of the morning mist, horses pounded into their little valley. Gunshots boomed all around her, so close the smell of gunpowder stung her nostrils. Acrid smoke billowed from the direction of the barn, filling the air and making her cough. The children whimpered and clung to Emily as they crowded on the porch.

Where was Amos? Sister Josephine? Had they been shot? Did they lay bleeding?

Untapped fear and rage boiled up from Grace's stomach.

"Willie? Where's Willie?" Emily cried above the fray.

In a blink, a numerically superior horde of mounted, blue-coated soldiers with shiny brass buttons circled the house, shouting and shooting their pistols in the air. One soldier urged his mount up on the porch. The children screamed and drew back into their mother's skirts.

The Yank captain's fingers wrapped tightly around the trigger of the gun he touted. "Get those children away from the house."

The soldiers lit torches as Emily's children were herded under the oak tree. The same tree Sister Josephine had drilled them in their school lessons.

"Please don't burn down my house," Emily pleaded.

Soldiers looted the house, carrying out clothes, paintings, household goods.

Grace refused to budge off the porch. Sister Josephine appeared beside her, her white cornette in stark contrast to her black tunic. "We aren't moving," said the nun.

A Yank took his gun out and aimed at Sister Josephine. "On the count of three, move or else."

Amos jerked the man off the horse and roared a terrible roar. "No one hurts, Sister Josephine!"

Yanks fell on him. He punched one in the nose, making a popping sound and dousing him in a shower of blood. He broke free and elbowed an oncoming Yank in the windpipe. The soldier took a convulsing breath and flipped over in the dirt.

Wide-eyed, Grace watched the gentle giant. No longer was he fearful. He rushed to meet their numbers. Just as bodies crashed together, he grasped one huge wrist and cracked it in two. He stopped and hit the next man with a massive right. He aimed another savage blow at the head of another Yank and cracked his jaw.

A gun fired. Blood flowed down Amos' dangling

arm. Still he fought with his good arm. A huge brute hit him in the pit of his stomach with the butt of his gun. Pure opposing numbers were Amos' undoing, grappling him to the ground, punching and kicking him.

Hysterical and sobbing, Sylvia and Renee tore free of their mother's arms and cleaved through the melee and collapsed upon Amos, protecting him with their little bodies.

Four Yank firebrands held up their torches eager to toss them into the house.

Grace raised her voice, commanding their attention. "I am Grace Barrett. My father was a famous surgeon who operated on many Yank soldiers."

"We know who you are. We came for you."

"For me?" she was incredulous.

"We're part of General Sheridan's cavalry," was all the information he'd allow.

"What are we waiting for? Let's treat these Rebs the way they deserve and burn down the house," bellowed a toothless Yank.

Grace saw Willie up in the tree with a gun. She shook her head. He'd be easy pickings for the Yanks.

Sister Josephine walked to the edge of the porch. Her voice lashed them in a most commanding manner. "I can tell by your accent that many of you soldiers are Irish Catholics, including you, Captain. This poor widow has her children to care for."

"Then why were Rebs using this as a camp?" contested one of the soldiers.

Grace clenched her fingers into the folds of her skirts, praying the soldiers would not see how badly her hands were shaking. "This was none of this mother's doings. Colonel Rourke seized her farm to use as a hospital. She had no choice in the matter."

"The Gray Ghost?" murmured the soldiers, their eyes spread wide with fear.

"Don't believe it. The woman and her children are southern sympathizers," spat another Yank.

As wild as the winds of the Cliffs of Moher, Sister Josephine marched down the steps and through the throng. The older nun's blazingly keen, gray eyes bored holes into every soldier. "Her husband died from a heart-attack tilling this soil."

"Her husband's a dirty Reb," confirmed a Yank soldier.

Sister Josephine's tall, lean body trembled not from fear, but righteous anger as she turned on the man and shook her fist at him. "If your sainted mother were here, she'd box your ears for such blasphemy. I can verify he was a good Christian man, minding his own business and providing for his family."

She swung in a circle, pointing a boney finger. "Like the magician's said to Pharaoh, 'This is the finger of God.' But did Pharaoh listen? No. For his hubris, he gained frogs, lice, boils, gnats, hail and darkness, and rivers turning to blood."

A brazen soldier whose complexion looked like he'd been in a war with an icepick and lost, dared to object. "But—"

Like thunder snapped from the heavens, Sister Josephine's voice cracked across the countryside. "There are no objections for every one of you will suffer the wrath of God if you do any harm to this family or their home."

The pockmarked soldier squirmed beneath her glare and the rest of the men shrank.

Grace kept her face blank with the whopper Sister Josephine told. Emily's husband was presumed dead in the war.

"Hold off," said the captain, doffing his hat. "Our quarrel is not with a widow and her children."

None of them dared to take on a holy nun and suffer Divine retribution. Soldiers dropped their torches.

Grace picked up her skirts, dashed off the porch and under the tree and to where the Yanks pulled up Amos and chained him. "You big oaf. Are you trying to get yourself killed?"

"They were going to hurt Sister Josephine, you and the children. I had to protect you."

She ripped a strip of linen from her petticoat. "Yes, you did, and you got shot, when you should have escaped. Fortunately, the ball went through. I shudder to think how it could have been worse," she scolded him.

She used the ruse of binding Amos' arm to whisper to Willie above her. "Get word to Colonel Rourke." It was her hope that Ryan might be reached in time and follow them. But that would take a miracle.

CHAPTER 30

THE CONQUERING SUN HAD DROPPED from the sky, and stars poked bright holes in the blackness overhead, leaving a suffocating darkness to spill over the Yank campsite. Grace welcomed the humid nightfall as opposed to the day's sun that had beat down on her furiously as the heat wave continued, oblivious to the chaos of war. Up close, she bore witness to Yank brutalities on the south by Sheridan's cavalry. Destruction of homes, towns, farmlands, carrying off all stock and leaving the Shenandoah Valley a barren wasteland. For two days, they had pressed their horses at a breathless pace, looking over their shoulders, no doubt fearful of the wrath of the Gray Ghost.

She passed Yank tents too innumerable to count, their miserable band moving her pathetically to her demise. Her exhausted mind drifted from one question to another but circled to one fact. How had the Yank soldiers found them in such a remote place?

The captain put up his gloved hand to stop.

She dismounted, and a soldier led her horse away. She swiped at a tear, and then glanced up to where a daunting moon rose in the west crowded out by the immensity of stars and planets and a far-off galaxy unfurling its menacing arms above her.

They tied their horses to a long rope, and she looked behind at Amos. Her gentle giant and protector was slammed with the butt end of a rifle in the back.

"Get going, Reb."

An angry snarl curled her lips. "The man needs medical attention."

A soldier with two missing teeth leered into her face. The animosity humming from him and others around the camp was palpable. "He's under Yankee hospitality now."

How courageous Amos had been to stop the burning of Emily's house, fighting off so many. His arm needed tending. Blood covered his knuckles and a nasty swelling closed his eye. She was sure at least one of his ribs cracked when the soldiers had kicked him so mercilessly. Never would she forget the little girls defending Amos in a futile attempt to shield him, crying over and over again how they loved him as if their love might take away his pain.

"Don't worry about me, Miss Grace."

I will find some way to help you, she mouthed.

He nodded as the Yank led him in an opposite direction.

In between endless rows of tents, a soldier ushered Grace down dark alleys, illuminated only by his lantern swishing light to and fro. With every footfall, her heart beat a dreaded tattoo in her chest. She was in the middle of the Yanks. Soon she'd be hanging from a rope for murdering her stepbrother. Why else would they have sought her out?

Bedraggled, exhausted, and starving, she was led to a man seated on a horse with his back to her.

The soldier with the lantern cleared his throat. "Brigadier General Jensen."

Her father's friend turned his horse. "Who are you?"

Brigadier General Jensen was an intense balding man with penetrating button-black eyes that scowled from a moon-shaped face, black mustache and ragged spade beard. He slid out of his saddle and faced into the firelight to reveal skeletal thin legs bowed like razor clam shells that looked entirely inadequate to support his big belly and broad, muscled torso.

He might not recognize her in her current state. She barely recognized herself with her dress torn and filthy. The Yank soldiers had moved at breakneck speed, spending minimal time to rest.

"Brigadier General Jensen, I am Grace Barrett. I believe you knew of my father." He was more than acquainted. They were best friends. Of course, Brigadier General Jensen knew who she was. Why the intrigue?

He held his hand up and, without a word, gestured rudely for her to go to the privacy of his tent. Not a warm welcome from someone who had intimately known her family. Inside, he settled in a chair behind a desk. Left her standing.

"Anything else, sir?" asked the captain who had escorted her from Rourke's camp.

"Have Sergeant Dollard bring in our other guest, and then you may retire for the night, Captain. Good job." The officer saluted.

Grace glanced over her shoulder to the departing soldier, and then returned her gaze to her father's best friend. He stared at her with hate-filled eyes. An iciness hit her core.

Grace waited. The brigadier general said nothing, devoting his full attention to his paperwork as if she weren't there. His meaty fingers wrapped around a dip pen, which he proceeded to plunge into the ink. How many times had this man been entertained in her home in Maryland? Her father had given him one of their prized horses, the bay gelding he rode, even bailed him out of bankruptcy when he made foolish financial investments. After so many years of a trusted relationship? How his betrayal came with an endless sting.

She laced her fingers over her stomach to quell the hunger pains. The bitter scent of burning lantern oil became a welcome temporary balm.

From the firelight outside, grotesque shadows splayed across the tent every time someone moved in front of the flames. A rustling, and then someone came up beside her. Sister Jennifer Agatha. Grace's stomach roiled. With dawning realization, the vindictive nun had pinpointed their camp's location and from the general's cold reception, had provided a twisted version of events. It was her own fault. She had not listened to Rourke's orders.

"I see they found you in your lair," Sister Jennifer Agatha baited her.

Brigadier General Jensen threw down his pen and crossed his arms. "I want this cleared up. Miss Barrett, were you taken against your will by Reb soldiers?"

"Yes," she said. She must exonerate herself, to beg him to help her.

"Did you treat Confederate soldiers of your own free will or did you resist?"

She fought to even her breathing. Was she on trial? No doubt the general had predetermined her culpability, swayed by the crafty nun who spoke mere portions of truth in order to deceive. Sister Jennifer Agatha had proven a dangerous adversary, as dangerous to Grace as hydrophobia to a dog.

She lifted her shoulders. "I treated the Confederate soldiers of my own free will as my father would have expected me to."

"She did more than care for them. Her whoring and behavior need to be curbed. She needs to be sent back home to face the authorities for the crime of killing her stepbrother." The nun's cold, amber eyes bore her triumph, delighted to have condemned Grace in the brigadier general's eyes.

Jensen's bulbous, bald head swung back and forth on something too short and thick to truly be considered a neck. "Jesus wept. My dear friend's daughter cavorting with the enemy. What would your father say?"

Grace blinked from the irony. Helping wounded Rebel soldiers was worse than killing her stepbrother? "My father would praise my efforts and trust in me. He often told me how easy it is to judge rightly after one sees what evil comes from judging wrongly and listening to vengeful gossip."

"Is this true?" He sneered at the nun.

Sister Jennifer Agatha's mole throbbed up and down, yet Grace knew the nun refused to be beaten. "She is everything and more than I told you. I saw her go into Colonel Rourke's tent countless and extended times, exceeding the bounds of decency. The Rebel, Rourke is a dictator and human scum and the north's greatest atrocity. Grace even traveled with him to show the Rebs where Union warehouses were located to pillage and steal."

With the nun's damning words, she drove more nails in Grace's coffin. Rourke had captured Jensen sleeping and spanked him, making him a laughingstock of all Washington. In addition, he lost his promotion—all acts of humiliation the brigadier general would never forget.

Grace glared at Sister Jennifer Agatha. "I've always learned the self-righteous scream judgments against others to hide the noise of skeletons dancing in their own closets."

Jensen slammed his fist on his desk. The ink bottle jumped and ink splashed out. "Enough. I can scarce believe my ears. You laid with that Rebel bastard? You are a scarlet woman."

The condemning eyes of Pontius Pilate scorned her. To inform him Colonel Rourke was her husband? No. The general was a vessel of venomous fury for the Gray Ghost. He'd burn her at the stake.

"Miss Barrett, your father must be rolling in his grave with the shame you have wrought. You will be placed under house arrest until further investigation. During that time, you will be assigned to our camp hospital to work with the staff. Is that clear?"

"Not good enough," said Sister Jennifer Agatha. "She should be tried for treason."

"I make the orders in my camp, Sister Jennifer Agatha. You are excused."

He waited for the nun to leave, and then addressed Grace. "You will have a guard posted on you and watched at all times. As of now, you are considered an enemy of the United States, do I make myself clear? And if your paramour decides to pay us a call, and I hope he does, we'll give the damned Rebel bastards a taste of our sting for Yankee bullets have a way of making vacancies."

CHAPTER 31

TWO DAYS PASSED AND GRACE attended to the sick and injured Yanks. Relegated to mundane tasks, she changed bandages and emptied bedpans. Disdain and contempt from doctors and soldiers alike made aware her treasonous associations with Rebels.

A young, sun-browned guard had been posted on her. He was a chunky little soldier, with a long body and short legs, not enough neck to hang him, and such long arms that if his ankles itched, he could scratch them without stooping. Finding her activity too dull to maintain his concentration, he spent his time napping in the corner.

A man with a chest wound from friendly fire lay on the table. The surgeon, a beady-eyed, sour-faced glutton with prominent jowls who seemed to snore even when awake shook his head and walked away.

"Wait." Grace grabbed his arm. "He can be saved."

He gave her a snide expression. "What would a traitor know? The man faces undeniable death."

Such arrogance. The doctor left and joined his colleagues outside. *Drunkards.* They couldn't wait to get to their whiskey.

The man gasped for breath. There remained little time for him. No way could she let him die. She glanced over her shoulder. The doctors would be well into their cups soon. She collected forceps, scalpels, chloroform, bandages, needles and a bottle of collodion solution. At the last moment, she placed two scalpels in her pocket.

The amputee on the cot next to her stared. He narrowed his eyes, gauging whether she was telling the truth.

Grace placed a finger to her lips. "I'm a doctor. I can save his life. I'm going to implement a risky procedure my father learned from French soldiers shot during the Crimean War that quadrupled survival rates."

After applying anesthesia, she made an incision, quickly cleansing the wound. She probed to remove bits of dirt, exploring farther and found the minié ball, plucking it out and placing it aside.

She prayed the man would survive her surgery and imagined what would befall her despite the fact she was attempting to save his life. She remembered it wasn't the wound itself, but the sucking. The negative pressure in the thorax created by opening the chest cavity caused the lungs to collapse, and led to suffocation.

Speed. She needed another pair of hands.

She looked at the amputee again. "I need your help."

He hobbled onto his one leg and used his crutches to prop himself up. She poured alcohol over his hands, and then instructed him to push the two sections of skin together.

Grace wiped the sweat from her forehead with her elbow and closed the wound with sutures. She alternated layers of linen bandages, and then added a few drops of syrupy collodion.

When finished, she nodded to the one-legged soldier who sat back down on his cot.

Grace held her breath and waited for the gooey substance to dry. The patient's chest moved up and down. He started to breathe. Joy bubbled over her. The collodion had formed a tenacious adhesive film when it dried and created an air-tight seal.

"Get away from that soldier," shouted the doctor and knocked her aside. Other doctors clustered around them. She held up the Minnie ball. "He's breathing."

"I helped her," said the soldier on the cot who had assisted her. "She saved his life when Sawbones…" he pointed to the other doctor, "…gave him up for dead."

One by one, soldiers murmured their approvals for what they'd witnessed.

"Well I never," sputtered the doctor.

Grace explained the procedure to the other physicians gathered around and who her father was. The doctors stared in awe. "We knew your father and had great respect for him."

"I would ask a favor. There is a Reb soldier who needs attending. I ask a mercy for me to treat his wounds."

Grace went outside in the torrid sunshine to get a breath of fresh air. Her peach-fuzzed guard from New York trailed her. How his eyes followed her with adulation and, oftentimes, she used cajolery to flatter him never knowing when he might be useful. She sat on a stump and arranged her skirts around her. Someone handed her a tin plate of beef stew, and with an unladylike gusto, she gobbled it down.

"Look there, Charles," she pointed with her bread. "Isn't that Brigadier General Jensen's gelding tethered with that line of horses and left to broil in the hot sun? A brilliant recruit like you might think that placing those poor animals under the shade of that live oak behind the tent would be an improvement. Far be it from me for anyone to suffer the brigadier general's wrath if he should learn his mount has not been properly cared for."

"You'll stay here? Not move away?" the boy begged.

"Of course, not." She bequeathed him with her most brilliant smile and, for one moment, she thought the boy would fall to his knees and sing *Hosanna,* so happy to perform the task *she'd* planted in his head.

Amos was delivered to her later that day and placed in a screened-off corner of the hospital tent assigned for captured Confederates and segregated from Union soldiers. Couldn't contaminate the Yanks.

She motioned for Amos to lay down on the cot. Leaning over him to tend his gunshot wound, she whispered, "There is a horse for you in the back. Cut through the canvas when everyone is unaware."

Amos shook his head. "What about you?"

"You need to escape. I'll get out later." She slipped one of the two scalpels from her pocket into his hand, dubious of any chance at her own getaway.

Startled when her young guard shuffled close,

she made a showy examination of Amos, and then straightened, shaking her head with dreaded woe that demonstrated the patient would not survive. She pushed back a curl of Charlie's hair that flowed from his hat just down over his ears, and then wiped a tear from her eye.

The boy colored from the gesture. Amos caught on, closing his eyes and eliciting proper moans with enough enthusiasm to convince an undertaker he had a prospective corpse.

Lacing her voice with the right amount of venomous fury and outrage, she said, "What's the use of doctors if they don't care for these men? This man has a severed artery and has not long to live."

Amos' bruising, swollen eye and bloody bandage lent credence to her grim assessment. If Amos' situation had been the worst-case scenario, mottled purpling of the skin, blood, and putrid gangrene would have appeared, but the young Union soldier didn't know the difference between a paper cut and a severed blood vessel.

Fortune shined. For Amos' wound was healthy. She went to work, cleansing the area that the ball went through, and then bound his cracked rib tight to give him stability for a fast escape. There was an ironic justice after all, for the huge bay gelding, a valued prize her father had given the duplicitous general, would serve perfectly for Amos' flight.

"I'll get you back in shape," she promised with the exaggerated sympathy a professional might give to a dying man. She coaxed down a tea of willow bark used to lower the possibility of any fever, and then leaned over to Charles and whispered confidingly, "Morphine. To make him rest quieter. In fact, he'll sleep solidly, and the medicine will ease his pain and be a comfort to him as he enters the next world."

Grace sat next to Amos' cot and folded her hands. "Now we pray."

"I ain't praying for no Reb," the young soldier said indignantly, and with his long arms, hitched up his pants and huffed outside.

Grace patted Amos. "Choose the giant bay gelding. He will ride upon the wind."

Amos nodded and she left to join her guard.

Normally shy, Charles became suddenly chatty. "What is the Gray Ghost like?"

A bevy of soldiers nearby pretended not to listen but were all ears as Grace settled on a three-legged stool. With an eager audience, she decided to regale them with ghost stories mixed with mysticism.

Why the charade instead of her silence? Part of her was filled with anger, shock, and treachery. Another part of her had become the embodiment of fear, defensiveness and vengefulness. Another part seized a rising amusement at making them fearful. Nevertheless, she was a woman alone, taken from her mate with an awful and unknown future ahead of her.

She smoothed some wrinkles in her white apron, and then shielding her eyes, looked up to her guard. "Sometimes the Gray Ghost appears by his own accord or can be summoned by magic."

Charles' eyes grew as big as saucers. "Magic, you say. What kind of magic?"

Grace shook her head. "The kind of magic you

don't want to know about. Sometimes he appears in the morning mist or in a bolt of lightning during a thunderstorm."

"It's going to storm tonight," a soldier predicted, his voice cracking. "I feel it in my bones."

She drew a quivering breath and continued. "Some say he is a spirit of the dead coming to gather souls to his bosom and carry them to the underworld."

A scraggly, bearded soldier clapped his hands on his knees in virtuous fury. "Those things can never happen."

Grace placed her tin plate on the ground and fanned her hands as if weaving supernatural incantations and mesmerizing them. "You never know when the Gray Ghost will appear. I've heard tell of men writhing and moaning, and then waking up in nailed coffins with six feet of dirt over them."

Another soldier yipped like a startled poodle. "My ma always believed in ghosts, said her house was full of them."

The men were all agog and she had to tamp down a grin. "Some say the Gray Ghost drifts over whole armies while they sleep, a specter, an apparition selecting his victims like a patron at a buffet."

A soldier with a thick gray compact beard on his chin spat a wad of spittle two feet away, the rest, nested in his beard. "Nonsense."

"Even larks and cicadas halt their songs when the Gray Ghost passes over." Weaving a grim and ghastly atmosphere, she snapped her fingers in the air for emphasis, "Just like that."

Charles' gaze darted from one side of the dark woods

to the other. "You hear that? Nothing but silence." He turned his fearful eyes to her. "Do you think he's near?"

A behemoth of a Yank got up and towered over her. "I don't believe in ghosts. Never seen one."

She cricked her head back to peer up at him. "Some people can't see the color red. Doesn't mean it isn't there. It's when the sun goes down and you feel something behind you, you hear it, you feel its breath against your neck, but when you turn around, there's nothing there."

Now, all the soldiers grouped around her, shuffled their feet in the dust, heads turned, their dark eyes flitting up and down and in circles around them. Soldiers were a species addicted to stories and she would use her tales as a most powerful weapon, creating fundamental human apprehension.

"You met the Gray Ghost. What is he like?"

"Like? He scares the bejeebies out of me." *He scares me with the desire lit in his blue eyes. He scares me when he palms me with his rough, calloused hands and leaves me pulsing and throbbing with a need so great, I can barely stand it. He scares me when he ravishes my mouth with his lips and teeth and tongue, burning a path across my neck, throat and breasts leaving my heart pounding so wildly that it would jump from my skin.*

Grace almost blushed with the thoughts. Thankfully, the soldiers misinterpreted her silence for extraordinary fear. The soldiers shook their heads, pitying her to have been pegged by a monster.

She took a deep breath. "All I can say is he is a vengeful spirit, starving and envious of the living, and anything taken from him that he has marked as his own will perish a horrid death."

Stepping back from her, the men crossed themselves.

Sergeant Dollard came to fetch her to Brigadier General Jensen's headquarters, and if he found anything unusual about the bevy of soldiers surrounding her, he said nothing.

Her arrival was announced and once more, she stood in front of the brigadier general's desk while he worked at his papers. This cooling of heels annoyed and infuriated her.

A flag snapped in the wind and drew her attention to the left. Two men engulfed in shadow sat eating their dinner as if they dined at the Willard Hotel. The blood drained from her face.

Her stepfather and older stepbrother.

In their fine clothes, they appeared out of step with military regalia. Her stepbrother, Carl Dawson, a slimmer version of his father, preened in his silk trousers, top boots, satin vest, black coat, silk tie, and pearl stickpin. On a table, lay his silk top hat. His narrow side whiskers, barber-trimmed, were like his long black hair, oiled smooth as jet, but it was his knowing eyes that rattled her.

The tent twirled. Her position was like steering between Scylla, the six-headed monster who lived on a rock on one side of a narrow strait in order to avoid Charybdis, a whirlpool that would devour her.

Her stepfather pointed a damning finger at her. "You think yourself high and mighty. You'll learn a lesson." He stuffed a hunk of beef in his mouth the size of Grace's fist. "You'll be taken back to Maryland to marry Carl."

How she'd like to wipe the smug smirk off her stepbrother's face. She almost laughed. *Bigamy?* She'd not tell them she was married to the Gray Ghost until she was in Maryland.

"You shot my son, Thomas, but it was a flesh wound and he recovered."

"He's not dead?" All this time she'd lived in guilt and fear for being a murderess.

"Of course not. Marry Carl, or it will be a long ride back to Washington where a trial awaits you for attempted murder. Your fate is entirely in your hands."

"Your son tried to rape me. It was self-defense."

"I have a witness to state you tried to kill him. You will have no defense plea." Senator swirled a piece of beef in gravy and popped it in his mouth and chewed noisily. "I do have authority over your inheritance."

Grace fancied she could see the gears of her stepfather's mind whirring like a timepiece wound to too tightly, rejoicing that he now possessed his bounty.

"Then why do you insist I marry your son if you have control over my money?" she challenged him. "Because you don't have the authority, do you?"

He finished gorging on his food. "Don't you worry your pretty little head over that. I make it my business to have the oversight. I'm just being noble to have your name purified by marrying my son. Saves you dishonor."

Brigadier General Jensen arched a stern brow. "I've informed your stepfather of Sister Jennifer Agatha's concerns over your bad choices."

"You are stuck in the tarpit, Grace. Hands and feet stuck," the senator mocked.

Despair clutched her heart. Ryan would try to rescue her and she didn't want him to get killed. The beast of loneliness scratched its fingertips over her soul and she'd no power over it.

To be married to such a monster as her stepbrother would be a life of hell. She shivered with images of his fingers rough against her skin. His repugnant face hovering over her, and his mustache curled up in an imperious sneer. No! She would shout from the rooftops, and then do everything in her power to escape.

Brigadier General Jensen cleared his throat. "In case you are with child, my dear, the senator has generously solved the situation by addressing the problem."

She narrowed her eyes on Jensen. "And how do you profit?"

"Now see here—"

Senator Dawson tapped his temple. "I have coaxed him into an agreement. His favorable attitude toward me will gain him promotion, and—a bit of money."

"My money, of course."

With a great degree of theatrics, Senator Dawson waved his hands, palms up. "Of course."

A sharp spasm in her stomach pulled her gaze from Senator Dawson to Carl, and then to the brigadier general, all of them forcing a charming and condescending expression. No longer could she bear to be in their company and turned to leave. "I will resume my hospital duties."

Her stepbrother blocked her way, gripped her shoulders, purring with a predatory leer. "Only a lovely lady like you can heal a man's scars."

She slid her eyes to where he dared to hold her, and then whipped a scalpel from her pocket and held it in front of his eyes. "Either you take your hands off me, or I'll take them off at the wrists."

Nonplussed, he grinned with a malevolence that iced her veins. "I like a woman with fight."

She flashed the scalpel in the light. "Think of being in a sound sleep and threatened with castration. As a surgeon, I know where to make the cut." He jerked back nearly tripping over his own feet.

She bit back a smile. She'd struck fear in him. A surge of elation swept through her. She was not the same person anymore. No longer would she take their abuse. She'd fight them with every breath she took.

A round of gunfire rattled in the distance. It was the third time that day. Part of her hoped it was Ryan for she missed him so much, but the rational side of her prayed he'd not be foolish for the Yank numbers were too many. He'd be caught in a trap.

Visibly shaken, Jensen barked to his lieutenant. "Has Captain Mohagen done anything to investigate the perimeter?"

"Yes, sir. The captain has ordered his picket lines strengthened and ordered a full company forward in an effort to pursue whatever enemy company is responsible."

Jensen snapped, "It has the sound of mounted troops. Does Captain Mohagen think foot soldiers can catch a cavalry patrol?"

The young lieutenant glanced downward. "I can't answer that."

Jensen stood abruptly and knocked over his chair.

"What can you answer?"

"It appears to be Rebel cavalry, sir. They seem to be attacking all around us, yet mostly to the west. The 75th Ohio has gone missing and we have to assume taken by the enemy. Some of the men are nervous and think it's the Gray Ghost."

Grace deposited her scalpel in her pocket and patted it there. "Plans seemed to go to hell when the first shot was fired."

Carl looked like he wanted to jump from his skin. "You think you're so smart."

With a defiant lift of her chin, Grace faced him. "I know I'm smarter than a snake."

"Shouldn't you capture the bastard?" Senator Dawson demanded.

Jensen slammed his meaty fist on his desk. "You can't pursue a flying enemy."

Grace's laugh came loud and unexpected surprising the men. "No, you can't pursue a flying enemy. It will be dark in a few hours. Ghosts are more powerful then and can sneak up on you while you are sleeping. Right, Brigadier General Jensen?" Was that a glimmer of horror showing in Jensen's eyes? A hint of a smile tugged at Grace's lips.

The senator donned his top hat and cleared his throat with uncharacteristic nervousness. "We will secure our train tickets and leave as soon as possible. We have nuptials to prepare and must get back to Maryland."

"Or perhaps you are afraid it is Colonel Rourke with long memories of your harangues in northern papers, Senator," Grace said, and at once felt victorious when her stepfather turned as white as a ghost.

CHAPTER 32

RYAN'S HORSE VAULTED OVER A fence and his men followed. He rode hard, his first thoughts to get to Grace. Hutchinson, Gill and his men matched his grueling pace across the Shenandoah.

Damn the war and Lee's orders that had taken him from his camp for so long. It was because of him that Grace had been left alone and vulnerable. He cursed. He'd failed to protect her.

How fortuitous to run into Willie Ferguson. The boy had ridden hours from home to inform him of one of Sheridan's men's raid. Ryan gritted his teeth. How had the Northern major general known the exact location of their camp and to come specifically for Grace?

The next stroke of luck was running into Amos who guided them to Brigadier General Jensen's camp. Amos unloaded on him everything that had occurred since he and Grace had been taken prisoner, and the gossip gleaned from the Yank camp. Like a lodestone around Ryan's neck came the news that Grace was being held for treason for aiding the Confederate raid on Union warehouses in Maryland. Even more alarming was Senator Dawson's appearance in the camp. The senator used his power to free Grace on the stipulation she'd comply to marry his son. Ryan braced himself for the worst of his fears. That he'd lose her forever, and without her, life meant nothing.

All day, he had savagely attacked the outskirts of the Yank camp. Now, Ryan put his hand up and led his men to an inner forest clearing, a predetermined rendezvous point where he'd meet with his scouts.

Gill and two other soldiers rode into their bivouac on lathered mounts. Gill slid from his saddle. "I have a friend who's the station master at Trevon Station, and he's learned that Senator Dawson has booked passage for three on an eastern-bound passenger train. A typical politician, Dawson has made fanfare of his trip. My friend gave me the timetable and we know to the minute when the train is due."

Ryan chewed on his cigar. "With certainty, Grace will be returning with him. I can't wait to get my hands on that bastard stepfather of hers." Ryan imagined all kinds of humiliations Grace had suffered during her capture and because of him. "We'll grab Grace, burn the train, create a sensation that will compel Sheridan to place stronger guards on the railroad. When is it due?"

"At two in the morning," Gill said.

Ryan smiled around his cigar. "We'll be able to travel under veil of darkness."

Gill interrupted his thoughts. "Need I remind you, Colonel, that throughout the summer we have kept up incessant warfare on Sheridan, the rail lines, and his communications to materially reduce the Yank's offensive strength. As a result, the Union is now engaged in repairing the railroads that brings Sheridan's supplies. As a consequence of your favorite point of attack on Sheridan's rear, the rail lines are closely guarded by a detachment of troops and will make Grace's rescue near impossible."

Ryan pointed at his captain with his cigar. "That's why we've attacked the pickets on Jensen's camp to draw them in a westerly direction. They will not be looking east."

Sergeant Hutchinson rode in with another scout. He dismounted and spread a map wide against his saddle. "We kept watch for unguarded points, and no opportunity was lost. We found a gap between the guards that we might penetrate and reach that railroad without exciting an alarm. The enterprise is hazardous as there are Yank camps along the line with frequent communication between them."

To save Grace will be like pushing a camel through the eye of a needle. Ryan rubbed the back of his neck. "Our greatest hazard will be discovery by patrols on the road."

Captain Gill fanned his face with his hat while behind him, men drank from their canteens.

"We can time our arrival to give us the shortest wait period."

Hutchinson splayed his hands. "Again, I caution there are camps heavy with Yankees all around, including where Grace is held prisoner. Our capture might be imminent."

But Ryan didn't hear him. He ignored the great risk. He ignored everything except the fact that Grace needed his help and he'd come for her.

Amos spoke up. "After the way she helped me escape, foregoing herself, I'd walk through fire for Miss Grace."

Hutchinson hesitated, and then said, "What if she's not on the train?"

Ryan swore, forcing himself to stay rooted. Helpless. If they failed, the Yanks would guard the railroads threefold. Rage blazed in his belly. "I'd burn the entire north to the ground. I'd scour the earth until destiny consumed me whole and hell tried to declare me, as it surely will unless I find her."

Beneath the light of a half-moon, a lovely night unfolded. Dog day cicadas droned endlessly, large numbers singing in synchrony from soft to loud, and then back to soft. The light breezy sage-like odor of purple aster seeped into the air. Sirius, the big star in the constellation Canis Major beamed brightly. Yet, Grace's absence left him colder, and he pulled his collar tighter to him.

Sergeant Hutchinson led them down a path, a rather dubious and uncertain one, along a long ridge of high bluffs that unfurled through a rolling broad-leaf forest peppered with mountain laurel to a deep cut on the railroad. No patrol or picket was in sight.

Hutchinson slapped a mosquito on his cheek, "Crazy how people are willing to risk travel on a railroad in a country where military operations are ongoing. Not that we're conducting an insurance business on life and property but derailing the train in a cut is safer than running it off an embankment and less likely for passengers to get hurt."

Ryan shifted his cigar in his mouth. Hutchinson meant it would be safer for Grace and Ryan was thankful for that planning. "Send mounted sentries down the line to keep watch. Get those rails pulled up." They dismounted and tied their horses in the trees.

His men sweated to curve up the rails, and then took their positions lying down on the banks of the roadbed.

He pinched his nose and scrubbed his face with his hands to tamp down the fatigue setting in. By God, there was no way he'd let Grace slip through his fingers. His mind drifted to earlier in the day when he'd harassed the fringes of Jensen's camp, scouted around and ascertained a weak spot in the brigadier general's lines.

Then on command, like the roar of Niagara, the Rebel yell drowned out everything. One hundred horsemen at full gallop came thundering down, capturing fifty infantry. One Ohioan fumbled for his pistol until he looked down the muzzle of Ryan's revolver and was compelled to surrender. They left the Yanks tied up miles away. They were lucky bastards because Ryan didn't have time to take the prisoners to Richmond.

The thought of Grace under the thumbnail of her wicked stepbrother, stepfather, and indifferent mother turned his stomach. The train was late, the cicadas stopped and mind-numbing quiet lit the countryside.

A million outcomes of what could go wrong sped

through his mind. Waiting stretched painfully. Hollow grief raged inside him. He couldn't face life without her.

With deep breaths, he gathered his defenses and reminded himself that patience was power, not an absence of inaction, but the timing, the right time to act.

All you have to do is sound commanding and the Yanks will do anything you want them to.

Grace's confident words called out to him. His battle instincts stirred, his senses lifting to the next level of acuity. He signaled to James.

The young soldier scuttled up and put his ear to the iron rail. "Coming fast, Colonel. Two miles off by the click of engine wheels."

"Don't be so buoyant to hope there isn't any peril," Ryan cautioned, keeping to the side of the embankment with his men, waiting for the fireworks to begin.

He stared down the distant rails, spotted a tiny yellow light, like a lantern of hope at the top of a dark well. The rumbling and clattering train inched forward at an excruciating pace. His men had their pistols primed.

"I'm coming to get you. I'm coming to get you," repeated the staccato, clickety-clack of wheels over rail joints into the hot and humid night.

Grace's wild heart saw blessings where others did not. Tirelessly, she cared for his soldiers, and for him. How her smile took on the same radiance as a whole tree of peach blossoms. How she endangered herself to keep a widow's home from burning. How brave she'd been through treachery, taken prisoner by Union forces and degraded, yet persevered to save men. How she helped Amos escape, sacrificing herself when her own freedom was naught.

But most of all, he recalled her bravery the day she made solemn vows to become his wife.

Ryan took off his hat, swiped his arm across his brow. A slight breeze ruffled and cooled his hair. He put his hat back on and waited.

The rushing and rumbling of tons of metal buzzed with vibration, bearing down on them. With certainty, the engineer saw the folly of the upended rails. Too late. A whistle blew an ear-splitting blast. Wheels skidded with the raucous, metallic shriek of brakes, skidding and sparking on hot iron. Percussive, roaring, sharp, shrill, deafening, the train plunged off the track.

The boiler burst. The air filled with red-hot cinders and the hiss of escaping steam.

Through a glittering shower and thick heavy vapors, Ryan ran down the line. "Get to work before the Yanks hear of it. Get those passengers off the train. No time is to be lost."

The cacophonous cries of confused travelers met his ears as Ryan swung on the train. His men filled the crowded cars, their guns ready. Women screamed. Children cried.

"Take the soldiers off first and tie them up," Ryan ordered.

Ryan passed from car to car looking for Grace. He could not find her.

One car, full of bearded German immigrants, refused to budge.

"They claim they've paid for their tickets, Colonel and will not give up their seats," said Hutchinson.

"Grab all those *New York Heralds* and set fire to the car and burn the Germans if they won't depart."

His men marshaled passengers out, but not quick enough. Ryan shoved them out of the way, moving from one car to another. What if she wasn't on the train? What if the information had been wrong? What if he'd been too late, or they decided to depart the next day? Ryan's skin burned everywhere. His skull went numb except for the ache in his head that pulsed with the accelerating rhythm of his heart.

Eyes wide, people pointed at him and crossed themselves. "The Gray Ghost."

On the last car, he elbowed men from in front of him. Hutchinson kept pace from behind. Captain Gill entered the car from the back, shrugging his shoulders.

Then Ryan's gaze fell on Grace. She was tired and worn, but she was his beautiful Grace.

Their gazes locked, and her dreadful misery was mirrored in her face, but it was the entreaty in her tear-stained eyes that came as sure as if she'd shouted the words.

You've come to save me!

Despite the indignities he was sure she had endured, she held her head high. She carried herself like a princess and, for that, he was proud.

He clenched his hands into fists. The dark circles beneath her eyes, her pale skin and loss of weight showed her ill-use where she'd likely been pushed beyond endurance on their travels south. Bred in his nature was the protection of women. He cursed Jensen, the senator and his stepson. They would pay for their abuse of Grace.

She attempted to rise but the portly man across from her showed the nerve to push her down in her seat. Senator Dawson, no doubt.

Like stalking into a den of rival wolves, Ryan swaggered up to them with full confidence that chaos and fear subdued the occupants.

"I told you I'd come for you." Ryan grabbed her hand but the man in the seat beside her with the well-oiled mustache dared to place his arm across her, barring her exit.

Ryan narrowed his eyes on him. He was obviously related to the senator. Younger version. Same lips, receding hairline, black eyes. He'd bet the spawn was the more dangerous of the two.

"You're not taking her. The lady is my fiancé."

With lightning speed, Ryan's pistol leveled right in between her stepbrother's eyes. One tap with a hammer would shatter him.

The younger Dawson threw his hands up.

Coward.

"That's right," said the senator, nodding with showy haughtiness. "The lady is engaged to be married to my son, Carl."

Ryan swung his revolver to him and the older man blanched.

"She will be my bride and there is nothing you can do to stop that." The younger Dawson's voice came nasal and whiny and grated on Ryan's nerves. From his vest pocket, Carl whipped a revolver and pointed it at Ryan's heart, flashing a pearly white row of teeth.

Ryan smiled a deadly smile at Dawson's bravado. As long as the gun was pointed at Ryan and not at

Grace. How many punches would it take to remove every tooth? "Don't tempt me to rip your yellow spine out through your throat," Ryan warned. How it would give him so much pleasure to put a bullet right through Carl's brain.

Captain Gill came up from behind and snatched Carl's gun. He glared at the senator's son. "The art of a moron."

Ryan planted his Colt against Carl's head. "I find arguing reductive and the poorer version of conversation. I'm assuming the dumber parts of your brain, Carl, are triggered and the smarter parts hold zero input. So, I'd suggest to keep me calm, you bow to my demands, and politely and quickly release the lady for my self-control is a finite resource. And right now, that inferno in my belly is as hot as any dragon ever flamed."

The senator jabbed a shaky, plump finger in the air. "She will marry my son."

Ryan drawled dangerously, "You have a problem then, gentlemen."

Grace pried her stepbrother's fingers from her wrist and sprang from her seat. Ryan put his arm protectively around her. Her warmth felt good.

"I will not marry Carl because I'm married to Colonel Rourke, and I love him."

How he treasured hearing her declaration and, in that moment, he found a thousand different things that he loved about her.

Very gently, Ryan kissed her with all the aching tenderness in his heart, and she laid her trembling fingers against his cheek and kissed him back.

The passengers on the train gasped. The women swooned with the news. "She loves the handsome Rebel colonel. How romantic," they murmured to the stern disapproval of their menfolk.

The senator's eyes bulged, and he grabbed hold of her again as if to stop his money pot from vanishing. "I'll have you know I'm an important United States Senator."

Ryan pondered the few observations he'd made about Dawson in the few seconds he'd clapped eyes on him. A man way above his station who conducted business with the unscrupulous desperation of someone living well above his means and, in this case, leeching off his stepdaughter's estate. He was fastidious, vain and greedy to the point of immorality. Like a rat from the sewers, he'd made a career of lying and subterfuge to get what he wanted. Visions of him locking Grace in the attic and beating her loomed, producing an angry red haze in front of his eyes.

"Senator Dawson, you seem to be getting the wrong impression of my Virginia hospitality. If you don't take your hands off my wife, you will be a dead senator. As far as I'm concerned, you deserve to be taken out and hanged."

Grace tugged her arm free and, again, Dawson forgot to be afraid for a second and his fat, dry lip curled up in an imperious sneer. "You may be the Gray Ghost, but you forget I'm protected by Federal authority."

"I'm sure Lincoln won't blink if I take a lying, corrupt politician off his hands." Ryan didn't only rely on observation.

"How dare you accuse me—"

"Of course, there is what you bragged to northern newspapers about all the things you'd do to the Gray Ghost. Instead of you lynching me and dancing on my grave, we'll be hanging you tonight."

The senator wheezed a breath so abruptly, he choked on his own spittle. "Now see here—"

A man dared to stand up between them. "Excuse me, I'm Darren Daniels from the *New York Herald*. My photographer," he pointed to the anxious man in the seat beside him. "May I get a picture and quote from you."

"I know who you are, Darren Daniels. You misquote me all the time and I don't forget liars. I'll be generous and hang you, too."

"Let's not take them prisoner. Let's gut them, Colonel," suggested Hutchinson.

The reporter blanched and sputtered.

Ryan's gaze flicked over the reporter. "I hate newspaper men. You are pariahs, bloodsuckers on society, extorting the most out of fraudulent headlines to sell papers. I'll spare your life if you run a story on Senator Dawson's theft. And if you don't tell it word for word, be rest assured that the Gray Ghost will pay you a nightly visit."

Like a woodpecker ready to strike, the reporter's head bobbed up and down in rapid-fire crusade. "Yes, sir!"

Ryan spoke loudly for everyone in the train car to hear. "Senator Dawson is a shameless self-promoter who has profited off the war machine including the United States Navy. He skimmed profits from several munition companies by taking backdoor bribes."

The news spread through the passengers like fire

through a haymow and their mutterings intensified. Worse than war were manipulative politicians who made gains for themselves.

The senator's face suffused a deep scarlet. "How dare you accuse me—"

Ryan clicked his Colt revolver and lifted it to the senator's head. "I state facts, and I don't take kindly to cowards who beat their stepdaughters, and then have the nerve to call me a liar."

"He beat his stepdaughter?" asked the reporter, scratching his pencil to paper.

"Wait!" the senator rasped, hacking up a last bit and pressing a trembling hand to his heart as though willing it to slow.

"Ryan?"

He looked down to where Grace's hand rested on his arm. "You—"

He knew what her feelings were, but the blackguard deserved to be lynched. "Take him, his son and the soldiers as prisoners."

"You forget we are in a war, sweetheart. The senator is now my prisoner. Boys, get everyone off the train."

"Take the Rebel whore," shouted Sister Jennifer Agatha, her eyes feral, as if preaching fire and damnation from a pulpit.

Ryan spun around, stood a hair's breadth from her. His towering presence made the old crone quake in her boots. "With certainty, now I know how Sheridan's troops found my camp. You know what we do with spies, Sister Jennifer Agatha?"

Hutchinson held up a nasty Bowie knife. "We gut them, that's what we do. Did I mention what I've always sensed about you, Sister Jennifer Agatha? That you've fallen from the ugly tree and hit every branch."

Ryan pointed his pistol at her and glared at the nun whose vengefulness had dictated so much trouble. "The night is fading, and I have half a mind to shoot you, but I don't kill women, and besides, it would be a disservice to the Confederacy when no doubt you'll cause horrendous damage to the Union."

The nun clamped her teeth together.

Ryan turned from Sister Jennifer Agatha and ushered Grace ahead of him. "I do love that sound she makes when she shuts up."

Soon the train was ablaze. Outside, he pulled Grace through the crowds to the horses. The Germans tumbled out of the flames and grumbled, gesturing wildly with their hands and with conviction, discharging what he interpreted were Hanoverian curses on his person.

"You can't blame me, blame General Sheridan," Ryan told them. "It's his business, not mine to protect you."

A rotund lady cried out, "My father is a Mason."

"Lady, if there was a hanging for idiocy, you'd be first in line."

Grace glanced over her shoulder. "Ryan, the passengers are trailing us. They appear to possess a curious admiration."

Ryan pivoted, noted the peculiar following, and then tugged her along. "The greatest lesson in life, my dear, is to know that even fools are right sometimes."

A hefty man with long sideburns steamed up to his side, huffing to keep up with him. "My good sir, I have immunity on the grounds that I'm a member of an aristocratic church in Baltimore."

The lunacy of the passengers gave Ryan a headache. "I can't help it." He bent over and kissed Grace. "Never underestimate the power of stupid people in big groups."

His men, Andrew Dear and Alfred Finney dashed up to him. "We've captured two U.S. Paymasters with their satchels of greenbacks."

"Lieutenant Smith, take Dear and Crawford over the ridge to our rendezvous and guard those satchels."

His men dipped into the ladies' pocketbooks, took watches and seized other valuable articles.

An old woman cried, "That is my wedding band and the only memory I have of my late husband."

Grace retrieved the ring from the Rebel soldier and gave it back to the woman. "Colonel Rourke's men may appropriate the enemy's goods as is a custom of war, but not the wedding rings of widows."

The old woman had tears in her eyes. "I'm forever grateful, Miss."

Toward the end of the train they stopped, and Ryan hauled Grace up beside him. "Senator Dawson, you and your son may strip."

Dawson's son threw a punch. Ryan ducked and the wild blow hit a giant German immigrant behind him. Ryan wanted to plant his fist in the younger Dawson's face, but a low hum of fury escaped from the German. He'd allow the giant to supply punches, which he did, until Ryan shot his pistol in the air. Openmouthed passengers grouped around with interest.

Ryan had enough of delays, and gritted his teeth while Dawson and his son, the latter now hosting two black eyes, stripped down to their long johns. Impatient, Ryan gestured with his pistol for the photographer. "Take two pictures. I'm giving one plate to the *Richmond Examiner* and the other is for you, Daniels, to be published in the *New York Herald*. I'm giving you a story of a lifetime. Not only do you get to reveal the embezzlement by a major United States Senator, you get a picture of him with the Gray Ghost. You can thank me later for your promotion but make sure you spell my name right."

With the fires from the train giving full illumination, Ryan put his arm around Senator Dawson and smiled for the camera.

Ryan called out, "Captain Gill, take the prisoners and half our men and head out. Leave Senator Dawson and his son. Let the vultures in the north pick his bones after the newspapers run his story."

***

Ryan clicked Archimedes a little ahead of his men. He held Grace in his arms and turned her face to him, making her look into his eyes to see the import of his words. "When Jensen and your stepfather had you in their grasp, when you were secured behind Yank lines, I went crazy."

"Oh, Ryan, I thought I'd never see you again. I worried that you'd be foolish and try and rescue me. I prayed you wouldn't come for fear of you getting shot, captured or killed. It broke my heart to *parley* such prayers, but I feared for your safety over mine. Even if it meant never seeing you again."

"Over and over, I played this out like an ominous

dance with death. All I could do was give in to it, step right inside the storm and pray it didn't swallow me up."

Grace drew him down to her, and he kissed her slow, thoughtful, his tongue tracing the soft fullness of her lips. His men cheered.

They reached the Shenandoah River and his rear patrol galloped up to him with Dear, Finney, Smith and the U. S. payroll. "A Yank cavalry is pounding on our heels. I'm guessing thirty or forty men, Colonel."

Grace slipped from his saddle and onto her own mount.

Ryan stood in his stirrups, squinted and noted the dirt spewing up in the road. "I'm speculating you're correct in your assessment, Lieutenant Smith. We'll divide and flank them." They retreated and hid in thick pine woods. Impossible for anyone to see them. When the unsuspecting Yanks pulled in between, Ryan's men fired from behind trees. The Yanks coming upon overwhelming forces easily surrendered.

"Who is your commanding officer?" Ryan demanded.

An officer pressed his mount forward. "That would be me. I'm Captain Maybee, Army of the Potomac."

"And who do you directly serve?"

"General Sheridan and Brigadier General Jensen."

"Well, Captain Maybee, the day couldn't get any better. You must appreciate we have the honor of meeting again."

"And who do I have the dishonor of meeting?" Maybee gritted out.

"The Gray Ghost or as you aptly named me, the

bogeyman. We met a few months ago and made a bet with a bottle of wine. Do you remember?"

"Impossible." His mouth slackened, he blinked several times, and then openly stared. The dawning realization of Captain Maybee was amusing. He ripped off his hat and pushed a hand through his long, thinning hair "I could have had you then."

"Yes, you could have, but not without a fight."

Maybee snorted. "Who would have guessed? Well, that's good then. Now I'm your prisoner."

Ryan said, "Since you've been so gracious in your surrender, it will be me who'll give you a bottle of wine."

CHAPTER 33

September 1864, North fork of the Shenandoah River

FOR A MONTH, GRACE HAD been set up in a new hospital in General Early's camp, seeing the impact of Grant's omnipresent and aggressive Army of the Shenandoah commanded by Major General Philip Sheridan. Presently, she dragged her feet through the multitude of wounded soldiers. A soldier patient reached out, grabbed her hand as she walked by. She inspected the filthy nails of the gunpowder-stained hand engulfing hers.

"Will you write my sweetheart a letter?" She could see he didn't have much time. Her eyes dimmed with tears. She procured a pencil and paper from her pocket and commenced to write.

His throat gurgled with his last gasping breaths. The death rattle. "I never imagined you loved me, but the action bade me hope that a kindly regard might develop into love, as the bud expands into the flower. I trust I shall meet you, my darling, in the world above."

When he died, she came out of the hospital and took several gulps of fresh air. Death was everywhere. Bluebottle flies swarmed over the bodies.

"Good to see you, Sister Grace. Oh, excuse me, it's Mrs. Rourke now."

Grace watched Colonel Lawler approach. He stood one foot from her, daring to intimidate her with his height. She stood her ground. "I'm not inclined to tell you how good it is to see you."

"Are your blessed nuptials in agreement with you, or dare I ask if the colonel is still among the living?" he laughed.

Oh, the man was filled with infinite spite and calculated vindictiveness and doubtless would be praying for Ryan's demise. "The only difference between an alligator and you, Colonel Lawler, is that the alligator shows its teeth before it bites."

Lawler put up his hands. "No need to get your airs up. Although, I'd not mind a nibble on a delicious morsel." He stared at her breasts.

"Beware of the snake. It's not the creature's bite, but the venom left behind," she said coolly. She felt her husband come up alongside her.

"Ah, Colonel Rourke, so glad to see you."

"I'm sure. What business do you have with my wife?"

Grace threaded her arm through her husband's. His muscles shifted beneath his coat.

"Just paying my respects. That's all." His voice seemed to originate in his extremely large nose.

"Pay your respects somewhere else."

"I'm preparing for the battle ahead."

"Prepared? You can't get your pants buttoned before noon."

"It would be unfortunate for you to get killed on the battlefield," warned Lawler.

Grace knew enemies were not just Yanks. From time to time, Confederate ranks solved the end of long-time feuds on the battlefield with no one the wiser.

Ryan stepped into Lawler's space, stuck his finger in the man's chest. "You'll be dead before you pull the trigger."

CHAPTER 34

IN THEIR TENT, RYAN STROKED Grace's hair, infinitely gentle, like the caress of silk against velvet. "If the improbable were to occur, my brothers, John and Lucas, will help you," he said. "I guarantee it."

"I don't want to talk about it. I refuse to let anything happen to you," Grace responded. He was being noble, that she would be cared for in the event of his death since, with certainty, her inheritance was null and void for marrying an enemy combatant of the north.

"Grace—"

She placed a cool finger against his lips and rose, wrapping the bedsheet around her. "I don't want to hear it." She picked at a plate of fried green tomatoes sprinkled with a pinch of sugar.

"Our children must have a father."

"Are you telling me something?"

She stopped licking her fingers, thinking of the dates

of her last course, and how easily she could deceive him. But she'd not play that game and give him more cause to worry. She shook her head. "Don't go. Let's leave this place, start a new life."

"So easy to weave a castle in the sky," he said wistfully, rolling on his back and linking his hands behind his head. "You know better than I of my duty. You cannot forget I leave in the morn."

"Likely so," Grace said, fury and frustration skirmishing in her gut. "Nothing feeds forgetfulness better than war. Most keep quiet while the majority tries to convince the rest of us that what we've acted on, what we've discovered about ourselves, and about others is a mirage, a fleeting terrifying dream. Wars hold no recollection, and nobody has the courage to comprehend them until there are no declarations left to disclose of what transpired, until the moment comes when we no longer identify them and they come back again, with a new face and a new name, to eat greedily of what they left behind.

"Give up this madness," she begged. "In a calvary fight, men die one bullet at a time. In an artillery fight, they die in bulk. I've seen and cared for what was left of that fight."

His lips drew back in a snarl and he sat up. "In the Peninsula Campaign, Longstreet played defense to McClellan's aggressiveness and kept on winning enough that the Yank general found himself back in Northern Virginia where he came from in the first place."

Grace swept her hair back over her shoulder. "This isn't McClellan you're fighting anymore. It's Grant and he is Lincoln's bulldog unchecked. He has unleashed his hound of hell, Sheridan. The Northern cavalry has improved. There is the repeater rifle and the carbine. You don't have a chance."

A vein throbbed in his forehead. "I'm heartily sick and tired of hearing what Grant will do. You talk as if he'll do a double somersault, and land in our rear and on both our flanks. Try and think of what damage we can do to him."

Grace argued hotly her contention. "Grant's strategy changed upon his promotion to command all the Union armies. He has concurred with Lincoln and Sherman and Sheridan about the scorched earth tactics required to defeat the Confederate forces, to destroy the Confederacy's economic base, striking at the heart of the Confederacy."

Ryan shot up from the bed. "And that's why I must fight that line of attack against the Shenandoah Valley. To divide the Confederacy would be a blow. Grant's strategy, if it works, will close the invasion route to the north and deny the use of its supplies to the guerrillas operating in the area and begin a campaign of destruction, including my home. Sheridan has defeated us at Winchester, Fisher's Hill. He must be stopped."

"Oh, how you wear your fallible pride like a suit of armor. You think it keeps you safe, but all it does is weigh you down and make it hard for you to move as this bloody war burns earth and sky."

Ryan blew out a breath. "In these few precious minutes we have left, I don't want to talk about war."

Grace narrowed her gaze, and then decided on another tactic as old as Samson and Delilah. She'd employ other devices to keep him from fighting a useless war. "Don't you have to be at a meeting? I take it you're not the kind of man who ignores rules."

With dainty fingers, she picked up a tomato slice and stared at him. She held it to her lips, hovering… drawing and nibbling between her perfect white teeth, and then sucking until nothing of the delicacy remained. Her voice came full-throated and carnal.

"Delicious."

He rose and stalked her across the tent. Backed her to the bed. "Have you known me to follow any rules in our acquaintance?"

Towering above her, his hips pressed into hers, he growled into her ear. "I warn you, Wife, you are making a grave error. Do you think your coaxing will make me stay?"

"I hope so." She reached down to stroke the hardening of his manhood.

"Patience is a virtue."

"Can't hurry up be a virtue?"

He threw back his head and laughed. "You are a temptress for sure." He pressed her back onto the bed and they made wild, sweet love.

CHAPTER 35

October 9th, 1864 Tom's Brook, Virginia

THE STORM HURLING ITSELF AGAINST the tent was the only sound ripping through her pounding head. The wind picked up, howling, crying, warning like a wolf in the night. The air lay heavy and dank and frightening.

Word had been General Jubal Early launched a surprise attack with Colonel Rourke's cavalry acting as a screen against the encamped army of now Brigadier General Sheridan, across Cedar Creek, northeast of Strasburg, Virginia. During the morning fighting, they came up against seven Union infantry divisions.

"Grace? Where is Grace?"

"Ryan?" She turned as men rushed through the door, allowing a swirling sheet of driving rain to soak her skirts. Captain Gill was lifted on the table. Shot in the chest. So much blood.

"Grace," Gill croaked. "This is mortal, no use telling me different."

His scream was silent, but it lashed to her like great shards of glass. The blood drained from her face, her heart thudded.

She sat next to him and took his hand, his voice barely above a whisper with his struggle to breathe and mirrored her terror.

"I have neither father, mother, nor sister. The love of my life, my wife died with our son. I will be with them before the hour." He panted, trying to catch his breath. "Reach in my inner pocket. Hurry."

Grace obeyed, held an envelope up for him to see.

He nodded. "It's yours, Grace, the deed to my farm. Not much, and rundown. I've no one to leave it to and have signed the property to you and Colonel Rourke. You are my only family. You can start a new life. Have the horse farm you dreamed of…in the Shenandoah."

A warm, sticky sensation pooled over her arm and her knee. Bile rose to her throat for fear of Gill's life.

"It's so cold," he said.

The warm liquid slid down her leg. Ryan covered him with a blanket and lit another lantern. Lightning flashed, illuminating the grimmest sight of the horror-filled night. She was a doctor. Had witnessed so much…but this was Captain Gill.

Blood. Spreading from the prone form across both sides of the table and onto the floor. Tears filling her eyes, she looked to Ryan for help. He shook his head. There was nothing anyone could do, least of all her.

Breath exploded from her chest; her beloved friend

wreathed in the golden glow of the pathetic lantern light. Hot tears blurred her vision.

"I can't see you anymore. Don't leave me."

He sounded afraid, which intensified her own despair. She moved to cradle his head against her chest, clutching him to her as though if she held on tightly enough, she could will life back into him.

"We're here," said Ryan. "We will not leave you."

Lightning slashed across the sky with the answering boom of thunder rocking across the valley. Immune to the storm, Grace's throat ached, moved by the depth of Ryan's feelings, his love for this man who was like a brother, and hatred for his useless death.

"Will you sing to me?" Gill rasped as a great wind gusted against the tent. "*Amazing Grace.*"

Her vocal cords paralyzed, Grace swallowed and forced the words through anguish and pain.

Amazing Grace, how sweet the sound.

That saved a wretch like me

Her voice rolled through the tent and over the hills in sorrowful waves. Swells of power rolled up in her throat. And her arms tightened around him. The music became her external heartbeat and the lyrics came from her soul in sweet vibrations, a song of love of one another, to nature and creation, life and death.

Grace held her cheek to the side of his bristly face as she belted out the final notes. Ryan touched his friend's hand and joined her song. Gill smiled, squeezed Ryan's hand, though blood leaked from the corner of his mouth and trickled into his hair. His skin was so cold, but the blood pumping out of him was warm, shrouding them both.

I once was lost, but now am found
Was blind but now I see…

Her voice snared on a sob. Then another, and she didn't think she could sing another note. Right then, as the storm raged outside, the sweet man's chest heaved one last time, his head dropped and he went limp, the last light of his life dimmed. She hugged him and rocked him. She cried and cried. This noble man who made her laugh had gone home to his wife and child.

"Grace, Captain Gill lived profoundly and had no fear of death. That part of him that we have known deeply, we can never lose and becomes a part of us. The utmost honor we can give him is not grief but gratitude."

Her husband peeled her away and held her in his arms. Cradling her head against his neck, he allowed her to weep.

Grace could not look at him.

He rubbed his hands up and down her back and led her away. "Death isn't kind, Grace. It doesn't pretend to care or to distinguish."

She knew that. How long had she been witness to death's talons, snatching where it could, taking those far too young and far too good. Again, death had ripped away another part of her and her world had gone cold. As the war beat on, so many more would be snatched away.

She went with Rourke outside the tent. "You are leaving again. Quit this war. Punishing yourself by denying the things that bring happiness. Lee cannot replace his soldiers or supplies. How long can he hold out?"

"We're back to that again."

"The real crux of it is that I cannot bear the thought of the war taking you."

"Don't you think I want the war to end? I'm in too deep. To fear that I'll die alone…with my eyes open to the sky in a field with no one to bury me?"

"Promise me you'll send a message to let me know you're all right."

"I promise."

"If anything happens to you, I could not exist."

"Nothing will happen to me, I promise. I must return—"

In a wisp of wind, he hopped up on Archimedes and departed. She watched him recede into the darkness of the starlit dawn.

CHAPTER 36

RYAN STOPPED WITHIN A TREE line, beyond which lay a meadow, and another tree line bordered the field. Calm. Peaceful. An owl crossed overhead. He recognized the cry of a barn owl and guessed it was coming home with a belly full of mice and frogs. Ryan gripped his reins. Sighting of a midday owl was a bad omen or had the creature simply been rousted from its nest?

They came to a river and the horses plunged their heads up to their eyes, so thirsty the poor beasts were. He shot a glance toward the defiant sky—or where the sky would be if it could be seen through gathering piles of thick gray clouds angrily pushing against each other. Bad feelings danced in his head. On the somber field of battle, nothing thicker than a knife's blade separated life from death. He should have listened to Grace. Gone someplace else. Started anew.

Ryan thoughts drifted to Grace. *How her pale blonde hair splayed over his chest. How she'd moved her arms about him, beckoning him closer to her as they lay on his bed. Her scent and heat surrounded him like a sensual miasma. The magic and memory swirled a potent brew that drowned him in heady passion as he rolled atop her, their bodies bathed in the slant of the moon's glow.*

She hadn't wondered at his thoughts—his body tensed and tightened, felt the cup of his hand upon her cheek, and before she could speak, he kissed her, forcefully, seductively, denying any chance of protest. In response, she weaved her soft arms about his neck, splaying her fingers down his shoulders and back. He liked her free response, moving her hands everywhere to pleasure him.

A hand upon his chest, she had pushed him back to his elbows. She leaned over him, her hair veiling them in a canopy of silk.

"Hungry?" she teased.

"Starving."

When her lips had met his, he needed no urging to part his own. Her soft breasts pushed into his chest. When he entered her, her eyes closed, and he saw the soft sweep of her lashes and heard the soft pleading moans as she cried out for him in a sweet pinnacle of release.

How much more entranced could he be?

How easy to be lured away. Yet this strange and unfamiliar fantasy in the middle of this bleak war beckoned him. Only one word carried through the quiet, still day, and braved the tumultuous storm swirling and screaming inside his skull.

Mine.

She was his and always would be.

How he hated to leave the warmth of his bed. The scent of their lovemaking. The feel of her skin against his. How he hated everything that was to come.

A muscle jumped in Ryan's jaw. Ever since General Lee had ordered the withdrawal of General Kershaw's troops to bolster Richmond defenses, Yank Brigadier General Philip Sheridan had struck ruinous casualties on the Confederate's forces. The day before, General Early had discovered a weakness along the Union lines. With boldness and, using surprise to his advantage, he planned an assault on the superior forces across the North fork of the Shenandoah River and Cedar Creek to attack the Union left. They had been successful in rolling up the line and defeating each part.

Exhausted and hungry, Early's men fell out of ranks to pillage supplies from the Union camps for they had won a stunning Confederate victory.

Ryan had not fallen to the plunder and had ridden a broad reconnaissance. The men at war were too complacent. He urged Archimedes across the lifeless river and stood in his stirrups once more. He pulled out his scope and scanned below, the broad level valley ran for miles with its fields and pastures shortened into a narrow band of green. After a few minutes, he caught a glitter, a reflection of the morning sun from a brass field piece, a glittering bayonet and masked barrels. It was a Yank turning column one mile ahead. He swung his scope. The colors of the Stars and Stripes appeared at the head of the column in the woods to his left flank, and then on the right side, a mile in length. Infantry and artillery.

He sent a courier to Early and watched in horror as

the Yanks continued to march. Would this be a rout? He plunged his horse forward into Sheridan's design of Thermopylae. His men followed.

They soon encountered heavy columns of the enemy with his probe. So ensnared by his orders, he fought the battle on the point of honor. Two great aggressive rabbles, driving into each other like hordes of savages. Yanks, in accordioned waves of horse drawn panic.

Musket fire burst. Artillery boomed and ripped the air. Smoke seared his nostrils.

To withdraw would have the appearance of defeat and give the moral effect of a victory to the enemy. He absorbed the terrain bursting with Yanks like a spreading disease. It was Green Tavern all over again and he froze.

He could not breathe. His skin became clammy and his hands shook. His heart exploded in his chest. His mind reeled, unable to comprehend or process the images sent by his eyes. He looked away, then looked back to see if the images were still there. Images that could not be erased.

Grace's voice cut through.

You must come back to me.

His training kicked in.

A bullet whistled close by his head. He couldn't see anything through the puff of gun smoke. He plunged his spurs into Archimedes' flank. The horse leaped, his front hooves plowing into the chest of a Yank. His mount reared and Ryan jumped away as Archimedes rolled. He slapped the stallion away from the intense firing, and then dropped into a ditch and fired his rifle.

He shouted for his men, and then realized many lay

dead or wounded. He fired blindly. The oncoming soldiers' lips were stained by black powder from biting cartridges, their faces wild with rage and excitement. The world was in chaos, nothing but a whirl of smoke and stabbing flame and men screaming defiance.

Colonel Lawler galloped up to him. He raised his pistol and pointed at Ryan.

"I'm going to kill you, you son of a bitch. I wish I could make you suffer for all the humiliations you have caused me."

Time stood still. Lawler, a man addicted to his rage and jealousy, possessed lunatic eyes full of venom. Ryan fumbled for his dagger, leaped forward, and swinging viciously with his right hand, sliced an artery in Lawler's thigh.

A Yank bullet pierced Lawler's brain, his horse reared, then fell, pitching his lifeless body face down in the grass.

Ryan didn't have time to think about the rot in Lawler's soul. Dazed, Ryan looked up. Where were his men? A total collapse. Men cried out and fell as volley after volley slammed into them. A tsunami of blue moved on top of them. It was hand to hand combat now.

"Retreat!" he shouted over the melee.

A riderless horse galloped by. Ryan rose to catch it, hooked his boot in the stirrup and seized the saddle horn. He pressed close to the animal's side, using the horse as a shield. A booming cannon caused the horse to reverse course. Fully exposed, a bullet hit Ryan in the gut. Blood sprayed through the air in a fine crimson mist. The horse carried him to another meadow.

Colorful spots contoured the sides of his eyes and he bit his lip from the agony. So fatigued. He struggled to hold on. His fingers slipped from the saddle and he plummeted to the ground.

He reached down, touched his abdomen, and then wearily lifted his hand. The blood that once flowed thick and scarlet in his veins now stained his callused fingers. In the bright light of October, it was indecently red, as red as any flower bloom. "No," he whispered. To die alone. To not capture the warmth of Grace's arms again?

Screams came from a place of terror, telling a mind of absolute fear and agony. His scream stayed silent, as he hunched up to see around him. His brigade was shattered, and a large portion were near capture surrounded as they were. To defeat the enemy with this slender means was like going to sea in a saucer.

He lay back down, his head pillowed by soft grasses. His life passed before him in an ever-shifting kaleidoscope. Lucas. John. Zachery. All the war years tattooed on his brain. The battles, campaigns, hours in the saddle. Grace the nun. Grace the healer. Grace his lover and wife. He had allowed the demon of hate and war to consume him and now he faced the terrible consequences of his obsession.

None of it was worth it.

His eyelids shut tighter through the pain. If only to see Grace one more time…

CHAPTER 37

AT THE EDGE OF THE field, so many men lay crying out in agony, so many of their brethren dead. Both blue and gray. The sun came out, bursting in full bloom over the sky as Grace, Clara and Sister Josephine climbed out of the wagon, their wide white cornettes, giving the appearance of angels' wings and their long cassocks identifying their calling.

They were at great risk. No one was allowed in the zone. The butcher, Brigadier General Sheridan's orders. No quarter was given for stretcher bearers to go in. Cold Harbor all over again. No truce to collect the injured or dead. Both sides had snipers keen to shoot anyone who defied the orders.

Known to both sides as battlefield angels for their devoted acts of mercy, it was Grace's hope, that the Sisters of Mercy would be spared. Grace gripped her medical bag and glanced at the guns aimed at them from both sides.

"There are pickets up in the trees that enjoy a clear target. I pray they do not shoot." said Sister Josephine who, with Clara, insisted on coming to help Grace find Ryan.

"They won't dare shoot a Sister of Mercy and risk eternal damnation," said Grace.

Sister Josephine pressed forward. "You're relying a little too strongly on that notion."

"Oh, ye of little faith," said Clara.

A Confederate officer had ordered them not to go and to move the hospital back ten miles.

Grace was through with orders. This was a man's world built on madness and chaos. No more would she succumb to the status quo and meekly sit back. She had grown beyond the naïveté that held her bound. Not when she held the hope that Ryan was alive, and she was the only one to help him.

Under a white flag of truce, Francis drove the wagon stocked with medical supplies and water. Lucifer perched on his shoulder, cawed.

Sister Josephine moved from injured soldier to soldier, giving each man a drink. She gazed out over the carnage. And shook her head. "For there lies the harvest they reaped, each sheaf distinctly labeled with the name of the reaper in the wound they received."

The sun sweltered. Men cried out for succor.

"Lower your guns, men." Grace heard a Yank soldier order, his Irish brogue evident.

"But there was to be no quarter given, sir. We were commanded to shoot," protested another.

"This is from a higher command. They are doing

God's work." The Yanks' guns were lowered.

Grace peeked from beneath her cornette to the other side. The Rebs lowered their guns.

It had been a serious rout for the Confederates. The dead and wounded still remained as they had fallen on the field of battle. The artillery had torn its sheaves out by the roots and scattered the fragments of human remains, while the infantry had mowed them down in the well-heaped windrows. One man drawn up in a ball died like a snail without a shell. So many begged piteously for water. She collected the canteens of both Rebs and Yanks and filled them from rain barrels on the wagon. Some asked to write their family final farewells, but there was no time. She had to find Ryan.

She went from man to man. Where was Ryan?

Lucifer settled on her shoulder. Strange, the bird rarely left Francis. She flicked her wrist and shooed him away, too concerned with finding Ryan. The bird alighted, and then resettled on her shoulder, loudly cawing. "Strange how Lucifer—"

"Stop." Sister Josephine stayed her hand before she flicked the bird away. "Angels can appear as animals."

Grace widened her eyes with dawning realization. "Lucifer, find Colonel Rourke."

The crow took off, his shiny black feathers catching the light. Grace shielded her eyes from the bright sun. Lucifer circled the entire field once, twice, and then landed on a tree in the corner and cawed. Grace forced herself to maintain her ruse as a holy sister and moved toward the crow, giving water to the soldiers, the ground so slick with blood and the stench overwhelming. One soldier grabbed her ankle and she fell, her palms skidding in the soil. As she tore his fingers from her, he went limp and died.

How many times did she resist the urge to pick up her cassock and run to where Lucifer perched. Finally, beneath the crow, under the broad branches of an oak lay Ryan. He'd been shot in the abdomen. She'd seen many wounds like this. Rarely did anyone survive. Grace tried to speak, but the agony was too heavy in her throat. A storm of her tears was beginning to gather the strength of the one raging inside. "You stupid fool, you promised me you wouldn't get hurt."

She reached into her bag and started doing everything she could to stabilize him.

Sister Josephine knelt beside Grace. "Knowing that however mysterious, God has a unique destiny for all of us, a mission that is longer on this earth for some than for others. Colonel Rourke will survive, but you must leave this madness behind. Start anew."

"I know." Grace probed for metal, found the bullet. Surgery on the field was not in her realm of experience but she worked at her craft. Anything to save him. "And nothing will stop me, not even General Lee."

⁂

Her heavenly voice had brought Ryan back from the beckoning abyss above which he'd feverishly drifted.

She held his hand and made him promise her he'd never let go.

And so, he had.

Through blackouts to consciousness, he fought the constant swaying and rocking of a wagon. He'd live only because she ordered him to.

Whenever death seduced him with an end to the agony, he waited to hear the soft resonance of her admonishments just one more time. The slide of her fingers against his palm somehow banked the terror of endless and fruitless battle. He measured time in the increments between awakening through a drug-filled haze and her concerned eyes focused on him, then in pain-numbing slumber. She didn't let go. Her hold on his hand anchored him to the world.

When his bandages were changed, she'd been there. Stroking him. Giving reassurances and extolling his improvement. Vowing he would recover.

She whispered to him. Her hopes a balm to his soul. What did heaven mean without her?

Nothing.

She was his light in the dark. His prayer at night, everything that remained of his wretched past and present.

She was his glorious future.

Finally, the wooziness abated and the ringing in his ears that pulsed like a plucked wire dimmed and died. He blinked, opened his eyes.

Violets danced in a blur of silver.

"My darling, can you see me?" She sobbed, making a pool of grief and rage in his palm.

See her? He absorbed her. Consumed her. There was nothing else he wanted to see. And never wanted to.

Her sweet face, her hair veiling him. He reached up to touch her and she held his palm to her cheek. A tear splashed from her eye and disappeared into the crease between his fingers.

A rut in the road jostled them with such force at

their frantic pace his chest heaved a scream into his throat, but it only escaped as a piteous, gurgling groan.

"Francis, be careful of the ruts in the road," Grace said, and then looked at Ryan. "Darling, a little farther and we'll be there. You're going to survive."

Francis? Where were they going? Before he could search for answers, his head was lifted, and he was forced to drink something bitter. His muscles relaxed and his head fell into her lap. Blessed sleep came upon him.

CHAPTER 38

West Shenandoah Valley, one year later

TIME WAS LIKE THE SHENANDOAH River. It slipped beneath her like water, and then flowed away. Change had come, her memories bookended to be forgotten, yet never forgotten. Since the Battle at Cedar Creek, the war trudged on to its awful and blessed conclusion. The North's Brigadier General Philip Sheridan had arrived just in time to launch a crushing counterattack, from which General Early's Rebel forces could not recover. Sheridan's victory at Cedar Creek extinguished any hope of further Confederate offensives in the Shenandoah Valley.

In November of 1864, General Sherman destroyed Atlanta's warehouses and railroad facilities with his sixty-two thousand men, and then began his March to the Sea. "I can make Georgia howl!" Sherman had boasted to the terror of southern residents. And he did.

The following December brought the news of General Hood's Rebel army of twenty-three thousand crushed at Nashville, ceasing the Confederates resistance in Tennessee. In January of 1865, the United States Congress approved the Thirteenth Amendment to the United States Constitution abolishing slavery. If there had been any good that came from the war, it was the termination of the horrific activity. In April, General Grant broke through Lee's lines in Petersburg with Union troops filling Richmond, the capital of the Confederacy. The Confederate battle flag was taken down and replaced with the Stars and Stripes.

In May, General Robert E. Lee surrendered his Confederate forces to General Ulysses S. Grant at the Appomattox Court House in Virginia. Ironically, the war had started and ended there.

Sad news came two weeks later of President Abraham Lincoln's death. He'd been attending a play at the Ford's Theatre when John Wilkes Booth shot him. The self-taught prairie lawyer had deftly led the nation through its worst crisis and preserved a shattered Union. His policy, "With malice toward none; with charity for all" demonstrated his compassion and extraordinary leadership to heal the divisions. Surprisingly, Ryan respected the man.

On her front porch, Grace gazed out over the valley where the green hues deepened and lightened over nodding heads of wheat and hay, and the air grew heavy with the sweet scent of sun-soaked grasses. Down the sloping mountain lay a lazy meandering river, the banks alive with nesting ducks and the sapphire depths abundant with fish.

She thought of Captain Joshua Gill and the precious gift he had given them and hoped her joyful gratitude reached him in heaven. In these moments, there emerged an eternity in each second, a delight that came in the free birdsong and a steadiness to her heart and soul. And supporting all this was the humble earth, that rich green that brought all this in concert with the sunshine. For this peace all around her, she could wish for no more.

She'd have to be blind as a bat to not see the rundown condition of the farm. Like an unleavened loaf of bread, half of the hay barn lay buckled. The other buildings lingered like columns of deflated mushrooms. Doors hung akimbo from rusted hinges and had surrendered to gravity.

The house possessed worn clapboard, and the planks on the porch rose and fell like a teeter totter depending where you stepped. At least the roof didn't leak and the brick fireplace in the kitchen kept them warm and comfortable from winter winds. She couldn't think of a more beautiful place on earth.

Akin to other southerners, they were broke, scraping by yet rich in happiness and wealthy with dreams of a promising future when money allowed. In time, they hoped to raise a new barn, purchase more land for extra pasture, and build a mill on the river. Lumber transpired a precious and needed commodity in rebuilding the south, and holding numerous acres of hardwood forests, might well produce a fruitful income.

Like nailing jelly to a wall, Grace had started renovations with Francis and Clara's help. During

Ryan's lengthy convalescence, he had proved a difficult patient and more challenging to keep down. How close he had been to death. The bullet had missed vital organs and stopped at his spleen. So he wouldn't bleed to death, she'd cut off and tied the vessels that supplied the blood flow to the spleen. She then removed the organ and sat back and prayed. Ryan was one of the lucky ones who had survived the procedure. With her warm stews and doctoring skills, he came back stronger than ever.

The chicken coop had been salvageable and now hosted several laying hens that scratched in the yard to the tune of a Leghorn rooster. In the rich soils, a garden yielded red tomatoes, green beans, and then potatoes, turnips and other root vegetables to roast in the autumn. A few scored fields had been plowed and now lay heavy with oats, wheat and corn.

Purchased with the last of Ryan's meager earnings was a newly acquired mare with excellent bloodlines whom they had paired with Archimedes. Next spring they'd have a new foal and thus, begin their herd.

Grace thought about all the people she had met during the war. Francis and Clara lived happily in one of the cabins on their farm with Clara expecting their first child soon. For the first time in their lives, the two had a home filled with an abundance of love.

Sergeant Hutchinson married and with his bride resided on a piece of property given as a wedding gift by his new father-in-law in Chester County.

The reporter, Daniels, did indeed print the story in the *New York Herald*, precipitating Senator Dawson's arrest. His hubris caught up with him and he reposed in prison.

Brigadier General Jensen was reprimanded for allowing so many of his troops to be captured by Confederates and his legacy remained the humiliation suffered by the hands of the Gray Ghost. He retired at war's end and died six months later from consumption.

Grace had sent her mother a letter detailing her happy marriage to Colonel Rourke and their home in the Shenandoah. Grace forgave her mother.

In the months that followed, she received correspondence from her mother who was combatting a long illness due to scarlet fever, leaving her weak. She had lost most of her hair. She admitted her wretchedness to Grace, stating that her own parents had little use for her. It wasn't an excuse for her own actions, but knowing her daughter's heart was happy to go to her maker with Grace's absolution.

She also wrote that when the senator went to jail for his crimes, his sons disappeared. Rumors abound claimed her youngest stepbrother, Thomas, had gone west and had been killed by Comanches. Carl Dawson, her older stepbrother had simply vanished.

With her mother's confession, Grace discovered a miracle in her heart by building a bridge of reconciliation. For the first time in her life, her shackled burdens lifted and she was set free.

She smiled thinking of Sister Josephine who had started a school near the town of New Market. She lived with the Fergusons while the citizens of the community built her a new home. The children flowered under her tutelage and were thrilled to have their teacher living with them.

Emily's husband was reported dead, presumed to have been burned alive in the forests that had caught fire during the Battle of the Wilderness.

Amos stayed on as a free hand finding love in the roots of a family that adored him. He rebuilt Emily's barn that the Yanks had burned down, plowed the fields and occupied himself with the myriad of chores that Emily's husband might have performed. According to Sister Josephine's letters, an inspiring romance was blossoming between Emily and Amos. Of course, encouraged by Emily's clever children.

Sister Josephine and Grace sent letters to Mother Superior regarding Sister Jennifer Agatha's conduct. For her penance, Sister Jennifer Agatha was confined to a cloistered abbey of the Sisters of Mercy, separated from human interaction, scrubbing floors in silence.

Letters flowed back and forth from Ryan's parents, with promises of a visit from the family as soon as his older brother, General John Rourke, fully recovered from his wounds. Good news came that he and his wife, Catherine, had a healthy baby boy who was sunshine and smiles, and not only walking but running. Ryan's brother, Zachary, was running the farm but getting antsy. There was talk of heading west again. Communications came from Lucas and his wife, Rachel, in Washington. Ryan was still unclear what role Colonel Lucas Rourke had performed for the Union but had his suspicions of it having to do with spying. They had the fortune to be blessed with a daughter, and both brothers espoused how there was nothing more contagious and magical than the laughter of young children. Grace hoped in days to come they would be blessed with a child.

Ryan had gone to get a pardon. These were dangerous times and he didn't know if the pardoning was a Union ploy to arrest him. He had been gone for three weeks and his absence worried her.

There was a storm coming and it agitated her. She hoped Ryan arrived home before it broke. Lucifer settled on the porch railing and cawed. He fluttered his jet-black plumage, flapped his wings, turned his dark head side to side, and then alighted, cawing with the clamor of an Irish wake. She frowned at his odd behavior.

Three men in the distance rode up from the river. Ryan? Hairs prickled on the back of her neck. She walked to the side of the porch and called for Francis. Nothing. She closed her eyes. They had gone berry picking that morn.

Grace picked up her rifle. In the wake of war, and the less than established peace, the countryside remained unruly and she never knew if a stranger emerged as friend or foe.

In the yard to the rear of the house, geese honked and rushed to the front. A rooster crowed uproariously. The animal's bizarre behavior rattled her.

Side by side, the men approached, bearded, filthy and desperate-looking.

"That's far enough." Grace pointed with her gun.

They stopped with her well-aimed message, loosened their reins and allowed their mounts to graze on the grass. Their calmness bothered her. Too calm. "What do you want?"

"You're not very hospitable for a sister who shot

me," one man said, then laughed.

"Thomas?" Never would she have recognized her stepbrother. Gaunt, teeth missing, bent over and looking years older. "Come any closer and this time I'll make sure my shot hits its mark."

Thomas flicked his gaze over her. "Not a drink of water?"

"I thought the Comanches killed you."

He waved his hands, palms up. "Here I am in the living flesh."

"Leave or I'll call for my husband. And you don't ever want to meet him," she bluffed.

Archimedes and the mare whickered. Their nostrils flared, snorting out an alarm. Her heart thudded wildly.

A plank creaked behind her. Suddenly seized by the hair, she was yanked viciously upward. Her rifle went flying and landed far off the porch. Above her, Carl's lips stretched in a cruel smile. His change was more dramatic than his brother's. Bloated, oily, greasy, heavily bearded, his normally fastidious appearance had devolved into slovenliness and grime. His breath smelled rank with alcohol. Cold, dark fear jagged up her spine.

"You've caused us enough trouble. My father was thrown in jail. Because of your husband."

"Your father's greed placed him in prison."

"I'll kill the Gray Ghost for what he's done to me. I've lost everything. Do you hear me? Everything." Carl wrenched her arm nearly out of its socket. "We've been watching you. Your husband has been gone for a long time, but I'm a patient man. I'll wait for his return and kill him."

"If you harm him, I promise I'll kill you," Grace gritted out between her teeth.

"Enough. I'll have you first, spread your milky white thighs and ram my cock into you until you scream for mercy."

"No," said the younger brother. "I get her first."

Grace's muscles went rigid. While the two brothers argued, she saw Francis edge to the lower side of the porch. She gave him a side eye, warning him away. Couldn't risk Francis losing his life and leaving Clara vulnerable. *Get Ryan,* she mimed.

"How did you find me?" She stalled for time, thinking what she could do.

"We broke into your home in Maryland," found a letter from you to your mother, and now we're taking you back to Maryland. Grace shot daggers at Carl. She did not shake with fear but anger with herself for being caught unaware.

Knowing there was a loose plank behind her, she shoved back against Carl. He stumbled, lost his grip on her, tripped a step back, and the plank swung up with force, and whapped him in the back of the head. He sailed forward and, arms flailing, fell down the steps. Grace took a step to run but, at the last second, he grabbed the hem of her dress and she pitched to the ground. She scrambled to her feet with Carl now clutching her petticoats.

Idiot. In one swift move, Grace hauled back and kicked with all her might, striking him in the groin, and then ran across the yard and into the woods. Pointy branches slashed at her skin and tore at her dress. She tripped on hidden tree roots and went sprawling, her hands skidding across sharp rocks. Palms smarting, she picked herself up and ran across an open meadow until her lungs felt about to explode, until her legs became leaden, until her breath came out in gasps. She bent over to catch her breath, then heard a thrashing noise. Heavy breathing came from behind her, and turning, she saw Carl stumbling, tripping, running faster than she ever imagined he could. She turned to run, but Carl grabbed her hair from behind and slammed her to the ground. Her breath whooshed out of her. Her head swirling, she rolled.

Carl laughed, then dropped down on top of her. "I do like a woman who fights," he said, pinning her to the ground. "So I can teach her a lesson." He raised his arm, fist clenched…then paused midair when a dark shadow swirled in a circle overhead. Then a caw sounded above them. "What the…" he sputtered.

Lucifer. She looked higher, saw the bird circling Hope filled her heart. Ryan. Had Lucifer summoned Ryan?

The bird cawed, then dove down, distracting Carl who turned to see where the crow had gone.

With Carl's fat body still pinning her down, Grace twisted her head to see.

Ryan, it had to be Ryan. Her heart leaped. "Ryan!" she shouted.

Suddenly, the ground beneath them thundered, and like a plague of ravenous locusts, a band of men burst from the woods, riding at an unbreakable speed toward them. Like a million teeming banshees their ferocious war cries filled the meadow. The Rebel Cry!

Carl cursed.

Gunfire came from behind where her younger

stepbrother fell from his horse and lay unconscious. Ryan's men headed forward toward her on their horses then stopped when Carl yanked her to her feet and, using her as a human shield, pressed a revolver to the side of her head.

Ice ran through Ryan's veins. He'd come so far. To lose Grace now?

Two remaining men aimed their rifles. Not the toughest Ryan had ever seen. Rough lives, and perpetual struggle in their ancestry. But they didn't have the customary war-torn look of a soldier.

He prodded his horse up close enough to get a clear shot. A bearded man dared to raise his gun to her head. He would die first.

The two men commenced shooting. Ryan lifted his rifle, primed and loaded, and at full gallop he fired, hit the closest man square in the shoulder, the shot flinging him off his horse. Ryan fired the next shot and winged the second man who fell to the ground unconscious or in a faint.

Ryan jumped from his horse.

"She'll be dead if you don't leave," said the man.

Ryan knew that nasal, whiny voice. Carl Dawson. Ryan drew his lips back in a snarl. "This day you will enter the gates of hell."

Carl stepped back, taking Grace with him. "You will not defeat me." He shifted his weight from one foot to the other, his prancing indicative of a less than assured victory.

Ryan took a step toward him. Carl pressed the

muzzle of the gun harder into her skull.

"Now," Grace yelled. She bit Carl's hand, slipped from his hold and dropped to the ground.

Ryan launched forward at Carl, slugged him with a colossal right, with all the inertia forward and as hard as he could. He caught Carl dead on the nose, a big target, and felt his fist drive through it, and beyond it, and then his falling body weight whipped his head out from under his moving hand. Carl went down, swung his leg out, tripped Ryan, and raised his gun. On his back, Ryan clinked his pistol against Carl's, the man's oily face glaring down at him and dripping sweat onto Ryan's face.

Carl's pistol went off and dislodged Ryan's gun from his grasp. With no weapon but his bare hands, Ryan reached for the man's throat, his fingertips right behind his larynx, squeezing and tearing. Carl's face reddened, his eyes slits of rage…his right hand grasped a knife… raised it…aimed at Ryan's heart.

A gun blasted from behind, lighting Carl's face with surprise as a bullet entered the back of his shoulder. Eyes wide open, blood spurting, he plummeted face first to the ground, flinging up columns of caked earth, and clutching his useless arm.

"I killed him. I told him I'd kill him if he tried to harm you." Grace's hands shook around the rifle.

Ryan leaped up and took her in his arms. "My brave sweetheart. For the second time, you saved my life." He prodded Carl with the toe of his boot and her stepbrother moaned. "You didn't kill him. Unfortunately, he'll live." He signaled to his men. "Take care of him and tie up the prisoners to take to the authorities." Ryan scooped her up on his horse, and then climbed up behind.

"Ryan, I thought I'd never see you again," she said, collapsing against his chest. "I love you so much. What took you so long getting home?" And then she peered around him. "What are all your men doing here? Sergeant Hutchinson? Francis?"

Francis nodded. "I jumped on Archimedes and told him to find Colonel Rourke. He took me right to him. Not only can that horse count, he has a sixth sense."

Ryan held her close, placing his chin on her head and explained his long absence. "Despite the implied safeguard from the United States Military authorities, we were uncertain of President Grant's pardon to me and my men's surrender. Dubious of the designs the Yankees had on me, we circled Lynchburg for a few days. Finally, I went to the authorities and gave cause as to my appearance. The provost marshal of the city was confused and unaware of the pardon arrangement. Under General Wells, we were surrounded by twenty Yanks and arrested, waiting until further orders were communicated through Washington. After several days, it came to light the misunderstanding of facts and we were released upon parole by specific and direct orders of President Grant, mine being included in the terms of General Lee's surrender at Appomattox."

"But why are all your men here?"

Ryan smoothed a hand down Grace's back to ease her trembling, then leaned over and kissed her. "We reconnected near Chancellorsville. My men offered to do the work of raising a new barn and building a sawmill."

He clicked his horse ahead of his men and, together, they watched huge distant clouds dragging their coattails of rain across the Shenandoah. "We were made to be together, Grace, and I can no more stop loving you than prevent the next tempest."

"We'll have many storms ahead of us, and we'll face them together and be stronger for it. I love you wholly and unconditionally And I will never ever stop loving you, of this I promise." Her gaze roved over his body inch by inch, from head to foot enough to harden his loins and roast his wits.

"Wait 'til I get you alone…" To repay her for the lingering glance she'd subjected him to, he whispered, "I will caress and stroke and taste—" He was rewarded when her breath rushed out of her in short pants.

Her fingers dug into his sleeves. Good. He quirked his mouth into a wolfish smile, and then dipped his gaze to linger on the rounded fullness of her breasts where they pushed up against her décolletage. "I'll strip you naked, suckle your breasts…ravish you with my mouth…until I stroke a hot fire in your loins, and have your legs wrapped around my—"

Caught between a sigh and a moan, she said, "You are the devil's own, Colonel Rourke. You will be punished." Her eyes lit with challenge and she ran her tongue across her upper lip with a soft, sensual lick. "What if I repay you in kind?"

How he wanted to gallop away, throw up her skirts and…she was far too proficient for her own good. "A wicked game you play, *Mrs. Rourke.*"

They cantered up to their home ready for whatever

his Grace had in store.

Except two men stood on their front porch... apparently waiting for them. Ryan's ardor faded like a quickly setting sun. He pulled his gun. "You better have a good reason for being here." He'd had enough of strangers and wanted to be alone with his wife.

They put their hands up. "We're looking for Miss Grace Barrett and were informed we might find her at this residence."

Was Grace in trouble with the authorities again? Had Senator Dawson performed one last manipulation to cause her harm? "You do realize I'm Colonel Ryan Rourke." He let that threat drift over them for a moment, hoping it might influence them to depart. He had just received his pardon and he wanted no more trouble, but his reputation as the Gray Ghost remained, so he might as well use it.

"The Gray Ghost? Of the Confederacy?" they said, mouths hanging open..

"Do you have a problem with that?"

"No sir, we have the greatest respect and admiration for you. I'm formerly Captain Jude Wenke of the Army of the Potomac. We came face-to-face once. I was your enemy and injured, yet you gave me a drink from a canteen. I'll never forget your mercy."

"I remember. Say your piece but it better be good. I'm of no mind—"

"Wait, hear us out. We bring bad... and agreeable news. We've been exhausted trying to locate Miss Barrett."

"Let the men talk, Ryan." Grace pressed his gun arm down, and then slid from the saddle. He followed. His men had their guns up. No one was taking his wife.

"I'm Grace Barrett Rourke and this is my husband."

She took his arm in hers, warning him with her eyes. Ryan didn't like it one bit. Not when there was a menace to her on his front porch. Nor did he miss their raised eyebrows as they inspected the ramshackle house and farm. He wished a loosened porch plank to rise up and catapult them all the way back north.

"Well, you found her. Now, move off my property. My men will escort you if you don't leave now. We don't need anything. We're happy to be poor but we'll make it."

"Poor?" Suddenly, both men commenced laughing uproariously, clapping their hands together, wiping their eyes, and then had difficulty catching their breaths. Ryan scowled. They raged with their hilarity at his expense? From behind, he heard several clicks of his men's pistols and questioned the intruders' sanity.

"Ryan, let the men talk," ordered Grace.

"I'm a banker," said Captain Jude Wenke, "and this is Samuel D. Laine, an attorney representing Miss Barrett, excuse me," he corrected himself, "*Mrs. Rourke.* Regrettably, we must inform you of your mother's passing and extend our condolences."

Ryan tightened his arm around her.

Captain Jude Wenke continued. "We went through your late mother's correspondence and found this address and, on a hunch and came to find you."

"You let her know of her mother, now get off my property," said Ryan.

Grace shushed him. "Go on, Captain Wenke."

Captain Wenke exchanged a knowing look with

his associate, and then turned to Grace. "You are far from poor. Your father, the late Edward Barrett's estate, which is now your estate, *Mrs. Rourke*, have tripled during the war."

Grace's mouth dropped open. "I thought my stepfather took everything."

Captain Wenke smacked his hand on his hat, the wind gaining strength and the air heavy with the scent of rain. "Senator Dawson had a stroke of bad luck. From a published account in the *New York Herald*," he dipped his eyes meaningfully to Ryan, "he shamefully resigned from his position due to scandalous and illegal war profiteering. He's in prison for his crimes. Nevertheless, he tried to tap your estate and inheritance. There was no way he could venture to get his hands on one penny of your assets. Your father had an air-tight will in case of such an event."

Directly, it began to rain, and it rained like a fury, too. Ryan had never seen the wind blow so as he attempted to grasp the news.

"Did you hear that, Ryan?" said Grace, rain pattering on her beaming face. "We can expand the horse farm."

The clouds were blue-black and lovely and lifted waves of rain, thrashing against a line of trees, bending them down like a genuflection, and then wildly tossing their arms up like a bright and glorified praise.

"My goodness, you could expand the horse farm to the size of Rhode Island, if you like," said Captain Wenke.

The wind whipped against them, tearing out the last of Grace's hairpins, lashing their clothes to their bodies. The warmth of it seeped into his bones. Grace threw her arms around Ryan, and he picked her up and swung her around. And all the while, Grace was laughing, and he was laughing too, loud, sweet, deep hilarious laughter and all for the sheer joy of it.

Ryan's men cheered and he walked up on the porch with Grace and shook hands with Captain Wenke and Samuel.

"Why didn't you say so in the first place?" Ryan said.

Captain Wenke chuckled. "It was hard to parlay any thoughts with a dozen guns pointed at me, and especially in the august company of the formidable Gray Ghost."

Glowing, Grace said, "Are my father's thoroughbreds still in Maryland?"

"Every last one of them," said Samuel D. Laine.

She was soaked from head to toe, her hair streaming down her back and she couldn't have been more beautiful. His Grace.

The men were ushered inside by Francis, leaving the two of them to gaze at the storm, the rain driving down the high mountain valleys, a stunning and awesome sight. The sun appeared in the wake of the tempest and shimmered through blustery riffs, igniting the mountain ridges here and there, while the valley below lay shrouded in lingering darkness. The peaceful, level rays fringed the pewter clouds with scarlet, and transformed the torrent into waves of golden rain; in the valleys the glistening mists were tinted every riotous color; and the farthest heavens were set fire with blazing glory.

Grace leaned into his side just as awed as he and whispered, "From the tempests of war, there are times when good luck comes, and then you can make something good and wonderful grow. And like I said before, sometimes a storm doesn't come to destroy you…it comes to clear a path."

She was right. Ryan recalled what President Lincoln had once said, "…all American citizens, brothers of a common country should dwell tighter in the bonds of fraternal feeling." No one desired peace more ardently than Ryan.

He would always remember this time, this moment, this memory engraved forever on his mind. War was behavior with roots in the earliest times of the world and had defined him both good and bad. There were no victory celebrations, no valued Cause, only suffering and a hallowed death for so many.

Yet, the storm of conflict was swept away, the past a dimming memory, and its story told. All that remained of what rested behind him was what rested before him, to what rested within him…a stirring desire for brotherhood to banish the temptation of violence and war…to gain harmonious reconciliation, and hope of a new era, an era of peace, welcomed from the depths of his heart.

The End

AUTHOR'S NOTE

This is a novel and to construe it as anything else would be an error. For the sake of storytelling, the timeline of fictionalized events, places and people was compressed. Colonel Ryan Rourke is an amalgamation of several of the famous cavaliers, with their histories woven and mirroring actual events. Somewhat romanticized, cavalrymen were forces that fought on horseback, armed with pistols, carbines, and sabers, that underscored their emphasis on screening, reconnaissance, raiding and harassment. Of particular note is Colonel J. E. B. Stuart, a prominent Cavalry leader, a flamboyant dresser and audacious commander who epitomized the chivalry and heroism celebrated by the South. There was also Wade Hampton, and John Hunt Morgan, and the most violent and ruthless cavalry commander, Nathan Bedford Forrest.

No other figure of the Civil War became during his lifetime such a storybook legend as Colonel John Singleton Mosby, the real "Gray Ghost". He was one of the most effective and resourceful leaders, leading his cavalry unit, known as Mosby's Rangers, and striking the Union army time and again with lightning raids, seemingly to then melt away by blending in with local farmers and townspeople. He succeeded in tying upwards of forty thousand Federal troops defending rail lines and logistical hubs with a hundred irregulars. At the war's end, he was pardoned by his enemy, United States President Ulysses S. Grant. Mosby became a Republican, supporting Grant, and later served as the American Consul to Hong Kong and the U. S. Department of Justice.

The truth is the handful of women doctors during the Civil War became pioneers in their field yet remained the recipients of hostilities from their male counterparts, who firmly believed that field medicine was a male environment. Of note, Dr. Elizabeth Blackwell, an English immigrant was the first woman to earn a medical degree in the United States. Dr. Mary Edwards Walker earned a Union army commission for her valuable skills as a surgeon. In 1864, she was captured and believed to be a spy, imprisoned in Richmond's Castle Thunder. She was later released via a trade. By 1870 there were five hundred and twenty-five trained women doctors in America. By 2021, nearly a third of the one million professional practicing physicians happen to be women and for the first time medical schools are graduating more women doctors than men.

The Sisters of Mercy and the Sisters of Charity, Catholic religious orders, left a legacy in the history of philanthropy, women's history, medicine and nursing during the American Civil War. The Sisters of

Mercy and the Sisters of Charity provided thousands of nurses serving the armies of both the Union and the Confederacy by caring equally for victims of war whether they themselves sympathized with the North or the South. Agents of change, the sisters broke down religious, social and gender barriers, and worked in a gamut of settings, from civilian and military hospitals, to medical transports along waterways, on blood-soaked battlefields, in prisons and isolation camps. These "Angels of the Battlefield" risked life and limb to serve the sick and wounded soldiers physically, emotionally and spiritually in cataclysmic conditions, yet their contributions have been sadly overlooked by history.

The Civil War was the bloodiest war in the United States. Approximately six hundred and twenty thousand people died in the conflict with more Americans dying in the Civil War than in all other wars combined.

Referred to the Middle Ages of American medicine, there arose the unfortunate circumstance that twice as many soldiers died from disease than in combat. Causative elements of combat-related deaths were inexperienced surgeons, deficiencies in an organized method to get the wounded off the battlefield swiftly, infections, no sterile techniques implemented because it was not discovered at the time as important, little sanitation, overcrowded camps, terrible diet, few specialized treatments.

However, numerous medical and surgical advances transpired during the War Between the States. Medical innovations included use of quinine for prevention of malaria, and the use of quarantine, which virtually eliminated yellow fever, successful treatment of hospital gangrene with bromine and isolation, development of an ambulance system for evacuation of the wounded, use of trains and boats to transport patients, establishment of large general hospitals, and formation of specialty hospitals, and prosthetics improvements.

New techniques in surgery included safe use of anesthetics, rudimentary neurosurgery, development of techniques for arterial ligation, performance of first plastic surgeries, resection or the process of cutting out muscle or bone to save a limb. Also, the closing of chest wounds to keep the lungs from collapsing, a technique learned by doctors during the Crimean War.

Dr. Ignaz Semmelweis was an Austrian doctor and pioneer of antiseptic procedures. Described as the "savior of mothers", Semmelweis discovered that the incidence of puerperal fever or "childbed fever" could be drastically cut by the use of hand disinfection in obstetrical clinics. Puerperal fever was common in mid-nineteenth century hospitals causing the death of many women. Semmelweis introduced the practice of washing hands to doctors with a chlorinated lime solution in Vienna's General Hospital, thus reducing the mortality rate to below one percent. Too outspoken of his discovery, his colleagues denounced his theories and had him committed to an asylum where guards beat him to death. Years later, Louis Pasteur confirmed the germ theory and Joseph Lister widely implemented the sterile technique. During the American Civil War, it was rare to find a learned and informed physician who exercised the antiseptic practice. Woefully disproportionate numbers of soldiers died from disease and most probably carried to them from their germ-ridden doctor's hands.

Battle at New Market: A makeshift army of forty-one hundred Confederates defeated ten thousand Yanks under Union Major General Franz Sigel and his Army of the Shenandoah, stopping Grant from threatening General Lee's eastern flank. Virginia Military Institute cadets or schoolboys were used to win the fight.

I always say that I'm a storyteller, not a historian, and as a storyteller, I'm more concerned with the what-ifs than the why-nots. I so enjoy taking a bit of artistic license in order to bring you the most exciting, sensual, love story that my what-if imagination can create.

ACKNOWLEDGEMENTS

Most books wouldn't be written without the help of some special people. I would like to acknowledge Caroline Tolley, my developmental editor, and Linda Style, my copy editor, and Scott Moreland, my line editor. Their insight and expertise were indispensable. Hugs also to my spouse, Edward, my right-hand man because without his support, none of my writing would be possible. Also, hugs to my five children, eight grandchildren, Eugene Dollard, Dr. Marcianna Dollard, Nancy Crawford, Brenda Kosinski, Paula Ursoy, and posthumously, Loretta Bysiek—your love and comfort surround me.

Many thanks to the gracious support of Western New York Romance Writers Group.

Finally, a special note of gratitude to my readers. You will never know how much your enthusiasm and support enrich my work and my life. You are the best!

ABOUT THE AUTHOR

Best-selling author Elizabeth St. Michel has received multiple awards for her work.

Her first book, *The Winds of Fate*, was a number-one hit on Amazon's list of best sellers and a quarterfinalist for the Amazon Breakthrough Novel Award.

Surrender the Wind, Elizabeth's second novel, received the Holt Medallion and the Reader's Choice Award and was a finalist of the National RONE Award, which honors literary excellence in romance writing.

Sweet Vengeance: Duke of Rutland I won the prestigious International Book Award.

Her fifth book, *Only You: Duke of Rutland Series III*, achieved the American Fiction Award and the "Crowned Heart Award" from InD'tale Magazine.

Her sixth book, *Lord of the Wilderness*, achieved the International Book Award, *InD'tale Magazine* RONE Award Finalist, *Forward Reviews* Bronze Medallion

Book of the Year, New England Readers' Choice Award.

Her seventh book *Surrender to Honor* received *InD'tale's* RONE Award.

St. Michel lives in New York and the Bahamas.

Dear Readers,

It has given me particular pleasure to write Surrender the Storm for you, which introduces General Rourke's younger brother, Colonel Ryan Rourke, the famed Confederate Calvary leader known as the Gray Ghost. Jaded from years at war, he is scornful enough to kidnap a group of nuns from beneath Yankee noses, stealing them to his Confederate camp to nurse his injured men. Yet Colonel Rourke acquired more than he bargained for. The youngest, Sister Grace, dares to challenge him and her provocations are not angelic at all. Why, she possesses a face and sway of hips that would make a monk lust.

In the shadow of fear, Grace Barrett has secrets and joins the Sisters of Charity to veil her identity. And while the beautiful Sister Grace has sworn to keep her vows, this wrong Rebel may be just the right man for her. Yet will Colonel Ryan Rourke's scars make him not only run from the world but from the woman who has the sole ability to heal his soul?

As you know, my first installment, *Surrender the Wind,* detailed the journey of legendary Confederate General John Daniel Rourke, the eldest son and his providential meeting of Catherine Fitzgerald from New York during the American Civil War.

The second installment, *Surrender to Honor,* acquainted us with Colonel Lucas Rourke head of Civilian Spying for the North. Colonel Rourke is honor bound to uphold the Union and responsible for a vast network of spies. When Confederates abduct him, his only hope is the enigmatic spy who surrenders her heart and soul to save him. Rachel Pierce is the notorious Saint. Witnessing her father's brutal murder by slaveholders, she emerges disciplined in the high art of spying, moving through southern latitudes like a ghost with no trace of her footsteps and defying every one of her enemies without the slightest hint of their knowledge. Caught in a dangerous web of intrigue, they uncover secrets that will prolong the war and cast them both in danger.

There is no greater compliment to me as an author than for my readers to become so involved with the characters that you want me to write more.

Although I can't tell you much more, I can promise you this: like my last novels, it is written with one goal in mind—to make you experience the laughter, the love, and all the other myriad emotions of its characters. And when it's over, to leave you smiling…

P.S. If you would like to receive an emailed newsletter from me, which will keep you informed about my books-in-progress as well as answer some of the questions I'm frequently asked about publishing, please contact me on my Facebook, Twitter or webpage at www.elizabethstmichel.com. I would be thrilled to hear from you!

Made in the USA
Middletown, DE
10 March 2024